PARABOLIS

A Novelzine by
Eddie Han

Art by Curt Merlo

Parabolis

Copyright © 2013 Eddie Han
All rights reserved. Published in the United States by Saboteur Press.

ISBN 978-0-9883981-0-8

All production, artwork and design by Curt Merlo

First Edition
Printed in China

This is a work of fiction. Names, characters, places, and incidents are either the product of the author's imagination or are used fictitiously, and any resemblance to actual persons, living or dead, business establishments, events, or locales is entirely coincidental.

www.parabolis.com

TABLE OF CONTENTS

Overture | 09

No. 01

Socks | 18
A Boy Counting Bubbles | 21
The Blacksmith | 27
Before the Dusk | 34

No. 02

War Machines | 50
A New Beginning | 57
On the Groveland Express | 63
Selah | 67
Home | 70
Carnaval City | 78
Fixer at the Broken Cistern | 85
Felix | 92
The Ass of the Velvet Fray | 101
Sanctuary | 107
An Evening with the Red Rabbit | 113
The Ghost and the Darkness | 122
Reaping the Rogues | 130

No. 03

Great Matters | 144
Stolen Morning | 149
Teardrop | 152
For Justice | 160

Midnight Macabre | 167
Encounter at Chesterlink Pass | 174
Alone with Death | 179
To Complete a Melody | 186
Not Doing Nothing | 191
SSC | 193
The Inquisition | 198
Charles Valkyrie | 204
In the Mirror Dimly | 211
Free | 218
Passing the Torch | 222
Blackout | 224
Shit Storm | 231
Into the Wilds | 236
The Kiss at the World's End | 240
The Sermon in the Mud | 248

No. 04

The Sad Boy and the Songstress | 260
A Promise Kept | 266
Living Forest | 270
The Guerrilla Resistance | 274
Evening Sun | 279
Borderland Ridge Run | 287
Casualties of War | 294
The Final Directive | 298
A Confession | 304
Shadow in the North | 311
Failed | 314
Muriah Bay | 318
A Measure of Peace | 325

FOR MONICA AND ERIC

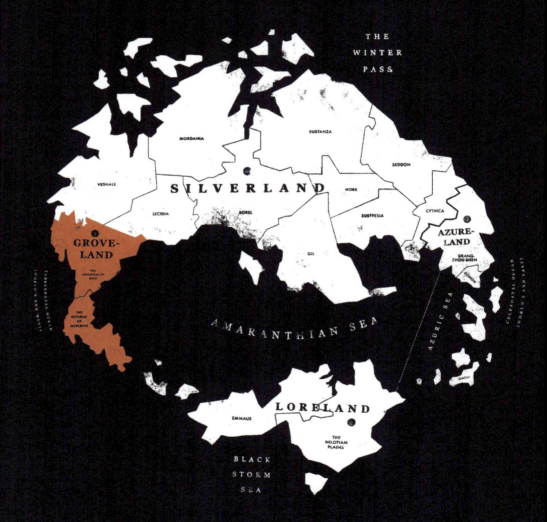

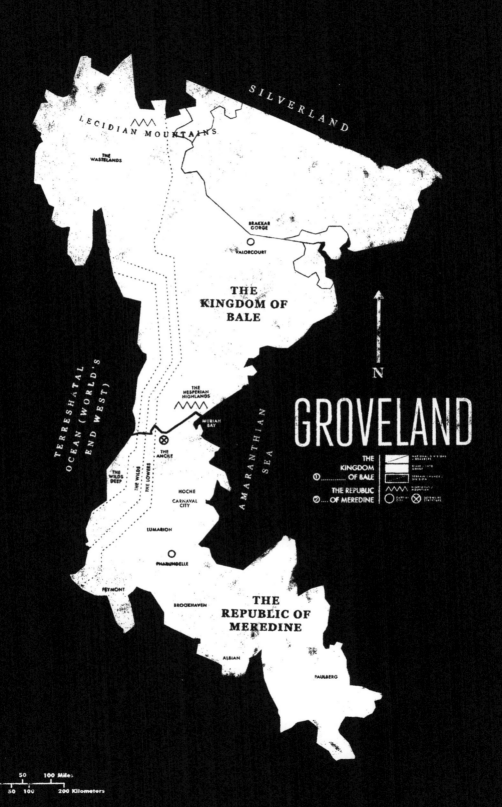

CH 00
OVERTURE

Twenty Shaldean Riders raced across the Saracen deserts of Loreland. Like a sandstorm, they sped toward the Emmainite village—a lone outpost in the vast emptiness. Keffiyehs covered their faces, scimitars were sheathed at their sides and long rifles were strapped to their backs. Behind them, a ruby sun melted into the sea of dunes.

"*Yeshalleh!*" the village gatekeeper shouted. "The Shaldea return!"

The chieftain emerged from his home. He was an old man with dark, leathery skin. His robes were made of airy white cotton, common to Emmainite tribesmen. When the Shaldean Riders entered the village, they were greeted with skins of water from the well. The lead rider dismounted and greeted the Emmainite chieftain with a kiss.

"Peace be upon you," he said. His face was sun scorched and heavily bearded.

"And you," the chieftain replied.

"Where is he?"

"In the parlor."

"Alone?"

The chieftain nodded.

"You sure it's him?"

"I have seen all matters of darkness in my life—none so dark as this one. I am sure he is who he says he is."

"How long has he been waiting?"

"Since before the sunrise. He hasn't

spoken a word. Hasn't eaten or slept. You have brought a great evil into my village, Shaldean."

"It is a risk we must take," said the lead rider. "We cannot defeat the Republic alone. This is the only way. I do this for us, for our land."

"Noble words. But I see no wisdom in summoning a Greater Evil to battle a Lesser Evil that Good alone has failed to overcome."

"The Republic is no 'Lesser Evil.'"

"Do what you will. But be quick about it. The sooner he leaves, the sooner God's grace can return to this village."

"God has long abandoned us." The lead rider walked past the old Emmainite into an annex of his home that served as both a meeting room and a reception for guests.

Inside a black-robed figure sat cross-legged in front of a glowing coal pit, the face hidden by a deep hood drawn over his head. He didn't so much as move. The Shaldean walked over to the basin and washed his hands. After drinking a ladle of water from a bucket he settled himself across from the dark figure.

"We are humbled by your presence," he began. "We did not think you would come. We hoped. But we did not think… forgive us for keeping you waiting. I came as soon as I received word. My name is Yusef Naskerazim. I am *Rajeth* of the Shaldean Riders."

The shadow said nothing.

Yusef cleared his throat. "Our people are known for their hospitality," he added. "I hope they did not disappoint."

The shadow finally spoke. "Why have you invoked our name?"

Relieved at the break in silence, Yusef was about to offer some food before he noticed an unmolested plate of cheese curds and a tea set sitting next to him.

"Can I have the chieftain bring you anything?" he asked instead. "Perhaps a smoke?"

"Why have you invoked our name?" the shadow repeated.

He had an accent that sounded vaguely like that of the gypsies of the Greater North. And he spoke without looking up from below the shroud of his hood.

Yusef took a deep breath to collect his thoughts. He stroked his thick black beard as he began.

"Because we need your help," he replied. "We want to see the Meredine Republic burn and we cannot stop them alone."

"Why do you seek its end?"

Yusef let out a bewildered chuckle. "The crimes of the Republic are too many to recount—like the grains of sand in the desert." He grew animated as he continued. "Everyday, we see more and more of their troops marching through our villages. Just last week, Republican Guards came through here, lined up the people like common thieves, women and children, and held them under the sword while they ransacked their homes."

"Looking for you," said the shadow. "You prod the beast and hide behind your kin."

"And what shall we do? Sit on our hands while they humiliate us and ravage

> **"The crimes of the Republic are too many to recount—like the grains of sand in the desert."**

our families, our children? They occupy our land, exploit our people, and rob us of our resources with their mines. They manipulate our markets and arrange unfair trade agreements with our ruling parties. Always meddling. Always deceiving."

"Then your grievances are with your rulers."

"Yes. They are weak. But whose

12

crimes are greater? The tempted or the tempter's?"

"We are not judges. Only equalizers."

"If equalizers, then you must see that the Republic's reign is an affront to any notion of equality. Our just struggle, they call terrorism. Their terrorism, they call justified occupation. This is not equal, *afendi*. This is tyranny."

"And not the first of its kind. This is the nature of men. What empire has existed before the Republic that did not abuse its power? Who would not do as they please if given the chance?"

"You do not," said Yusef. "You exercise restraint even in the face of injustice. Even when it is in your power to intervene."

"You assume to know much about us."

"Please, *afendi*. We merely want to see the end of the Republic. We want justice."

"Justice or vengeance, Mister Naskerazim? What price are you willing to pay? Would you, yourself, die to see the destruction of your enemies?"

Yusef recoiled. Softly he asked, "Why must the innocent die with the guilty?"

"You are not so innocent. What you fail to understand, Mister Naskerazim, is that today's rebels are tomorrow's tyrants. The lust for power is great. Were your people to reign in the Republic's place, you would be different only in nationality. And I would be sitting across from another, negotiating the terms of *your* end."

"I would not have braved this meeting if…" Yusef's voice trailed. He knew better than to appeal for sympathy from what the village chieftain referred to as "a Greater Evil." His gaze fell.

There was a long pause. Then the shadow said at last, "The balance of power will be reset. The Republic *will* be destroyed."

Yusef's eyes widened with renewed hope. "Then, you *will* help us?" he asked.

"We help no one. You and your Shaldea would be wise to simply fade into obscurity. For when we undermine the Republic, we will undermine with it those who would try and profit from its end."

The shadow looked up for the first time. He was a young man with a pale face, marked with what appeared to be a broad smudge of dried blood around his mouth. Upon closer examination, Yusef realized that it was a dark crimson tattoo—a tattoo of a handprint covering his nose and mouth. His teeth were silver and his eyes like that of a coiled asp. "In the reckoning, we will destroy *everyone*."

Leaving the speechless Shaldean to mull over the catholic threat, the dark figure stood and left the parlor. The others waiting outside parted as he passed. Then he disappeared into the evening desert like a ghost.

PARA

BOLIS

№ 01

CH 01

SOCKS

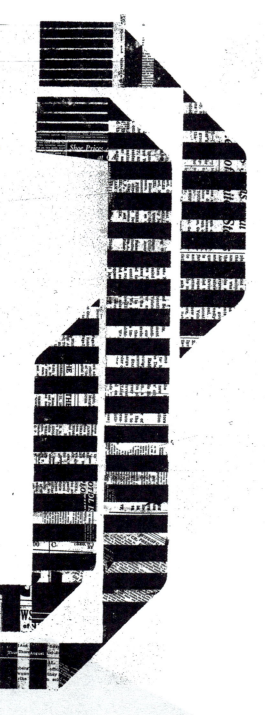

D ale Sunday was clever enough; he had a quick wit. But in class he pulled middling grades. He wasn't particularly handsome, nor was he of any great stature. He didn't come from wealth. He was not the strongest, not the most athletic. He was not popular. Dale was fairly artistic; he could hold a tune, but he wasn't a talent. By all standards, Dale Sunday was mediocre. Yet, he thought himself special—set apart. Because while most children his age were thinking about school and play, boys and girls, and holidays, Dale was thinking about things like mortality, the origins of man, the longing heart.

He was different. And he knew it.

It was this self-aggrandized sense of purpose juxtaposed against an ambivalent world that made Dale a brooding, temperamental adolescent. The world didn't care what he thought of himself. In its busyness, in all its moving parts, Dale Sunday was just another kid—a dreamer put in his place by the overwhelming reality. At twelve years old, not many saw past his mediocrity, no one knew his musings. He was noticed instead for his socks. Long, black-and-white striped wool socks pulled up to his knees.

The previous summer, when the heat of the Westerlies blew away the temperate effects of the bay, Dale had taken the liberty of cutting his school uniform pants into a pair of shorts. Months later, his shortsighted alterations left him with nothing but his wool socks to fend off the winter chill.

"Don't be a weasel," Dale said to his friend, Arturo Lucien.

"I'm not. We never shook on it. You have to shake on it."

For Dale, knowing he had beaten Arturo at arm wrestling was reward enough. The money didn't really matter. It was the principle.

"Says who?"

"Everyone knows you gotta shake on it!"

"Give me my shilling."

And that's when Marcus Addy approached with three of his friends. "Would you look at these little dipshits. *Give me my shilling!*" he said.

At fourteen years old, Marcus was the only one in his class with a mustache. A head taller and a budding acne problem made it clear to all that Marcus was superior. He was also the son of Count Nigel Addy, the school's largest donor and one of Carnaval City's premiere aristocrats.

"We were just talking about whether or not you have to shake on a bet for it to count," Arturo bumbled. "I was saying—"

"Shut up, twerp!" barked one of Marcus' friends. "No one cares."

Marcus looked at Dale. Then, at his socks.

"Does your mommy know you stole her knickers?"

Everyone began to laugh. In his nervousness, even Arturo forced a chuckle. Dale felt the heat rise from his chest, through his throat, and to his ears. It wasn't the first time someone had commented on his socks. Mostly, it didn't bother him when people commented on his socks. But this was Marcus. And he made mention of a mother Dale did not have.

"I don't know, Marcus. Does *your* mommy know you stole her mustache?"

Everyone gasped. Arturo masked a burst of laughter with a cough. And then he slowly inched away.

Dale stood alone, his chest up, a defiant look on his face. As Marcus stepped up to him, the anger and the defiance faded, and they were quickly replaced by fear.

He grabbed Dale by the collar and cocked his fist.

"What'd you say?"

"I think you heard what I said."

Having sealed his fate, Dale braced

"Does your mommy know you stole her mustache?"

himself for the beating. Arturo waited wide-eyed in morbid fascination. The bell rang signaling the end of the lunch period. The teachers appeared on the schoolyard to round up the children. Marcus released Dale with a shove.

"You're dead."

Then they all slowly merged with the rest of the shuffling bodies back into the school hall.

"Are you crazy?" asked Arturo. "What's the matter with you?"

"You still owe me a shilling."

"Here." Arturo handed him the coin. "A lot of good it'll do you when you're dead."

CH 02

A BOY COUNTING BUBBLES

Like every other day, as soon as class got out, Dale went over to the first-grade trailers to look for his cousin, Mosaic. Every day he walked her to and from his uncle's bakery in the Waterfront District. On this particular day, Mosaic was not outside. He stood, waiting, his eyes darting from one end of the schoolyard to the other for signs of Marcus. The urgency inside him seemed to slow time. When he could stand still no longer, Dale stepped around and peered through the small window on the door. The teacher was addressing the class. Mosaic sat attentively in the back row.

When the class finally emptied, Dale grabbed Mosaic by the wrist.

"Let's go, Mo. Hurry."

Dale walked as quickly as he possibly could with Mosaic in tow.

"Dale, why are we walking so fast? My feet hurt."

"I know, but we have to hurry."

"Why?"

"Because."

As they passed the laundry service, Dale got a waft of that distinct bay smell—of fishy gull droppings and salted air. They turned into the alley that cut across the block and into the waterfront. They were almost home.

"Hey, dipshit!"

Dale turned, still holding Mosaic's hand. Behind them, Marcus and his three friends approached from the end of the alley.

"Dale, who are they?" asked Mosaic.

Dale looked at her, then to the alley opening ahead. They were just half a block from the Waterfront District where at this time of day there were sure to be familiar faces—mostly fisherman and merchants—who knew them by name. He could've made a run for it, if it wasn't for Mosaic. Dale looked down at her. He tried to smile.

"Mo, can you get to the bakery by yourself from here? I just need to talk to these guys."

Mosaic looked at him dubiously. "No. I'll wait."

"Just get going. Listen to me. I'll be right there."

The four boys were almost upon them. Dale nudged Mosaic behind him and gave her a firm push. "Go on, Mo. I'll be right there."

She took a few half-hearted steps toward the other end of the alley.

The boys surrounded Dale.

Marcus knocked Dale's books out of his hand. He shoved him toward the side of the alley. "What? You got nothing clever to say now?" He punched Dale in the stomach.

It was the first time someone had hit him. It startled him more than it hurt. As he doubled over, Dale noticed Marcus' brand new, red leather shoes.

"Who's the jackass now?"

One of Marcus' friends stood him up. Before Dale could look up, he was punched in the nose.

Through the shouts and laughter, through the salty blur, Dale turned to see where Mosaic was. He could see her standing there. Frozen. Frightened. Again, Dale tried to smile at her.

"Look! He thinks it's funny. Hit him again!"

A punch landed on the side of his head. And then they were all on top of him. Dale curled up and covered his head.

Mosaic screamed, "Stop! Stop it!"

Dale tried to stand up, but he couldn't. Again, he curled up. He could hear Mosaic crying. The boys were now on their feet, kicking him.

Then it suddenly stopped.

The kicking stopped. Mosaic was quiet. Dale opened his eyes to see Marcus sprawled out on the ground next to him, unconscious. The other boys had taken a few steps back behind Marcus, stunned, staring at the small boy who stood over their friend, who had just knocked him out with one well-placed punch. They hadn't even realized he was there until Marcus was flat on his back.

Dale looked up. Standing above him was his best friend, Sparrow.

Of the proverbial four corners of the world, Sparrow was an immigrant from the shores of Azureland, or the Far East. Common to people from Azuric nations,

his fair skin was tinted yellow, like the color of dried bamboo. He had a shallow brow, high cheekbones, dark almond-shaped eyes, and hair as black as a raven. Like all boys of the Far East, his head was kept closely shaved, as they were not allowed to grow their hair out until their coming of age.

Sparrow had permanently swollen tear-troughs that made him look like he'd just woken up after crying himself to sleep. And he had a scar that ran horizontally across his cheekbone just below his left eye, from the slash of a blade. Unable to afford proper schooling, Sparrow was an apprentice to a blacksmith who ran a disciplined shop. He was trained daily not only in the art of weapons crafting, but in all matters of martial skills including weapons and hand-to-hand combat.

Marcus began to come to. One of the boys said to the others, "Get him." But no one moved.

Sparrow's thoughts seemed to be elsewhere, his expression like a boy counting bubbles in a fountain drink. Sparrow wasn't violent by nature. He just lacked the basic inhibitions that most people possessed, and that, combined with his training, proved useful in a fight.

"C'mon, let's get him," another urged as Marcus recovered.

One of the boys lunged at Sparrow. Sparrow sidestepped the assailant, swept his legs as he stumbled past. Before he could regain his stance, the other two boys jumped him. Together they managed to grab Sparrow and hold his arms behind him.

"Marcus, we got him! We got him! Hit him!"

As Dale staggered to his feet, Marcus punched his friend with vengeful fervor. Overcome with rage, adrenaline coursing through his veins, Dale plowed his shoulder into Marcus' side and drove him into the ground. He began swinging his arms wildly. And as each blow landed on Marcus' face, blood streaming out of his nose and over his fuzzy little mustache, he couldn't help but feel sorry. For himself. For Marcus. For all of their losses.

"A lass will lose her innocence making love," a naval officer had once told him, "and a lad, making war."

"Dale!" Mosaic screamed.

Sparrow broke free by running backwards up against the alley wall and upon impact, throwing his head back into one of his captor's noses. Just then, the sound of a whistle pierced the air. It blew again, louder, closer.

"You lads, stop right there!" From the far end of the alley, a constable came running toward them holding a club in his hand.

Dale immediately jumped up off of Marcus, grabbed his books, and ran toward Mosaic.

"Come on! Run!"

Sparrow followed them out into a sea of people along the busy streets of Carnaval City's Waterfront District. When they could see the constable was no longer in pursuit, they stopped below an overpass.

Dale's hands were still shaking, his knuckles swollen and bruised. Mosaic was still crying in rhythmic sniffles. Dale set his books down in a neat stack and crouched down beside her.

"*Shh*, it's okay, Mo," he tried. "We're okay, now. See?"

He patted her on the back as her sniffles slowed until she finally slurped up the

---

"A lass will lose her innocence making love...and a lad, making war."

---

air and sighed.

"I want to go home," she whimpered, her face still glistening with tears.

Sparrow was holding his ribs, one of his eyes ballooning shut.

"You all right?" asked Dale.

Sparrow looked up and nodded. He wiped the blood from his nose with the back of his hand and sat propped up against a column supporting the overpass.

"I'll be right back. Come on, Mo." Dale rushed Mosaic across the street, around the corner, down a block, and around another corner, up to the front of the bakery.

Just before she walked through the door, Mosaic stopped.

"What's the matter?"

Mosaic looked at Dale, a little wrinkle forming between her brows. She rubbed her eyes and frowned.

"I'm telling on you!"

Then she ran in.

When Dale got back to the overpass, Sparrow was reading one of his books.

"We're doing a series on classic novels," said Dale, crouching down beside him. "We have to read two of those every month. You know how to read?"

"Some," Sparrow replied, gently placing it back on the stack. "Master T'varche taught me. *The sharpest weapon in the world is a well-read mind.*"

They sat a moment, staring into nothing.

"I think you might have broken that kid's nose," said Dale.

"Maybe. Nothing compared to what you did to Marcus."

"What *I* did to him? You're the one who knocked him out."

Dale still took an occasional peek over his shoulder for the constable.

"Master T'varche told me that if a man strikes you, it's okay to strike him back," said Sparrow. "But if a man strikes your brother, that man must die."

Sparrow never asked how the fight started. To him it didn't matter.

"You really believe that?" asked Dale.

Sparrow shrugged. Then the corner of his lips slowly curled into a smirk.

"What?" asked Dale, pressing the tender bruise forming around his left cheek.

"Nice socks."

CH 03

THE BLACKSMITH

I gotta go."

"Yeah, I'd better get going too," said Dale.

He was supposed to go to his father's ship-breaking yard, or in local parlance, "the breaker," to see an old decommissioned naval frigate. Dale had been anxious to see the ship ever since his father had told him about the holes and scoring on the deck from battles with Submariners. It was a parcel of common interest he shared with an otherwise absent father.

The son of a poor Albian immigrant, Dale's father was a hard worker and a fair businessman. He had poured his life into building a business—a business of disassembling things of the past, piecing it out, selling and trading. It provided a stable living for Dale and his older brother, Darius, but his commitment to his work mixed with an already somber disposition made him an absent father, even when he was physically present.

"Hey, how do I look?"

"Like you've been in a fight."

Dale despaired at the thought of spoiling the rare engagement with his father wearing blood and bruises and having to explain himself.

"You think I can go with you instead? To the shop?"

Sparrow shrugged. "If you want."

People from all over made their way through Carnaval City. It was the trade capital of the West, the hub of Meredine's thriving economy. Strategically positioned along the eastern seaboard, the city boasted one of the world's largest seaports and busiest train stations. Like most Azuric immigrants, Sparrow lived in the lower Southside of the Central District, or Azuretown. Though it was only a fifteen-minute walk from the waterfront, to Dale it felt like another country. The strange smells of herbs and spices, the chaos of vendors and traders speaking over one another in foreign tongues, men with distant faces squatting along the wall—it all heightened that sense of *elsewhere*. Even the signs were written in Azuric characters.

Sparrow had taught Dale how to distinguish between the three dominant tribes of Azureland by the way the older men wore their hair. The Shen wore long braided tails, while the Omeijians shaved the crown of their heads and intricately folded their ponytails onto the bare pates. The Goseonites, Sparrow's people, simply gripped their hair together into a short topknot.

"I'll start growing my hair out next year," said Sparrow.

"You going to have a topknot?"

Sparrow shrugged. "My mom will probably want me to."

It wasn't until their thirteenth birthday that Azuric boys were permitted to grow their black hair out. Traditionally, they would then wear it as the men of their respective tribes did. But most of the Azuric youths in Carnaval City were assimilating to the culture and customs of the city. Shedding the particularities of their fathers, they were becoming increasingly indistinguishable.

They walked past the old yellow building where Sparrow and his mother rented a room. In the seven years they had known each other, Sparrow never invited Dale to his home. Dale had never met Sparrow's mother. All Dale knew of her was that she worked late nights and slept all day. As for his father, Dale got bits and pieces of a traveling soldier Sparrow never knew. The closest thing to a father he had ever known was the blacksmith, Master T'varche.

"Hello, Dale."

"Hello, Master T'varche."

Aleksander T'varche hailed from the mountainous regions of Cythica, where the Greater North stretched east into the borders of Azureland. He was lean with big arms and big hands. He had a full head of blonde hair and a thick sandy beard. His eyes sat deep in hollowed sockets, his ears cauliflowered from many years training in various wrestling disciplines. Strange tattoos covered his rosy skin. As for work, he possessed a particular expertise in forging blades.

Without so much as glancing up or disrupting the rhythmic blow of his hammer on glowing steel, he asked in his thick

Silven accent, "What happened to your face?"

"Some boys from my school—" Dale paused, not looking at the Master. "They—we got in a fight."

Master T'varche slipped the shaped steel back into the embers and stoked the flames.

"How many were there?"

"Four."

"Four against one? That's hardly fair."

"It wasn't until Sparrow showed up."

The blacksmith looked at Dale.

"Your first fight?" he asked.

"Yes."

Dale wondered what clued him in.

"Not very pleasant, was it? It never is. Not even when you win."

Master T'varche removed the glowing blade from the coke and hammered out its edge.

"But it is good for you to experience such things, Dale," he added, the steel hissing as he dunked it into the slack tub. "It is good for a boy to grow accustomed to pain."

When he drew the steel from the tub, the short, double-edged sword appeared menacing.

"Most things of value are born of pain and refined with suffering," he continued. "You see this sword. A mere piece of steel. But once tempered in fire and shaped under the force of the hammer, it forms an edge sharper than a jester's wit." He held

> *"It takes a great deal of trauma to make a masterpiece."*

the blade up to the light. "It takes a great deal of trauma to make a masterpiece."

Suddenly, Master T'varche's eyes darted toward the door. Two members of the Kangozen entered. The Kangozen was an Omeijian crime syndicate with roots in Azureland. In recent years they had aggressively expanded into the Republic.

"Afternoon, Cythic. Is the sample ready?" one of them asked.

The blacksmith nodded and quietly disappeared into the storeroom.

While they waited, the younger of the two looked over at Sparrow.

"Oy, aren't you No-ran's boy?" he asked.

In his reticent fashion, Sparrow stood looking nowhere and saying nothing. The gangster walked over and raised Sparrow's head by the chin until their eyes locked.

"I asked you a question. What's your name, young Goseonite?"

"Jūng-geun," Sparrow replied.

Dale hadn't heard that name in a long time. Not since they'd first met. The Goseonite name had never rolled easily off his Grovish tongue.

"Jūng-geun what?" the young gangster pressed.

"Sae," Sparrow replied.

Years before, when Dale had discovered Sparrow's surname translated in Common was "bird," he had said, "Like a sparrow!" And as nicknames among children often do, it stuck.

"So you *are* the son of my favorite whore," said the young gangster. He studied Sparrow for a reaction. "And what happened to your face, Jūng-geun Sae? Were you in a fight?" He leaned in for a closer examination. "Looks like you took a beating."

Then he released him with a snicker just as Aleksander T'varche re-emerged from the storeroom with an ornately decorated oak scabbard. Sheathed in it was the finest benkei backsword west of the Amaranthian Sea. The legendary katanas were rumored to be the sharpest in the world. With a slight curve, the light, slender two-handed single-edged blades were designed for slicing. And it was understood that none other than an Omeijian master smith knew the secrets of forging one well. Aleksander T'varche was the exception to this rule.

The older gangster carefully took it and unsheathed it, his eyes tracing the blade's hamon.

"I wouldn't be surprised if you had Omeijian blood running through your veins, Cythic," he said, studying the craftsmanship. "I'm sure the Orushin will be very pleased with these. They admire your work."

The blacksmith nodded indifferently.

"Now, we'll need fifty," the gangster added.

"It will take a month."

"You have three weeks."

"Polishing alone requires a full week."

"Then you'd better get started."

The Kangozen had been ramping up their orders the last couple years. At its inception, they were no more than a group of street thugs. They operated in relative obscurity. Their activities were random, unorganized—mostly burglary and neighborhood extortion. As they grew in number and as some of the original members grew older, they, like all others in their trade, became increasingly driven by money. Money led the Kangozen to narcotics and then later to human trafficking. Their emergence beyond Azureland gained them notice by both the authorities and the more established underworld presence—the Carousel Rogues.

If such a thing as a moral high ground existed in the criminal underworld, the Carousel Rogues saw themselves on it. Founded as a thieves' guild based in the South District, the Carousel Rogues had evolved into the largest and oldest criminal organization in Carnaval City. With the charm of gangsters of old, they operated in what they considered "legitimate" criminal activities—gambling, racketeering, prostitution. But the Rogues' greatest asset was their stranglehold on the city's black market trade. Their deep pockets bought them association with prominent civic and community leaders, who did not mind the association so long as the Rogues ran their criminal enterprise with a certain delicate touch. They did just that, priding themselves on a certain set of values—discretion being of the highest. For the Rogues, the rise of the Kangozen not only threatened to destabilize their criminal enterprise, it was an offense to their sensibilities. Their reckless, wanton ways could not be tolerated; war was an inevitable future.

The older gangster signaled his minion who then removed a pouch full of gold coins and tossed it on the blacksmith's tool bench.

"An advance for your faithful service," he added. "There will be twenty more when you complete the rest. I'll return in three weeks."

As the young gangster followed him out, he looked again at Sparrow.

"Give your mother my regards. And come see us when you want a real job."

Aleksander walked them out and watched as they marched down the road. Then he turned to Sparrow.

"Go and see your mother before she's off to work. Then return here. We have much to do."

"Yes, master."

"Go in peace, Dale."

"Okay. Bye."

Dale walked with Sparrow back toward the yellow building.

"Who were those guys?"

"The Kangozen. Gangsters."

"What did he mean when he called your mom his favorite whore?"

Sparrow didn't reply. He just hung his head and quickened his steps.

"Is it true?" Dale pressed. "Is she—"

"I don't want to talk about my mom." The tone in Sparrow's voice prompted no further questioning from Dale. They walked along quietly. But then Sparrow started again, almost as if talking to himself. "I'm not ashamed of my mother."

"I'm sorry. I shouldn't be asking about…well, it's none of my business."

"I should go," said Sparrow.

"Okay."

"See you."

"See you."

And as they parted ways, Dale stopped.

"Hey, Sparrow."

The Goseonite turned.

"Thanks, for helping me out today with those guys."

"*Rohar*," Sparrow replied, having always referred to Dale by the endearing Goseonite term literally translated, *My Brother*, "you're my friend. You don't have to thank me."

"Come by when you're free."

"I will."

CH 04

BEFORE THE DUSK

Dale anxiously awaited the arrival of his father. He was later than usual. On occasion, his father stopped by his uncle's bakery after work. The bakery was only a few blocks from the breaker. Dale hoped that on this day, his father was just held up at work.

Just as the house crossed the threshold into needing light, his father walked in holding a bag of day-old bread, two potatoes, and a pot of mutton stew.

"Your auntie fixed us a proper meal again." Dale's father looked at him and added, "Be sure to thank her when you visit."

"Yes, sir."

Dale was now certain his father had heard everything from his uncle, Turkish Shawl, who had heard everything from Mosaic. *Why else would he not be surprised by my bruises?*

"Boil some water for the potatoes and go wash up."

When Dale returned to the table, his father blessed the food and began to eat. Too anxious to eat, Dale just watched as his father's spoon rapped against the side of the soup bowl.

"You're not eating."

"I'm not hungry."

"Auntie Cora Tess went to a lot of trouble to make this for us. Eat."

Dale took a couple disinterested bites

of the bread. He could feel his father's eyes on him, probing.

"We started on the frigate today. I thought you were going to come by."

"I didn't feel like it."

"You were looking forward to it all week."

Dale tore a pinch of white from his bread and rolled it between his fingers into a doughy ball. He took a peek. His father stuffed his mouth with soup-soaked bread. Dale had always admired the way his father ate—tearing away at his portion without a hint of delicacy, chewing with conviction, the muscles in his jaws visibly flexing with each bite. As a child, Dale would stand in front of a mirror compressing his molars, studying his own cheek and temple for some semblance of his eating father.

"There's something we need to talk about, son."

Dale felt his stomach drop to his toes. His father wiped his bearded chin with a napkin, stood up, and walked over to his leather pack on the kitchen counter. He removed from it a book entitled, *The Walgorende's Last Stand*. He brought it over and placed it on the table.

"This belong to you?"

Dale said nothing. His father opened it and on the inside of the cover was Dale's name printed in his own handwriting.

"A constable brought it by my office. Found it in an alley not far from the breaker. A civil complaint was filed by Count Nigel Addy. It said you and your friend beat up his son. Is that true?"

Dale sat quietly rubbing his palms against his trousers, his eyes fixed on his untouched soup.

"I asked you a question."

"Yes, sir. But he started it."

His father folded his arms on the edge of the table and stared at Dale from below his brows.

"He was taken to the hospital."

Dale looked up.

"He's going to be all right, but the school's been notified. You've been expelled."

Dale turned his gaze back down. He clenched his teeth at the injustice of it all.

"Did you hear me, Dale?"

"That's not fair. They were beating *me* up! Four of them! Why am I getting expelled?"

"Expulsion is the least of your concerns! The count was pushing to have you sent to a juvenile detention center. He wanted to press charges for assault."

Dale had heard stories of the detention centers—how it was full of hardened criminals like the Jones' kid who stabbed his foster father in the leg with a pair of scissors.

"Sparrow too, if they knew who he was and where to find him."

"Did you tell on him?"

"You worry about yourself!"

Dale's eyes welled up with tears. The bitterness pushed on his chest until he could not stand it anymore. He wanted to flail, throw something, kick. The acute awareness of his powerlessness made him long for the ability to do something, to exact revenge, to kill Marcus Addy. "I should've killed him," he blurted.

He felt a stinging jolt across his face and the force sent him spinning.

"You watch your tongue!"

There was silence. Silent tears began to flow.

"Do you have any idea how much trouble you're in? I had to ask the constable to speak to the count. I had to plead with him."

"I'm not scared of the count," Dale mumbled.

"What did you say? What did you say? You're not scared? Who do you think you are?"

Dale didn't care anymore. He got up and through streaming tears yelled, "Dad! Four kids attacked me. Because I wouldn't let Marcus pick on me. He's an asshole. He said something about Mom. And then he followed me and Mosaic. Why don't you say something about them? Why don't you stand up to the count? Why are you pleading?"

His father stood dumbfounded.

The silent stare was stifling. Dale wiped his tears. The rage was gone. It was replaced by fear. He had lost control; he had said too much. Then he saw an expression on his father he'd never seen before. Dale learned then that his father's searing glare of disapproval was more bearable than the look of sadness and shame that had replaced it.

His father slumped back in his chair. "This is my fault," he said quietly. "I'm sorry, son. I've failed you as a father. I see now that you are of age—" before Dale could wonder, *of what age?* his father added, "—when you will either become a man or, like so many of us, remain forever as something less. I won't let your fate be determined by my failures. You're going to the Academy. It's time you followed in your brother's footsteps."

Dale's brother, Darius, was already a cadet three years into the Academy of the Republican Guard. Having quickly climbed the ranks, it was expected that he would graduate at the top of his class. He was the pride of their family.

"Darius will be taking his first leave in about a week," his father continued. "When he returns to Pharundelle, you'll go with him. Enrollment begins at the end of the month."

There was a long pause. *It's fair*, thought Dale. It wasn't his father's fault. His life was just how it was. And his father didn't know what to do with him. Dale's eyes were on his toes, chin to chest. His father looked at him for what felt like the very first time.

"You're excused if you've no stomach to eat now."

Dale turned and fought the urge to run into his room. He took slow deliberate steps as his father added from behind, "Ice that cheek and dress your knuckles. We'll talk more about it later."

That night, lying awake with swirling emotions and racing thoughts, Dale began to worry. The romantic in him found the idea of becoming a soldier appealing. But he knew enough to know it would push him to his physical and mental limits. He thought about Master T'varche's words: *Most things of value are born of pain and refined with suffering.*

He worried about whether or not he'd really be able to take a life if he were in battle. That was his last coherent thought before his mind fell under the narcotic spell of exhaustion. Without a drift, he was fast asleep.

When Darius arrived a week later, he was taller and broader than Dale remembered. And seeing him in uniform only reassured him. His anxieties gave way to anticipation. Darius, the same brother he'd grown up with and followed, playing, scrapping—the same brother that would pin him to the floor and spit on his face or punch him in the arm just to remind him who was older—had left Dale's childish world to become a man. A soldier. And suddenly, Dale could hardly wait to join him.

A few days before the brothers were to leave, the entire family gathered at the bakery in the late afternoon, passing time over frosted fig cakes and Dale's favorite, chocolate milk.

"So it was just the two of you against four?" asked Darius, proudly tussling his kid brother's hair.

"Let's hear no more of that," said Dale's father.

"Yes, don't encourage him," Cora Tess added. "A boy shouldn't be fighting in the streets like some hooligan. What is this world coming to?"

Mosaic sat with a slice of cake in her two little hands, frosting all over her mouth. She was softly humming to herself. Her big brown eyes darted from face to face, amused by the grown-ups' idiosyncrasies—the bulbs of saliva that would gather on the corner of Dale's father's lips as he chewed, the way her own father would blink in rapid flutters while he listened to someone speak, how her mother would touch her ear whenever she laughed. Then suddenly, Mosaic noticed someone at the window.

"Look," she said, pointing. "It's your friend, the sad boy." She waved. "What happened to his face?"

Peering in, his scarred face covered in soot, was Sparrow.

"You tell him you're leaving?" asked Dale's father.

"Not yet."

"Go on. You better tell him."

While Dale removed the copy of *The Walgorende's Last Stand* from his bag and walked out to greet Sparrow, Dale's father recounted how the two had become friends.

"When Dale was six years old, he was eating lunch in the schoolyard with the other kids. And he saw that boy drinking water from a drainpipe."

Darius cocked his head to the side, his brows colliding in bewilderment. "Why was he drinking water from a drainpipe?"

"Because some kids couldn't afford food so they filled their stomachs with water while the other kids were eating."

Cora Tess put a hand to her mouth and looked out the window at the Azuric boy. "Oh, the poor thing," she lamented.

"When Dale saw him, he gave him half his potato," Dale's father continued.

"They've been friends ever since. I remember when he told me that story, I kept thinking how proud his mother would've been."

"Aye, she would've been," said Uncle Turkish.

"Imagine, having nothing to eat in this day and age. It just breaks my heart, it does."

"Where are his parents?"

"From what I understand, his mother's a prostitute in Azuretown. He has no father."

"Oh dear."

"What's a pasta toot?" asked Mosaic.

"Never mind, young lady. Go bring him some of this cake. Go on now."

Just outside, Dale greeted his friend.

"Hey."

"Hey."

"What're you doing here?"

"We finished most of the swords," Sparrow replied. "We still have to polish them but—hey, is that Darius?"

"Yeah."

Sparrow waved, and everyone within waved back.

"He's big. How long has he been gone?"

"Three years. We're eating cake. Wanna join us?"

"That's okay," he replied. "I just came by to tell you that we're almost done with the swords."

Mosaic struggled the door open with

"I remember when he told me that, I kept thinking how proud his mother would've been."

---

a slice of cake in her hand and held it up. "Here. Mama told me to bring it out to you. She made it."

Sparrow hesitated.

"Go on," said Dale. "She makes the best fig cakes ever."

Sparrow cautiously took the cake and true to Azuric form, he looked in at Cora Tess through the window and bowed his head in gratitude, then again before Mosaic. Mosaic bashfully twirled her skirt back and forth and watched as he bit into it.

"*Ith good.*"

Mosaic giggled.

"Okay Mo, go back inside," said Dale.

"Why?"

"Because I need to talk to Sparrow for a minute."

"About what?"

"Grown up stuff."

"You're not a grown up."

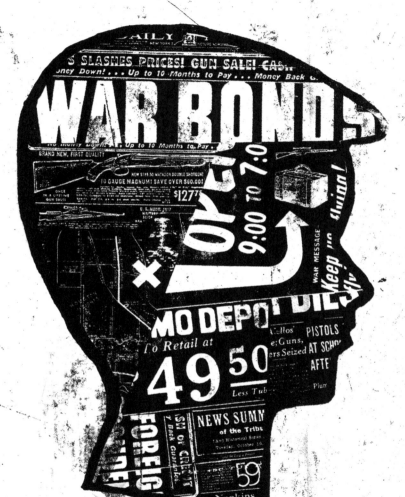

"Am too. Now go on before I make you."

She waited until Dale reached for her and then rushed in with a squeal.

Sparrow finished the cake in four bites.

"Want more?"

Barely able to close his mouth, he shook his head and wiped his hands on his pants.

"So guess what?"

"What?"

"I got expelled."

"Really?"

"Marcus was taken to the hospital so his dad told the school. I'm lucky I'm not going to a detention center."

"Gosh. Sorry to hear that."

"It's not your fault. I mean if it weren't for you, *I* probably would've been the one in the hospital."

"How upset was your dad?"

"Pretty upset."

"Did he beat you?"

"No. But he's sending me to the Academy."

"Really?"

"Yeah. I'm leaving with Darius in a few days."

"For how long?"

"I don't know. Until I graduate?"

"So you're going to be a soldier?"

"I guess," Dale replied with a tinge of pride. "It beats being in school, right?"

Sparrow shrugged.

"Trust me, it does," Dale added. "Although, I bet you would've done well if you stayed in school."

"You think?"

"Better than me. Here." Dale handed him his book. "I never read it but it's a classic. It's about a Mystic king during the crusades or something. Anyway, I thought you might like it."

Sparrow hesitated. He was not accustomed to receiving gifts. Growing up, his mother had instilled in him an aversion to receiving anything. *Never allow yourself to be indebted to another*, his mother had said.

"Take it," Dale insisted. "You can read it when you get a break or something."

Sparrow took the book with a kind of reverence that made Dale chuckle.

"*Rohar*, thank you," he said.

"You're my friend," Dale replied. "You don't have to thank me."

Sparrow smiled. He ran his hand across the cover of the book and slipped it into his pocket. Then his smile faded and his gaze slowly fell.

"So I guess I won't be seeing you around anymore, huh?"

Dale felt guilty, as if he were abandoning his friend to weather the world alone. Like him, he knew Sparrow had few friends. And he had no reliable family. Other than a mother he seldom saw and a strict taskmaster of a blacksmith, Sparrow had no one.

"I don't know. I mean, I'll come home

on leave and stuff so I'll probably see you then," Dale tried. "And you can always come visit me too. Pharundelle isn't *that* far. Only like two days by train if you take the express."

Sparrow knew he could never afford a train ticket. And new cadets weren't permitted to take leave for the first three years. As they spoke these last few wishful words, the two boys had no idea that by Dale's first visit home, his Goseonite friend would no longer be there, swept away in the wake of tragedy. They could not imagine that more than a decade would pass before fate would reunite them.

Sparrow looked up with a glimmer of hope in his eyes contrasted against an otherwise expressionless face.

"That'd be neat," he replied.

And for the moment, they stood beside each other with their backs up against the bakery glass window, watching in silence as people passed by, trying to enjoy their fleeting hours of friendship. The sun was low. The shadows were tall. Everything was saturated in gold.

DEPARTMENT OF THE REPUBLIC GUARD FIELD MANUAL

SURVIVAL MANUAL

HEADQUARTERS, DEPARTMENT OF THE REPUBLICAN GUARD

SM 56-37

9731
NUMBER

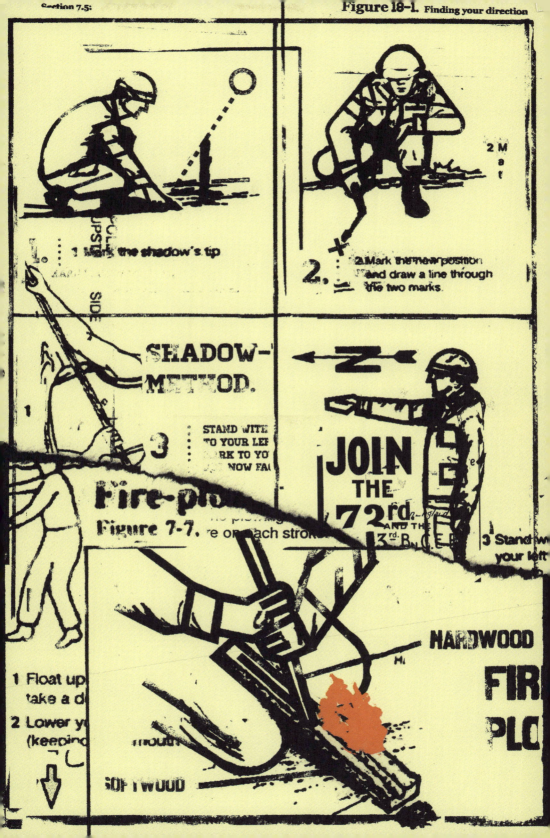

CARNAVAL-CITY NEWS

KING OF THE NORTH DEAD!

Duke Thane takes throne: Could this be the end of Grovish peace?

DEFENDING THE REPUBLIC: OR PLAIN PREMATURE?

Construction of defensive fortresses along border land approved.

JOIN THE

FIGHT FOR PEACE!

Final Edition PHARUNDELLE DAILY

THE SILENT TREATMENT

ALL MEREDIAN RELATIONS WITH BALE SEVERED!

№ 02

CH 05

WAR MACHINES

The first light of day was filtering through an icy haze. It was a cold Balean morning, colder than the starless night before. Thawing inside Castle Verona's War Room were two bearded men with fair, rosy skin and long braided hair—Duke Merrick Thalian and his advisor, Eli Sorensen. They sat waiting at a table with a map of Groveland spread out in between them and a great fire blazing in the hearth behind.

"The people love you, Your Highness," said Eli, the firelight dancing in his eyes. "You are a just ruler. A reflection of our late king."

The duke smiled. "Is that what your Ciphers told you?"

Eli Sorensen was both advisor to the throne and the director of the Royal Intelligence Brigade, commonly referred to as the *Ciphers*. As the head of Balean intelligence, it was his job to oversee the collection of sensitive information. He was constantly analyzing and re-analyzing, sifting through countless documents and sources of information. The duke knew what he was getting when he appointed Eli. He wanted someone cold and calculating in his political corner, someone who could navigate that treacherous terrain of "snakes and thespians," as he would refer to politicians, without turning into one himself.

    Following the untimely death of the late king, Aegis Leawen, the duke was elected regent. As a man who despised politics, it was a position he had accepted reluctantly.

    "It's not their love that I desire, Eli." He looked down at the map. "It's the preservation of the oldest monarchy in all of Parabolis. To see it handed down to its rightful successor in its rightful condition."

    Groveland was separated into two global powers: the Republic of Meredine to the south and the Kingdom of Bale to the north. The kingdom's borders were marked on the map with a red outline stretching from the Hesperian Highlands

> **"As you know, General, wars are won with money."**

to the Lecidian Mountains of Silverland.

"And its rightful condition will be the glory into which you will lead it," Eli replied.

The duke looked at his advisor from below his brows. He was about to say something, cast some doubt on their undertaking, when General Arun Kilbremmer entered. His eyes still had sleep in them.

"It's colder than a spurned lover," he said, cinching his collar. He was clothed in a fur-lined, leather uniform. He had platinum hair and was older than both the duke and Eli. His face wore many years of hard decisions but his body was fitter than those of men half his age.

He walked over to the hearth to warm his hands and looked around the room. "Where are the others?"

"There are no others," the duke replied. "Sit."

Merrick waited until the general took his seat beside Eli. "This meeting is not for the Royal Court," he added. "Not for now, at least."

"Why the secrecy?"

"We've decided to act."

The general sighed through his nose. "And how long have you known this?"

"For as long as our benefactor has funded this initiative."

"'*Benefactor*.'" The general grunted. "I don't trust that man, Merrick. You know this. I don't trust anyone who wears a mask."

"Trust him or not, General, he has delivered on every account," said Eli. "We now have international support."

"You call a handful of wealthy men 'international support?'"

"I call it money. As you know, General, wars are won with money. And with our funds secure, we will proceed as planned. We enter Meredian soil on the night of their Harvest Festival and take Carnaval City. We take Carnaval City, we take Pharundelle. And that means the Republic."

The general pressed his finger down on the map along the borderland marked by a star, northeast of Carnaval City. "What about this?"

"Yes, the Gateway to the Republic. What about it?"

"You still don't understand the implications of what it is that the Republic has managed to construct here, do you?"

"Enlighten me, General."

"The Ancile is a star fortress. Unlike your conventional fortresses with high walls and rounded turrets, this intricately designed structure is composed of low set, thick walls made of brick, reinforced with an external shell of iron. Here, several armed bastions extend out into diamond shaped points, designed to prevent storming infantry cover from defensive fire. Run between them and you'll be met with an onslaught of rifle fire and arrows. A conventional approach will do us no good."

Eli smiled. "I couldn't agree more. Consider for us an *un*conventional approach then."

"To the west, you have the Wilds, the World's End beyond that. To the east, the Borderland Ridge overlooking our own highlands as far as Muriah Bay. There's no way around it but by the Amaranthian. And we'd risk forfeiting the element of surprise and invite a swift counter-offensive, assuming, of course, the Royal Fleet's successful engagement with their blockade. There is no strategically advantageous approach."

"I'm disappointed in your lack of imagination, Arun," said the duke.

The general sighed again. "For more than a millennium we have managed to coexist in relative harmony with our neighbors to the south. Perhaps it is not too late to reinitiate dialogue."

The duke sat back in his seat. He folded his arms and cocked his head. "You don't think this Ancile, which you've described in great detail, sitting there on our border, poses any threat to our sovereignty?"

"Of course it does."

"You've no stomach to fight, then?"

"The question is not what is in my stomach," the general's voice grew louder as he continued, "but whether or not an open war is what the king would have wanted."

"The king is dead. I am regent until the child returns. All I want to know is if I take a course of action that leads us to war, will you fight for us?"

Arun's eyes lit up, brighter than the fire. Through clenched teeth he replied, "With all due respect, *Your Highness*, I was Bjorn of the Crimson Knights while you were still a hairless pup! Never again will you question my loyalty to the throne. Regardless of who sits on it, I would die for my kingdom."

The duke smiled. "That's all I wanted to hear." Both he and Eli then rose from their seats. "Come with us."

"Where? What's this all about?"

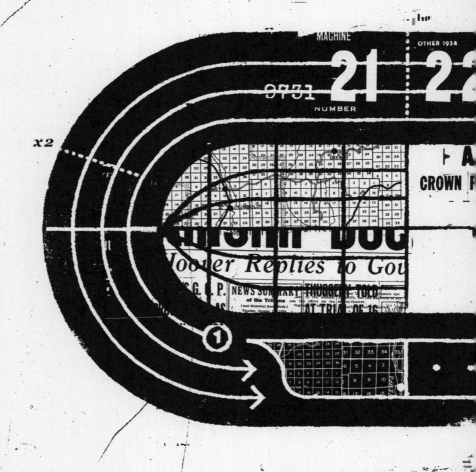

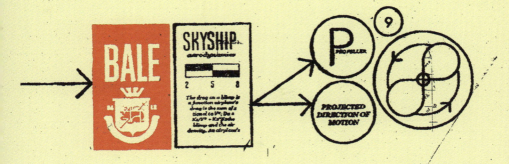

"Our answer to the Ancile. Bring your coat."

The three men shared a carriage into a barren field behind Castle Verona, heavily guarded by a series of checkpoints manned with the Cipher's own security detail. They stopped just short of a steep hill and hiked to its icy precipice overlooking Brakkar Gorge. Welding sparks flew like confetti below, the finishing touches of a war machine in assembly. Another completed just beyond.

"Have you gone mad? You're building ships in a canyon."

"Skyships, General," Eli replied. "A galleon of steel and oak designed to sail the clouds. It's amazing what a balloon, some propellers, and wing flaps can do. That's the prototype there."

"It flies?"

"It flies."

There was a moment of pause—an appreciation for the fact that the world would never be the same again.

"Incredible. How many?"

"Just the two there for now. But we plan to have a fleet of twelve ready for the Harvest Festival."

"And the benefactor knows about this?"

"It was his idea," Eli replied. "His blueprints."

They watched as the operational prototype was being fitted with artilleries and munitions.

"Merrick, what exactly do you know about this benefactor?" asked Arun, his eyes never leaving the skyship.

"His name is Magog Siberion," the duke replied. "A Veshalic national who believes the whole of Groveland should be united under the crown, as it was in the days of old."

"Why should a Silven care what becomes of Groveland?"

"He doesn't. He cares what becomes of the Republic. Before he founded the Machina Investment Group, he was a Red Dragon in the Reznevayok Special Operations Command in the Liberation Army of Veshale. He is no friend of the Republic."

"An 'enemy of my enemy.' But do you trust him?"

Duke Thalian faced Arun. "I have seen him without his mask. He wears it to conceal a grotesque bloodstain in the shape of a handprint tattooed across his face. Not many are privy to that. And then, there's this." The duke held out his hand over the gorge. "So yes, Arun. I trust him."

The general nodded, eyes still glazed with wonder. Then he softly said, "This will change everything, Merrick. Forever."

CH — 06

A NEW BEGINNING

Thirteen years had passed since Dale left for the Academy, seven since his graduation and subsequent enlistment, four since his commissioning, and three days since his resignation. At twenty-five years old, Dale's military career had come to an abrupt end.

He had since learned to enjoy the simple pleasures of life—the scent of a bathed woman's hair, a ballad on the oboe, a smoke in the cold, and not least of all, a long, quiet, train ride. He watched the world scroll past the windows, the canopies of trees mushrooming over the morning mist, the migration of buffalo across prairieland, the grass swaying in the wind, and wild horses under the moonlight. The world on the other side of the train window was a world unlike the one he'd known for the past thirteen years—a world full of tightly structured days and nights, of endless duties, of class after class. There were training camps, anxious patrols through dangerous trade routes. And death.

"Life," Staff Sergeant Weylin had said while leading Dale's company through a village they had just raided. "So frail and so goddamn meaningless. Pile 'em up and burn 'em!"

It was a world growing distant with each rhythmic rattle of steel on tracks. And Dale couldn't be happier for it.

As a commissioned officer, Dale spent

"I'm not giving up. I'm moving on."

---

most of his tour in the south patrolling bandit trade routes and protecting Republic interests in Loreland; that is to say, protecting Republic-occupied natural resources on foreign soil from the Shaldean Riders. His first kill was a Shaldean, an Emmainite villager barely old enough to be considered a man.

In retaliation for a string of attacks on copper mines owned by Republic corporations, Dale's unit had been sent in to a nearby village suspected of sheltering a Shaldean cell leader. While investigating his whereabouts, a mob of loyal Shaldean sympathizers attacked them with nothing more than daggers and farming tools. Dale's unit suppressed the village uprising. Some were shot and the others scattered. The village was left with only a handful of frightened women and children.

Contrary to the expectations of those who knew him, and to his own expectations most of all, Dale excelled in the Academy environment. He didn't enjoy the daily regimen of training, but he developed into a good soldier. His superiors took notice and before long, Dale was given broader areas of responsibility. Once in the field, he discovered that he flourished in the heat of a fight. Coming off the adrenaline highs, he quietly reveled in the courage he did not know he had. But there was no reveling in taking another's life. Once he had shot the young Shaldean and sent him across that irreversible line, he discovered it became easier to send others. The act became easier, but the ease became unsettling.

"If it wasn't them, it would've been us," his fellow soldiers reasoned.

For Dale, it wasn't so simple. Dale had always been content with ambiguity when it came to questions of faith and religion. In the midst of his duties as a soldier, to remain ambiguous grew increasingly uncomfortable. Despite a context in which killing was sanctioned, even justified, he couldn't help but feel a growing, looming judgment from some cosmic judicial system that would one day summon him to settle accounts. The feeling, corroborated by his conscience, would not leave Dale alone. He began to question the Republic's policies.

What rights, if any, did the Republic have on Emmainite land?

He began to question himself—who he had become.

Dale's career in the Republican Guard ended the same year his father passed away. Stationed in a remote Loreland outpost along the Saracen, Dale was unable to attend the funeral. He mourned alone. And it was then that he decided he was going to resign.

Days before his decommissioning and scheduled departure, Darius visited him in Pharundelle.

"You're making a mistake, Dale."

"Maybe."

"No, you are. After you've worked all these years, you're just going to give up now?"

"I'm not giving up. I'm moving on."

"To do what?"

Stuffing his duffle bag with what little possessions he had, Dale replied, "I'm going to take over Dad's breaker."

"Dad's breaker? What the hell do you know about running a business?"

"Nothing yet."

"Dad poured his life into that thing so we wouldn't have to live like him. So we could have opportunities he didn't have. You want to do something for him, make captain."

"I don't want to make captain and I'm not doing this for him. You make it sound like wanting to live a quiet life is asking too much."

"Not too much. Too little. A quiet life isn't living, Dale. Life is about being a part of something greater than yourself. It's about sacrifice."

It was regurgitated propaganda straight from the Republican Guard's cadet training. Dale knew it well. There was a time when he believed every word.

"Well, that's not what I'm about. I'm not like you."

In the early years at the Academy, Dale had begun to suspect that he and Darius were very different. After graduation, as he began to serve, the difference grew increasingly apparent. Dale knew that if he stayed with the Guard, it would be for different reasons than his older, more ambitious brother. When Dale began to grapple with the moral implications of his career, there was no doubt that he and Darius were destined to take divergent paths. He wasn't a warrior. At least not in the way Darius seemed to embody it. A major at twenty-eight, Darius was the consummate soldier. He followed orders well. He was competent, dutiful, and a natural-born leader. And when he killed in the line of duty, he did not seem to give it a second thought.

"I know what this is about," Darius tried. "I know it's not easy, the things required of us."

"You don't need to coddle me. That's not what this is about."

"Then what *is* it about?"

"Everything. This whole system. Us. The Republic."

"What're you talking about?"

Dale walked over to his inventory chest at the foot of his bunk, removed an old textbook and held it up. "You remember reading this in the Academy?" He tossed it on the cot beside Darius. "The Siños Uprising. You remember what happened? The massacre? Why it happened? That course was all about how we stopped them. But no one ever talks about how it started."

"I know how it started. The mining corporations."

"*Meredian* mining corporations. We started it. The Shaldea are no different from the Siños Nacional Movement. It's just a different era, different people, different resources."

"The Shaldea? You're talking about the Shaldea? We've got a warmongering pretender to the throne rallying his army

to the north, and you're talking about sandworms?"

Dale realized there was no reasoning with Darius. He shook his head and started for the latrine. Darius followed.

"You know what your problem is? You're a romantic. You have unreasonable expectations of life."

Dale stopped, appalled by the accusation. "Wait, *I'm* a romantic?"

"At some point, you're going to have to just accept it for what it is and stop living with these silly ideas of how you think it should be—"

"You're the one talking about glory and sacrifice, and you're calling *me* a romantic?"

"You're not a kid anymore."

Dale threw up his hands. "No shit."

"Calm down."

Nothing made Dale more upset than being told to calm down.

"I am calm!"

Trailing him into the latrine, Darius persisted. "You think working at the breaker will make you any happier?"

"Maybe."

"It won't. You know why? Because you're the kind of guy who can't be happy unless there's something to be unhappy about."

Dale scoffed and squared up to the toilet. "You going to watch me piss?"

When he had finished relieving himself, Darius was waiting back at the bunk.

"Look, you know I'm being transferred to the Ancile."

"Yeah, I know. Congratulations." Dale resumed packing.

"It's only a matter of time before Bale invades. You know that too. The Ancile is going to be the front line."

"Well, I'm not worried. That thing is supposed to be impenetrable."

"My point exactly. It's where you want to be when the shit starts flying. You should come with me, Dale. I can put in a word for you. It's not too late."

"Dare—"

"Just think about it, all right? This isn't about protecting corporate interests. Duke Merrick Thalian is a real threat to our world. They invade, you can forget about Dad's breaker and you can forget about your quiet little life. It's up to you whether you're going to do something about it or not. But you can't just ignore it. So think about that before you get on that train. All right?"

"I've already thought about it."

"Dale! Just think about it, for God's sake!"

"All right! All right. Calm down."

And Dale thought about it. He thought about it as he was debriefed and decommissioned in the days that followed. He thought about it on the Groveland Express, watching the world change outside his window, bound for Carnaval City. Bound for the quiet life.

CH 07
ON THE GROVELAND EXPRESS

On the second morning of the two-day trip from Pharundelle, the Groveland Express pulled into a small station in a rural village called Lumarion. A handful of passengers boarded. During the stop, Dale stepped off the train to stretch his legs. He snacked on some candied ginger that he had purchased from a local vendor and had a smoke before returning to his seat, content. With two-thirds of his journey to Carnaval City behind him, he looked forward to a few more hours to himself. The first few days back, he anticipated, would be busy with seeing people and sorting through the state of affairs at the breaker. There had been little solitude over the past seven years since the Academy, so he relished the time on the Express, alone with his thoughts. He sat back and thought of Sparrow.

During his first visit back to Carnaval City, three years into the Academy, Dale went to Azuretown looking for Sparrow. After a year of letters trickled back and forth, the sparse communication stopped.

Dale had assumed he would find things as he'd left them. But Master T'varche's forge had been sold to another smith, who had explained to him that Aleksander T'varche practically gave him the business and left the country. Dale went looking for Sparrow's home, the yellow building into which Dale had never entered. Sparrow was not there. When he asked around, he learned that Sparrow's mother had passed away under unfortunate circumstances not long after Dale had left for the Academy. No one had seen him since.

Dale's thoughts of Sparrow were interrupted by the sight of a young woman, a cleric of the Benesanti, walking down the aisle looking at the seats and the ticket in her hand.

She was beautiful. The modest appearance required of a Holy Order acolyte did little to hide her simple beauty. Her short, espresso hair was cut in a unisex fashion. She wore a cleric's habit in standard gray, marked with the red and white crest of the Benesanti on its shoulder. The unflattering dress and the haphazardly cut hair only highlighted her face—fair with blue-gray eyes, full lips, and high-arching eyebrows that gave her the uninviting weightiness of a full presence, concerned more with what she was doing than who she was.

She took a seat, four rows up, facing Dale. He could neither look away nor sit staring directly at her. He was like a man pained by the setting sun, the unapproachable brilliance, the beauty of what he could not touch, slowly and inevitably slipping away. After thirty minutes of stealing glances, Dale got up and walked to the back of the train in agitation.

The last time he'd felt like this was when he first set eyes on Johana Sagan, a nurse-in-training at an all-girls school near the Academy. She had chestnut hair and a kind face. Dale couldn't stop obsessing over her. After months of misery, he had an opportunity to talk to her. Like any boy his age, he feared rejection. Still, he tried. And to his surprise, Johana reciprocated his interest. They began seeing each other as frequently as they could. But with each encounter, the enchantment began to peel away layer by layer until at last, there was no more depth to their notions of love into which they could fall. He realized then that it was never Johana with whom he had been smitten, but rather a meticulously constructed idol in his mind bearing her likeness—a far cry from Johana the real. Before graduation, Dale called off the relationship, vowing never to make the same mistake again. A vow he could hardly remember standing there in the back of the train.

Darius was right. Dale was a hopeless romantic. When he returned to his seat, he couldn't help himself from thinking about what might be. His approach, her reaction. For the three remaining hours,

this cleric was his singular focus. At one point, he took an unnecessary trip to the toilet in the next car so he could get a closer look. In the bathroom, Dale was disgusted with himself. He was determined to stop obsessing. Then he went right on obsessing until the train finally pulled into Carnaval City's Central Station.

As the passengers began to collect their belongings, Dale knew it would likely be the last he'd see of her. If there were to be any chance of either realizing or dispelling what only existed in the realm of possibility, he would have to exercise some sort of bold initiative. When the doors opened, Dale was one of the first to stand. He slung his duffle bag over his shoulder and weaved his way up the aisle. To calm himself, Dale remembered, *I'm a soldier, I've been in battles. I've killed people.*

The cleric had her back to him, gathering her belongings—a small satchel and several books. He tapped her on the shoulder.

"Excuse me."

She turned to him with an inquiring look.

"Yes?"

"I…" Dale went blank.

When Dale said nothing, she quickly assumed he was trying to get by.

"Oh, sorry."

With a "thank you," Dale walked past her. He stepped off the train, rolling his eyes and shaking his head. Walking through the station, his cognitive capacity coming back to him, Dale ran through all the things he could have said. It was so plain to him. It seemed so simple. He thought of how different the last leg of the trip was from the quietness of the first. How easily life is disrupted. Dale thought he had better find a place for a drink.

CH 08

SELAH

The cleric emerged from the train after Dale. Alaric Linhelm, Marshal of the Vail Templar, was waiting to greet her on the platform.

"It's been a long time, dear child," he said, bowing.

His voice was a raspy whisper. It suited his weathered face, generously marked by battle scars. A prominent scar ran down his right eye, leaving it with a colorless iris. Even as he greeted his guest with warm words, his expression was stoic, firm.

"Champion Alaric Linhelm," said the cleric. "I'm pleased to see that the years have been kind to you."

"And you. You've grown into your own, haven't you? A proper sister of the Benesanti now."

"The Maker has been gracious to me on this side of life."

"Shall I call you Prioress Evenford, then?"

"Selah is fine."

"The name suits you, Selah."

In Balean fashion, they spoke humorlessly, without inflection, like mathematicians or librarians.

"You sound local," said Alaric, taking note of the cleric's Meredian accent, or rather, the lack of a Balean one.

"I should hope so. It's been quite some time since I've taken to life in the Republic."

The templar paused, suspicious of every passerby within earshot, before finally snatching her books and satchel.

"Come. This is no place to dawdle." He hurried out of the station where his coach was waiting for them. Four more templar guarded it. They wore polished helms, breastplates, gauntlets and greaves. Their armor shimmered in the morning sun as they stood vigil with their tower shields and their signature broadswords that measured shoulder high from tip to pommel.

After loading her belongings and settling into the car, Alaric seemed more at ease.

"Forgive me for rushing you, child," he added, "but there are eyes lurking in the shadows. And this city has many shadows."

The carriage started toward the temple.

"That dangerous, is it?"

"Carnaval City is no Lumarion."

Gazing out the window, Selah softly muttered, "Brilliant."

"You have nothing to worry about. I'll keep my good eye on you."

A small patch of fog formed on the window from Selah's breath. She poked two eyes into it and completed a smiling face with a swipe. Then she turned to Alaric. "Just the same, I'd feel safer with a sword of my own."

"You still know your way around steel?"

"Of course."

"All this time in service of the cloth has not softened you?"

"Is this a challenge?"

Alaric huffed.

"It's not easy to forget when I've learned from the best," Selah added.

Alaric folded his arms across his chest and sighed. "Aye. The best I most certainly *was*, before my body began to betray me."

"Making excuses? That is unlike you, Alaric."

"Be mindful of the robes you wear, child. A sword has no place in the hands of a cleric."

Selah glanced out the window just in time to catch a group of mischievous children fleeing a candy store. Tracking them with her eyes until they disappeared beyond view, she said, "If I were born a man, I could've been a templar."

"Aye. A fine one at that."

Then she looked at Alaric.

"And had you been born a lass, what kind of cleric would you have been? I wonder."

Again, Alaric huffed.

"I would've been far too pretty to be a cleric."

Selah smiled. But the smile faded as quickly as it had appeared. She looked over at this old man and her thoughts drifted into a distant past when she knew Alaric only as her mother's friend. A past

> **"...there are eyes lurking in the shadows. And this city has many shadows."**

---

when her smiles were more frequent.

The carriage pulled into the West Gate of the temple grounds. At its center was one of four temples in the entire world, ornately decorated with reliefs carved into its whitewashed façade, and skyscraping spires guarded by gargoyles perching on every corner. Flanking it on either side was the College of Sisters for the clerics and the barracks of the Vail Templar.

Serving as monuments of the Benesanti's vast global influence, each temple had been erected in four select cities in each of the four corners of Parabolis. This one, in Carnaval City, represented the whole of Groveland.

"There are rumors," said Selah, unmoved by the architectural marvel.

"What kind of rumors?"

"I've heard that Duke Thalian is preparing for an invasion. Is this true?"

"I don't know," Alaric replied. "But pray that it is not."

CH 09

HOME

The city teemed with traders, sidewalk musicians, street performers. A prophet stood on his soapbox. And in the shadows lurked the swindlers and strangers. Progress had changed the backdrop; the buildings were newer, taller, shinier. Most of the street vendors had given way to rows of storefronts. But the feel of Carnaval City endured. Dale hailed a cabriolet and took it to the waterfront, hoping to find his bearings in more familiar surroundings. As he rode into the old neighborhood, Dale saw that it too had transformed under the hand of progress. There was now a large cannery where there once was an outdoor market. Beyond the wharf was the monument of modern progress known as the Spegen. It was a contraction of "Steam Powered Electric Generator," or the "S.P.E. Gen," a smaller counterpart to the massive thermal power plant in Pharundelle. Its steady hum, and not the crashing waves of the bay, had become the new ubiquitous sound of the waterfront.

The familiar smell of freshly baked baguettes drew Dale into the old bakery. It was smaller than he remembered. A little rusty bell rang as he entered. There was a young woman wiping down the counter, her fingernails painted dark purple. She had a delicate frame and a porcelain-sculpted face. Her ears were poking out of her dark brown hair that fell short of her shoulders and naturally curled up just below the jaw line.

"Mo?"

"Excuse me?" she asked, startled.

Her voice was soft as a song. Her eyes lit up. Though nineteen years old, Mosaic Shawl still had the face of a child with full triangle lips. Her large doe eyes were kind and curious.

"Dale? Dale! Papa, it's Dale!" she yelled as she ran around the counter.

Before he knew it, there was an onslaught of hugs and kisses. And questions. Finally, Uncle Turkish burst out. "Okay, hey, let's give the boy some room." With that he led Dale to their table in the corner and placed a plate of fresh bread in front of him. "It's damn good to see you, boy."

"You too, Uncle."

"How was the trip?"

"Nice."

"Long, I imagine."

"Long, but nice."

"How about some port to wet your beak?"

"You got anything lighter?"

"Sure, we've got some white wine and I think I've got some bottled ale in the back."

"Actually, could I get some chocolate milk?"

"Heh! Did you hear that, love?"

Turkish poured himself a glass of port while Cora Tess prepared a cold glass of creamy chocolate milk for Dale.

"Just the way you like it," she said, setting it down in front of him.

She watched with satisfaction as Dale cleared half its contents.

"Gosh, I missed this," he said. A cocoa mustache coated his upper lip. "This really is an art, Auntie. That golden ratio of powdered chocolate, sugar, and milk. I don't know how you do it."

She touched her ear and laughed.

Mosaic smiled in the back. "Never knew you were a connoisseur of a five-year-old's drink," she said.

"Never mind her," said Cora Tess.

"You just let me know when you want a proper drink," said Turkish, lifting his glass of port. "I've got an excellent bottle of brandy at home I've been meaning to open."

Cora Tess then clasped her hands together, an epiphanic expression on her face. "I'll whip up a fig cake just for you."

"No, don't trouble yourself, Auntie," Dale tried.

"Nonsense. There's always a lull in the afternoon. Might as well make myself useful."

Cora Tess grew up in an era of wars and famines. She was familiar with both and what they did to the value of food. For her, love was feeding someone a good meal. Whenever Darius and Dale would visit as kids, she'd give them a big hug and with great enthusiasm say, "Auntie will make you boys something really good!"

Having finished wiping down the tables and packaging orders placed for pickup, Mosaic quickly changed out of her apron. She stopped by the table, apologizing that she had to get to rehearsals for an upcoming performance at the Halo's Concert Hall. Apparently, she had taken up the piano a few years back as a part of her studies and turned out to be quite a talented musician.

"I wish I could stay and catch up."

"Don't worry about it," said Dale. "We'll have plenty of time for that. Get going."

"Will you be home for dinner?" asked Cora Tess.

"I don't think so." Mosaic gave her a peck on the cheek.

Seeing her interact with her parents only made their age difference more pronounced. They'd had Mosaic late; Dale's uncle and aunt were old enough to be her grandparents.

"Well, don't be too late."

"Don't wait up. Love you."

She slipped into her coat and gave Dale another hug.

"It's good to have you back," she said.

Then she walked out, shoelaces untied. She hopped on her rusty old bicycle and waved through the window before peddling off.

"There she goes again," said Turkish, shaking his head. "Always on the go, that one."

"I hardly recognized her. Can't believe it."

"Can't say much about her fashion sensibilities, but she's blossomed into quite a beautiful young lady."

"Bet there's some boys sniffing around here, huh?"

"Keeps me up at night," Turkish replied. They all laughed.

"Don't worry about it, Uncle. Just give me a list and I'll take care of them."

"No! There is no list. That's the problem. She's too busy for boys. Every morning, she's in here with us, and every afternoon, if she's not buried in her books, she's off to the Concert Hall. She has no interest in boys at all. Is that normal?"

"Really? That's a good thing, isn't it?"

"I don't know. It just doesn't seem right. Most boys and girls her age are given to some chasing. Not Mosaic. Not that one."

"Can't rush a lass into love," said Cora Tess from behind the counter.

"Love? I'm not talking about love. I'm talking about marriage. Grandchildren."

"There you go again."

"I just want to know when," Turkish directed over his shoulder. He turned back to a smiling Dale and gave him a wink. Then he poured himself another glass. "Speaking of love, anyone in your life?"

"No, nobody."

"Well, I'm sure you'll have no trouble finding a nice girl to settle down with in town."

Dale shrugged.

"What about Darius?"

"He settles down with someone new every time he's on leave."

Turkish gave an approving smirk. Then they both burst into laughter.

"By the way, he sends his regards," Dale added.

"Oh? He visited you?"

"In Pharundelle just before I got out. He tried to talk me out of it. He wanted me to join him at the Ancile."

"So why didn't you?"

"I don't know," he replied, swirling the chocolate milk around in his glass. "I was just done."

There was a pause.

"Well, probably for the best. You pay your respects to your parents yet?"

"I came straight here."

"Right, well, you make sure you do that."

"I will."

"When was the last time you saw your father?"

"When I graduated."

Turkish shook his head. Then he disappeared behind the counter and returned with an envelope.

"Here," he said, removing some documents and sliding them across the table. "I had these prepared as soon as I received your wire."

They were the deed to his father's house along with a key and an application for a business license.

"Now, I've registered you with the Department of Commerce, but you'll have to go in yourself to change the title of ownership on the breaker when you apply."

"Thanks for taking care of that," said Dale.

"If it were anyone else, I'd tell him that it's not a good time for business. But you're your father's son. Your father knew how to thrive wherever he was with whatever he had. I'm sure you'll do the same." Turkish took a shallow sip of his port. Then he stared off into the distance. "You know, I never told you this, but I didn't like him very much when your mother first introduced me."

"Why's that?"

"Same reason you don't like the idea of boys sniffing around here. I wasn't about to let my baby sister get swept up by just anybody. And especially not some poor kid from Albia."

"What's wrong with Albians?"

"They had a reputation back then for being passionate. And by passionate, I mean short tempered and impulsive. You know anything about that?" Turkish asked with a smirk.

"Little bit."

"I still remember the first time I met him. I was a few years older than you are now, and he and your mother were, what? Seven years younger? They were just kids, the two of them. We had him over for dinner and I remember he was terribly nervous. You couldn't tell by the look on his face, but he kept rubbing his palms against his trousers. He didn't say much. Didn't eat much, either. I asked him what he did. He looked me straight in the eyes and told me he shined shoes at the Central Station. That's what he was doing at the time, he and your grandfather. Shining shoes. It paid for his schooling and school is where he met your mother. You know that. Anyway, I laughed at him when he told me what he did—a shoe shiner. I asked him how he expected to support your mother. I asked him if that's the kind of life he thought my sister deserved. And I still remember the look on his face. He looked at me like he was about to jump the table. He said, 'Your sister deserves to be happy. And I will do whatever it takes to make her happy.' He wasn't rubbing his trousers anymore. The following week, he dropped his classes and took up a second job as a hired hand at the shipping yard. Every morning, before shining shoes, your father broke his back working at the docks. He worked those two jobs for over three years. For peanuts. But he saved every bit of it and put it into that house—your house. Then he asked your mother to marry him. Your father understood the meaning of love. I didn't laugh at him much after

> *"...you're your father's son. Your father knew how to thrive wherever he was with whatever he had."*

that."

"When did he start the breaker?"

"When Darius was born. Your grandfather passed away around the same time and left him some money. He put all of it down on some abandoned docks and turned that thing into the ship-breaking yard. Who's ever heard of a ship-breaking yard? But that's what he did. Found himself a niche and started his own business. Your father was a clever man. And a damn hard worker."

"Aye, he was a good man," chimed Cora Tess, coming out from the kitchen.

Turkish tossed back the remaining port in his glass.

"A man of his word too," he said. "He

made your mother very happy. Gave her everything she deserved and more."

"I wish I knew her," said Dale.

"Your mother?" Turkish snorted. "Oh, there wasn't a creature alive that didn't love her. She was a beauty. She didn't think about herself much. And saw the best in people. She could see way back then what your father could be when he was shining shoes at the station. It's almost like he lived up to what she saw in him."

Turkish sighed and poured himself another glass of port. Dale sat staring at the keys in his hand.

"Go on, now. You've made a long journey. Go home and get settled in. After you visit your mother and father, come by the house for supper. We'll have a feast ready. And maybe even open that bottle of brandy."

"What about the cake?" Dale asked.

"We'll have it for dessert," said Cora Tess. "Now off with you."

Dale thanked them and wandered back into the streets, heading to his father's house. The house he'd grown up in. He was relieved to see it unmolested by modernity. Just as he remembered it, the house sat nestled in a row of old shops and eateries along the boardwalk. As he approached the house, he paused to take in that familiar smell, the fishy, salted air of the bay.

The doorknob was loose. Inside, there was a musty odor of an abandoned home. Dale walked toward the kitchen and saw a thin layer of dust on the dining table. The wall clock was still ticking. He ran his fingers along the old cast iron furnace. Cold. Then he noticed the faded black and white photographs lined along the fireplace mantle. They were the same photos of Darius and Dale as young children. At the end were two recent graduation photos from the Academy. And then there were the two pulled in front of his mother. Dale studied each closely as he had just about every day growing up. The mother he had never known, frozen. In one she looked serious. In the other, in which she stood in his father's embrace, his mother smiled almost in laughter. His father looked especially strange. He was smiling. Beaming. Suddenly, Dale realized he couldn't remember the sound of his father's laughter. He realized his father had never known a day of joy since his mother's death—since Dale's birth. A lump formed in his throat. He cleared his throat and went over to the kitchen cabinet where his father used to store his liquor. There was a half-emptied bottle of bourbon.

Thanks, Pops.

Dale sat at the dining table, lit a smoke and sipped from the bottle.

After he'd finished settling in, he hiked up to the cemetery by the abandoned lighthouse overlooking the bay. His father was buried beside his mother. The grave was marked with a simple stone block that read: *Mikhail Sunday, proud father, loving husband, faithful servant.*

Ever since he received news about his father's passing, Dale thought about this moment. He played through in his mind the things he would say: the apologies, the gratitude, the things he should've said to his living father. Standing there over his grave, Dale could not bring himself to say anything. He took a quick scan of the empty cemetery. Then he muttered under his breath, "I hope you see her now, Dad."

As night fell, his coach arrived in Hoche—a quaint village just outside of the main city where the Shawls lived. From a distance, Dale's uncle's cottage looked like something out of a painting, softly glowing against the backdrop of lush rolling hills. Smoke rose weightlessly from the chimney into the cool autumn air. Dale took it all in, overwhelmed by the feeling of childhood—the feeling of holiday and home.

CH 10

CARNAVAL CITY

Dale could not reopen the breaker for a couple weeks. Upon his initial survey, it was apparent to him that he had to first figure out the business. He started with trying to understand the shop's set up—what went where and why? His father's idea of a filing system was stacks of paper on desks, and more stacks in boxes. But after two days of investigative work, Dale began to see that there was an organization to the chaos. A hidden system. Once he could see it, he began to understand what his father was doing. Those two weeks, Dale was in early; he left late. With the daylight, he made slight adjustments to the yard—placement of certain containers with specific types of scrap. Nights were spent in the office poring over the books, receipts, and records of business dealings. It gave him a sense of the business, a business built largely around salvaged scrap parts.

Organizing inventory and pushing papers at a desk was quite a departure from his former life. At first, being "your own boss" was a welcome change from the regimented life of a soldier. But once he got past the challenge of getting the shop operational, Dale grew quickly bored. It didn't take long for him to realize that he lacked that certain penchant for business; namely, he lacked the love of money.

Without proper motivation, Dale spent hours at a time swiveling in his father's leather chair, wondering how his life had become an aimless routine of disassembling ships and selling their salvageable parts for scrap.

After closing shop one evening, Dale wandered along the docks. Under fading light, the still surface of the Amaranthian Sea beyond the bay looked like a sheet of glass. Along the harbor were anchored ships—an entire community of seafarers with their laundry hanging on cables across obsolete masts, smoke stacks rising from the galleys above deck. The scene brought to mind his childhood fantasies of setting sail toward an endless horizon into the unknown beyond, free and elsewhere. A life at sea that ended drearily in a stinking bay. He had grown so far from that boy for whom it was so normal to dream.

Dale walked beyond the boardwalk and into the streets of the waterfront. There, he stopped at the overpass, the one he and Sparrow crouched under after the fight with Marcus.

Then he made his way along the main streets of the Central District toward the Southside, toward Azuretown.

Although most of the residents of Azuretown were still Azuric, it was no longer uncommon to see hip, young urbanites patronizing businesses for an exotic experience. Where there were once herbal apothecaries and merchants selling live chickens, there were now trendy nightclubs and fusion restaurants. The unthinkable a decade ago—seeing a non-Azuric sitting among the locals, shoveling mouthfuls of noodles with a pair of chopsticks and drinking rice liquor around smoky food stalls—was so common now that it went unnoticed. Even the signs and menus had been changed to accommodate the outside world.

Dale barely recognized the place Sparrow had shared with his mother. Like the rest of the block, the yellow building had been renovated. It was no longer yellow, nor was it a housing complex for the underprivileged. It had been converted into some high-end bathhouse. Venturing further into the neighborhood, Dale came to an entire fenced-off block full of dirt mounds and broken slabs of mortar and brick. There was a construction site where the forge used to be. Azuric men covered in dirt and dried sweat shuffled out with their pickaxes slung over their shoulders.

"What're you doing here, peach?" asked the foreman, "peach" being the pejorative for people of fair skinned ethnicities. Namely, the Grovish and the Silven.

"There used to be a forge here," Dale said.

"There used to be a lot of things here."

"What're you building?"

"A glue factory, not that it's any of your business. Now, move along. The suits don't like outsiders snooping around. Especially on Rogue turf."

"The Rogues? The Carousel Rogues?"

"Yeah, the Carousel Rogues. What's the matter with you?"

"In Azuretown?"

The foreman chuckled.

"Listen, you better get going. Curious people are even less welcome."

Dale turned and took a few steps. He stopped and walked back to the foreman. "You wouldn't happen to know where the nearest brothel is, would you?"

"Ah. So that's what this is about. Damn peaches, always looking for some exotic flesh to poke. The only brothel we've ever had in Azuretown was the Lotus House. And ever since the massacre, they shut it down. Now you have to go to Central's Red Light District. They've got whatever you're looking for over there, if you can afford it." Then he leaned in with his shifty, narrow black eyes and a change in tone. "But if you're interested, I can point you to some massage parlors, if you know what I mean. Easier on the wallet too."

"Thanks," said Dale. "But I'll pass."

"Suit yourself."

Dale walked back toward the waterfront. Along the boardwalk, just a few blocks from his house, he noticed a soft glow coming from within the windows of an old shop, a shop he hadn't noticed before. The sign with the image of a grinning pig read, "The Broken Cistern." He poked his head in to discover a desolate tavern. He was greeted warmly by the barkeep.

"Welcome, friend. We've got seats if you've got a bottom."

Dale approached the bar. There were three fishermen huddled around a table going on their sixth or seventh round. And another two men sat in the back commiserating over a bottle of whiskey. None took notice of him.

"What'll it be?"

"Bourbon on the rocks," Dale replied.

"You got it."

The barkeep was a short round man with a red face, bulbous cheeks, and a twinkle in his eyes. His thin lips stretched into a permanent smile and his voice possessed a cheer in it that seemed inconsistent with the setting.

"You from around here?" he asked, sliding Dale his glass.

"Born and raised. Never seen this place before, though."

"Yeah, we don't get much traffic down here anymore, what with all them fancy pubs sprouting up everywhere 'round the Central District."

"Interesting sign you got out front."

"Eh?"

"The sign with the pig."

"Oh, right! We've been meaning to change that. And by 'we,' I mean 'me.' The place used to be called the 'Happy Ham' until recently."

"So you the new owner?"

"I'm the old owner. Been here since—well, since it used to be called the 'Blue Turnip.' And the 'Fishbowl' before that. I like to change the name every few years when business slows down. Brings in new customers."

He winked.

Dale couldn't help but smile. He sipped his bourbon and took another look around.

"It's quiet."

"*Real* quiet. Feels more like a monastery than a bar," the barkeep said with a hearty laugh. "But what we lack in revelry, we make up with longevity. Thirty years we've been open."

"That's a long time."

"You bet it is. We've had our ups and downs so I don't fret the slow seasons. Those old sods there were about your age when they started coming here."

Dale looked back at the fishermen.

"Anyway, business will pick up, what with all this talk of coming war," the barkeep added. "Nothing like anxiety to make a man thirsty."

He laughed at himself again.

"Hey you wouldn't know anything about a massacre in Azuretown, would you?" Dale then asked. "About ten years ago, maybe?"

"The Lotus House Massacre?" The barkeep scoffed. "Sure I do. Lost two of

> *"Nothing like anxiety to make a man thirsty."*

my regulars in it. Why?"

"What happened?"

The barkeep leaned over and propped his arms on the bar. He brimmed with enthusiasm as he started to tell the story.

"Well, it all started when the Grim Fox was killed in a freak accident," he began. "That's the old guild master of the Carousel Rogues. He ate eggplants that had been accidentally slipped into his lunch or something. Apparently, he was hyper allergic to eggplants. Can you imagine? You're the most powerful underworld boss, and an eggplant gets you. I just think that's so funny. Anyway, his three sons started fighting over who would take over. The second-born killed the oldest, which upset the youngest because he was closer to the oldest. So he had one of his guys kill his only living brother to avenge the murder of his other brother. Being the only living son of the Grim Fox, he took over. They called him the Little Fox. But he was still young and didn't really know what he was doing. So you had some other guys trying to muscle their way in. Meanwhile, the Azuretown gang started making a name for themselves."

"The Kangozen."

"Yeah, that's right. So you've heard of them. Well, they raised their own little army, every one of them armed with swords, you know, the Omeijian type. Katanas. Next thing, they're moving in on the black market, expanding their business and such. No one wanted to mess with them at first. Not even the Rogues. Not with all the in-fighting. But once the Kangozen started taking over territory outside of Azuretown, that's when things got real ugly. That's when the turf war began. Now, everyone thought that was the end of the Rogues. I mean, no one thought they'd survive a turf war, right? How could they? But then some underboss comes along and just takes over. Cleans house. I'm talking about Felix 'the Fat Fox' Eglon, of course. You heard of him, right?"

"No."

"Well, you better get familiar with the name. He runs the show now. So one morning, Felix takes some of his men and marches into Azuretown. They walk into the Lotus House and just started killing everyone in sight. And I mean everyone. Yeah, most of 'em were Kangozen. Thugs and smugglers. But there were some regular, ordinary folks in there too. Like I said, a couple of my customers. You know, just looking for some fun. All of them, the clerk at the desk, everybody, murdered. Over twenty killed. It was all over the papers for awhile."

"Damn."

"'Damn' is right. Now with the Kangozen out of the picture, Felix got to work on his own house. See, Little Fox didn't sign off on the killings. On one hand, the Kangozen was gone. On the other hand, you can't have somebody doing things like that without approval. So one night, the Little Fox invites Felix over for dinner. He tells him that they're celebrating. But he was going to kill him. Everybody knew this. Even Felix. And he wasn't about to roll over. So Felix gets his guys outside the restaurant and tells them to listen for a scream. When they hear the scream, they go in and kill everybody. Well, the story goes, during dinner Felix lunged across the table and shoved a fork in the guild master's eye. There was a scream all right, and everyone got killed. And that's how the Fat Fox single-handedly saved the Carousel Rogues and became the guild master."

Dale was rendered speechless.

"That's not someone you want to cross. You want another?"

"Sure."

"You know," the barkeep continued, pouring the bourbon. "When I was young, the old folk used to say that the times have changed. That the world was becoming a crueler place. But old folk have been talking like that forever, haven't they? So I just figured nothing's really changed at all. I thought people only say things like that because they become more aware of how it really is. You get jaded as you age, right?" Then he shook his head. "But, son, I was wrong. Times *have* changed. And take it from me. The world sure as hell ain't getting any kinder. I dread the thought of what it'll be like when it's your turn to start talking like that."

The barkeep then draped his shoulder with the dishrag he'd been wiping the counter with. "Be right back."

He left the bar to clear some tables and exchanged a few words with the other regulars. Dale quietly nursed his second round. He was staring into his glass, brows furrowed when the barkeep returned.

"What you thinking so hard about?"

"Huh? Oh, nothing."

"That's pretty hard for nothing."

"Well, for one, I was thinking it makes sense, why you changed the name of this place."

"How's that?"

"This, and you—nothing really happy about this ham."

The barkeep burst into laughter. He walked around the bar laughing, unable to contain himself. He stopped in front of Dale, coughing, chuckling, and wiping his tears. When he finally managed to collect himself, he let out a winded sigh. Still grinning, he looked up to say something to Dale, but his eyes were diverted to a man standing at the door wearing a suit.

"Come in. Come in, friend. Take a seat. You'll have to go somewhere else if you want anything other than the city's finest ale."

Dale glanced over his shoulder. He thought nothing of the man.

CH 11

FIXER AT THE BROKEN CISTERN

The thin man in the suit pulled up a stool at the bar. His face was pasty white, his cheeks were gaunt, and his hair—what there was left of it—was scraggly and oily. His eyes, however, were bright and alert.

"What can I get you?" asked the barkeep.

"Whatever you got on tap," the thin man replied. He turned his gaze toward Dale, holding it until he got Dale's attention.

"How's it going?" asked Dale.

"I'm sorry," said the thin man. "It's just that you look so familiar. Your name wouldn't happen to be Dale, would it? Dale Sunday?"

"Yeah. Who are you?"

"It *is* you!" The thin man grabbed his mug of ale and moved over to the stool next to Dale. "I knew it! Arturo Lucien." He held out his bony hand. "We went to the same school when we were kids, remember?"

Dale was more relieved than anything. "Arturo. Yeah, how you been, Art?"

He looked nothing like Dale remembered. And he spoke fast.

"Better than I deserve. Gosh, it's been what? Twelve years or something?" Arturo swilled his drink and wiped the foam from his lips with the sleeve of his shirt. "How strange to randomly bump into you here like this. Look at you. You look good. Last I heard you were with the Republican Guard or something. That true?"

"Where'd you hear that?"

"That was the rumor after you left. So you a soldier now or what?"

"I was. Not anymore."

"Oh? Why's that?"

"I decided it wasn't for me."

Arturo waited for Dale to elaborate. And when it was apparent he wasn't going to, Arturo was quick to fill the silence.

"Sure, sure. It's a good thing too. Word on the street is we might go to war with Bale. Can you imagine? Probably just posturing, but still. Duke Thalian can't be that dumb—going up against the Ancile. You ever seen it? The Ancile?"

"Only in pictures. My brother recently got transferred there."

"No shit! That's kind of a big deal, isn't it?"

Dale shrugged. "I guess."

Arturo suddenly sat up and took inventory of his surroundings as if it had only just occurred to him where he was. His head darted back and forth in short rapid bursts like a perching bird just before it takes flight. His eyes finally settled on the old fishermen quietly imbibing at their lonely tables. He didn't recognize any of them. Satisfied, he slumped back into his seat, took out his smokes and offered one to Dale.

"Thanks."

After lighting them, Arturo seemed to ease with his first pull. He released a thick plume with a sigh and shook his head. "Imagine, the last time I saw you we were just kids. Now look at us. Seems like a lifetime ago, doesn't it?"

"It was."

"You remember Marcus Addy, right?"

"Yeah, I do," Dale replied with a chuckle.

"Of course you do. Boy, I still remember when you beat him up real good. Everyone at school was talking about it for weeks." Arturo smiled, his eyes fixed on the memory. "Anyway, he became some sort of a corporate big shot a while back before he sold his company. Bought a few mines and now he heads the trade commission in Pharundelle. I heard he works directly with the prime minister."

"Good for him."

"And you remember Beryl Davies?"

"No."

"She's the one that sat behind Gordon Hemlock in science."

"The blonde?"

"Word on the street is we might go to war with Bale. Can you imagine?"

"Yeah! That's the one. You think she was a looker back then—" he sucked air through his teeth before continuing. "She grew into one fine woman. It's a shame that one got away. And not for the lack of effort on my part. But that's another story. Anyway, she ran around with some famous bard or playwright or something like that for a few years, then separated, and then became a physician's assistant. She finally settled down, if you can call it that, with a humanitarian." Arturo paused to track the barkeep making his rounds. "Last I heard, she's somewhere in Loreland running an orphanage or hospital or something. A beautiful girl with a golden heart. Who would've thought? Right up there with unicorns and flying pigs."

Dale drank and nodded with ambivalence. His peers had gone on to greater things while he was back where he'd started.

"So anyway, what're you up to if not soldiering? You back for good?"

"Yeah, just figuring some things out," Dale replied.

"You got a job at least?"

"Sort of. I'm trying to run a business."

"No kidding. A businessman, huh? That's a jump from the Guard, isn't it?" Arturo took a sip of his ale. He did not bother to wait for an answer and just kept going. "I'll tell you a secret. Business is all about making the right connections. Networking. You don't have to be very bright or possess any particular skill, really. You just need to know how to butter people up and sell them the same lies you're selling yourself. Eventually, if enough people start believing it, it becomes true."

"I guess that's one way of looking at it."

"Well, it's true in my business."

"What business is that?"

"I'm a fixer."

"A what?"

"A fixer. I work with clients who are in need of very specialized services. I connect them to those specialists who can service them. Introduce them to the right people, the right products. I'm basically the guy who gets you whatever you want whenever you want it. And depending on the client and what they're looking for, it can be a lucrative line of work."

"How'd you get into that?"

"I used to be a sea merchant, so I got around a lot. Got to know pretty much everyone that's worth knowing. And every now and then, someone would ask me if I knew someone that could get them this or help them out with that. Pretty soon, word got out that I was the go-to guy. Next thing I know, I'm making enough to quit my merchant trade and the rest is history." Arturo paused and glanced over at the barkeep. When he was out of earshot, he quickly put out his smoke and leaned in. "Hey, so how much are you pulling in a week, anyway?"

"What?"

"How much do you make?"

"Not much."

"How much? Give me a figure."

"Why?"

"Amuse me."

Dale shrugged. "Right now, about four hundred maybe," he replied. "And I'm sitting on another three in inventory."

Arturo scoffed.

"What if I told you I could set you up with someone who would be willing to pay you up to two thousand Republican marks in one night?"

Dale looked at him, more skeptical than impressed. "I'd ask you for what?"

"It's all about making the *right* con-

nections." Arturo did another scan around the room and continued in a hushed voice. "All the guy needs is a safe place to dock a ship for an hour. Maybe not even an hour."

"What's he smuggling?"

"*Shh*. No, no. Look, it's not like that."

"Then what do you mean by 'a safe place to dock?'"

"It's a simple transport."

"If it's so simple, why doesn't he just use the harbor like everyone else?"

"Look, he's offering two thousand marks and all you have to do is open your breaker. You don't even have to be there."

Suddenly, it occurred to Dale that his reunion with Arturo in the obscure tavern might not have been so serendipitous after all.

"Wait, do you live around here?" he asked.

"No. Why?"

"How'd you find this place?"

"What?"

"This bar. It isn't exactly the city's main attraction. And you're obviously not a regular."

"So?"

"So what are you doing here?"

"What do you mean? I just happened to be walking by." He looked at Dale, incredulous. "I was thirsty."

"I never said I was running a breaker."

Arturo stared blankly for a moment.

"I just assumed—it's what your fa-ther did, right? I mean, what other kind of business could you be in? Textiles?" He chuckled nervously.

"Did you follow me here?" asked Dale.

"No! What? No, of course not." Arturo scoffed. "What are you, paranoid or something? Why would I follow you?"

Dale shrugged and went back to his bourbon.

"Okay, fine," Arturo surrendered. "I followed you, all right? I did. I'm sorry. I'm a fixer. It's my job to keep an eye out. To know who's where and doin' what. Anyway, your breaker is perfect for what my client needs and it worked out even better that *you* run it because this is an opportunity for you to make in one night what would normally take you five weeks. So I get to help you out in the process. Everybody wins, right?"

"I'm not interested."

"Look, Dale—"

"Really."

Arturo sighed, scratched his chin, and rubbed the back of his neck. Then he chuckled. "How do you like that? I'm a fixer and you're a breaker."

Dale shook his head. "It's kind of creepy, actually, that you followed me," he said.

"I was trying to be tactful."

"You didn't do a very good job."

They both quietly finished their drinks.

"You want another one?" Arturo asked.

"I'm all right."

"No, no, come on. It's the least I can do for not being straight," he insisted. He flagged the barkeep. "Whiskey. Two."

"On the rocks?"

"Neat."

When the barkeep had poured them a shot each, Arturo held up his glass.

"To old times."

Then they tossed them back.

Dale's stomach felt warm as the whiskey poured in. He hadn't eaten dinner yet. Three drinks on an empty stomach were enough to get him tipsy.

"I need to get some food."

"Well, you're in luck," said the barkeep. "I happen to make the best potato fish stew in the city."

"Sounds good."

"Give me five minutes."

"Can we time you?" asked Arturo.

"Be my guest."

As soon as the barkeep went into the back kitchen, Arturo stood and stretched. "Well, I should get going now. I mean, all stalking aside, it was good seeing you again, Dale. Honest."

"You too, Art."

Then he started for the door before Dale stopped him.

"Hey, aren't you going to pay for your drinks?"

"Oh! Right." Arturo chuckled and shook his head as he returned to the bar. "Been so absent minded lately."

He removed some coins from a leather purse and tossed them on the counter. It was more than enough to cover all of their drinks and Dale's potato fish stew.

"Oh, and listen," he then added. "If you change your mind about my business proposition, you can find me at the Velvet Fray. You know where that is, right?"

"No."

"Well, you can't miss it. It's the casino near the Halo. The biggest and brightest. I'm there pretty much every night, so just ask around. They know me there. Everyone knows me."

"I meant 'no,' as in, nothing's changed in the past five minutes. Not interested."

"Of course. Of course you're not. I'll see you around, Dale," he said with a warm smile and darting eyes. And then he walked out.

CH 12

FELIX

Dale sat in his office, feet propped up on the old wooden desk cluttered with receipts and other dated documents. It had been another slow day. He was near nodding off when a visitor knocked on the frame of his open door. The man was in a tailored suit complete with top hat, an opera cloak, and a brass-handled cane.

"Can I help you?"

"Mister Sunday? Mister Dale Sunday?"

"Yes?"

The man had sharp features. He spoke clearly, careful to enunciate every word. At a salvage shipyard, the man was conspicuously out of place. Dale noticed a black

"Who I am is hardly important. What is important is that I represent the Fat Fox."

rose on his lapel and thought it peculiar. Just as the thought crossed his mind, the visitor removed his hat, bowed low with one arm out, as if a thespian about to exit the stage.

"My name is Remy Guillaume. I am a representative of Felix Eglon." He paused to study Dale's reaction. When it was obvious he was not getting one, Remy Guillaume continued. "He requests your audience."

"I'm sorry. Who are you?"

"Who I am is hardly important. What is important is that I represent the Fat Fox. He has sent me here to present to you an invitation to a late lunch—" He checked his watch and corrected himself.

"An early dinner with him."

"What's this about?"

The visitor studied the office, walking around it slowly with an air of someone about to purchase the place. He stopped at the window overlooking the breaker's hangar. "This will do," he said to himself. Then he turned to Dale. "Mister Sunday, you are familiar with Mister Eglon and his organization?"

"What do you mean?"

"You have heard of him—of us? You have heard of the Carousel Rogues, yes?"

"Yes."

"Then I do not have to tell you that accepting this invitation is not a matter of convenience."

"Again, Mister—"

"Remy. Please, call me Remy."

"Remy, what exactly is this regarding?"

"We have been informed that you have graciously volunteered your facilities to us for an evening. We intend to take you up on your offer."

"Excuse me?"

"All the arrangements have been finalized but there are a few items the Fat Fox would like to discuss with you regarding the transport."

"Look, there must be some mistake. I don't arrange 'transports.' This is a shipbreaking yard. Whoever informed you—" It dawned on Dale. "It was Arturo, wasn't it? You're his client, right? I don't know what he told you, but I told him I wasn't interested. And I'm not."

"Mister Sunday, please. If you will come with me."

"Where?"

"I have a coach waiting for us outside."

"What? Now?"

"Yes, now."

"Look, I'm not trying to be disagreeable here. I'm just trying to run a legitimate business so I'd rather not get involved."

"I am afraid you are already involved. As I mentioned, the arrangements have been finalized. If it is legitimacy that concerns you, the transport will not involve smuggling of contraband and your role in the operation will be quite minimal. As for compensation for your services, I am sure you will find that the Fat Fox is quite fair. Perhaps even generous. But all of this you can discuss with him in person. Now, if you will."

"I can't just leave now."

"Mister Sunday, if you do not accept his invitation now, then Mister Eglon will be forced to come visit you. I assure you, that would not be in your best interest so I suggest you accept his invitation while it stands."

"I'll have to close up."

"You have—" Remy glanced at his golden pocket watch, "—precisely four minutes and forty-eight seconds to do so. Forty-seven. Forty-six. I will be waiting outside. If you do not join me in the allotted time, I will relay your answer to the Fox."

Dale stood behind his desk dumbfounded. He ran over to the window and saw a limousine stretch-coach waiting in tow behind four draft horses. There was a guard and a driver, both large men with hardened faces. They too wore black roses on their lapels, and they were armed with flintlock pistols holstered at their sides and short swords sheathed at the hips. Remy was already outside, standing in front of the coach door, taking frequent peeks at his watch.

"Shit."

Dale locked up the gates and hangar bay doors. It was nowhere near closing time but the last thing he wanted was another visit from the Carousel Rogues. He looked at his own short sword, a standard issue from his service as a Republican Guard that he kept hidden in his office bureau, but decided against taking it with him. When the guard frisked him before he boarded the coach, he was glad he'd left his blade behind.

The interior of the coach smelled of cigars. They traveled from the waterfront over to the Central District's entertainment quarter on the upper westside. Dale looked out onto the streets lined with exotic restaurants, fancy hotels, and various overpriced specialty shops. At a glance, the people he saw walking along the sidewalk and sitting in restaurants appeared to Dale as happier and healthier than their counterparts on the other side of town. At the center of the five-block radius, under a constant fog of confetti and dizzying lights, was the Halo. It was an arrangement of buildings in an enclosed ring featuring the Opera House, the Theatre, the Arena, the Circus, and the Concert Hall where Mosaic occasionally performed.

The limousine coach came to a stop in front of a restaurant sandwiched between the Opera House and Theatre. The building was an extravagant display of wealth and excess. A relief was carved into the Seddonian granite surface just above the large vaulted doors that read "The Loviett."

Walking through the forecourt of the lobby where the upscale patronage waited for a table, Dale could see he was underdressed. The restaurant had ceilings decorated in glass and crystal, with golden crown molding framing walls of imported marble. An orchestra provided mood music in a recessed stage at the bottom of the main floor.

Dale followed Remy, who nodded occasionally at various Loviett staff members. They reciprocated as if recognizing him. Dale was led to the back of the restaurant where the Fat Fox sat at a cozy table facing the lobby. There was an entourage standing behind him. They were well armed. Dale was searched again by the guild master's right hand enforcer—a tall, imposing figure with deep-set eyes, fair skin cratered with pockmarks, and a lipless sliver for a mouth that looked as if it had been carved into his face with a knife.

"Come," said the Fat Fox. "Take a seat."

Felix "the Fat Fox" Eglon was a portly man. He was well groomed, donning a smart three-piece suit with, as Dale came to realize, the guild's signature black rose on his lapel. A diamond-encrusted chain led to a vest pocket which, Dale assumed, must contain a very expensive watch. His ashy hair was slicked back with oil. He was clean-shaven. As Dale approached the table, he smelled the heavy, musky cologne.

The waiter in a full tuxedo, accompanied by the restaurant manager, brought out a cheese and caviar platter with tartar of Borellian beef and Nalic oysters. A rare bottle of Poulain was uncorked. What sat on that table cost more than a year's wages, Dale thought.

"Please, Master Eglon, let us know if there's anything else I can do for you," said the manager, as the waiter filled his glass.

Then he mumbled some sort of warning to the waiter, his face stern, before they both quickly disappeared as if on a timer with grave consequences when expired.

Studying Dale with beady eyes, Felix started on the caviar.

"Do you know who I am?" he asked, nibbling bits and pieces.

Dale nodded.

"Who?"

"Guild master of the Carousel Rogues."

"That's right. Take a good look. This is the most wanted face in Carnaval City. Now, do you think all these people in here know who I am?"

"I don't know," Dale replied.

"They do. They know who I am and what I do. They know that I kill, I steal, and sleep in the sewers. And yet they don't seem to mind that I crawl out from below the city to eat in their fancy restaurants and attend their social galas. Do you know why? Because I dress like them." He laughed heartily and stopped abruptly. He continued, "And if you can do that, these people don't care to know the difference. There is no difference. Everyone here has something in common. Greed. I break the law, they buy it. Wealth is a moral equalizer. Which begs the question: What's an honest, hardworking young middleclass nobody like you doing here?"

"You invited me."

"Yes, I did, didn't I?" Felix smiled. He gave a chuckle. "That was a rhetorical question but you knew that. You're a clever one aren't you? That's good. I have an appreciation for wit. It's irreverence I cannot abide. There are two kinds of people I disapprove of. The irreverent and the womanizer. And I'll tell you why. The irreverent have no respect for anything or anyone, including themselves. They have no standards by which they govern their lives. You can't do business with someone like that. As for the womanizer, now he is just weak. These kinds of men, men ruled by their loins, they have no self-restraint. Men of compromise. And you can't trust a man like that. You're not a womanizer, are you, Dale? No. No, you don't look like one. You're not rich enough. And you're neither handsome nor charming. So just don't be irreverent and we'll carry on just fine."

The waiter brought out a small plate decorated with some variant of scallops and mushrooms, the second of a six-course meal.

"*Soliveres scallops au black truffle mer'dure*," said the waiter.

Felix ate the fine delicacy like a peasant eats food from a pushcart vendor. He held his fork in a fist and he wrapped his whole, pudgy hand around the wine glass. With the fork he shoveled the scallops in, swallowing before chewing. And washed them down with a mouthful of wine.

"You're here, Dale," he continued, when the waiter was gone, "because, as I'm sure Remy's already explained, I have a very important transport coming in. Unfortunately, we don't know when exactly that'll be. It could be tomorrow night. It could be in three weeks. What we do know is that it'll be arriving within the month at an absurd hour when decent people are deep in slumber. People like us, we'll be awake. And when it arrives, you will be there to open the breaker and receive it."

"Do you mind if I ask what the nature of the transport will be?"

"Yes, Dale, I do mind. That's a privileged matter. But I will tell you that it's not illicit. Now, I have a question for you. Can I trust you?"

Dale glanced at Remy, then the enforcer, who suddenly moved his hand ready on the grip of his pistol tucked into his pants and underneath his coat. Felix wiped his mouth, slid the plate aside, and leaned forward with his hands folded in front of him. After he motioned to one of his men to keep the wait staff away, the Fat Fox stared intently into Dale's eyes. Something in Dale told him not to avert his eyes.

"That was not rhetorical."

"I—trust me with what?"

Felix sighed with growing impatience. "Do you believe in fate, Dale?"

"I don't know," Dale replied. "Sometimes."

"'Sometimes?' You *sometimes* believe in fate? Well, what if—what if someone dear to you, a family member or, or a lover, let's say, was dying of an illness. An extremely rare one. One that requires an organ transplant." His expression hardened and his tone grew grave as he continued. "And suppose the only donor is this young, healthy fellow. As fate would have it, one evening, you alone stumble upon him, the donor, lying unconscious along the tracks from a long night of heavy drinking. And a train is fast approaching. If you do nothing, he'll surely die. Yet his organ will remain intact for argument's sake and with it the chance to spare your loved one's life. If, however, you risk your own life to deliver him from certain death, all hope will be lost for yours truly. Tell me, Dale, what would you do in that situation?"

"I don't know."

His palms were sweaty. He rubbed them against his trousers.

"Indulge me a moment. Consider this a personality test, if you will. How you answer gives me insight into your character."

Dale said nothing.

"It's a simple question, Dale," Felix added. "Do you let the donor die or do you try and help him?"

"Is the donor a derelict?"

"What's revealed is all you know."

"You're asking me to choose between a loved one and a stranger."

"I suppose I am."

"Then I'll let him die."

"Why?"

"Because I value the life of those I love more than a stranger's."

"And you find that morally justifiable?"

"I don't know. I don't think I'm responsible for his irresponsible behavior."

"Yet fate has brought you to him."

"After it abandoned him on the tracks. Who am I to meddle with fate?"

There was a long pause.

Dale held his breath, half-expecting the Fat Fox to pull a blade and stab him from across the table. It would not have been out of character for him to do something so callous and erratic. The Lotus House Massacre aside, it had happened before. During a sold-out gladiatorial event at the Arena, the Fat Fox resolved a verbal altercation by stabbing his combatant. No witnesses testified. He was never charged.

To Dale's relief, a smile slowly stretched across the Fat Fox's face.

"I like this one," he said, looking up at Remy. "Congratulations, Dale. You passed the test."

The enforcer removed his hand from the pistol. Remy placed a satchel in front of the Fat Fox who slid it across the table to Dale.

"I hope two thousand marks will suffice. You will find there a deposit of five hundred in banknotes. A gesture of good faith. If you have any plans to travel outside the city, cancel them. I expect you to be available when we send for you. Remy and my men will provide you with the remaining balance of fifteen once the transport has safely docked. Any questions?"

"No."

"Good."

Felix signaled his guards who made way for the waiter with the next course.

"Here we have Feoldis supreme bestend with Listain veal reduction."

"Get me a bottle of Tartarus Raki," said the guild master, waving the waiter away.

"Of course, sir."

He returned with a sealed bottle the size of an inkwell and presented the weathered label. When the Fat Fox nodded, the waiter laid out two thimble-sized glasses and carefully poured.

"I insist you have a drink with me before I send you on your way."

When the waiter had finished pouring, the guild master sprinkled a pinch of sugar into both glasses. He held it up between his thumb and index finger, admiring its contents.

"This little serving would go for about eighty marks, you know. Takes twice a lifetime to process a single bottle's worth to perfection, so enjoy it."

Taking his cue from Felix, Dale slowly sipped. Barely a drop touched his lips and he immediately felt the burn rolling down his throat. Dale would later describe it as "a sweet concoction of molten lava."

"My predecessor once said that friendship is forged between a shared drink," the Fat Fox added. "This makes us friends."

Remy leaned down and whispered something in his ear. Felix nodded, clarified something or another, and then returned his gaze to Dale. "I don't know what you've heard about me, but I want you to know that I'm an incredibly resourceful man. I know you were a lieutenant in the Republican Guard, that you're a trained soldier. I know you have a brother who is a major, recently transferred to the Ancile. I also know that your uncle owns a bakery near the waterfront and you have a cousin that performs on occasion at the Halo. I share all of this to illustrate a point. I'm choosing to trust you, Dale. And though I'm sure it's unnecessary to remind you, given the nature of this particular operation, I can't stress enough how important it is that all of this, and especially everything you'll bear witness to, remains in the strictest of confidence. If you betray this trust, you will cease to be my friend. I only have friends and enemies. Nothing in between. If you betray me, you will be my enemy and nobody wants that. Are we clear?"

Dale nodded.

"Good. We'll be in touch."

CH 13

THE ASS OF THE VELVET FRAY

Located not far from the Loviett was the Red-Light District. At its center was Fancy's Alley, a short back street lined with window displays of scantily clad men and women. Some were in costume, others in chains and assorted bondage devices, and still others were put on display stark naked. It was all there, no matter the particularity of taste or want, for the young and old, locals and tourists, nobles and commoners, the curious, the discreet, the shameless.

Nestled between the Red-Light District and the entertainment quarter was the Velvet Fray Hotel and Casino. Not by design, it served as a buffer between the two extremes in recreational indulgences. The Velvet Fray could not be missed. It had a gaudy glowing sign, a white palatial façade

replete with columns and archways, and a garden atrium housing a fountain of fake pearls. Its bright marble hall presented a contrasting background to the somber late afternoon scene. A handful of men with long faces were putting down the last of the little they had on losing bets. They had been at it so long, having won and lost so many times, they were no longer thinking.

Dale walked on to the main floor and stopped the first hostess he saw.

"Excuse me, do you know where I can find Arturo? Thin guy, dark hair. Looks a bit nervous."

Her nametag read "Doris." Unlike the nightshift hostesses, Doris was an unattractive, older woman. She wore heavy make-up, which accentuated her yellowed teeth.

"Arturo Lucien? Why? You a friend of that rat?"

"Not quite," Dale replied.

"He's over at the Caravaggio tables in the back."

"Thanks."

"If you're looking to collect, don't hold your breath. Bastard still owes me a bundle. Do me a favor and tell him he's an ass for me."

Dale tossed a copper coin on her drink tray and walked over to the tables in the far corner of the casino floor. Sure enough, Arturo Lucien was sitting with his eyes fixed on the Caravaggio wheel. He held a smoke close to his face, but wasn't smoking.

"Arturo. Hey, we need to talk."

"Dale! I didn't think you'd actually come. Sit down."

"That's all right. Can we step outside a minute?"

"Sure thing, buddy. After this spin. Georgie, give me three on the odds and a high pass."

Dale had been thinking about Arturo Lucien ever since Remy Guillaume walked into his office. All through Dale's meeting with the Fat Fox, he thought of Arturo Lucien and the reason he was there. And so on his walk over to the Velvet Fray, Dale had grown increasingly agitated. Dale did not like being forced into a bind. The Fat Fox annoyed him from the moment he laid eyes on him. An annoying man pushed him around and then for good measure, threatened his family. All because of Arturo. So when Arturo told him to wait, Dale could not contain his anger.

"Did you tell the Fat Fox that I was volunteering my breaker for some sort of transport?" Dale blurted.

The dealer and the two others sitting at the table looked up at him, startled.

"Because I just had a meeting with him. And somehow he's got the impression that I did."

"Georgie, cash me out, will you?" Arturo asked in a hushed voice. Then he turned to Dale, and said with a nervous chuckle, "Not sure what you're talking about." He kept chuckling. "Fat Fox? Come on man, I don't know. Hey, look, first of all, let's just calm down."

Dale grabbed him by the back of his jacket, and said into one ear, "I am calm. If I were not calm, I would be choking you on this floor."

"Okay, okay. Let's sort this out outside."

"Let's."

Arturo quickly gathered his winnings, shrugged and said, "Gentlemen." With that, he left the table and led Dale back across the casino floor out into the atrium.

"What's wrong with you? You can't just walk into a joint like this and talk about his business like that."

"What did you tell them?"

"Nothing."

"Don't bullshit me."

"I swear. I mean, all I said was that you *might* be interested, for the right price. That's it. That's all I said."

"I told you I wasn't interested!"

"Calm down."

"You tell me to 'calm down' one more time, and I swear to God, Art, I'm going to start swinging."

"Sorry. I'm sorry."

"If I knew it was the thieves' guild you were talking about—"

"Keep your voice down," Arturo whispered, as he moved further away from the door and into an isolated corner of the garden.

"Are you one of them?"

"You see a black rose?" asked Arturo, holding up the bare lapel of his coat. "Look, I didn't have much of a choice here, okay? I needed something to offer him. My contact at the port who was supposed to set me up with a dock got pinched. I already made the deal; I needed another spot for the transport. Your breaker's perfect. It's right on the edge of the bay, hidden from the main port, and you've got a sheltered hangar. What was I supposed to do? I mean, if I didn't get him what he needed, if I don't deliver, that's it for me. It's just a transport, Dale. For me, it's life or death. Now, you have every right to be upset. I understand. It's just, I had nowhere to go. And, I know you don't want to hear this, but it really is easy money."

"I don't want to be involved with those guys."

"Why not?"

"Because I'm trying to run an honest business."

"Did you listen to the deal, though? There's no contraband. You don't know what it is. You don't have to be there. Is there an easier two thousand marks anywhere?" Arturo looked genuinely puzzled by Dale's reluctance to seize an opportunity at easy gains.

"I don't care about the money. I just don't want to end up in the Fat Fox's pocket. I know how things like this work."

Arturo dismissively swatted the air.

"I don't care about the money. I just don't want to end up in the Fat Fox's pocket."

"You're not going to end up in anyone's pocket. Not if you're smart about it. And it's not like you owe him anything. If anything, you're doing *him* a favor."

"What if something goes wrong?"

"What can go wrong?"

"That's the question you ask before everything goes wrong."

"Look, it's just a simple transport, okay?"

"What's he transporting then?"

Arturo scoffed. "You think the Fat Fox would tell me something like that? It's my job to get him what he wants. Not to know his business."

Dale would've found the inconsistency in Arturo's deductive reasoning amusing if he weren't so annoyed. "Then how the hell do you know it's just a simple transport?"

Arturo opened his mouth as if he had an easy explanation. But he stammered, then started again and stopped, until finally he gave up with a sigh.

"I swear, Art, if it turns out to be slaves or drugs or something like that—"

"Come on, Dale. It's nothing illegal or, or, criminal. Do you think the Fat Fox would go to the trouble of lying to you about that? You're not going to get in trouble. Trust me."

"Trust you? Trust *you*?"

Arturo Lucien looked back at Dale, curiously fearful. He stood in a pathetic slouch. The expensive clothes hanging on his thin, drooping frame made Arturo look like a kid wearing his father's clothes—an old-looking kid with a receding hairline. Dale could not remain angry at the tragically absurd figure.

"You're a real piece of work, you know that?"

"I'm sorry, Dale. I had no choice."

"Of course you had a choice. You always have a choice."

"No, Dale, I didn't. Really. You don't understand. There are no second chances with the Fat Fox. I promised him a dock and arranged the transport. And he paid real well for both. If I didn't come through for him, he wouldn't have just killed me. He would've killed my wife and my kids."

"You have a wife and kids?" asked Dale, taken aback.

"Ex-wife, actually. My boy and two girls live with her."

His eyes fell.

"Well, you didn't give me much of a choice either," said Dale. "Now you got my family by the gallows."

"I know. And I'm sorry. Really, I am. But if we play this right, it could turn out real good for both of us."

Dale gave him an icy glare.

Arturo rubbed the back of his neck. Then he pulled out a smoke and lit it. Dale resigned to his fate. With a weary look, he told Arturo that he was heading home.

"Good idea. Get something to eat and don't worry so much. It'll be a piece of cake. Just keep thinking about how you're going to spend your two thousand when you're up. You'll see. You'll thank me later."

As far as Dale was concerned, encouraging words from Arturo was like a gift-wrapped box of spring-loaded shit.

"I doubt it," he replied. "By the way, Doris says you're an ass. When you see her, tell her I agree."

CH 14

SANCTUARY

In all of his years of service as the Marshal of the Vail Templar, Alaric had never noticed the ceiling of the training barn. The oak beams, the thatched roof, the cobwebs in the corner. He was lying on his back in the middle of the matted floor trying to catch his breath. He had a wooden sword in hand. Both hand and sword lay passively on the floor. The end of a different sword was to his throat. Holding it there was the young blue-eyed cleric.

"Yield," said Selah, hovering over him with a look of self-satisfaction.

It was a victory she wrested from the templar while he was distracted by an intrusion. Aided, but a victory nonetheless. And she had no qualms about claiming it with enthusiasm.

"I yield," Alaric finally said with a grunt, before rising to his feet and turning his attention to the intrusion. His junior, Sir Thomas Grail, stood at the entrance. "What is it, Thomas?"

"Forgive me, m'lord," said Thomas. "The Bene-seneschal would like a word with you regarding the prisoners."

"I'll be there shortly."

"Yes, m'lord."

The younger templar bowed and left the barn.

Selah approached Alaric as he removed his sparring vest.

"I thought the role of the Vail Templar was to protect the clerics, the temple and its relics. To keep the peace."

"It is."

"Since when did that include the taking of prisoners?"

"Since the SSC began unlawfully detaining Emmainites under allegations of collaborating with the Shaldea."

"The SSC?"

"The State Security Command," Alaric replied, wiping his face with a towel. "It's the Republic's equivalent of the Ciphers."

"What exactly is the nature of our relationship with them?"

"As you know, the temple ground is an autonomous state. So the SSC brings suspects here since we are not under the legal codes of their command directorate. We are commissioned to conduct the investigations. An inquisition, as we call it."

"So we're basically the Republic's proxy torturers?"

"Hardly, child. Torture is never sanctioned and certainly not on hallowed ground, which is why *we* conduct the inquisitions, not them. Our approach is one of mediation rather than enforcement. I prefer to think we're guardians of the people caught in a war between the dissidents and the establishment. Furthermore, we offer those found innocent Sanctuary."

"And if they're found guilty?"

"The SSC takes them." Alaric stored his equipment and took up his templar sword. "Now, enough of this," he then added. "You better return to the college before the matron begins asking about you."

Selah gathered her cleric's robes and started for the bathhouse adjacent to the training barn. She stopped at the door.

"Alaric? What does the SSC do with suspected Shaldea collaborators? After they take them away, that is."

The templar paused, fishing for the right words. "Nothing you need to concern yourself with, child," he finally replied. "Now, off with you."

Alaric had no time for a bath. He left the training barn after Selah and entered the temple sanctuary. He passed the main altar and made his way down the south transept into a corridor at the end of which was a door that led into the Bene-seneschal's study. It was guarded by a templar squire.

He knocked.

"Yes?" said a voice from within.

"Champion Linhelm here to see you, Your Grace."

There was a brief pause.

"Show him in."

"*Alunde andra*, Champion," said the Bene-seneschal, without looking up at Alaric.

He stood, focused over a chessboard in the corner of the study. Judging by the many pieces on the board, the match was in its early stages.

"*Alunde ver ti*," Alaric replied

"I'll be with you in just a second. Please, sit."

The room was lined with stocked bookshelves. An ancient manuscript was unfurled on a side desk, sitting under a magnifying glass attached to an arm lamp.

After some thought, the Bene-seneschal moved his white bishop to complete a *fianchetto*. With a self-assuring nod, he looked up at Alaric.

"Such a fascinating game. Do you play?"

Alaric shook his head. "Who's your opponent?"

"Enlil Fairchild."

"The patriarch of Parallel Mining Corp?"

"The wealthiest man in the Republic. Perhaps the world."

"Is he any good?"

"Good enough to beat me, twice. This is my third attempt. Then again, I may not have a knack for this game."

He chuckled as he settled into his seat.

The Bene-seneschal was nearly fifty years old. His face was cleanly shaven and he had a full set of lightning white hair. As the highest appointed overseer of both the clergy and the templar in Carnaval City, his customary gray habit was accessorized with a hooded shoulder cape and a tasseled stole draped over a scapular. It bore the regional crest on either end.

"You wanted to see me about the prisoners?" Alaric asked.

"Yes. I understand you have six men in the holding cells."

Alaric nodded.

The Bene-seneschal dug up the prisoners' files from below a small pile of documents.

"Have they already been subjected to an inquisition?"

"Only the Tobias bandits and Omar Basiliech. Not yet the ranger."

"And?"

"The Tobias bandits are nothing more than their name suggests. They are common bandits. As for the ranger—"

"*Charles Valkyrie?*" asked the Bene-seneschal, noting the conspicuously non-Emmainite name from the file.

Alaric nodded. "Sayeed Errai, prior to his departure from Loreland. He confessed he used to live in a village under Shaldean protection, but that was more than ten years ago. He has since been wandering the Wilds. He claims he has no affiliation but we won't know for sure until after the inquisition."

"I see. And Omar?"

"It's difficult to tell. He seems to be hiding something but the inquisition itself revealed nothing."

"That was three days ago."

"Two and half."

"Not according to the logs. His family has already contacted the local barrister. If you don't plan to turn him over to the SSC, I suggest you save us all the headache and release him immediately."

Alaric hesitated.

"*With* Sanctuary," the Bene-seneschal added, handing the templar a signed release form.

Sanctuary was an official document that provided immunity from further investigation for terrorist affiliations. Any future allegation brought up against a bearer of Sanctuary was to be considered a harassment of the Holy Order itself.

"I can't," said Alaric. "I can't guarantee yet that he isn't Shaldea."

"The time to determine that has passed. We need to make concessions to appease his family. Release the bandits as well. Without Sanctuary of course."

"Of course." The marshal rose from his seat. "Your Grace."

He started for the door when the Bene-seneschal stopped him. "One other thing, Alaric. I understand you've been sparring with a cleric?"

Alaric looked back at the Bene-seneschal with his good eye. "Yes," he replied. "She's an old family friend."

"You have family?"

"Is this line of questioning a prelude to an eventual order, Your Grace? Because if it is, just say the word and it shall be done."

The Bene-seneschal held up his hand and shook his head. "No. No, forgive me for prying. Keep me briefed on the ranger."

"Your Grace."

Alaric left the study and made his way

down to the holding cells below the templar barracks where the six Emmainites were waiting. The four disheveled bandits were huddled in the corner and the ranger stood in the back with his arms folded over his chest. He was in his late thirties. He had olive skin and black hair, thick and as wild as his beard. And much to the annoyance of his captors he wore a perpetual look of amusement, like he was taking everything in stride. In contrast, Omar was sitting alone in the middle of the cell with a bitter scowl.

Alaric first ordered the release of the bandits. They cheered and made crude comments and snickered as they were escorted out by a detail of templar.

Alaric then entered the cell and handed Omar Sanctuary. "We, the Holy Order of the Benesanti, find no cause to suspect you of collaborating with the Shaldea or any other terrorist organization. With the power vested in me as Marshal of the Vail Templar, I hereby release you with Sanctuary."

"What about me?" the ranger asked.

"We haven't made up our minds about you yet."

Omar looked back at him. "Say nothing. You don't need to justify your existence to these peaches."

Then he stormed off.

The ranger shook his head. "You're going to let *that* guy go? If he's not a terrorist, then I'm a goddamn peach."

> *"Say nothing. You don't need to justify your existence to these peaches."*

"Did he say anything to you?" Alaric asked with sudden urgency.

"Maybe," the ranger replied, with a coy smile. "Maybe he did."

"You can tell me now or I can extract it from you."

"Listen, Sir—"

"*Champion*," the marshal corrected, "Alaric Linhelm."

Like the military in structure, titles among the templar were not to be taken lightly. Where "sir" was the appropriate prefix for addressing all anointed templar from the most junior to senior, "Champion" was reserved strictly for the Marshal of the Vail Templar. To mistake one for the other was like calling a tiger a cat.

"*Champion* Linhelm," the ranger redressed, "grant me Sanctuary, and I will tell you what he told me."

"Squire! A flogging for the ranger!"

The ranger's face changed, cocky ambivalence giving way to a taut tension.

"Hey, hey! No need to get excited, Champ. I'm just giving you a hard time. I thought the guy was mute until a minute ago. That's the first I heard him speak since you dragged me in here. I swear."

"Are you certain? He said nothing?"

"Not a word. He's been sitting there like that the whole time, like he'd been sucking on a lemon. Those bandits though, they wouldn't shut up."

Convinced, Alaric exited the cell. "Apparently, a contagious condition," he thought aloud, dismissing the squire ready with a whip.

"Hey! Wait!" the ranger cried from behind. "How long am I supposed to wait here, anyway?" The door slammed shut. "Hello?"

CH 15

AN EVENING WITH THE RED RABBIT

The voluptuous woman with mocha skin sparkled in her violet dress. She swayed as she sang. Her voice was rich, silky, sad. Accompanying her on the piano was a petite pianist in a red rabbit costume. The red rabbit provided backup vocals—a tender voice to complement the sultry, a bit of sweet with the sad.

"That's my cousin," Dale would've boasted of the red rabbit. But he was not the type to bother a stranger with boasting. Turkish, on the other hand, had no problem with it.

"That's my daughter," he said, loud enough that the people two rows up could hear.

Cora Tess gave him a disapproving poke.

Backstage, after the show, Mosaic came out to meet them with her rabbit-eared hood pulled off. She was greeted with hugs and praise. Mosaic asked Dale, "You really liked it?"

"Like it? You're amazing."

They lingered for an obligatory mingling session in the lobby of the Concert Hall. Mosaic enthusiastically introduced her family to some of the other performers and theatre workers. Cora Tess and Turkish retired for the night beaming with pride. Mosaic thanked them for coming, told them not to wait up, and invited Dale to join her and her friends for a little gathering at a nearby pub.

The last time Dale had seen Mosaic was a week after his return to the city. They had met for brunch. Mosaic had filled him in on the details surrounding the pieces of news that had trickled down to Dale at the Academy: her studies, music, the health of her parents. She had spoken in rapid bursts, jumping from one subject to another, exploring tangents like a child exploring an unfamiliar room, realizing every now and then that she had strayed and needed to retrace her steps. She would suddenly realize she'd been going on and on and stop to chastise herself, grinning. "Enough about me. What about you?"

Dale had responded with brief stories from his time at the Academy but tried to quickly volley the conversation back to her. He enjoyed listening to Mosaic more than speaking himself.

On the way to the pub, Mosaic explained the inspiration and subtext behind the music. As they walked, people stared. Dale could not tell if the stares were in recognition of the sylphic talent from the concert or because Mosaic was still in costume—a hooded bodysuit with a white cottontail.

Dale had asked if she wanted to change before they'd left, but she had simply shrugged and sauntered ahead, arms swinging, as if she were above the suggestion.

When they reached the pub, the host greeted Mosaic by name and a kiss. Then he studied Dale with a suspicious smirk.

"So is this the lucky man that's finally managed to capture our Mosaic?"

"*Eew*, this is my cousin," Mosaic replied, laughing. "He was a Republican Guard so watch what you say around him."

"My apologies," he said smiling.

Dale smirked and nodded. He looked around the bar and wondered, *how do these people, who can't be much more than a few years my junior, look so much like children?*

"So how was the concert?" asked the host.

"It was nice. You should come see me sometime."

"Oh, how I long to. But ever since you've scorned my advances, it'd be like bathing open wounds in citrus to see you up there with your siren's voice."

"How poetic, Terry." Mosaic gave him a demure smile.

"Thank you. Nice outfit."

"Thank you."

"Right this way."

The kitschy pub called Rapture was quite a departure from Dale's newly preferred watering hole, the Broken Cistern. It was lively for one. A collage of chatter and laughter, tied together by some background music. Under a hovering layer of smoke, men and women filled the seats around tables crafted by local artists.

Being the first in their party to arrive, Terry showed them to a large, empty booth reserved in the back. Dale fetched himself a glass of bourbon from the bar while Mosaic settled in, nibbling an olive from the appetizer platter. When Dale asked about the host, Mosaic explained that she knew Terry from her classes at the university. Herself aside, she'd be hard-pressed to find a girl in town that hadn't shared his bed. Supposedly, he possessed an irresistible charm. Talk of Terry led to talk of their non-existent romantic lives.

Mosaic studied her own dim reflection in the window looking out into the evening promenade. She ran her hand, fingernails polished in green, through her disheveled, grown-out pixie cut. She pulled her hair up to see how it'd suit her. Dale noted the wispy threads of baby hair tracing her hairline and thought to himself how she still looked so much like the child he used to walk to school.

"Dale, am I weird?" she asked, still looking at her reflection.

"You're dressed like a red rabbit, Mo."

Her eyes were made for a smile. They became large, twinkling half-moons. She let her hair fall and pinned her side-swept bangs up with a barrette. "Seriously."

"I suppose that depends on your definition of normal. Why do you ask?"

"I think Papa is worried. He wants me to find someone and settle down. But I don't know. I don't have much of an interest in all of that. Never really have."

"In settling down or in boys?"

Mosaic shrugged. "Both?"

"Do you mean in the celibate sense or," Dale hesitated, "are you interested in girls?"

"No, nothing like that," said Mosaic with a giggle. "I just always felt like I wanted something different, you know? I don't want to settle on some guy just for the sake of settling down. I'm perfectly content being alone, learning, growing, and making music. For now, at least."

"Nothing weird about that."

"I don't know. You know I've never even kissed a boy before?"

"Good for you."

"There was Eugene Burnham but that was when I was in the third grade. And *he* kissed *me*. Does that count?"

"No. Eugene doesn't count."

"You know what it is? I don't think boys are interested in me."

"What? That's not true. Any guy in here would be lucky to be with you. That Terry kid there, he was practically drooling all over you."

"He's like that with *all* the girls."

"Mo, listen to me. You're smart and talented. You're lovely. Anyone who says otherwise is an idiot."

"You're just saying that because I'm your cousin."

"No, I'm not," said Dale, lighting a smoke. "And even if I were, doesn't make it any less true. Hand me that ashtray, will you?"

Mosaic slid one over from the far end of the table and watched as Dale blew out two steady gray streams from his nostrils.

"You shouldn't smoke, you know."

"Why not?"

"I heard it causes the black lung. It can kill you."

"Everything kills you."

"Well, I don't see the rush," said Mosaic, fanning the smoke away from her face. "And you don't have to take me with you."

"Fine."

Dale took one last heavy drag, put it out, and rinsed his throat with a mouthful of bourbon.

"While we're on the subject of dying, let me ask *you* something," he then began. "If Uncle Turkish had a rare disease and his only chance of survival was an organ transplant and the only donor was some perfectly healthy guy, and one night you found him—the donor—lying drunk on the train tracks, would you try and help him or would you just let him die so Uncle Turkish could get the organ? Assuming the organ stays intact, of course."

Mosaic stared at him with her big brown irises that gave her big round eyes that look of youthful wonder.

"Maybe weird runs in the family," she replied.

"Seriously, what would you do?"

"I don't know. What kind of question is that?"

"A hypothetical one. It gives you insight into a person's character. Just answer it."

"I'd try to help him."

"You mean the drunk donor?"

"Yeah."

"Really? Even if it means Uncle Turkish dies."

"Of course! Wouldn't you?"

"No, not necessarily."

"Really?"

"I don't even know him. You're not responsible for what happens, right? It's not like you put him there in that situation. The guy got drunk and passed out. And you'd still choose to save him over your own father?"

"Did you see someone lying on the tracks or something? Dale, did something happen?"

"No, no. It's just, someone asked me the same thing and I wasn't sure how to answer it."

Mosaic poured herself a cup of tea. "Well, sometimes doing nothing is as bad as doing what's wrong."

Dale gave it some thought and was about to comment on how wise beyond her years she sounded when Mosaic jerked back in her seat.

"Hot!" she cried.

Despite hovering over the teacup and blowing on its contents, she had taken an

> ## *"Well, sometimes doing nothing is as bad as doing what's wrong."*

eager sip too soon. Dale burst into laughter.

"It's not funny. I think I burned my tongue."

"Are you okay?"

"*Psh.* Now you ask?"

"Be careful."

"Yeah, yeah." Mosaic tapped her tongue with the tip of her finger before adding, "So what did my answer tell you about my character?"

"That you really are weird."

Mosaic rolled her eyes and popped an olive into her mouth. Dale went for a sip and got only ice.

"I'm going to get another. You want anything?"

"No, thanks."

By the time Dale was well into his second drink, the rest of the party had begun to trickle in. Mosaic's friends were of the sort that made her appear about as exceptional as a plum hanging from a plum tree planted in the middle of an apple orchard.

There was Rudy, short for Ruadah—the voluptuous mocha-skinned singer from the concert. As soon as Dale met her in person, sans stage make-up and elaborate costume, he could see why Mosaic was friends with her. She was loud, crass and fun, full of unbridled energy. Beside her was a lanky-framed bespectacled young man with a receding hairline hidden below a bowler cap. He had a thin mustache under a pointy nose. Under his arm was a book penned by some obscure author only literary elitists were familiar with. His name was Sebastian, an eccentric intellect. Whether anyone cared to listen or not, he'd carry on about the injustices of the world and the Republic's need for political reform.

"The Republic? It's just a farce," he said. "Just like every other government. The true god of Parabolis is gold. And where is the gold? Look around. The nobles know. The bankers know. The bureaucrats. They own the unions and the lobbyists. They fund the senate. They hold the strings from within the shadows. They've taken the throne and nobody's doing a thing about it."

"Oh dear," said Rudy, rolling her eyes. "Here we go again. Don't mind him, Dale. Sebastian grew up in the slums so he's always vilifying anyone who can afford a ruffled tunic."

"Mock it all you want. But when you're on the short end of the stick, soon enough, you'll be wondering how we ended up under the thumb of a plutocracy."

"Not me. I plan to marry a noble and end up on top. I always end up on top." She winked.

"Herein lies the problem," Sebastian continued. "The majority of us are sedated like good sheep, content to jest and squabble and graze on the latest and greatest at the Halo. No offense, Mo, but it's true. It's all just smoke and mirrors, a propaganda machine to keep us preoccupied, dumb and numb, while they rob the world from beneath our feet. If this government spent more time on education than they did protecting business interests, then maybe our country wouldn't be spiraling into the shit storm that it is. Never mind a Balean invasion, which, mind you, is nothing more than a contrivance of the profiteers invested in our military industry."

The others around the table had already tuned out just as Dale's interest piqued.

"What do you mean by that?" Dale asked.

Sebastian was taken aback. It had been so long since someone had listened to one of his diatribes.

"Well," he hesitated, gathering his thoughts, "take the Ancile for example. Everyone thinks it was about national security, right? Consider who profited from it. Mining corporations who provided the resources to build it. And construction firms who secured the contracts. And the politicians who were bribed, in essence, to ensure its necessity. Did we really need it? Well, we never did before."

"That's because Duke Thalian was never on the throne before," Dale offered.

"Everyone paints him like some warmonger. But he's only reacting to the threat the Ancile poses. You can't wave a sword at someone and then decry a defensive response. Call me a traitor if you want but our government is the real traitor. Our senators, the warmongers. Think about it. The mining corporations that sponsor them win on both ends of this conflict. Regardless of the outcome, they come out with the gold."

"How's that?"

"It takes resources for Bale to raise an army too. That means more iron and copper sales. You see? It's all one giant, sinister plot right under our noses. Far more sinister than the threat of some foreign invasion. This is treason at the highest levels. A domestic conclave of the powerful elite whose corruption knows no end. Our government has betrayed its people."

"Aren't you just a wellspring of good cheer," said Rudy. "So little faith that justice will prevail in the end."

"Not in this world. Not unless there's some higher power willing to intervene."

"There is. It's called God."

Sebastian scoffed. "Don't get me started on the Benesanti."

"Well, what are you going to do about it, Sebastian?" asked Mosaic.

"Yeah," Rudy added. "Do something instead of just going on about how utterly shit it is."

"I am doing something."

"And what's that?"

"I'm raising awareness."

Rudy laughed. Mosaic shook her head. Sebastian smiled at his own absurdi-ty. But Dale was not amused. As a veteran, he was constantly curbing his disdain for civilians who tossed around their theoretical opinions on politics and war. And even more so for those who trivialized it with indifference.

He left the booth to order another drink. By his fourth, the entire party had arrived—members of the cast, friends of the members, artists and musicians, until even the bar's quieter back was full of revelry. Then came the beautiful blonde Anika, who turned heads as she sashayed in on the arm of a tall, handsome young man that made Terry the host frown.

"Well, Mosey, aren't you going to introduce us?"

"Dale, this is Anika. Anika, my cousin Dale."

"A pleasure to meet you," said the blonde, holding out her hand palm down for him to kiss.

"And you," Dale replied, gently shaking it instead.

"Careful, Dale," said Rudy. "The lass may bed you if you stare too long."

To which Anika replied, "Oh, the whale and her tales. By the way, great show, Mosey. Rudy, you were flat."

She lit up a smoke on the end of her long stem filter and introduced her companion, who had a firm handshake and whose name Dale had made no effort to remember.

As the night wore on, Dale qui-

etly fixed himself full of bourbon while a battle to monopolize attention ensued between Anika and Rudy. Rudy with her humor, and Anika with a desperate peddling of her beauty. When she found herself losing, she feigned boredom. Then she sought attention away from the table. Her eyes wandered as she tossed her hair and fired off rapid, random smirks all over the room. A woman in need.

As the room began to spin, Dale excused himself. He sought the relief of the cool night's air. A group of young women dressed in short skirts and low bust lines shuffled their way in past him.

"Anika's competition just got stiffer," Dale mumbled to himself.

The evening was crisp. The night was quiet. Nothing spoke of an imminent invasion. No domestic conclave of the powerful elite. And no justice.

He moved into the alley beside the pub, hugged the wall and vomited. Mosaic came out after him and asked if he was okay.

"Fine, I'm fine," he replied, lighting up a smoke to mask his breath. "You know something? You have some interesting friends, Mo."

"Let's get you home," she said.

"No, no, you go back inside. I'll walk it off."

She looked at him skeptical.

"Really," Dale insisted. "I'm fine, now. I got most of it out."

"You sure?"

"Hey, just don't stay out too late, okay?"

"Okay."

He then thanked her for inviting him to the concert and for the great company. Before parting, they agreed that they should try to see each other more often.

Back at home, Dale lay in bed swirling in a haze. He stared at the white ceiling supported by dark alder beams wondering, *if there was an earthquake, would the ceiling hold?* He thought about how those were the same alder beams his father saw every night falling asleep. He closed his eyes and thought about his joyless father. He tried to define joy. Settled on likening it to the scent of something caught only on its way out, he rolled over and drifted off to the music from Mosaic's concert still fresh in his memory.

Nearly two hours passed.

Dale was stirred awake by an incessant rapping on his door—the sound of brass against oak. It wasn't a rushed knock, intended to alarm him; just steady and patient like a metronome. Unable to ignore it, he crawled out of bed and cursed over a throbbing head. When he opened the door, he saw a man holding a brass-handled cane. He was wearing a top hat and a black rose on his lapel.

"Good evening, Mister Sunday," said Remy Guillaume. "It is time."

CH 16

THE GHOST AND THE DARKNESS

It was just past midnight. The sky was without a moon. The air was heavy and cold. And the city around them was especially dark.

"The lights are out," Dale observed.

The street lamps were unlit. Every building, black. The only sources of light were, for a time, the limousine lamps that guided the horses. But even those were extinguished as they neared the breaker.

"Yes. We put the Spegen temporarily out of commission," Remy replied. "Just until the transport arrives, of course."

With control over the unions, it was no secret the Carousel Rogues had set themselves up to profit from the Spegen. Right at the onset of its operation, the Rogues siphoned a percentage from the payments. For the Rogues, shutting down the Steam Powered Electric Generator was a voluntary closing of a very lucrative spigot. They also risked a very public display of strength and the range of their reach in Carnaval City, a display the Rogues characteristically tried to avoid. The blackout revealed to Dale the importance of this transport to the Rogues and the Fat Fox.

Arturo Lucien was waiting in front of the breaker with two more stretch limousine coaches. They were guarded by a small entourage of Rogues. Dale passed them as he entered through the office and into the hangar. With no electric power, the gates had to be opened manually. He worked a mechanical crank that was connected to a pulley system. The chains rattled as the steel gates opened into the black bay. There were patches of thinning fog in the middle-distance like slow departing ghosts.

Meanwhile, Remy motioned one of the Rogues over. The Rogue carried in his arm a flare secured to a tripod. A bellow-like contraption was attached to it by a hose. He prepared it at the end of the dock, hidden deep below the hangar in the direct line of sight from the sea beyond. There was a burst of light as the flare ignited before it settled into a steady blue flame. Remy stood at the gates, eyes scanning the darkness.

Arturo walked up beside Dale, blowing into his hands.

"It's freezing," he said.

"What happens now?"

"We wait. As soon as the transport passes the naval blockade, it'll surface in the bay where the water is shallow. Then hopefully, it'll spot the flare and cruise straight in before anyone notices."

"So it's an underwater vessel?"

"What did you expect?"

"You said this transport wasn't going to be illegal."

"Not all underwater vessels are illegal."

"Oh, so these guys are marine surveyors? Just a couple of scientist, right?"

"No. They're Submariners."

"You mean 'pirates'."

"Look, nothing *you're* doing is illegal, okay?"

Shaking his head, Dale lit up a smoke. He then followed Arturo down to the dock where Remy waited.

"Let me get this straight," Dale said, walking behind Arturo. "I'm an accomplice in a smuggling operation conducted by pirates and the city's most notorious criminal organization, but it's not illegal?"

"Just relax, will you?"

Dale blew out a plume of smoke. "Don't I look relaxed to you?"

"Yeah, but the way you're making all this sound—it's making me nervous."

Remy checked his watch, looked up, and suddenly raised a hand. Everyone held their breath and peered with him into the darkness.

"There," whispered Arturo, pointing into the void.

Remy tapped his cane against the docks and the Rogue underling immediately began working the tripod contraption. The flare signaled in bursts of rhythmic pulses.

It took him a moment before Dale noticed the large moving silhouette emerging out of the darkness. A mass, swiftly and silently gliding toward them. The steam engine had been shut off. Purely on momentum, the stealth vessel settled into the docking bay. Stenciled into the side of the matte black iron hull was its name in

weathered gray paint: The Saint Viljoen.

Dale recognized it immediately. And something stirred within. He was a child again, marveling at a sea vessel in his father's breaker. "That's not a Submariner. That's *the* Submariner."

"Yep. He's a good friend of mine," Arturo replied, brimming with pride. "We did a lot of business together in the past when I was still a sea merchant. It's all about making the right connections."

The first to disembark was its captain, Leon Getty, a Submariner whose name was widely recognized among seafarers. He was one part charming gentlemen, two parts ruthless murderer. He climbed out of the hatch and swaggered down the docking ramp, his long navy coat hovering just above his ankles. Down his chest, holstered in two rows of three on either side of his suspenders, were percussion-pin pistols, and two more on his hips. His bronzed skin was weathered and leathery. His dark hair was pulled into a neatly folded back-knot. The tightly pulled hair and the large hoop earrings in both ears accentuated his narrow face. When he spoke, the deep voice came with a noticeable lisp.

"Traversed have I from shore to shore in the womb of the Amaranthian. But none have my eyes beset a friendlier face than this," he said, clutching Arturo's arm. He greeted him with a kiss, as it was customary among men of the sea. "It's good to see you, old friend," he added, with an affectionate gaze.

"You too, Leon."

"He looks like shit," came a sultry voice from behind the captain.

"And you, lovelier than ever, Cassiopeia," Arturo replied.

Cassiopeia, "Siren of the Saint," was rumored to be as fetching in form as she was dangerous. Dale had heard of her generous bosom, hips of an hourglass, and long striding legs that men would fall on their swords to part—embellishments of libidinous men who'd been at sea too long. Other than a plunging décolletage, chocolate brown curls, and a saber sheathed at her side, Dale thought Cassiopeia's colorful language was more notable than anything in her appearance.

"Come here and let me greet you proper, you filthy brack swab."

Arturo couldn't help but blush when she kissed him on the cheek, giving hue to his otherwise pasty skin.

Leon gave Dale a nod. "So is this handsome fellow the face behind our darkly encounter?" he asked.

"No, this is my friend, Dale Sunday," Arturo replied. "He owns the breaker."

Cassiopeia looked at Remy. "And who's the ass in the hat?" she asked.

"I am Remy Guillaume of the Carousel Rogues," Remy replied, with a formal bow, top hat in hand. "Perhaps the lady can take greater care with her choice of words."

"Perhaps I can take care to stick the heel of my boot in your throat, Mister Top Hat."

"*Hetep*, Cassiopeia," said Leon, in the pirate tongue. "You'll forgive my first mate," he added, stepping forward. "She is especially temperamental after a long journey."

The Submariner's eyes were fixed elsewhere. Dale followed his gaze over his shoulder and noticed that the entourage of Rogues had positioned themselves all throughout the hangar, overlooking the dock with their missile weapons trained on Leon.

"Your reputation precedes you, Captain Leon Getty," said Remy. "We know who you are. We know to whom you answer. And at sea, you may be an unrivaled bunch. But I would like to remind you and your first mate that you are currently standing on land under the protection of the Carousel Rogues. We expect you to behave accordingly."

Leon immediately raised a hand and silenced Cassiopeia before she could respond.

"We understand," he replied. "And we have no intention of overstaying our welcome. We only need to complete this exchange and then we'll be on our merry way."

The Rogue who had been working the flare had put it out and was now standing beside Remy with a large leather suitcase in hand.

"As agreed," said Remy, "we will give you your payment once we can verify that the passengers are indeed who they say they are."

"And what fool would pretend to be when they are not?" said Leon. "Tread carefully, good rogue. These are no ordinary men."

He clapped his hands twice. On cue, a fellow pirate waiting at the mouth of the Saint Viljoen's cargo door opened it. A tall, broad-shouldered man emerged in a tieless black suit. His face was hidden behind a ghostly, expressionless mask made of porcelain. He descended down the docking ramp alone.

Remy bowed and introduced himself.

"Where is the Fat Fox?" asked the man in the ghost mask.

He had a slight Silven accent.

"We will take you to him, shortly," Remy replied. "But first, I must confirm your identity. A mere formality, you understand."

The Ghost curiously cocked his head.

"You wish me to remove my mask, Remy Guillaume of the Carousel Rogues?"

"No. You only need to answer a simple question."

"Wouldn't cutting your throat be confirmation enough?"

Before he finished speaking, a figure stood behind Remy, holding a blade to his throat. No one, not Remy, Dale, nor anyone else had noticed this dark figure disembark and sneak up behind Remy. It was as if he appeared out of thin air. All of the Rogues in the breaker shuffled alert at the threat. They aimed their weapons, but too late. The rest looked on, stunned and immobile.

Remy signaled his men to stand down with a raised hand. He moved slowly.

"*Qi a santom rachnya fad espel?*" he then asked.

Remy spoke to the Ghost in a dead language—a language with which only scholars of ancient languages were familiar.

The Ghost paused and studied him.

"*Espel a santom nai,*" he finally replied, rolling up his sleeve just enough to show Remy a tattoo on his left wrist. It was of a compass marked with ancient runes, framed in a machine cog.

"*Mora a'unde espel si yakovz.*"

The Darkness then released him, sheathed his blade, and stepped away. As he did, he moved unlike anything Dale had ever seen, like a figure from a feverish nightmare, deliberate and menacing.

The Darkness wore a lean-fitting outfit of charcoal gray dappled with black, rendering him nearly indistinguishable against the backdrop of night. And over his head was a matching mottled balaclava with two separate holes cut out for his ink-black eyes. He wore thin gloves attached to bracers of matted black leather and boots fastened with wraps nearly up to his knees. Sheathed into a shoulder harness under the arms on either side were two throwing knives. And running horizontally across his hips just below the small of his back was the scabbard housing his blade. Nothing of him was uncovered.

The blade itself was similar in form to an Omeijian wakizashi, too long to be a dagger and too short to be a sword. But to the trained eye there was no mistaking it for anything other than a customized variant. It was simpler and more pragmatic in design, with a straight single-edge as opposed to the curve common to Omeijian blades. And there was no guard between the collars separating the blade from the

> ## *It was as if he appeared out of thin air.*

handle. The bladed half measured slightly longer than the length of its wielder's forearm, while the braided grip was nearly equal in length for two-handed leveraging.

Remy rubbed his throat where the Darkness had pressed his blade up against it. Then he signaled the Rogue standing beside him who handed the suitcase over to Leon. While the Submariners checked its contents, counting the bundles of banknotes, Remy looked at the Ghost and gestured toward the breaker exit.

"Please, if you will come with me."

The Ghost and the Darkness followed Remy out and disappeared into one of the guild's stretch coaches. Remy then returned with a satchel containing the rest of Dale's pay.

"You have seen nothing and know nothing," he said. "Our business is complete."

And then he left.

When the small convoy had set off, Dale was left with Arturo, the Submariner and his crew. There was a collective sigh.

"What the hell was that?" asked Arturo.

"We almost got killed," said Cassiopeia. "That little rat hat cocking Rogue nearly got us all killed."

"What was that?" Arturo repeated.

"That, my dear Arty, was the Samaeli," Leon replied. "Had I known they were the cargo, I would never have agreed to this transport."

"What's a Samaeli?"

"The scariest thing in Parabolis. They are the shadows within the shadows. Until now, I knew them only to exist in tavern tales."

"Why would the Fat Fox hire them?"

Leon shook his head and wagged his finger. "Dear, dear, Arty, nobody hires the Samaeli. They're not petty bounty hunters, freelancers to be contracted. They do not give audience to those they mean to service, or rather, use."

"So, if they weren't hired, what are they doing here?"

"The darkness weaves what terrors it pleases and no prey knows its reason."

"We need to get out of here," said Cassiopeia. "I've got a bad feeling about this."

"Agreed."

"But you just got here," Arturo tried.

"And we've got what we came for," said Leon, holding up the large suitcase.

"What're you going to do with those? You can't just spend that anywhere."

"Republican marks are worth twice their value in gold in some places."

"Muriah Bay?"

"Precisely."

Muriah Bay was a small coastal village hidden in a cove just north of the Republic's border. Because of its remote location, it was a common stop for smugglers and black market traders.

"We'll need to settle for a few months

to resupply anyway before the long voyage back," Leon added. "The crew's getting restless."

"As am I," said Cassiopeia. "Captain, please."

"Gentlemen, I have washed my hands of this and you would be wise to do the same. These men of shadow bear ill omen. Neither strength nor cunning can deliver you from such evil. Cast not your lives to the winds of chance and depart with me from the very memory of this night."

"Here, here," said Arturo, raising an imaginary glass.

"Arty, this is no joke. Stay away from them. The Lords of the Sea know I'd hate for something terrible to happen to you."

Dale found the exchange fascinating. Despite all of his misgivings about Arturo, warranted or not, in some select part of the world, within some select circles of self-serving fortune hunting pirates, Arturo was actually cared for, his friendship valued.

"Those men, they aren't human," said Cassiopeia, clutching his arm. "Even the Pirate Lord Del Rasa shudders at the thought of them. The Rogues don't know what they're getting into. You'd be wise not to make the same mistake. And take care of your skin. You look sick."

She climbed the ramp and disappeared into the hatch.

"Too brief, I know. But as always, it was good seeing you, Arty. And Dale, it was a pleasure. Any friend of Arty's is a friend of mine. Remember that. Gentlemen." The captain then boarded the vessel after his first mate, turned to his crew below and barked, "*Nosere vai!*"

As the steam engines began to spit and knock before settling into a soft steady hum, he looked down at Arturo and Dale from the opening, blew a kiss, and closed the hatch.

The Saint Viljoen drifted back into the bay as quickly and quietly as it had come. Dale couldn't tell at what point it had submerged, having lost track of the hull against the black horizon. He only saw the wake of the water until that too, disappeared, and all was still again.

CH 17

REAPING

Built a century ago by its founder, Petra Le'Viscante, the Carousel Rogues' secret lair was an intricate subterranean network of tunnels. Only sworn members knew of its existence and, once within its catacombs, how to navigate the maze.

Remy led the Ghost and the Darkness through the sewers until they arrived at a dead end, a bare concrete wall. One of the Rogue henchmen turned various wheels attached to a piping grid on an adjacent wall in a dizzying array of combinations. When he finished, Remy approached the wall, pressed down on a barely visible button along one of its many fissures. Steam began to spit from one of the pipes. The entire wall rotated clockwise twenty-five degrees, with grating sounds of cogs and chains. An opening wedge appeared to the right. One by one, the group slipped

THE ROGUES

through and collected in the next chamber. Once the wall shut behind them, they were trapped. Only an iron portcullis now separated them from the lair of the Carousel Rogues. On the other side was a vault where a guard sat beside two levers: one black and one red.

"Mister Guillaume, how many hares in a hat?"

"None if you are blind as a bat," Remy replied.

Upon hearing the passphrase, the guard pulled the black lever, raising the portcullis. Had Remy or any other person appearing before the guard spoken the wrong words, the guard was to pull the red lever without any further consideration. The red lever triggered a mechanism designed to open the entire chamber floor, the contents of which would then drop into a collecting pit with no access, to be sorted and dealt with appropriately.

The thieves manning the passage watched and muttered to one another as the guests were ushered in. The lair was a large fortress carved into a cavern, complete with storage spaces, sleeping quarters, a bathhouse, and training rooms. One of the training areas built into a large recess of the cavern was a life-size replica of a surface street corner. Designed with no detail overlooked, the replica served as a staging area for final "run-throughs" of various Rogue exploits. Beyond these features, at the heart of the fortress was a heavily guarded cast-iron door, the entry to the den of the Fat Fox. Two elite guards stood watch.

"Mister Guillaume, we'll have to confiscate all weapons here."

Remy looked back at the Ghost apologetically.

"This is the first time outsiders have been permitted to venture this far into our lair," Remy explained. "In light of your, ah, *unique skill-set*, you must understand my employer's cautious disposition."

The Ghost turned to the Darkness.

"*Azash et a'boujan*."

The Darkness reluctantly pulled his prized blade from its scabbard and surrendered it to the guard. He did the same with his throwing knives. The Ghost held open his coat and performed a slow pirouette to show that he was unarmed. Then they followed Remy through the cast-iron door into a narrow hallway marked by floor lighting. At the end of it was another thick cast-iron door with a view hole at eye level. Remy knocked. The view slid open and a set of eyes peered out. They darted between Remy and his two guests. Then it closed. There were three clicks and the heavy door slowly opened. Two of the Fat Fox's most trusted bodyguards showed them in.

The den was spacious with high ceilings. It was furnished with the finest oak cabinets and bookshelves, modern sculptures, and paintings. A beautiful tapestry adorned one of the concrete walls. Imported fur rugs covered the cold cement floor. From this main room, other doors led to multiple chambers: bedchamber, dining room, cigar room, and personal toilet and bathing quarters. At the end was a large granite surface desk behind which the Fat Fox sat on a tall, leather chair. As always, he was impeccably dressed in a smart three-piece suit, pressed and prim, polished shoes, hair oiled back, cleanly shaven.

Remy removed his hat, walked over to the Fat Fox and whispered in his ear. Then he took his place beside the enforcer behind the guild master.

"Gentlemen, please take a seat."

The Ghost took a seat on the small wooden chair in front of the desk. He crossed his legs and appeared at ease. The Darkness stood beside him, mirroring the guild master's enforcer.

"You must be Felix Eglon," came a muffled voice from below the eerie porcelain mask.

"Yes. And you must be Magog Siberion. It's good to finally put a face to the name, so to speak. Is the mask really necessary?"

Magog glanced over his shoulder at the men standing guard and replied, "Are you in the habit of discussing privileged matters so openly?"

The Fat Fox smiled. With a wave of his hand, he dismissed his two bodyguards at the door. When they stepped out into the narrow hallway, Felix replied, "You've met my counselor and personal liaison, Remy Guillaume. And this is my chief executor, Vicente. They are my most trusted confidants." Then the Fox looked up at the Darkness. "What's his story?"

"He's not your concern."

"He can't speak for himself?"

"He's not your concern," the Ghost repeated.

Felix opened his drawer, pulled out a cigar, slid it under his nostrils and clipped the end. He placed it between his lips unlit and took in the flavor. All the while, he kept his eyes fixed on the silent Darkness. Neither averted their gaze. He attempted a condescending smirk, but the muscles in his cheek quivered, pulling the upper lip into shaky lift. With his face betraying him, Felix thought he had better start talking.

"So, what's this all about?"

When Magog didn't immediately respond, Felix shifted in his seat, lit his cigar, and filled the silence. "Let me guess. You want me to invest in your Machina Group."

"The Shaldea have contacted you. Why?"

"Excuse me?"

"Why have the Shaldea contacted you?"

"That's my business."

"Mister Eglon, you have led me down into this—this monolith you call a home. Into your elaborate paranoia. Tell me, do you suppose all of this will keep you safe?"

The Fat Fox's eyes took on the look of a lost child. His lips turned pale and dry. "Is there a problem?"

The Ghost removed his expressionless porcelain mask. His face was the same shade of his mask—cold, white porcelain. He had a crimson handprint tattooed over his mouth. His menacing face, barely human, solicited the same response that it had years ago in the desolate Emmainite village. At the sight, the Fat Fox recoiled in his seat. Vicente felt his legs go limp.

"We require a base of operations and a temporary funding stream. Your little club of thieves here will suffice. Unfortunately, you will not survive the acquisition."

With Magog's words still hanging in the air, Remy Guillaume pulled his cane apart revealing a single-shot pistol, the grip of which was its brass handle. In one fluid motion, he pressed the barrel against the side of Vicente's head and pulled the trigger.

Magog extended his hand toward the Fat Fox as if he were signaling him to stop. The Fat Fox, with horror in his eyes, back-pedaled in his leather chair, his short legs kicking frantically, ineffectively. From within the sleeve of Magog, a needle laced with paralyzing poison shot out. It pierced the guild master's chest.

At the sound of gunfire, both elite bodyguards rushed back toward the den. The Darkness, anticipating their response, was already positioned at the door. He grabbed the first from behind and snapped his neck while simultaneously relieving him of his dagger. Before the first hit the floor the dagger was plunged into

The Fat Fox's gasping for air was amplified by the sudden silence that befell the room. He was slumped in his chair, a small crimson speck on his shirt where the needle had penetrated his skin, his teeth clenched, straining. His cigar was on the floor, slowly burning through the rug. Remy stamped it out and stood before the Fat Fox.

"Everything casts a shadow, Mister Eglon," he said. "Even a sewer rat like you." Then he unbuttoned the top half of his shirt and pulled it open. In the center of his chest was a cogged compass tattoo like the one on Magog's wrist. "I am and have always been a Shadow of the Samaeli."

He got up close and gave the Fat Fox a consoling look. Then he picked up Vicente's blade and stabbed the Fat Fox in the neck.

Magog sat once more in the small wooden chair.

"Vengian," he said, summoning the Darkness over, "take the first train to Pharundelle in the morning. Treat the senator quickly and return. We have much to do here."

The Darkness nodded in the affirmative.

"Master," said Remy, wiping his bloodstained hands with a handkerchief, "our Shadow in the north has confirmed your suspicions. The Shaldea have involved themselves."

"Secure your position over this guild," Magog ordered. "Once you have established your leadership, meet with the local cell."

"Yes, master."

"We will kill them all."

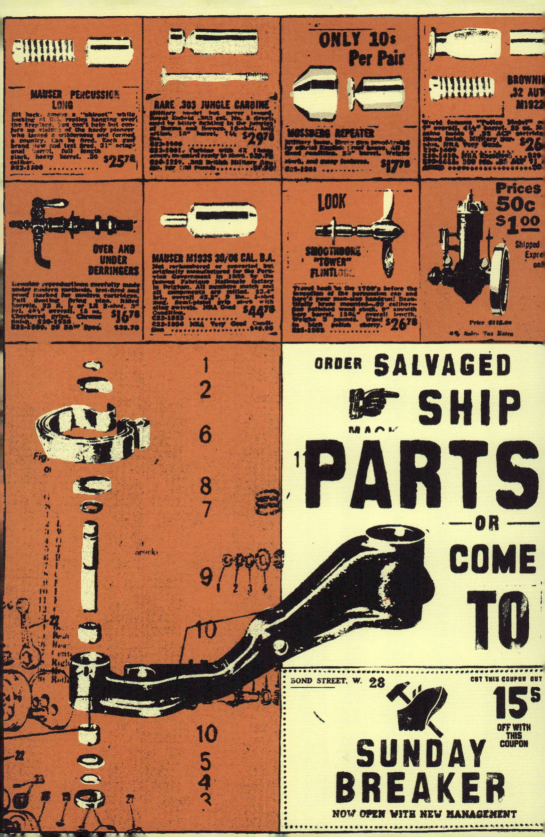

Carnaval City Goes Black.

Spegen goes down, was it the Rogues?

BULLETIN.

Lakehurst, N. J., Tuesday, Oct. 16.—(Special.)—The Graf Zeppelin was berthed inside the navy hangar here alongside the Los Angeles at 3 o'clock this morning. The great bulk was hauled from the mooring mast, about 200 feet away, in little more than an hour.

BY TOM PETTEY
(Chicago Tribune Press Service.)
(Pictures on back page.)

BLACKOUT!

New Name

10's

Same BEER!

Used to be THE HAPPY HAM

Now  THE BROKEN CISTERN

OPEN AGAIN AFTER REMODELING

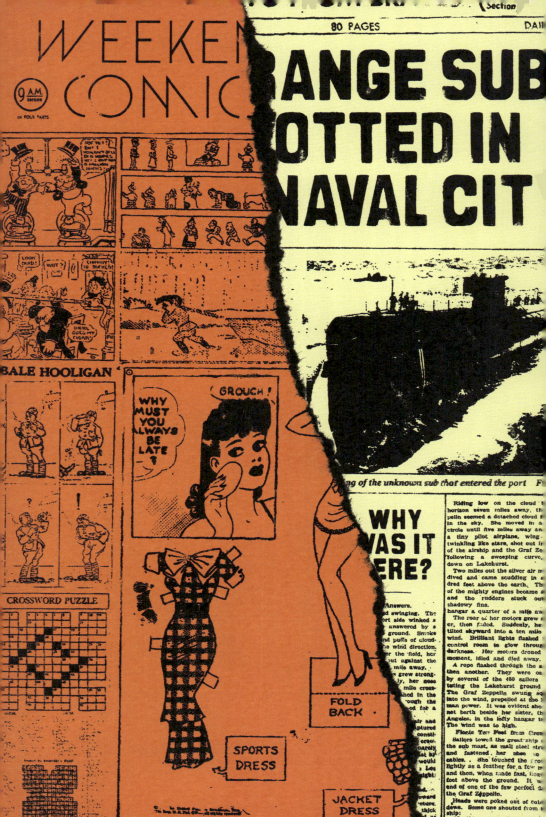

№ 03

CH 18

GREAT MATTERS

"P lease, follow me."
An Emmainite messenger led Remy Guillaume into a web of narrow alleyways cut through the slums beyond Trivelka Square. Eyes peered out of sandstone buildings. Children played, half-naked in sewage run off. Older women with gaunt faces and hollowed eyes crouched in doorways. A young mother among them nursed her babe. They all took notice of the stranger. No one spoke a word. After a series of turns, they came to the door of an old pottery shop.

"Saffi!" the guide shouted from the entryway.

An old Emmainite man poked his head out. He glanced up at the guide and then at Remy. Then he showed them into his shop. Without a word, he led the two through the store lined with barrel-sized clay pots. Remy recognized them as storage pots and cisterns. Once they were at the back end of the building, the old man pointed to the section of the storeroom partitioned off by a makeshift curtain, a printed fabric hung on a wire strung along the ceiling. He left the visitors there and returned to the front. Standing guard at the partition were two men, their faces covered by black keffiyehs, each armed with a janbiya. Without bothering to frisk Remy, they pulled back the curtain, admitting the two visitors.

The air in the back of the storeroom was pungent with tobacco and spice. The smoke from a long-stem pipe danced in the streak of the late afternoon sun beaming through a single tarnished window. The cell leader sat against the far wall.

Omar Basiliech had rounded, dark eyes with heavy lids set deep below his thick brows. Under his prominent nose was a thick, black mustache to match his brows. Around him stood a retinue of armed men.

"The Maker's peace be upon you," he said, after excusing the guide. "Welcome. Please, sit."

Remy sat in a leather chair that had been brought out for him.

"Care for some tea?"

"No, thank you."

> *"You are dealing with demons... Nothing good can come of this."*

One of his guards poured Omar a glass from a tea set resting on top of an adjacent bureau. The rising scent of sweet mint added to the strange medley of smoke and spice.

"Mister Guillaume, is it?"

"At your service. And you must be Mister Omar Basiliech—am I pronouncing that correctly?"

"Perfectly. But please, call me Omar."

"Very well, Omar."

"You'll forgive me for making you come all this way. But we have not managed to elude the Eagles' eyes for as long as we have by any lack of caution."

"You preach to the choir, Shaldean."

Omar smiled.

"Not to sound rude, Mister Guillau-

"Yes, well, he regrets not being able to be here in person. He is tied up at the moment. But rest assured, I have been given authority to speak on his behalf. Now, what can we do for you, Omar?"

Omar gave his words careful thought before replying.

"We have a shipment coming in next week. We would appreciate it if the local authorities were preoccupied during that time."

"Give me a name and the Fat Fox will make sure your shipment is safely delivered," offered Remy.

"Cain Stoyanov."

"The Lecidian arms dealer?"

"Yes. We are always in need of arms."

"Of course. Is that it?"

"There is one other thing. On the night of the Harvest Festival, we need you to shut down the Spegen."

Remy sat back in his chair and folded his hands over his crossed knees. "That is quite a request."

"But not beyond your means. We are prepared to pay handsomely for it." Omar waved his hand. A large duffle bag was brought out and placed on the table. "In that duffle bag, you will find one-hundred thousand marks."

Remy cocked his brow. "An impressive sum."

"For both the Spegen and our ship-

Remy removed from the bag a bundle of banknotes and studied it under the afternoon light. "I would be remiss if I did not ask for what purposes you are making this request."

"I'm afraid I can't say."

"I see." Remy tossed the bundle back into the duffle bag. "You will have your shipment of arms. And the Spegen will be shut down on the night of the Harvest Festival. You have my word. But keep your money."

The men in the room exchanged glances and muttered in disbelief.

"What I want instead is information," Remy added.

"Mister Guillaume, I can not tell you the nature of our business."

"I already know the nature of your business. You are terrorists. The information I speak of is the whereabouts of one Yusef Naskerazim."

Omar went silent.

"Surely you have heard of him. He is a former *Rajeth* of your Riders."

Omar emptied his pipe and set it down and took a sip of his tea. "I don't know anyone by that name," he replied.

"We are intelligent men, Omar. Let us not insult each other with falsehood."

"Who is asking?"

"Men even the Fat Fox cannot refuse. The Samaeli."

The name got Omar's full attention.

an opponent who has pushed in a sizable bet. When he could see that Remy was not the bluffing sort, his face sank. Unable to hide his distress, through clenched teeth he whispered, "*Zaal'mavorte*."

"Yes," said Remy. "The *Zaal'mavorte*."

"They are here?" Omar asked.

"Yes. And if you will not tell me where Yusef Naskerazim is, they will come looking for you." Remy then leaned forward and spoke in the ancient Emmainite language. "*Al Zaal'mavorte saf'ha sha mut'lark, sayif Omar. Mu'hana al avela. Ve avela sha hari'yarde.*"

The men standing around the cell leader looked at one another, their surprise written on their faces. Even they did not understand everything Remy had said. But Omar did: *the Samaeli deal in absolutes, Omar my friend. They are the shadows. The shadows are everywhere.*

Omar gave deep thought to the demand. He looked at his men and found no help.

"You are dealing with demons, *afendi*," he said in Common. "Nothing good can come of this."

"Then you understand why I cannot leave here without an answer."

Omar folded his hands and bowed his head. He took a deep breath.

"Out," he said. "All of you."

When the backroom was cleared, Omar stood. He began as he paced, "*Afendi*, I do not concern myself in great matters or in things too difficult for me." He stopped, licked his lips, and started again, "Yusef Naskerazim is here in Carnaval City. Yes. But no one knows where. No one has had any direct contact with him in years."

"This is what you want me to relay to my clients?"

"This is the truth. I swear it. Who would dare withhold from the *Zaal'mavorte?*"

"Yes. Who would dare?" Remy rose from his seat and buttoned his coat.

"Please, *afendi*," Omar tried, "take the money."

Remy smiled. "It is not money that my clients seek."

As Remy turned to leave, Omar held his hands out to the side and pleaded, "Tell them I have withheld nothing."

Remy glanced back, bowed, and said, "Thank you for your time, Omar," just before stepping out through the partitioned curtain.

WINTER PEARS 35¢

Sept Values SALE 35

Buy ...etime!

CH 19

STOLEN MORNING

The week leading up to the Harvest Festival, Carnaval City was abuzz. The streets were decorated with lights and ribbons. Banners hung from light posts and streets signs. Colorful masks and costumes were showcased in various stores. The influx of tourists and pilgrims meant an infusion of money to the city, even trickling into the scrap business.

For weeks, Dale had been overseeing the disassembling of an old freighter. He used the money from the night of the transport to purchase salvage from expedition projects. The rest he used to hire a few temporary yard hands to help with the extra work. With the spike in scrap inventory, Dale attracted a number of new buyers. Even before Dale could spread the word, developers looking for raw materials began to show up at the breaker. Savvy businessmen knew raw materials outside the mining industry were both rare and sold at bargain prices—prices too good to pass up.

After securing a contract with one such buyer, Dale stopped by the Marketplace to pick up some winter pears for his uncle, auntie, and Mosaic. It was Cora Tess' favorite, but an indulgence she seldom allowed herself. "It's just too much for a mere piece of fruit," she would say. "Why, if I were in the Hesperian Highlands, they would cost me near nothing."

Imported winter pears ran somewhere between fox pelts and pearls. With business finally picking up, Dale felt like splurging on the family.

While he leaned in to look for the perfectly ripe ones, Dale felt a rustling in his coat pocket. When he glanced down, he saw a little hand slip out. Dale darted around and saw a freckle-faced boy with copper-colored hair. He looked about ten years old, skinny as a rail. In the boy's hand was Dale's leather coin purse.

"Hey!"

Wide-eyed, the boy spun and bolted. Dale gave chase.

The boy was quick and light on his feet, weaving through the crowded street. Rounding a corner, the boy looked back to see if he was still being chased. There was no one in pursuit. He took the corner briskly. He reached in his pocket, pulled out the coin purse, and checked its contents. There was more money in it than the boy had seen in his lifetime. He closed the purse, gripped it tight in his fist, and started to sprint again. He turned into an alley, then another, and as he burst out into a large plaza, the boy crashed into a passerby.

"Careful," said the stranger.

The boy tore away and began to almost skip through the plaza. At the north end of the plaza was the Temple of the Benesanti. A number of clerics stood outside taking a mid-morning break. A few tended to a group of orphans playing in the courtyard. As the boy strode toward the temple, he was grabbed violently from behind.

"Got you, you little rat," said Dale.

The boy curled up into a ball, tucked the purse back into his trousers, and started kicking and pulling.

"Hey! Calm down, kid."

The boys and girls in the courtyard stopped their play and stared. One of the clerics approached.

"Excuse me, is there a problem?"

Dale looked up and saw the beautiful cleric that had so captivated him on the Groveland Express.

"Well?"

"Huh?"

"Is there a problem here?" Selah repeated.

"Uh, no. This kid just snatched my coin purse."

The cleric knelt down beside the boy. She grabbed him by the shoulders. He looked down at his shoes.

"Give it back to him, Mouse."

With a crestfallen gaze, he slowly pulled the coin purse from his pocket, and without looking at Dale, handed it to him.

"Now apologize," Selah added.

He pounded his chest twice with a closed fist, then opened it and bowed his head.

"Hold on," said Dale. Then he removed a few coins from his purse and handed it to the boy. "Here, kid. Your finder's fee."

"What do you say, Mouse?"

The boy pressed his hands together and bowed his head. He ran through the courtyard and into the temple.

"That was very gracious of you."

"It's nothing," Dale replied. "I was a kid too, once."

Selah looked at Dale. She appeared to him perfectly unaffected. "Unfortunately, this isn't the first time with that one. Children in want of love will do foolish things. My apologies on his behalf. If you'd like to report the incident—"

"No, no, that's not necessary," Dale said with a scowl.

"Blessings to you then, good citizen."

She turned to leave, but Dale was not about to let another opportunity pass. After failing to mount even an attempt in the aisle of the Groveland Express, Dale had sternly chastised himself. In the station, after some choice words, he had told himself something to the effect of, *If you ever get another chance…*

And here it was.

"You're from Lumarion, aren't you?" he asked.

Selah glossed him over with a curious expression before replying. "I'm sorry. Have we met?"

"No. Not really. I remember seeing you on the Groveland Express a few months ago. I was on my way back from Pharundelle when we stopped in Lumarion."

"I see."

"Your face is difficult to forget, Prioress." Dale let the words hang in the air between them. He hoped to see something in her to direct a way forward—a lilt of an eyebrow, a light stroke of her hair, a blush or a sheepish grin. Something. Nothing. Not even disinterest. Wavering, but undaunted, he introduced himself. "I'm Dale Sunday."

"Selah Evenford."

"A pleasure to meet you, Prioress Evenford."

"And you, Mister Sunday. Are you a member of our temple?"

"I…no, I'm not. I'm not very religious."

"Compassion, justice, peace is our religion. If not these, then what are you?"

"Discontent. Mediocre. Hungry."

"Is that an attempt at humor?"

"Yeah, but I guess it'd be funnier if it weren't mostly true."

"You sound like a troubled soul."

"Don't I?"

A templar approached the two. He was large like a castle tower, with glimmering armor and a plank-sized sword strapped to his back. Without acknowledging Dale, he spoke to Selah.

"Prioress Evenford, you should take the children back into the temple," said Alaric.

Selah nodded. She turned to Dale as she walked away. "We have worship services every week. I hope you'll join us at the temple, Mister Sunday."

She returned to the courtyard. Dale watched as she herded the children together and led them into the temple. Alaric stood next to Dale, unnoticed. Once Selah was out of sight, Dale turned and looked up at Alaric, who was looking down at him. Neither of the men said anything. Dale offered a friendly grin. It was not reciprocated. Seeing he was not welcome, Dale left Alaric in front of the temple. Walking toward the south end of the plaza, a dumb grin plastered across his face, Dale thought of the merits of a religious life.

CH 20

TEARDROP

Back at the breaker, Dale was useless. He could not stop thinking about Selah. It was well past noon and he had done little more than file a few forms, shuffle some papers around. From his office, he watched the workers strip the freighter of its last salvageable pieces. Any other day, he would have been working right there alongside the men. This day, they were coming into the office every hour to get directives they would've gotten on the yard. Finally, Dale went out, and put one of the men in charge. Then he gave the crew instructions on closing up the shop and took the rest of the day off. Having been a lieutenant in the Republican Guard with men under his command, what Dale lacked in administrative skills, he made up for with his ability to lead, to communicate and delegate responsibility.

With a bag of winter pears in hand, he started for the bakery. Just outside the gate, a well-dressed Azuric man stopped him. Dale recognized him as a Shen by the way he wore the long hair on the back of his head in a braided tail.

"Mister Sunday?"

"Yes?"

"Detective Graham Lei with the Metropolitan City Guards," said the Shen, flashing a badge. "May I have a word with you?"

"What's this regarding?"

"Did you recently loan out your breaker for use as a dock?"

"I'm sorry?" Dale's stomach turned.

"On the night the Spegen was temporarily shutdown, was your breaker loaned out to the Carousel Rogues?"

Dale felt that numb emptying inside. His mind went into a swirl. Unable to give an answer, Dale did all he could to project a calm demeanor.

"You didn't think we'd find out?"

"Am I being charged with something, Detective?"

"That can be arranged."

"Well, unless you are going to charge me with something, I don't have anything to say. Excuse me. I have some errands to run."

As Dale turned to walk away, he grimaced, a pained scowl spreading across his face. The detective yelled out to him, "There's something you should know, Dale. It's about your friend, Arturo Lucien. We believe he may've been murdered."

Dale stopped. He managed to restore a serene expression before turning around to face the detective. His thoughts went to his auntie, uncle, and Mosaic. They were in danger. The urgency swelled in his chest. He needed to get to the bakery.

"I thought that might get your attention," the detective added, approaching Dale.

"Look, he's a guy I knew as a kid," Dale replied. "Ran into him a couple times since I've been back but that's it. I'll answer whatever questions you have, but right now, I need to be somewhere."

"If it's the Fat Fox you're worried about, he's dead too."

A five-minute walk later, Dale was sitting across from the detective outside of a quiet café. Lei ordered himself a cup of coffee. Dale wasn't much of a coffee drinker, but on occasion he ordered a specialty drink called "the teardrop." It was three-fourths steamed milk and a fourth, or a "teardrop," of coffee.

Taking a sip of his coffee, staring into the street, the detective started, "You know, I was the first Azuric in this city to make detective. Ever since I was a kid, ever since a local constable helped my father fend off a robbery attempt at our little store, I'd always dreamt of becoming a lawman. Never thought it possible being Azuric. But here I am. That's what I love about this place. It doesn't matter where you're from because everyone is from somewhere else. This city was built on the backs of immigrants."

"You from Shangzhou-Shen?" asked Dale.

"You know your Azurics. But don't let the tail and eyes fool you. I'm only Shen in appearance. I was born and raised right here in Carnaval City. My family's actually been here for three generations." He took another sip. "You know what's missing? A little spiced rum in this. I love rum."

After a pause, he continued, "I met my great grandfather when I was a little kid. I don't remember him but he lived a long time. My dad said he swore by baijiu. He drank a glass everyday. You ever try baijiu?"

"No," Dale replied, deadpan.

"It's a variant of rice liquor indigenous to Shangzhou-Shen. I don't have much of a palate for it. It all tastes the same to me—baijiu, Goseonite soju, Omeijian shochu. Sort of like whiskey, scotch, and bourbon. Anyway, he'd be rolling in his grave if he knew my poison was rum. What do you drink?"

"Chocolate milk," Dale replied.

"What?" the detective asked with a laugh.

"Bourbon."

"'Chocolate milk?' You're funny."

"Detective, was there something you wanted to talk to me about?"

The detective set his cup down and leaned in.

"I'm going to be frank with you, Dale. I've been contacted by the SSC. The Eagles. And they're coming to town because they think what you got yourself mixed up in is a big harping deal. Now, I'm offering you a chance to come clean with me and I suggest you take it because I guarantee you'll fare a lot better with me than you will with them."

"What do you want to know?"

The detective sat back, studying Dale before he asked, "Do you know who Jan Vandermeer is?"

Dale shook his head.

"What about Baron Francis Koch?"

"No."

"Victor Madhaven? The Chief of the International Banking Exchange?"

Dale held a blank expression.

"Grayson Ur? Senator Arlen Prescott?"

"I've heard of Senator Prescott," Dale finally chimed. "He's the one that recently committed suicide."

"Right. Suicide. Now, do you know what all these men have in common?"

Dale shrugged.

"They're all dead. All within a six month period. They also happened to represent a constituency of shareholders in a little investment group called Machina. Now, it doesn't take a genius to see this and begin to wonder. The SSC believes there's a conspiracy—coordinated assassinations. And they're coming here to look for possible suspects."

"Okay. What's that got to do with

me?"

"Days after the senator was found dead, Felix Eglon's body turned up in the canals."

"And?"

"Come on, Dale. Let's dispense with all this nonsense. You helped him smuggle some shady characters into the city. Arturo told us everything. He told us about how he made the arrangements with you and the Fat Fox. About the night of the transport. Everything. The men you smuggled in. He said that they were some special breed of assassins."

Dale shook his head in disgust. It was just like Arturo to roll over—whatever would work to his own advantage. Few standards, even fewer morals. But Dale realized immediately there was nothing to be gained by ire directed toward the dead.

"And that's why they killed him? Because he talked too much?"

"He got spooked once he found out about the Fat Fox and told us he'd get back to us with more details. We let him go and that was the last we'd heard from him. We haven't found a body yet."

"Wait. Then how do you know he's dead?"

"Look, Arturo isn't a hard guy to find. We've worked all of his contacts. The casino regulars. They're all saying the same thing—haven't seen or heard from him in a week. That's not a good sign."

"What about his family?"

"What family?"

"His ex-wife and kids."

"Is that what he told you?"

Dale had never considered Arturo's shifty business methods would include fleecing sympathy. *That rat bastard.*

"The only family he had was a widowed mother that passed away three years ago," the detective added. He sat back and took a sip of his coffee. "Not to sound grim, but it's only a matter of time before his body turns up."

"Yeah. And then mine."

The detective's expression hardened. He leaned forward, "On the contrary. I'm trying to keep you from getting killed. You see, you can avoid the gallows by helping us catch some very dangerous people."

"The gallows? Are you kidding me?"

"Smuggling alone gets you at least three years. Add conspiracy, conspiring with a known criminal organization, and accessory to murder, the way I see it, your life's over either way."

"Okay, look. Yes. I opened the breaker. Okay? I told Arturo that I wanted nothing to do with this whole thing when he first approached me. But then I got dragged out to see the Fox, and he threatened my family. So, I opened the breaker. I had no idea what was coming in."

"How do we know that, Dale?"

"They assured me that none of it was illegal. That no one would get hurt. I'm a victim here, Detective."

"And how much did you make as a victim?"

"I didn't have a choice."

"You always have a choice."

They were familiar words. But unlike Arturo, the threat to Dale's family was real.

"I told you, the Fat Fox threatened to kill my relatives. And when a man like that makes threats, you listen."

"I know you were a Republican Guard. I want to believe you. But it doesn't buy you a free pass."

"I'm not looking for a pass. I was trying to protect my family. You want to get to the bottom of this? So do I. If you're right, and Arturo is dead, then my family is still in danger."

"Okay, suppose I believe you. You need to give me some more information. What kind of assassins were they?"

The anxiety returned. The relief that poured over Dale at the news of the Fat Fox's death was now being dispelled by the growing belief that he was mixed up with something far more menacing than the Carousel Rogues. He recalled what he saw step off the submarine that night. What the pirates had said. And he felt again the urgency to get to the bakery.

"I don't know. There were only two of them. Detective, can we do this later? I really need to be somewhere right now. I promise to come by your office. You tell me when, I'll be there," he replied.

The detective pulled out a notepad and pen from his coat pocket. Without looking at Dale, he denied him. "No. We're doing this now. What did they look like?"

Dale thought about running. He lit a smoke instead and determined to answer the questions as fast as he could.

"They both had their faces covered. One of them with a white porcelain mask, like in a masquerade. And the other one was wearing blackish gray camouflage with a matching balaclava. I didn't see any faces."

"What else?"

"The one with the white mask did all the talking," he continued. "He had a slight accent. Northern."

"Balean or Silven?"

"Not Balean. I don't know. I'm not the best with accents. But he was definitely foreign."

"Foreign," the detective dictated to himself as he scribbled into his notebook. "And what about the other one?"

"He didn't say anything. I don't even know if he was human."

"What do you mean?"

"He moved quick and quiet. Like a shadow. Literally. It was like nothing I'd ever seen."

"Were they armed?"

"The shadow guy was. A blade."

"Anything particular about it?"

"One of those Omeijian types. Sin-

"I don't even know if he was human."

gle-edged."

"Did Arturo mention anything like why they were here, or what they wanted, or who they worked for, who they were?"

"The pirates who smuggled them in, they called them 'the Samaeli.'"

"'The Samaeli?'"

"Yeah. They—the pirates—were really nervous about these guys."

"That seems to be the trend."

The detective sipped from his cup while reviewing his notes, his mind trying in vain to wrap around all the peculiarities of the case.

Dale finished his smoke and put it out. He noticed another man had settled into a nearby seat with his face hidden behind the paper, spread open before him like a map. The headline read: *Carnaval City, a haven for immigrants or criminals?* He was dressed in suit and tie. *A professional*, thought Dale. Not being able to see his face, Dale grew suspicious. *Why with all these empty tables, did he take a seat near us? There aren't very many people in suit and tie in this part of town.*

The detective asked for the check. The waiter returned with the bill on a saucer. All the while, Dale kept his eye on the stranger. The man with the paper briefly set it down to check his watch. Then he glanced up at Dale. They locked eyes. The man smiled and picked up his paper again.

The detective threw some coins on the bill and got up. Dale got up with him, eager to leave. Putting the notebook back in his pocket the detective said, "That's it for now. Hopefully there's enough here to keep the SSC off your back. I'll be in touch. Don't go anywhere."

Dale gave a nod. He was taking steps away even as the detective was speaking. Just as he turned in earnest for the bakery, the detective called, "Dale, one more thing. Be careful."

"Yeah, thanks. And thanks for the teardrop."

CH 21

FOR JUSTICE

Balean soldiers dangled off the highest turret of Castle Verona. They were harnessed to ropes, one for every crenel along the parapet. The ropes fell deep into the chasm below the crag on which the castle was built. At the rappelling instructor's command, they each loosened their grip and zipped down the line into the void. The rappel was an important part of their air assault strategy. The training had gone on for weeks to ensure precise timing.

Duke Merrick Thalian and Eli were standing along the wall of the castle watching the exercise. A herald approached on the run. He came to a halt before the duke, snapped his heels and saluted smartly.

"The guests are waiting in the Great Hall, m'lord," he said.

"How many?"

"More than twenty riders strong."

"Their horses?" asked Eli.

"The stable master has taken them under his care."

"Good. These men, they love their horses more than they do their wives. Have their *Rajeth* meet us in the War Room."

"Yes, m'lord."

The herald snapped his heels again and disappeared. Eli peered over the ledge.

"General? We're waiting on you."

"Don't rush me!"

General Arun Kilbremmer was among those rappelling. He was still hanging over the side of the turret. Below him, a blanket of mist covered the chasm floor.

"What's the matter, Arun?" asked the duke. "You afraid of heights?"

"I'm afraid of nothing."

"On your way then."

"Easy to bark with sure footing beneath you."

"Thank the Maker, yes. In return for your troubles, you will bask in the glory of leading the Royal Army to victory."

Arun scoffed. "Hell of a price to pay for glory."

"That's why you wear the stripes and I hold the scepter, old man."

> *"Hell of a price to pay for glory."*

Arun looked down past his dangling feet—should his rope fail—into certain death. Then he looked up at the duke, fear masked in umbrage. "Curse you and your war, m'lord."

He opened his grip and rapidly descended down the face of the castle and into the mist. Near the bottom of the chasm, he slowed and came to a complete stop, just a standing man's height from the ground where other rappelling instructors were waiting for him.

"Ah-hoon-da!" they shouted.

The instructor's counterpart at the top turned to the duke. "He's fine, Your Highness."

"Of course he is. Have him meet us in the War Room."

"Yes, m'lord."

Duke Thalian and Eli returned to the warmth of the castle walls and started down the spiraling staircase.

"I could never do that," said Eli. "I'm terrified of heights."

The duke smiled. "Yes. It takes a special breed of man to mimic a bird, doesn't it?"

"It seems the general still questions our undertaking."

"That's because Arun is of another age," Duke Thalian replied. "He was once the king's most trusted knight. He believes in using military might judiciously. For protecting the crown."

"Yes, it's all very noble. But so impractical."

The duke gave Eli a look of disapproval. "It does make one wonder. Perhaps we've been too hasty in moving off this old way."

"Are you beginning to share his doubts?"

Duke Thalian stopped and turned to Eli. "And if I were?"

Eli shrugged. "You are the regent, Your Highness. Only say the word and we will turn back."

"There is no turning back. Not since the day your Ciphers made ships fly in Brakker Gorge." As they rounded the last flight of stairs into the halls of the keep, the duke continued, "Eli, do you know the legacy of King Leawen?"

Eli gave no reply.

"Justice. It's what drove him to take his own life."

"I always thought it was depression," said Eli.

"It was. But the depression was caused by the demands of justice. The death of the queen. Ordering her execution was the beginning of his own end. Never did I question the king's love for her. Imagine then the torment he endured to do it. King Leawen, high ruler of the Kingdom of Bale. He could have simply waved his hand and the charges against her would have been dismissed. He had absolute power. No one would have challenged it. But he chose eternal grief over tyranny. It inspired in me both reverence and dread. Now look at us. Do we carry his legacy forward? Is this just, Eli? To aggress war undeclared, unprovoked?"

"The Ancile was provocation enough."

"Was it?"

Eli gave it some thought. "Our opposition always compares the monarchal rule to that of a despotic regime," he then began. "What they fail to understand, however, is that there can be no justice without a ruthless, uncompromising fealty to the letter of the law. Under the banner of freedom, the Meredians eat from golden bowls, willfully turning a blind eye to the degradation of their own society. If not blind, they're stupid. And if not stupid, depraved beyond what is tolerable."

"What man, Meredian or Balean, is above reproach?"

"There are degrees to reproach, Your Highness. I read not long ago that the daughter of some magistrate in Feymont, unable to bear the shame, took her own life after it came to light that her father had forced himself on her. If that were the most horrific thing I'd read, I'd consider morality in the Republic something yet salvageable. In Carnaval City, an abandoned wife became so agitated with the cries of her nursing babe that she dashed his head against the wall."

The duke scowled as Eli continued, "And in Pharundelle, just last year, a deranged man was found guilty of kidnapping children, cooking them alive, and feeding on them. When questioned for a motive, he replied, 'Because it's cheaper than bread.' Forgive me, Your Highness, for relaying such horrors. If only they were mere stories from the imagination of a twisted mind. They are not. This is the state of Meredine. We must see it as it is—a nation that has forfeited its humanity in the name of limitless self-indulgence. A disease. We attempt only to be a cure."

"By the Lords, Eli. You're starting to sound like the Shaldea."

"The Shaldea hate the Republic out of passion. They seek its end out of vengeance."

"And us?"

"By our king, our legacy is justice. And what greater justice is there than ridding the land of such corruption and wickedness?"

Duke Thalian smiled. "You and your silver tongue, Eli. Oh, that the princess would return to claim her family's crown and relieve me of this burden."

"Perhaps she will when Bale is the whole of Groveland."

"We'll have to find her, you know."

"Yes, but will she want to be found?"

Four flights of stairs and a long corridor's walk later, they entered the War Room. Waiting by the hearth was a Shaldean Rider. Like all Shaldean Riders, his skin was dark and weathered. He wore a fur blanket over his shoulders and the look of misery on his face.

"Duke Merrick Thalian. It is an honor to meet you," he said.

"The honor is mine, *Rajeth*."

"Please, call me Haddu."

"My royal advisor and director of intelligence, Eli Sorensen. Please, sit."

The Shaldean Rider sat across from the duke, Eli to his right.

"I don't know how anyone can suffer this cold," he said, blowing into his hands.

"Yes, the cold. As foreign to you, I imagine, as the sand dunes of Loreland would be to me. Can I offer you some tea?"

"Please."

The duke poured him a cup. It was small relief from the effects of the northern chill. In the North, it was not uncommon to have snow as early as autumn.

"I'll have my servants prepare a hot meal for you as well."

"Tea is fine for now, thank you."

"Quite the journey you made with your Riders."

"We wouldn't miss a chance at an assault on the Republic's beacon of pride."

"I understand you brought your own horses. We could've spared you the expense and provided our own."

Haddu smiled wryly. "There is no substitute for a purebred Saracen Glider."

"Of course. Fine horses from what I've heard."

"The finest in the world."

Arun entered the War Room, groomed and dressed in formal regalia. His appearance showed no signs of a man who just minutes prior was hanging off the side of the castle. He saluted the duke.

"Ah, General, please, join us. Haddu, this is General Arun Kilbremmer, who will be leading the assault. General, this is the latest *Rajeth* of the Shaldean Riders, Haddu."

Arun greeted the Shaldean leader and took his seat to the left of the duke. "How many of you are there?"

"Twenty-four, General."

"A full cavalry, then."

"A single Shaldean Rider is as effective on the battlefield as three light cavalry troopers bearing any standard. And we would welcome the chance to prove it."

"The general has agreed to allow you and your men to lead the assault ahead of our forces."

Haddu gave Arun a grateful nod. "I do have a question, however," he said. "According to our last correspondence, you claim the general will lower the Ancile's impenetrable defenses prior to the assault?"

"Yes."

"How exactly do you intend to do that?"

The duke and Eli exchanged glances.

"We don't want to spoil the surprise. But have faith, *Rajeth*. All will be as it should be before you ride."

"It's not that I doubt your assertion. Well, it's just that if we ride, and the—"

"I understand," the duke interrupted. "If the defenses are not lowered, you and your riders will have nowhere to go. But the rest of our army will advance right behind you. If the defenses are not lowered, we all have much to lose. Trust us. We would neither send you nor our own men if we knew the Ancile could not be breached."

Haddu appeared satisfied.

"Now, what news have you of your counterparts in the city?"

"Omar has been released," Haddu replied.

"Good. We were concerned his detainment would affect our plans."

"Their electric generator will be out of commission. My brethren have made an agreement with the local thieves' guild. As you so eloquently put it, 'all will be as it should be.'"

The duke nodded. He looked to Eli and Arun to see if they had anything to add. When they said nothing, he placed his hands on the table and sat up.

"Gentlemen, it appears then that history has brought us together for an undertaking greater than any of us could have imagined. A strange alliance between snow and sand. May the Maker and our Lords have mercy on the Republic, for we will not."

CH 22

MIDNIGHT MACABRE

"It's all been delivered as instructed, sir."

"Good," said Cain Listoyanov, loosening his tie.

He had arrived that morning and spent the better half of it making sure his delivery of arms was squirreled away as instructed by his clients.

"Goddamn sandworms. This is the first time I needed a treasure map just to bury the loot."

Cain settled into his penthouse suite in the Rue Ayan, Central District's finest luxury hotel. It was situated in the entertainment quarter not more than a block from the Halo. No expenses were spared in his lodging, which included a panoramic view of the city below and a built-in spa. Though it was a welcome end to a long journey at sea, and a long morning, it had little effect on his foul mood. He had it in mind to attend an underground slave auction, only to discover it had been recently shut down. The hotel staff was especially concerned because Cain Listoyanov was a man of very particular tastes, and notorious for erratic behavior when his demands were unmet.

During his last stay in another hotel from which he'd been subsequently banned, he'd set fire to the bed because he'd discovered the thread-count on the sheets was less than advertised. He ended up paying for the damages, but it was of little consequence to him. He possessed enough wealth to burn a thousand beds. Following news of the cancelled auction, he may have again been so inclined to try had he not received a timely notice.

One of his two bodyguards handed him an envelope.

"What's this?"

"From the concierge, sir. Also—" The bodyguard shifted uncomfortably.

"Also, what?" Cain asked, carefully tearing along the fold.

"There's a woman waiting for you in the lobby."

The arms dealer gave his bodyguard a curious glance before reading the note within.

Mister Listoyanov: As always, we appreciate your timely shipment. We hope you find your accommodations agreeable. We've also made available the services of our associate, Hilda Bern. She is an excellent resource and at your complete disposal. We look forward to our final meeting tonight. –Friends

Cain scoffed and tossed the note in the waste bin.

"Shaldean flattery," he thought aloud. "I'll be impressed if they actually get me that contract with Bale."

"Shall I summon the girl?"

"You remember the last one they set me up with?"

"This one's different."

"Is she?"

His bodyguard nodded.

"If it's another mule—"

"She's not, sir. I'm sure she'll be to your liking."

Cain would have reprimanded his bodyguard for being so presumptuous had he not been intrigued. "Well, send her up."

Less than five minutes passed before a young redheaded woman in an emerald green evening dress entered.

Cain was pleasantly surprised. What a woman wore was just as important to him as what she looked like in the nude. He assessed the value of a woman much in the same way he did any object he intended to purchase.

"Mister Listoyanov," she said, holding up her hand in a silver glove, palm down.

Cain gave it a gentle peck. "Miss Bern, I presume?"

"At your pleasure," she replied, with an inviting purr.

He paused to study her in detail. Her red hair was in curls. She had a symmetrical face, lightly made up, though a little heavy on the lips.

Noticing his culling eyes, she mocked a turn. He passed quickly over her bust and backside, for they were of little consequence to him. "May I see your feet?" he asked.

"Excuse me?"

"Your feet. May I see them?"

"You can see whatever you like, hon-

> **The Carousel Rogues often employed them to elicit sensitive information from people of interest.**

ey," she replied with a wink.

Then she pulled her evening dress up to her ankle with one hand, slipped her right foot out of her gold pumps, and held it just off the ground.

"And the other one?"

With a bemused flick of the brow, she repeated with her left.

"Satisfied?" she asked.

Her feet were just the way he liked them. The toes, treated and perfectly scaled in length, each slender but none too boney. Fair and flawless.

"Quite," he replied, excusing his bodyguards.

An hour later, the two of them had brunch in the hotel restaurant; they exchanged a kiss and a promise of another rendezvous later that evening before Hilda left. Like a child who'd just been dropped off at boarding school, Cain watched her round a corner and disappear. He sighed.

Hilda was one of several affiliated girls under Rogue oversight that had that effect on men—the ability to scale an impenetrable façade and leave a lasting impression, even after a single tussle. The Carousel Rogues often employed them to elicit sensitive information from people of interest. And that was why the new guild master had contacted Hilda just days before to take on the role.

Three blocks from the Rue Ayan, Hilda stopped to rest her feet. She sat on a park bench occupied by a man reading the daily paper, a black rose on his lapel. She removed her heel and began massaging her sole.

"He's in room one-five-zero-two," she said, as if speaking into the wind. "The meeting will be at midnight, pink factory, old garment district."

The man abruptly folded his paper, stood, and walked away, leaving in his place an envelope filled with cash. She took it and disappeared.

By eleven forty-five that evening, a Shaldean convoy was traveling down Seventh Street through Trivelka Square.

"Was it all there?" asked Omar.

"Enough to arm every one of us twice," his minion replied. "Rifles, scimitars, and kegs of powder. We are all ready, *afendi*. Nothing can stop us now."

"Pride before the fall, Amsa. Our vengeance comes on the coattails of the Balean Kingdom. Be wise with your words lest the Maker foil our plans."

The road carried them through the warrens. Beyond that was the old, abandoned garment district on the edge of the bay, now little more than a cluster of rusted steel structures—skeletons that spoke of an industry passed, remnants of investments lost. Surrounded by water to the north and northeast, and bordering Trivelka Square on the slum-side was a large, empty warehouse. It was once the factory for a line of women's intimate apparel. On the roof, there was an old, sodden advertising board where traces of faded paint had in the past displayed a reclining woman in her undergarments. A slogan across the bottom now barely legible, read: *Think Pink!*

There was a back entrance in the loading dock on the east end of the warehouse. A carriage was parked there, its tow-horse buried in the provided trough. Omar Basiliech and his entourage of nine men pulled up beside it. Two guards dressed in black suits, heavily armed, were waiting for them by the entrance. They introduced themselves as Cain Stoyanov's bodyguards before one of them showed Omar and all but one of his men in.

Omar was led through the dark warehouse by Stoyanov's guard. Concrete pillars partitioned off what were once sewing stations. At the end of the north side, there was a soft glow coming from an executive meeting room. The meeting room was bare but for a few chairs, a conference table, and a large window overlooking the bay. Even the doors had been removed from their hinges. Cropped through the doorframe, Omar could see a lantern placed on top of a conference table. And sitting in a swivel chair with his back to the entry, silhouetted by the light, was Cain.

"Peace be upon you, Mister Stoyanov. We received your…" Passing the threshold, Omar noticed another man in a black tieless business suit sitting at the head of the table on the east end of the room. He was wearing a white, ghostly mask. "You did not mention any guests."

There was no response.

Stoyanov's guard spun Cain around in his chair. Omar recoiled at the sight and his entourage immediately drew their pistols and daggers. The arms dealer's eyes were open, his jaw slack, head hanging to the side from an open throat that had stained the white of his shirt with blood.

"What is this?" asked Omar.

Amsa clutched the duffle bag and backed into a previously unaccounted for apparition that had appeared in the entryway behind him—the Vengian, standing as still as a stone.

Amsa dropped the duffle bag and raised his pistol. The Vengian came alive like a flash of lightning. Movement of his black camouflage created a dissonance against the darkness behind him that revealed his form. He grabbed the Shaldean's wrist, twisted it back, drew his blade, and jabbed it in and out of his chest like a sewing needle, striking the heart. As if their deaths had been coordinated, five more Shaldea were dispatched in a matter of seconds, the sound of misfired pistols followed by bodies hitting the floor in rapid succession. There were no unnecessary acrobatics and no style in the way the Vengian took life. Just perfectly calculated, efficient movements with dexterity and speed that left the dwindling witnesses in awesome terror.

At last, he sheathed his blade, grabbed the two throwing knives tucked under his arms and, with a flick of the wrists, sent them flying into the heads of the remaining two Shaldea who were huddled in a corner shielding their leader.

When the smoke cleared, Omar was standing alone, surrounded by a disarrangement of bodies.

"Who…who are you?" he asked,

blood pooling around his shoes.

"I wish to illustrate a point, so pay close attention," Magog replied.

On cue, the Vengian walked up behind Stoyanov's guard, who was in fact a Rogue in disguise, assigned to this detail by Remy. The Vengian then stabbed him in the back through the lung.

"Do you know what I have learned in all my years wandering to and fro throughout the world? The futility of it all. That the sanctity of life is a lie. We are no more precious than dust and stones." Magog removed his mask revealing his tattooed face. He then leaned forward and looked at Omar with the fury of hell in his eyes. "Death is the only absolute."

"*Zaal'mavorte!*" shouted Omar. He fell to his knees, his hands trembling, the scent of blood and feces in the air churning his stomach. "Please, *afendi*. I have withheld nothing. I don't know where Yusef Naskerazim is. I swear it! All of our dealings with him are conducted strictly through a proxy."

"*Shh*. I believe you, Omar." Magog stood and walked over to where Amsa lay. He picked up his duffle bag, placed it on the table and opened it. From it, he drew a bundle of Balean crowns. "What is the name of this proxy?"

"Enlil Fairchild. He is a wealthy man. A mining mogul."

"'A mining mogul.' Is there no limit to Shaldean hypocrisy?"

At the command of Magog's glance,

the Vengian pierced Omar just below the skull, severing his cervical vertebrae. And like a marionette snipped of his strings, he crumpled to the floor into a contorted pile.

The lone Shaldean standing guard outside was already dead when Magog and the Vengian exited the building. The Stoyanov-guard-disguised Rogue was waiting anxiously by their carriage.

"He tried to run when he heard the shots," he explained. "What happened in there? Where's Trevor?"

"He was killed," Magog curtly replied. "Now set it ablaze."

Despite lingering questions, the Rogue was under strict orders from Remy to minimize his interactions with their Samaeli guests and obey their every command. He quietly carried a keg of kerosene into the warehouse while Magog and the Vengian boarded the carriage.

"I will find you, Yusef," Magog thought aloud.

Then came the low, unexpected voice from the hidden mouth of the Vengian. "*Tsarevet*, I have a favor to ask you."

For a moment, Magog was at a loss for words. It was one of the few times he had ever heard the Vengian break his silence, let alone reveal himself as vulnerable with a personal request. Intrigued, Magog replied, "Certainly."

CH 23

ENCOUNTER AT CHESTERLINK PASS

The afternoon Dale had run to the bakery from his meeting with Detective Graham Lei, he had been relieved to find everything as it always was—Mosaic behind the counter reading, Cora Tess and Turkish in the back making preparations for the following morning.

Aside from an occasional walk-in, the bakery had been as empty as it usually was in the afternoons. After Dale caught his breath, they gathered around the table next to the kitchen. And after some unconvincing chastisement from Cora Tess, they sampled the winter pears together.

Dale had been quiet that afternoon; he'd done his best to keep his troubles hidden. It required no less effort today. Three days had passed and Cora Tess was still raving about the delicious winter pears. Mixed with her exuberant comments were admonishments to never waste that much money on fruit again.

"Are they gone?" Dale yelled back into the kitchen.

"Those things don't last around here. Between Mosaic and your aunt, I barely saw one," Turkish said with a smirk.

Dale sat at the table with his uncle, some tea and a warm baguette. He kept quiet, stealing glances out the window. The late autumn sky was already darkening.

"I'll get some more tomorrow," he called to his aunt.

"Don't you dare," said Cora Tess, storming out of the kitchen. "I've had my fill for this season. Don't ruin 'em for me. Not having them is part of what makes them so good."

"Okay, okay," Dale relented.

"You two want anything else? Something to drink?" his aunt asked.

"Why don't you come on out here? Sit with us," said Dale.

"Almost done. I'll be right out."

Once Cora Tess returned to the kitchen, Uncle Turkish said, "Just don't get too many. She really does feel bad about it. She counts the money as she eats them."

"Okay, I won't. Just a few," Dale said with a smile.

"Hey, is everything okay with you?"

"Yeah, why?"

"This is the third day in a row you've visited."

"You getting tired of me already?" asked Dale, trying to make light of his uncle's question.

"Nonsense. But you do seem a bit anxious. I wouldn't have said anything, but I notice you're wearing steel."

Dale forgot he was armed. When he was in the service, it had become second nature to him—an extension of his uniform. It didn't take more than a day to get re-acquainted with that familiar feeling. Ever since his meeting with Detective Graham Lei, the short sword from his office bureau was sheathed at his side. Every morning, he'd wake up, brush his teeth, shave, slip into a pair of trousers and boots, button up his shirt, arm himself, and throw on a coat. By the third day, it had become so comfortable that he forgot to conceal it at the bakery.

"You in some sort of trouble? Mosaic told us you were asking strange questions about a train accident or something."

Dale laughed. "Everything's okay, Uncle. Don't worry."

"Don't you lie to me, boy. I have a sense for these things."

"I'm fine. Honest."

"Then explain to me why you're armed."

"I've had this thing buried in my

drawer since I got back. I took it out recently to give it a polish and I've been wearing it since. I've got all the papers for it. Nothing to worry about."

"You'd be a man and tell me up front if there were some sort of trouble now, wouldn't you?"

"Of course."

Turkish examined him for any sign of withholding. Cora Tess came out and took a seat at the table. "What's this about?" she asked.

"Nothing. Uncle thinks I'm in some sort of trouble. I'm not. And I'd tell you both if I were."

The rusty bell on the door jingled as Mosaic entered. She was wearing theatre prop dragonfly wings on her back, her nails painted a sapphire blue.

"What in the Maker's name are you wearing?" asked Cora Tess.

"What?"

"Those!" she said, pointing at her wings.

"Oh. It's for the concert. I'm a sprite, see? Hi, Dale!"

"Hey," said Dale.

"Bring any more winter pears?" Mosaic asked.

"Nope."

"Rats."

"We have one left in the icebox," said Cora Tess.

"Mine!" Mosaic ran over and snatched the orb from the cooler and bit into it. "So good," she said, wiping the juices dribbling down her chin with the sleeve of her shirt. "This the last one?"

"Yes. And Dale is under strict orders not to purchase any more. At least not again this season."

Seeing a frowning Mosaic, Dale shrugged his shoulders.

"So, you coming?" Mosaic asked.

"Where?"

"The Harvest Festival concert," she said, showing off her wings.

"Maybe," Dale replied. "When is it?"

"Um, on the day of the Harvest Festival."

"That's two days from now."

"I told you about it last week."

"You did?"

Mosaic rolled her eyes.

"I'll be there," Dale finally replied.

"Good. Because I'm singing lead this time. And don't forget. The actual show's going to be at the Flora Crystal, not the Concert Hall."

"Where's that?"

"Here." She handed Dale a flyer. "Oh, and wear a costume."

"A costume?"

"It's the Harvest Festival."

"Precisely why we're not going," said Turkish. "Hooligans will be out in throngs, no doubt. Never understood why we have to celebrate the Harvest like a bunch of crazed lunatics."

"By the way, your friend stopped by

today."

"What friend?"

"Some Azuric guy. He didn't leave a name."

"Was he Shen?"

"I don't know. I can't tell."

"Did he have a braided tail?"

"I don't remember. He just asked how you were doing. That's about it."

"And he came by the Concert Hall?"

"Yep."

Dale thought it peculiar. *Why would Detective Lei visit Mosaic at the Concert Hall?* He knew where Dale worked. Probably knew where he lived. Dale checked his watch.

"Thanks for the tea. I have to get going."

"You barely touched it."

"I know, but there are some things I need to take care of."

"What about supper?" Cora Tess asked. "Will you be joining us?"

"No, not tonight."

"Well, you know where we are if you change your mind."

"Thanks. I'll see you later."

The chill in the air penetrated to the bone. Dale pulled his jacket tight around himself and propped his collar up. With the recent breaker contract signed, he could afford a cab ride to the City Guard Headquarters, but he didn't mind walking. It gave him time to think. He stuck to the back alleys, a straight shot from the Waterfront District to Central, streets he'd taken countless times since he was a child. A few blocks from the bakery, alone in one of these back alleys, he got the feeling he was being followed. He quickened his pace. The feeling intensified.

As he turned the corner of Chesterlink Pass, a T-intersection that led north into Chesterlink Avenue and south toward Trivelka Square, he darted around half-expecting to catch a figure slipping behind a building wall or some conveniently placed waste crate. There was no one. The alley behind him was empty. All he heard was the soft hum of the Steam Powered Electric Generator in the distance.

He turned back and realized his hand was still on the hilt of his sword. He thought about what he must have looked like. Spinning around, wide-eyed. The spin, the stance, declaring into the nothingness, "Aha!"

With a nervous chuckle, Dale turned back in the direction he was headed. Standing before him was Remy Guillaume in his top hat and brass-handled cane.

"Shit!" Dale blurted.

"Good evening, Mister Sunday. It is a pleasure to see you again."

"You scared the hell out of me."

"Please, come with me."

"Where?"

"There is a carriage waiting for us this way."

He began walking north toward Chesterlink Avenue.

"I'd rather not."

Remy sighed, turned around, and faced him. "Once again, this is not a request, Mister Sunday."

Dale drew his sword. "Like I said, I'd rather not."

He felt a prick on the back of his neck and swatted it, half expecting a mosquito or a bee. There was a needle. He removed it and was looking at it when something moved in his periphery. A figure. He couldn't focus on him. His eyes were failing him, not to darkness, but to dreams. The walls of the buildings along Chesterlink Pass came alive, expanding and contracting with each breath. He was hallucinating.

"Do not fight it, Mister Sunday," said Remy.

He tried to speak, but his words came out in a low drawn-out moan. His legs turned to liquid and he folded under his own weight. Two men appeared next to Remy. They looked like black voids—holes in the shape of men cut out of canvas. They grabbed him and dragged him into a carriage.

Then it all went black.

CH **24**

ALONE WITH DEATH

H*ow many hares in a hat?*
None if you are blind as a bat.

The ring of hammering steel in the distance stirred Dale into a limited form of consciousness. He could not move his extremities. He couldn't speak. It felt to him like sleep paralysis. Interspersed with the hammering, he heard strange voices.

Enlil Fairchild is preparing to leave the city, Master. His assets and operations have already been moved to Brookhaven. We must make haste.

Dale slipped back into dreams. Coming in and out of consciousness, he could not distinguish between his dreams and the waking world. Hours could have been years, the minutes like days. When he finally opened his eyes, there was a sudden rush. The world took shape before him. The various sounds became defined. He was weak, but he could feel his body. He was awake.

Beneath him was a soft, comfortable sofa. The air was damp. There were wire-guarded barn lights hanging from a high ceiling directly above him, a halo of fog around each. Dale blinked several times and rubbed his eyes. He tried to connect his present circumstances to his last conscious moment. He was in need of some context. Groping into a cloudy mind, Dale suddenly remembered Remy at Chesterlink Pass.

He shot up, flushed with anxiety, like a child in a bazaar who discovers that the hand he is holding is not his mother's. Dale swung his head from side to side to take inventory of his surroundings. Rusty pipes, valves, and mossy vents cut into caverns composed a contrasting backdrop to the office furniture, imported rugs, and oil paintings. The nearest door was made of cast iron. Standing guard on either side were two Rogues.

"Eat." The voice reverberated off the walls of the hollowed cavern.

Dale saw a meal set on a small, wooden table in the middle of the room. The table was set for two.

"Where am I?"

"You are in the lair of the Carousel Rogues."

Dale again looked into the lights and saw the halos.

"Something's wrong with my eyes."

"Effects of the somnidrone," Remy replied. Remy Guillaume was sitting at the other end of the room behind the large, granite desk, once belonging to the departed Fat Fox. "It will wear off soon."

"Somnidrone?"

"An opiate. Unfortunately, reactions to the alkaloids found in the pods can have varying effects. You have been unconscious for thirteen hours."

"You drugged me."

"Poisoned, technically. And it was not me."

Remy made his way over to the small wooden table and took a seat.

"I apologize for the discomfort," he added, "but we could not risk compromising this location. You understand."

"Something wrong with a blindfold?"

"You are a trained combatant. You were armed and appeared reluctant."

Dale noticed he had been disarmed.

"Come, join me. You must be famished."

"Where's the Fat Fox?"

Remy smiled. "All responsibilities concerning this organization have fallen to me."

It's true. But Felix Eglon's death was no consolation for Dale. Remy Guillaume's treatment of Dale was proving far less cordial than his predecessor's. As far as he knew, Remy was capable of the same ruthlessness with which Felix had conducted his business. And he had yet to figure out who was behind all that Detective Lei had told him. In the quiet days following their meeting, Dale did not know what to believe. *Were all these men really killed? Was Arturo Lucien dead? Who killed the Fat Fox? The assassins?* He couldn't piece it together. There were too many gaps. Sitting in the bakery, the possibility that none of it was true had dawned on him. The detective could have been trying to squeeze him for information.

Now, Dale knew the Fat Fox was dead. And that Remy, at least in part, had something to do with it. *If the Fat Fox was dead, then Arturo was probably dead too,* thought Dale as he got up from the sofa and walked over to the table.

"What about Arturo Lucien?" he asked.

"What about him?"

"You kill him too?"

"Mister Sunday, please take a seat."

Dale did not immediately oblige. Between them was a loaf of bread, two bowls of wild boar pasta, and two pints of beer.

"Everything will be explained. For now, let us eat." Seeing Dale's apprehension, Remy tried to reassure him. "It is just food."

"You poisoned me and brought me here against my will. You'll excuse me if I'm a bit skeptical about anything you have to say."

"Fair enough. Would you like me to take a bite from your bowl, a drink from your pint?" When Dale did not answer, Remy continued to try and reason with him. "If I wanted you dead, Mister Sunday, you would already be dead. Would I drag you here to revive you so I can poison you again?"

The new guild master seemed to grow weary of entreating his prisoner, and so started into his bowl of boar pasta. Dale finally sat. Remy took notice but continued to scoop in the pasta without a hitch, only stopping to take generous gulps from his glass. Dale took a drink of the ale. It was refreshingly cold with just the right blend of malted barley and hops. Once he tasted it, he couldn't stop drinking. He emptied the glass without setting it down. With a smirk, Remy gestured to one of his men who filled Dale's glass from a flagon. With his apprehensions quelled, Dale shoveled in the pasta. The two men ate with a steady vigor found in places where men worked hard from the rising of the sun to its setting. There were active hands, steady chewing, and the distinct sound of heavy breathing through the nostrils.

With a mouthful of food, Dale asked, "So what's this all about?"

Remy set his fork down and reclined with his beer in hand.

"We brought you here to warn you, Mister Sunday."

"Warn me about what?"

Remy signaled the guard who promptly disappeared through the cast-iron door.

"The Balean Kingdom is about to invade."

"Yeah? And how's that?"

"I am not at liberty to speak to you about details. What I can tell you is that it is in your best interest to gather your family and leave the city as soon as possible—before the Harvest Festival."

"How do you know this?"

"We know a great many things, Mister Sunday. There are people, and they know other people. These people are privy to some highly sensitive information."

"Look, we've been talking about the Baleans for years. It's no secret. And even if it's true, the Republic nearly bankrupt itself erecting an impenetrable structure just for this occasion."

"Mister Sunday, listen to me very carefully. I will try to make this as simple as possible. There is only one day until the Harvest Festival. You have one day to get out of Carnaval City. If you do not heed this warning, you and your loved ones will die."

"And if I don't believe you?"

"That is your choice. We cannot force you to leave."

Remy set down his glass and returned to his meal. Dale had steadily curbed his eating and drinking. Now he sat motionless and watched as Remy recommenced on his pasta. He did not appear to be a man interested enough in Dale nor in Carnaval City to be lying about the invasion. Dale weighed his options. When Remy looked up to check on Dale's motionless countenance, Dale said, "You're telling me the truth."

Remy wiped his mouth with his napkin and tossed it on the table. "Yes," he replied, "I am." Then he rose from his seat. "Now, if you will excuse me." He buttoned the bottom of his coat and fixed his collar as if preparing for another appointment.

Dale's mind was racing. He tried to piece together all the information. But between what he had just heard and all he had learned from Detective Lei, there was too much to sort. In the midst of the confusion, a clear question dawned.

"Wait. Why me?" he called as Remy started toward the door. "Why warn me?"

"Perhaps he can answer that for you."

When Remy opened the door, the Vengian was standing on the other side. He was unmasked, shirtless, wearing dark

> *"If you do not heed this warning, you and your loved ones will die."*

pants. In his hand was a sword wrapped in cloth. He had the face of an Azuric man and appeared to Dale to be about his age. He had raven-black hair sans the customary style that would have been telling of his tribal origins. No topknot, no braided tail. It was instead cut short, barely long enough to run his fingers through. He had a sinewy, muscular cut from hours of rigorous physical training. His arm and back were heavily tattooed. On the side of his neck, the Samaeli machine cogged-compass tattoo was conspicuously displayed.

As Remy stepped past the Vengian he turned back to Dale and added, "Oh, and Mister Sunday. To answer your previous question, we did not kill Arturo Lucien."

Dale was alone with Death.

He needed no introduction. Even unmasked and shirtless, Dale recognized the man he had helped smuggle in. It was in his gait, his countenance, his aura, the darkness—a darkness that was more than the absence of light. In the Vengian's world-weary eyes, there was an absence of a soul. Dale was certain he was going to unwrap the sword and cut him to pieces with it. As his body instinctively prepared to fight, Dale tried to think of a way to defend himself. Still sitting, he took a firm grip of the back of the chair, and prepared to jump to his feet.

The Vengian walked slowly around Dale, giving him plenty of space, and sat in the seat previously occupied by Remy. He looked straight at Dale with those empty eyes and asked, "Do you know who I am?"

Dale, still with a tight grip on the chair, was startled by the Vengian's quiet voice.

"No," he managed.

"Did Remy tell you why you're here?"

"He told me that he brought me here to warn me." Cautiously, he pressed, "Why *am* I here? I mean…is that the real reason?"

The Vengian didn't respond.

There was no comfort in silence. Dale couldn't shake the vision of the Vengian lunging at him with the sword. He held fast to his chair.

"I saw Mosaic yesterday," the Vengian said. "She's beautiful."

Dale realized he had assumed incorrectly. The "Azuric friend" she had spoken of was not the detective. With the realization, he felt a chill in the back of his neck. *This thing was standing next to Mosaic.* His dread turned to rage.

"Stay away from her," he said, as firmly as he could.

The Vengian calmly reached into his back pocket. He brought forth a small, tattered book and tossed it on the table. The dulled cover read *The Walgorende's Last Stand*.

"You don't remember me, *rohar*, do you?"

The Goseonite term for *My Brother!* The memories came flooding in. Dale looked up, wide-eyed as if seeing a ghost. The swollen tear-troughs. The prominent scar below the left eye.

"Sparrow?"

CH 25

TO COMPLETE A MELODY

Dale looked across the table at the man who was once his childhood friend. There had always been a blank, distant look about Sparrow. Dale would often catch him staring out into nothing. He was quiet, seldom volunteering his thoughts. But even as odd as Sparrow had been as a child, no one could have anticipated that a poor, skinny Azuric boy would become the man now sitting across from Dale. A killer. The overall appearance was intimidating, but the brutality was mostly in the eyes. The blank eyes that used to dart around and avoid direct contact were now fixed on Dale. Unmoving, staring through him. They had lost their humanity—that connection to fear, to a conscience.

The reunion was unlike those that Dale had dreamt. There was no excitement, no embrace. There wasn't the customary exchanging of rushed, choppy stories. Just stunned disbelief. Even after the Vengian revealed himself, Dale was not convinced that his old friend hadn't been sent into the room to kill him. Before Dale could fully accept the revelation, Sparrow had moved on to confirming Remy's story. Dale had indeed been brought to the lair to be warned.

"Take your family south to Brookhaven before the Harvest Festival begins tomorrow night, maybe even as far

as Loreland. What the guild master told you is true. The Balean invasion is imminent. Carnaval City will fall first."

"Wait. What happened to you?"

"Get your family out of the city. Leave today."

"I can't. I can't just leave. I mean—Sparrow, where have you been? On my first leave, I looked for you but no one knew where you were. Where'd you go? What happened?"

Sparrow was quiet for a moment. His face remained expressionless.

"Do you smoke?" he asked, as he reached into his pocket.

He produced a package of smokes and extended it to Dale. Dale took one and leaned in as Sparrow lit his smoke before putting the match to his own. Sparrow took a deep drag, blew the smoke through his nostrils, and started talking. Once he began, he spoke in a steady, well-paced monotone as if he were trying to get somewhere quickly. It was sparse in detail and his pacing did not allow for Dale's questions.

"After my mother died, Master T'varche took me with him. We left the city. We traveled the world taking odd jobs and training. Always training. When I had become a man, he told me he was part of an organization. And that all the years of training was in preparation to initiate me into this organization. I was initiated and then soon after, Master T'vache was killed. I've been working as a part of this organization since."

"I heard about your mom. I'm sorry."

"Death was better for her than life," Sparrow answered quickly.

"So, is that your philosophy on life? Death is better? I mean, you are an assassin, right? Your organization, the Samaeli, right?"

"Where did you hear that?"

"I've heard plenty in the last month. That's what you are. You kill people professionally."

"Yes. No different from a Republican Guard, who kills on order and collects his monthly pay. Only, my loyalties are to an order, not to country."

"It's different. Wars are declared. Soldiers are armed."

"Is it? That's what you tell yourself. But it doesn't matter to me. What matters is Bale is going to attack. And you must leave today. If not for yourself, get your family out. Get Mosaic out."

"You ever question what you're doing? What you've done?"

Sparrow sighed a reluctant sigh.

"Some people were born to paint, play music," he replied. "I was born to do this."

"Sparrow, murder isn't like playing the piano or making music. You're not making anything. You're destroying."

"The Samaeli destroys what needs to be destroyed. You judge as if the world has two clear notes. But the piano has no right or wrong key. Each note serves its purpose when played in the right arrangement. Likewise, death and destruction may be, in its time, necessary to complete a melody."

"You sound crazy."

Sparrow smiled and replied, "I am crazy."

Dale chuckled back. And for a fleeting moment, they were kids. "When did you become such the philosopher?"

"I read a lot," Sparrow replied.

"Right. The sharpest weapon's a well-read mind."

"Yes. You remember."

"I do remember."

> ## *"Some people were born to paint, play music...I was born to do this."*

"I read everything and anything I could get my hands on. Starting with that." Sparrow pointed at the old copy of *The Walgorende's Last Stand*. Then he leaned forward. "*Rohar*, enough about what's become of me. You have to get out of the city today."

"How do you know all this?"

"That's not important."

"What about the Ancile? How is Bale going to get past the Ancile?"

"Nothing is impenetrable. Everything can be breached. Anyone, killed."

"I have to warn someone."

"There's nothing you can do."

Dale shook his head.

"It doesn't make any sense. Why now? Bale's been posturing for years. Nobody believes they'll do anything about it."

"Unseen forces dictate the course of

history. The Samaeli exist to restore balance. The Republic is drunk with power and covered in the filth of corruption. Its time has come."

"Wait. So you're doing this? You're behind all of this?"

As quickly as the bond between the two friends had re-emerged, it vanished. Once again, Dale saw a cold killer, a representative of some shadow league with geo-political machinations. His old friend made the Carousel Rogues seem benign in comparison. The Vengian did not answer his question. He continued to try to convince Dale of the urgency of the situation.

"Get your family together. Don't waste time with your possessions. Head south."

Sparrow then unwrapped the sword in his lap and handed it to Dale. It was Dale's sword, only the blade had been reinforced and the hilt ergonomically reshaped. Dale held it up. The slightly curved grip was taped in ridged rubber, designed to keep his hands from slipping even when wet with sweat or rain. The cross guard had been shortened to perfect the overall weight balance in the hand and the blade was now the color of gunmetal. The same dark steel found on Sparrow's blade.

"I made a few modifications," Sparrow added. "I hope you don't mind."

As Dale admired the craftsmanship, the cast-iron door opened and a Rogue messenger entered.

"The Silver Fox would like to speak to you. He's waiting for you in the forge. He says it's urgent."

Sparrow then stood and summoned the messenger over who handed Dale a black cotton sack.

"What's this?" asked Dale.

"The Silver Fox says that you're welcome to choose between this or another dose of somnidrone," the Rogue replied.

Dale took the sack, stood, slipped the old copy of *The Walgorende's Last Stand* into his coat pocket, and sheathed his sword.

"When will we meet again?"

"Hopefully, on the other side of the coming storm," Sparrow replied. Then he grabbed Dale by the arm. And with the end of the world in his dark narrow eyes, he added, "*Rohar*, take care and make haste."

Then the Vengian vanished through the cast-iron door. Like a dream. Like a nightmare.

"Let's go," said the Rogue.

Dale threw the sack over his head and walked in the direction he was shoved. A walk through what felt to him like humid tunnels and caves, followed by an hour-long carriage ride, and then Dale was back on the streets of Carnaval City.

CH **26**

NOT DOING NOTHING

The coach dropped Dale off in front of his house. In all appearances, it was like any other morning. With the ever-present backdrop of ships both launching and coming into port, the Waterfront bustled with pre-festival activity. Sailors and merchants were at work to wrap up business before the holiday. It was all perfectly ordinary. Nothing spoke of the looming threat from the North. Standing in front of his house in the crisp morning air, it felt like a dream to Dale—poisoned, taken thirteen hours into the lair of the

Carousel Rogues, re-united with Sparrow, and warned of an impossible invasion. It all felt like a distant, fuzzy-haloed dream.

Dale checked his watch. Had it not been the Eve of the Harvest Festival, he would have been late for work. Yet, like most small businesses, the breaker was closed for the coming holiday. He would have been waking up late this morning, looking forward to sharing in the events of the festival with his uncle, auntie, and Mosaic. With some new deals locked up, Dale would have celebrated knowing some lucrative work awaited him on the other side of the festival. As it was, there were no guarantees there would even be a day after the Harvest Festival.

Dale walked to his door recounting the events leading up to his fateful re-union with Sparrow—the systematic assassinations of high profile targets, rumors of war, the emergence of the Samaeli. Put into context, the warning took on a different level of urgency. Without entering his house, Dale started for the bakery.

He walked briskly through the crowded waterfront. Every face he saw represented a life. Faces in anticipation of the festival. Faces of workers. Of men, women, children. They were like sheep, completely oblivious to the slaughter gathering at the gate. Dale began to jog. And with each step, with each passing face, the foreboding grew until he was in a full sprint.

"Uncle," he called, as he barged through the door.

"Dale?"

"Uncle, listen, you need to get Auntie and Mosaic out of the city."

"Is everything all right?" asked Cora Tess.

"I'll explain everything later. Right now, we all need to get out of the city."

Turkish looked at him, alarmed.

"What in the Maker's name are you talking about?" he asked.

"Where's Mosaic?"

"She's at rehearsals. Dale, calm down. Now, whatever this is about, I'm sure we can figure things out. But first, you have to tell us what is going on."

Dale tried to compose himself. He said as calmly as he could, "There's going to be war."

"War?" Turkish blurted. Cora Tess had been standing quietly. There was terror in her eyes. They had never seen Dale approach an excited state before. In light of his usual demeanor, Dale appeared to them on the verge of hysterical.

"Yes. The Balean Kingdom is going to invade tomorrow."

"Are you sure?"

"Yes."

"Where did you hear this?"

"I can't tell you where I heard it. But

CH 27

listen—"

"You've been acting mighty peculiar this past week. And your auntie and me, we don't like it. If you're in some sort of trouble, you tell us right now. And don't you lie to me, boy."

Dale grabbed Turkish by the shoulders and looked him in the eyes. And with as much gravitas as he could muster, he said softly, "We're all in trouble, Uncle. Bale is going to invade this city."

"Nonsense. Last I heard we still had the Ancile."

"The Ancile." Dale suddenly remembered Darius. Then instantly, Mosaic's words rang in his ears. *Sometimes doing nothing is as bad as doing what's wrong.*

It was so clear to him. He had to warn Darius. He had to warn the Republic, his fellow countrymen, everyone.

"The Ancile is going to fall. You have to believe me, Uncle. Auntie. You have to believe me."

Turkish and Cora Tess looked at each other. Without a word, it was confirmed.

"Okay, Dale. We believe you."

"Good. Now find Mosaic and get everyone to Hoche. There isn't much time."

"What if you're wrong?" asked Turkish.

"Pray that I am." Dale rushed out the way he came in.

SSC

The headquarters of the City Guards were located in the government quarter of the Central District. It was surrounded by the City Hall, the High Courts, and various other marble structures dating back to the founding of the Republic. The lobby of the headquarters was crowded and noisy. On the third floor was the Criminal Investigations Department. Detective Graham Lei's desk sat in a row of desks. Detective Graham Lei was not at his desk. He was behind a closed door with two sentinels of the State Security Command.

The sentinels wore their customary sheen black suits, black ties, and red armbands bearing the crest of the Republic. The crest was a white eagle, wings spanned wide, carrying in its talons a star framed in a crown of laurels. The older sentinel, Norman Walsh, was an out-of-shape veteran who seemed to always be out of breath. In contrast, his junior partner was tall with an athletic build. An ethnic descendent of the Nilotian plainsmen of Loreland, his skin was as dark as the harvest earth, his head polished—bald with a tuft of a black beard just around his lips and chin. And his voice was deep and commanding. His name was Gabriel Helell.

"How many?" Gabriel asked, referencing a case report folder.

"We're guessing twelve," the detective replied.

"All Shaldea?"

"Mostly. Hard to tell when all you have are bones and ashes. But we found scimitars. They were dead before the old factory was set ablaze. Some of the more intact bodies showed signs of stab wounds. A skirmish."

While the sentinels quietly tried to piece it together, Detective Lei continued to postulate. "According to their records, Machina invested primarily in securities, raw minerals, and various construction projects outside of Republic soil. Now, we all know the Shaldea have never been keen on Republic investments abroad, right? So I'm thinking maybe they had the Machina investors killed. And in retaliation, the Machina hired some goons to torch them."

"Not that simple," Norman replied. "If anything, it was the other way around. All of the Machina deaths were ruled something other than murder. The Shaldeans could never have pulled that off.

> **"No one knows where they come from...They appear and disappear. Dead men in their wake."**

And even if they could, there aren't any investors left to retaliate. Senator Prescott was the last of them."

Gabriel closed the report. "You sure your source said the 'Samaeli?'" he asked.

"Yes. It's right here. I wrote it down," the detective replied, flipping his notepad open.

"Detective Lei, if your source is correct, if the Samaeli are in this city, then you're in a world of trouble."

"Look, who or what exactly are these guys? And why would they kill Machina investors *and* the Shaldea?"

The sentinels exchanged glances.

"No one knows for sure who they are," Gabriel replied. "That's the problem. No one knows where they come from, where they're going, and what they want. They appear and disappear. Dead men in their wake. Some will tell you that they're agents of death. Highly trained, highly specialized assassins. Others say they're from another world, born of demons."

"Sentinel Helell here is a specialist on the Samaeli," Norman added.

"Detective, we'd like to speak to your source."

"My source? My source is just a small-businessman. He doesn't know anything."

"Given the Samaeli's apparent access to some high profile subjects, our best guess is that they employ sleeper agents to infiltrate various networks. And based on the information you've provided, we think your source may even be one of them."

"As far as we're concerned, *you* could be one of them," Norman quipped.

"Funny," said the detective. "But you know he was a Republican Guard."

"We know. Sleeper agents come in many forms, Detective," Gabriel continued. "The proximity of the events to the smuggling operation and the fact that Mister Sunday is the only one who has seen the Samaeli and isn't dead yet, indicates his involvement may be more than cursory. Now, where can we find him?"

Just then a clerk knocked on the door. He poked his head in. "Detective, there's a Dale Sunday here to see you."

After a pause of pleasant surprise, the detective indicated for Dale to be shown in.

Dale entered. The blinds rattled against the frosted glass as Sentinel Helell shut the door behind him.

"Take a seat," Detective Graham said. "We were just talking about you. This is Sentinel Norman Walsh and—"

"Sentinel Walsh and Sentinel Helell with the SSC," said Walsh, cutting off the detective. "We're glad you're here, Dale. There are some questions we'd like to ask you."

Dale had come with a plan. He was going to drop in to tell Detective Graham Lei what he knew of the invasion. In his mind, it was going to be a way to make the most of his time. *Get the word out to proper authorities and they'll handle it from there.* He would have done his part. Be absolved of the responsibility for all of those nameless faces he passed on his way there. But one look around the room, and Dale knew his plan had hit a serious snag. It was time to forego his conscience. He needed

to get out of that room as quickly as possible. And the best way to do this, Dale resolved, was to play dumb.

"Oh, yeah? What about?"

"Look, Dale," said the detective, "twelve more bodies turned up just a few days ago. Shaldea. We believe the Samaeli were involved."

"What do you know about it?" asked Sentinel Walsh.

"I don't know anything about it."

"You don't know anything?"

"No. Why would I know something about dead Shaldeans?"

"Like the detective said, we believe it was the work of the Samaeli. You may be the only person alive who has seen the Samaeli in the city. As far as we know, you brought them here. Now, think. Do you have anything you want to tell us?"

"Look, I don't know what you've been told. But I was forced by the Rogues to lease out my breaker. I had nothing to do with what came in. I don't know where they came from. I don't know where they went. Nothing. You want details, ask the Carousel Rogues."

"It's obvious your intent is not to cooperate," said Gabriel.

"If I was involved, do you think I'd be walking into the headquarters of the City Guards?"

Both sentinels rose from their seats. Dale jumped to his feet. The sentinels grabbed him before he could fully stand and held him down.

"Like I was saying," said Gabriel, "it's obvious to us you are not going to cooperate. We have some things we can do to get you more interested in working with us. Now if you'll come with us."

"Wait! Wait a minute! Okay. What do you want to know?"

"It's too late for that."

Dale began to struggle. The sentinels responded with force, throwing him to the floor and pinning him down with a knee on his back. When he had been subdued and shackled, they lifted him to his feet.

Dale pleaded with Detective Lei, "Please, Detective, you can't let them do this. I came here to tell you something. You want to hear what I have to say." As he was dragged to the door, his voice rose. "You can't let them take me! We're all in danger!"

Detective Lei looked at him apologetically and shrugged his shoulders.

"Detective! Doing nothing is just as bad as doing wrong! Damn it! Detective!"

CH 28

THE INQUISITION

The unmarked carriage pulling a prisoner's trailer arrived at the West Gate of the Temple of the Benesanti. Six templar stood guard at the gate. One of the six approached the carriage window and knocked, while another inspected the horses and cab. The portly Sentinel Walsh lowered the window and presented a badge and passport identifying himself. Sentinel Helell did the same. Once they cleared inspection, the carriage was driven up to the portico. They stepped out and started up the gray marble steps to a set of massive double doors. The doors were two stories high, solid oak, and held in place by iron hinges. They were surrounded by ornately decorated archivolts. A watchman cleric within the vestibule opened the door.

"Welcome, sojourners," she said, with a bow and a blessing. "*Alunde andra.*"

"*Alunde ver ti,*" Norman replied.

They surrendered their swords and percussion cap pistols and were consecrated with a sprinkling of myrrh from a chrismarium before given the blessing to enter the temple halls. As they made their way through another set of large doors into the softly lit nave, they passed through a draft of burning incense. On the other side, two more templar stood holding their shields to their chests.

A haunting choir's chant echoed off the high vaulted ceiling. There were frescos, sculptures, and stained glass windows. Stone tracery and tapestries depicted stories found in the sacred texts of the Benesanti. Directly below the dome of the sanctuary was a golden seal on the marble crossing. Engraved on the seal were lesser gods recognized by the Order. And kneeling in the center of it all before the Great Altar was Sir Thomas Grail.

The sentinels approached down the aisle, past the empty pews. Just before they reached the crossing, Sir Thomas Grail rose and turned around to greet them.

"Blessings of the Maker be upon you. Can I help you, gentlemen?"

The sentinels removed their badges from their inner coat pockets and held them up.

"I'm Sentinel Norman Walsh and this is my partner Sentinel Gabriel Helell with the Republic of Meredine's State Security Command. We're here to see the marshal."

"May I ask, what is the nature of your business with the marshal?"

"I'm afraid that's classified."

Virtually everything the State Security Command dealt with was classified.

"Is he expecting you?"

"No."

"Then I will summon him."

"Have him meet us by the monument. We have a prisoner with us."

"Very well."

They took the carriage around the north end of the temple, near the barracks, and stopped next to a rounded building that appeared to be a mausoleum. Adjacent to the round structure was a large monument dedicated to the brethren lost in the Battle of Geraloki. The towering sculpture was of a wounded templar on horseback, doubled over. In one hand, the immortalized figure gripped his mid section while with the other hand he held a banner with their coat of arms.

Sir Thomas Grail emerged alone from the marshal's building along the Northern Wall.

"Champion Linhelm is in a meeting with the Bene-seneschal. I've been sent in his stead to oversee the inquisition."

The sentinels opened the back of the prisoner's trailer. Sitting inside with his arms shackled behind him was Dale. The prisoner squinted as he looked out into the noon sunlight.

"Out," said Sentinel Walsh.

"He's not an Emmainite," observed Thomas.

"He's affiliated with the Samaeli."

"I already told you—" Dale began, but was quickly squelched.

"Quiet! You'll have your chance to make a statement. Not here. Not now."

"Then hurry up! Get me to the judge! Who's in charge around here?"

Sentinel Walsh punched him in the gut.

"I said quiet!"

"That's not necessary," said Thomas.

"Please conduct yourself with more restraint. You are on sacred ground."

"Just take us below."

"You intend to join us?" asked Thomas.

"This is our prisoner. We intend to conduct the investigation ourselves."

Thomas noticed Sentinel Gabriel Helell was carrying a large leather medical bag. "From my understanding, the Mizraheen Treaty states—"

"Get the marshal," Sentinel Walsh curtly injected. "We don't have time for a history lesson."

"Like I said, he is occupied with other matters. I'm here to oversee the inquisition."

"Listen Sir Grail, we are looking into over two dozen assassinations. Some of the most influential figures around the world have been murdered. Now this prisoner may have vital information regarding what we believe is a conspiracy. The longer you keep us from accessing that information the further you jeopardize this investigation. Get out of the way and let us do our job."

After a momentary hesitation, Thomas signaled for a fellow templar standing guard to escort them into the holding cells below.

"I will relay your urgency to Champion Linhelm," he said. "Do not proceed until I return."

Then he departed for the North Wall.

Dale and the sentinels were taken through the stone doors of the rounded building. The walls were decorated with more reliefs—the Lords of Emmaus, their judging eyes, cold and colorless. A spiral staircase led them underground into a deceptively long hall. At the end of the hall was a door that led to the holding cells be-

---

"Only a citizen can commit treason."

---

low the templar barracks.

Dale was led into a small room and he was shoved into a chair. His wrists and ankles were shackled to it. The sentinels spoke briefly with the templar outside of the room to reassure him that they were following protocol.

The sentinels entered with the templar. Sentinel Walsh removed his coat and rolled up his sleeves. As he paced, he fixed his beady eyes on Dale.

"I don't understand what I'm doing here," said Dale.

"You don't understand?"

"No, I don't."

"You're here because you're a Samaeli sleeper agent."

Dale shook his head in disbelief.

"A what?"

"Tell us when you became activated. And then you can tell us your role in these assassinations. What's your interest in the Machina Investment Group? What is your agenda? Why are you in the city?"

"I was born here, you idiot."

Sentinel Walsh reared back and threw a punch at Dale. At the last second, Dale turned and recoiled to make the strike a glancing one. The sentinel then punched him in the stomach. Strapped to the chair, Dale could do little to avoid the second blow.

"Just because you're a citizen, it doesn't make you innocent. Only a citizen can commit treason. Your contact with the Samaeli and the fact that you're not dead either makes you a liar or one of them. If you're lying, you're a fool. If one of them, you're a traitor. We think you're a traitor. And traitors have one thing waiting for them—the gallows, unless you're willing to cooperate. Now tell us about these killings, your role in them, and disclose the location of the Samaeli."

"I don't know! How many times do I have to say it? You have the wrong guy. Yes. I saw the Samaeli because the Fat Fox forced me to open the breaker. I had no idea what was being transported. I didn't know what they were when I saw them. I never even heard of the Samaeli until someone told me. That's it. The whole thing, I wanted no part of it. That's all I know."

"We'll see about that."

Sentinel Helell walked up from behind Dale and drove a syringe into the side of his neck. As his vision blurred, Dale's last cohesive thought was, *I can't believe I'm being poisoned again.* This time he did not black out. But as the drug took full effect, Dale wished he had. Unlike the effects of somnidrone, whatever was injected in him put him into a heightened, sensory nightmare. It was as if the drug stripped Dale's body of its ability to acclimate and dull its senses—the very ability to make living tolerable. Under the drug's influence, the clothing was heavy, scratchy; the shackles cut on his wrists and weighed down on his ankles; the sentinels' voices were like shrill screams. Everything was spiked to extremes. With no reprieve, Dale's mind began to fragment. Time seemed to pass in staccato. He blinked and he was no longer in a chair. Instead, he hung from the ceiling, shackled by the wrists, naked.

Sentinel Walsh had in his hand a cat o' nine tails. He vanished behind him. There was a crack. Dale cried out. The sting turned to a burn. The sentinel reappeared. He asked some questions. Dale couldn't understand the questions. Disoriented and writhing in pain, Dale blurted

out things to try to make the whole thing stop. He didn't know what he was saying. The incoherent babbling did not satisfy the sentinels. Another crack. And another. More questions. More random babbling. More lashings. Then suddenly the lashes stopped. Both sentinels were in Dale's face, a stalactite of saliva hanging from his chin.

"What did you say?"

They struggled to get his attention.

"Hey! Did you say Enlil Fairchild?"

It was a name Dale had heard while under the spell of somnidrone the night before. He wasn't aware he had slipped the name or why.

"What about him?" the sentinels continued. "Did he hire the Samaeli? Is he the next mark?"

Norman slapped him.

Just then, Champion Alaric Linhelm came barging through the door with Sir Thomas Grail.

"What in the Maker's name do you think you're doing?" Alaric shouted.

There was a lot of shouting.

The sentinels were cornered and stripped of the whip and their medical bag.

"Don't come in here and tell me how to do my job when you failed at your own!" Sentinel Walsh shouted. "You're in over your head, templar. Let us get the answers we need from our prisoner and—"

"This man ceased to be your prisoner when you brought him here! I must remind you, Sentinel, that you are on sovereign ground. Ground under the dominion of the Holy Order of the Benesanti. In accordance with the Mizraheen Treaty, the authority of the Republic is abnegated within these temple walls. That means this is no longer your prisoner. He's mine."

"I beg to differ."

"Beg all you want. But do it on your soil. Thomas, show them out."

"Yes, m'lord."

"This isn't over, templar. You'll be hearing from the Command Directorate."

When they were ushered out, Alaric approached the half-conscious Dale.

"M'lord...forgive me," stammered the templar guard who had been watching the inquisition from afar. "I didn't know—"

With his good eye still fixed on Dale, Alaric addressed the templar guard. "Summon a cleric. Get him cleaned up and properly treated. If this one dies of an infection, you'll be hanging from this ceiling."

"Yes, m'lord."

"And I want a full report of what he disclosed to those barbarians."

"Yes, m'lord."

Alaric stormed out.

The templar guard released Dale from the chains and gently laid him down on the stone floor. Then he injected him with a tranquilizer.

CH 29

CHARLES VALKYRIE

Dale was on his stomach, lying on a cot. He was groggy and shirtless. A damp towel had been placed on his wounds. It did nothing to ease the throbbing, burning sensation. When he gathered his wits about him, he sat up and looked around. It was another holding cell—concrete walls, an iron door, a wire-guarded light on the ceiling, a washbasin and faucet beside the cot, and a toilet along the far wall.

He heard whistling from the next cell over.

Dale sighed. "Shit."

The whistling stopped.

"You all right in there?"

"No. Who are you?"

"You can call me Charles Valkyrie. You?"

"Dale."

"Well met, Dale. Wish it were under different circumstances."

"What day is it?"

"The evening of the third."

There was still time before the Harvest Festival but time was running out. And he still had to make sure the Shawls had heeded his warning and were long departed from Carnaval City. He then had to get word to Darius at the Ancile.

Dale got up and began a close examination of his cell. Starting with the door, he worked his way looking high and low throughout the cell. Other than a food hatch in the door that could only be opened from the outside, there was no sign of structural vulnerability. Dale sat back on the cot, put his head in his hands, and sighed deeply.

"Man, I feel like shit."

"You got the serum."

"Serum?"

"A chemical compound designed to extract truth. That's what they stuck you with. A closely guarded secret even within the SSC. Consider yourself lucky, kid. A cat to the back is a hell of a lot worse without it. Although you do pay for that numbing with a piece of your mind."

It was true. As much as Dale tried to command his mind to focus, he could not do it. The part of him that was aware of the gravity of the situation urged him on. *Think. Think. How do you get out of here?* But another part of him, still awakening from the drug's effects, betrayed him, ushering him towards passivity. His mind and body kept telling him to lie down. It was all so tedious—the burden, the problem solving, the lethargy.

"So what brings you here, Dale?"

Conversation. Dale gave no reply to Valkyrie's question. *I have neither time nor the energy to talk to this guy.* He got up again and, without much hope, began to look around his cell. Undaunted, Charles Valkyrie proceeded with a one-way conversation.

"Probably some hogwash reason,

right? I was caught selling elf ears to local apothecaries as karis truffles. In case you don't know, elf ears are common mushrooms virtually identical to the truffle variant found in the Wilds Deep. Of course, the mushrooms lack the healing properties of its identical counterpart. But it's a chance to quadruple profits. Anyway, never thought swindling folk could be mistaken for terrorism but hey, if you're an Emmainite, you're as good as a Shaldean in this part of the world."

"You an Emmainite?" asked Dale, as he continued his half-hearted search for some exploitable weakness in his confines.

"Why else would I be stuck here?"

Dale thought of all the Emmainites he saw on his raids into suspected Shaldean burrows during his time with the Republican Guard. He wondered if his neighbor looked like any of the men he'd killed in the name of service.

"'Charles Valkyrie' doesn't sound very Emmainite."

Charles chuckled. "You got me there. I was born Sayeed Errai. Left the name when I left my home. You? You got a family name?"

"Sunday."

"Dale Sunday. That doesn't sound Emmainite either."

"It's not."

"Well, it's not Ka'eedish or Drashalmec. You even Lorean?"

"I'm half-Albian, half-Meredian. Full Grovish."

"The Shaldea don't recruit peaches. What the hell you doing down here?"

"That's what I'm trying to figure out. They think I know something about some assassinations."

"You're an assassin?"

"As much as you're a terrorist."

"That doesn't make any sense."

"You're telling me."

Dale gave up the futile search. He sat back down on the cot and buried his head in his hands. He thought about Uncle Turkish, Auntie Cora Tess, Mosaic. War was at hand putting the lives of his loved ones in peril, and he was locked in a cell. The feeling of helplessness welled into anger. He felt betrayed by the State Security Command, by the Republic for which he had made great sacrifices. The irony of being locked up by the very Republic he was trying to save wasn't lost on him. Despair set in. *What if I never get out of here? Dying, caged like an animal.* He wondered if this was reparation for the lives he took. Maybe he wasn't so innocent after all. Maybe this was a fitting way to pay for the crimes he had committed.

He rummaged through his pockets looking for a smoke and found the copy of *The Walgorende's Last Stand*. On the inside of the cover was his name written in his twelve-year-old hand. It was faded, the ink bled and dried. He wondered what that little boy would think if he knew where he would end up thirteen years later. He turned to the first page and started reading.

A Mystic king about to be executed by a mage awaited his fate in a dungeon cell. How fitting, thought Dale, reading about a man in a dungeon while sitting in a dungeon himself. The king prays.

Deliver me from this spellbound world, the filth, the fog, the appetites, the noise. Deliver me from my flesh and bones born unto slow decay, this murky dream and the darkening days. And remember me, my Maker, when you come in your Kingdom that I may be with you in paradise when I wake.

As if his life were synched to the narrative, just as the executioners entered the dungeon to fetch the Mystic king, Dale heard a heavy door down the corridor open and close. He stopped reading and waited, listening as the voices and footsteps neared his cell. They stopped just outside of his door. Keys rustled. Dale set the book down. The sound of a click followed the sliding of a steel bolt. The door swung open and standing in the threshold was Sir Thomas Grail.

"Dale Sunday," he said, crossing his arms. "Upon examination, you have been deemed a saboteur."

"What?"

"In keeping vigilance against the threat of radicalism, heresy, cultism, cabals, and all other subversive elements, all groups disseminating their agenda or doctrine in secrecy, or without recognition of the Benesanti, or in violation of international laws, are considered threats to the peace in accordance with the Mizraheen Treaty, section four, article nine. And all affiliates of said groups are deemed '*saboteurs* of the peace.' Thus, you will not be granted Sanctuary."

"But I'm not affiliated with anyone."

"The Samaeli would fall under the definition of 'subversive elements.' Your friendship with one of its assassins is something of an affiliation. You also assisted a criminal organization in smuggling the Samaeli into this very city."

Dale thought, *I must have sung like a bird under that serum.*

"Nevertheless, you will be free to go after our verdict is forwarded to the State Security Command."

"When will that be?"

"Tomorrow."

"That's too late," Dale blurted.

The templar did not acknowledge Dale. He stepped aside. Selah stepped forward into the cell holding a wooden bucket, some cotton wraps, and a lidded wooden cup.

"Mister Sunday."

"Prioress."

"When I extended an invitation to the temple, this isn't what I had in mind."

"Me neither."

"Lay on your stomach, please." When Dale hesitated, Selah explained, "I'm here to treat your wounds."

Dale did as he was told. Selah slowly peeled the cotton cloth from his back and reached down into the bucket to draw from it a sponge soaked in calamine soap. As she did, she whispered in his ear, "Is it true?"

"Is what true?"

"What you said about the Balean invasion—is it true?"

"Uh, what did I say?"

Then in her speaking voice, she added, "This may sting a bit."

It burned like ice. Despite the gentle touch, Dale flinched and clenched his teeth.

"Bear with me." Selah blew on his back with little effect. Once she finished washing his back, she applied some aloe ointment and redressed the wounds with a blanket of gauze. "Drink this." She held up the wooden cup. "It's water from the seed of a tropical drupe. It'll restore your spirit."

Dale sat up and took the cup, the contents of which were a clear liquid, sweet and nutty. He paused, wiped his mouth with the back of his hand. He turned to Selah. She was the only person to whom he could make an appeal.

"I need to warn my brother," he tried. "He's at the Ancile. And I—"

Selah put her hand toward his mouth. "I believe you. I'll be back," she whispered.

Then she took up the bucket and left the cell. Thomas shut the door after her, locked all the latches into place, and shouted, "Lights out!"

On command, the lights went out. Dale sat staring at the door through which Selah had left. *Could it be true?* he wondered. *Why would she believe me? What did she know?*

Based on the templar's pronouncement, it was clear Dale had divulged much during the inquisition. There was no way of knowing what he had said. Like the fleeting memory of a dream, the bits and pieces of the inquisition continued to fade away until there was nothing. The only things left in Dale's mind were

> *"When I extended an invitation to the temple, this isn't what I had in mind."*

the lashes to his back and the name *Fairchild*.

Dale got up and washed his hands and his face by the soft glow of a burning oil lamp left hanging just outside his door. The warm light seeped in between the cracks of his cell door. As he gently laid himself down on his stomach, he allowed himself to hope. With time running out, everything depended on Selah's promise.

"Zaal'mavorte," Valkyrie said into the silence.

"What?" asked Dale.

"*Zaal'mavorte*. 'Shadows of Death.' Or what you call in Common 'the Samaeli.' Is it true? You got a friend in the group?"

"I'd rather not talk about it."

"Probably for the best. But if it's true, I must say, it's a wonder you're still alive."

Valkyrie's words simmered in the silence. Dale considered how dangerous Sparrow had become—how precarious his reunion with him had been.

"What do you know about them?"

"I can't say I've ever had any contact with them," Valkyrie replied. "At least, not that I'm aware of. But when I was younger, I remember a man came crawling into our village one day. I grew up on the outskirts of the Saracen and the nearest village from ours was more than five thousand strides away. We didn't know how long the man had been traveling, but he was delirious, dehydrated, on the brink of death. And he was covered in dried blood. He kept whispering, '*bezazu*.' Means devil in our ancient tongue. He didn't survive the night. But from what he'd apparently told our chieftain, the Shaldean Riders had met with the *Zaal'mavorte* in his village. A few days later, he woke up covered in blood. All of the horses had been slaughtered. And his entire village was gone. His family. Everyone."

"You mean dead?"

"I mean gone. Vanished. Without a trace. Like they were never there."

It had the makings of a legend. But the uneasiness in his neighbor's voice told Dale it was true.

"Like I said, kid," Valkyrie added, "it's a wonder you're still alive."

CH — 30

IN THE MIRROR DIMLY

Count Enlil Fairchild was a private man. Only a few people knew what the head of the Parallel Mining Corporation looked like. Even fewer saw the old man on a regular basis. However, the name *Fairchild* was known in every corner of the developed world. He was, after all, one of the wealthiest men in one of the wealthiest cities in Groveland.

His primary place of residence was the largest estate in the exclusive gated community called the Foothills. It was located far above Carnaval City on its upper westside. A private enclave of the wealthy elite, the community had a twelve-foot wall along its entire perimeter. There was only one gate in. Most in Carnaval City only heard what was behind that wall. Though a small fraction of the city's population lived in the Foothills, it represented more than half of the world's wealth.

Each year, there was also a ball held at his estate on the eve of the Harvest Festival—a ball to which an invitation was considered somewhat of a measure of one's position in society. Count Fairchild himself rarely made an appearance at his own events. This year, his estate was eerily quiet. Parallel Mining Corporation had just completed a move of their base of operations to Brookhaven in the South. It was an administrative nightmare that yielded Fairchild hardly enough time to attend a luncheon celebrating an old associate's retirement. Even then, Fairchild excused himself early from the small gathering citing exhaustion, and he was home before sundown.

Aside from the servants who knew to stay out of sight, at home Fairchild would, at last, be alone. Over the years, he had grown increasingly weary of company. In fact, the exhaustion he was experiencing had little to do with the relocation of Parallel Mining. It was the mingling with people he found tedious. As he grew in stature, all of his relationships were with those who could gain something from the association with him. His friends had become panderers. All he saw around him was the pretentiousness brought on by competition. All he heard was gossip and empty flattery. There wasn't an honest person among them. Their company had grown worse than isolation until isolation became his only reprieve—an escape from the loveless network. He was glad he would soon be free of them for good.

The majordomo greeted him at the door.

"A storm is coming."

"Good evening, Master Fairchild," he said, taking his coat and hat.

"Evening, Nicolas."

Around him was his personal security team, a hand-selected group of men from a private security firm known for attracting mercenaries looking for easy work. Once Fairchild was at the door of the house, the security team broke formation. Two went to man the gates, six to patrol the grounds, and three to enter before Enlil and inspect every room.

Thunder rumbled in the distant gray.

"A storm is coming."

"That it is."

Nicolas then handed Fairchild an envelope. It was sealed with the crest of the Bene-seneschal.

"Ah!" Fairchild took it with enthusiasm, broke the wax seal, and ripped the envelope open. Then he adjusted his glasses and read the note: *Thank you for your faithful service. May the Maker's blessing go with you. Bg2.*

"Shall I run the bath, sir?" asked Nicolas.

"No."

"And what of supper?"

"I'll take a late meal on the train. Which reminds me, have Philippe ready the carriage by six. Departure's at eight."

"Very good, sir."

The majordomo disappeared down the gilded hallway into the east wing where the servants' quarters were.

Fairchild sat in the foyer as always until the head of security returned from his personal bedchambers.

"You're all clear, sir."

"Thank you, Quintus."

Fairchild climbed the grand staircase that stopped at a landing before curving up on either side to the second story. On the landing wall overlooking the foyer was a large, oil-on-canvas painting of himself, a rendering of his younger self. He posed with a victor's stance—the chin cocked up, looking out into the distance, his right foot set on a conquered stone, fist over chest. The painting was commissioned by his sons and presented to him on his fiftieth birthday. He stopped at the top of the stairs to take a last look. It was something he never did. Looking at the gallant figure, he was reminded of how fleeting time was. The painting would remain with most of his furniture and his other less valuable possessions for the looting that would surely ensue. Even his servants—trusted servants—would be abandoned. The company relocation was a logistical nightmare but a necessary one. His estate and staff, however, were deemed expendable.

He had to consider that a move would have raised questions. There were already questions about the move of Parallel Mining. Had he moved out of his private residence, there were bound to be more questions. Fairchild had been warned of the Balean invasion by a trusted source.

And the less evidence of foreknowledge, the better.

Fairchild passed the ambassador's suite on his way to his bedchamber. In his room, he switched on the lamp beside his bed, casting a soft drowsy glow into the darkening dusk. He made his way over to the chessboard beside his work desk and studied it. Referencing the note, he then moved the white bishop accordingly.

"Bishop to g-two. A *fianchetto* is it?" he muttered to himself. He flipped the note over, grabbed a pen, and jotted down the piece placements. "We'll have to continue this in Brookhaven."

Then he unbuttoned his shirt, poured himself a glass from his nightcap decanter. He took a seat in his leather chair and sipped on his brandy. His thoughts went to all that would ensue in Carnaval City in the first hours of the Harvest Festival. In the silence, alone with his drink, the gravity of war descended on him. He thought about the children of the city. The coming death and destruction. Just as dread began to fill him, the bell from the front gate rang.

Fairchild set his glass down on top of the note beside the chessboard and went back out into the corridor. He buttoned his shirt while standing against the rails overlooking the foyer. Quintus was there to ask, "Are you expecting anyone, sir?"

"No."

Nicolas was already at the door.

"Is Mister Fairchild in?"

"May I ask who's inquiring?"

"Sentinel Walsh and Sentinel Helell of the State Security Command. We'd like a word with him."

"And what is this regarding?"

Immediately, Fairchild thought of his ledger. His lies.

When frequently asked by his colleagues for the secret of his success, he had always proudly answered, "I understand that a business thrives only if the community around it thrives with it. Do you know why terrorists haven't attacked my mines? I build schools and wells in Emmainite villages."

The lie wasn't in his philosophy of mutual prosperity. It was in the talk of schools and wells. Fairchild's mines were no less guilty of exploitation. But they were left unmolested by the Shaldea only because he had entered an agreement with them—to be a funding vehicle for their cell groups within the Republic. A trained eye would have easily been able to detect the discrepancy in his accounts—the large sums of untraceable monies laundered through Parallel Mining prior to its eventual integration into Shaldean hands.

Remembering he had already destroyed the ledger just days earlier along with other incriminating evidence, he descended the stairs with aplomb.

"It's okay, Nicolas. Show them in."

"Sorry to disturb you," said Sentinel

Walsh, flashing his badge. "Sentinel Norman Walsh of the SSC. This is my partner, Sentinel Gabriel Helell."

"This way, please."

Fairchild showed them into his study just beyond the foyer. Quintus and his comrades stood guard just outside.

"Care for a drink?"

"No, thank you."

They all took a seat around the coffee table on the leather sofa set.

"Again, our apologies for dropping in unexpected," Sentinel Walsh began. "I'm sure you're very busy, but we believe you may be in danger."

"Danger?" It wasn't what he was expecting.

"We believe the deaths of the investors in the Machina Group is part of a larger plot. We believe they were, in fact, assassinated by members of a highly sophisticated subversive group known as the Samaeli. We recently interrogated a suspected affiliate and your name came up."

Fairchild's expression changed. "Why would my name come up?"

"We were hoping you could help us answer that."

"Excuse me a moment." Fairchild rose from his seat, opened the door and invited Quintus into the study. "I'd like my head of security to hear this."

"Of course."

"Sentinel, no one believed the official reports," Fairchild added, as he returned to his seat. "You'd be a fool to think every lead investor of Machina fell ill or died in an accident in a span of mere months. But what does this have to do with me?"

"Mister Fairchild, how familiar are you with the Machina Group?"

"I've done business with some of its members at one point or another. But that's the extent of it. I knew better than to get involved in Machina. I'm no traitor."

"Could you clarify what you mean by that?"

"Isn't it obvious?" Met with blank stares, Fairchild cocked his head. "You don't know." The old mining mogul sat back in his chair, relishing the fact that he knew something the Republic's premiere intelligence agency did not. He pressed his fingers together as he explained. "Machina is supporting the Kingdom of Bale. They have been for years now. Of course, they have investments in publicly traded assets as well, securities and such. But that's just a ruse. The Machina Group has been directly financing the Thalian Regime. All of them, set to reap great fortune from a war. Hence, the mounting tension along the borderlands, the construction of the Ancile—it was all by elaborate design."

"Mister Fairchild, are you talking about a conspiracy?" asked Norman.

"Of the highest kind."

Norman looked as if he had just learned of a loved one's infidelity. While the sentinels were reeling from the implications of this revelation—that Dale had been right, that war was coming—Fairchild added, "War can be quite profitable for those who stage it. Perhaps these assassins are trying to prevent that."

"Then why would your name come up?"

Fairchild smiled. "Surely, this isn't the first time my name's been mentioned with ill intentions."

"Mister Fairchild, the Samaeli—"

"Is not my concern. I trust Quintus here will see that no unwelcome guests breach my personal space."

"All of the assassinations were successfully carried out in spite of heavy security. This may be beyond your scope to appreciate."

"Then so be it. I appreciate you coming all this way to warn me." Then he rose from his seat, walked over to the door and held it open. "Now, if you'll excuse me, gentlemen, I have a train to catch. Quintus, show these men out."

"Yes, sir. This way."

As they made their way out of the study, Sentinel Walsh stopped at the door. "Mister Fairchild, if I may, one final question. Do you know who the chairman of the Machina Group is?"

"If I knew that, I would already be dead." Fairchild held up a finger and stated what the sentinels were already thinking. "Perhaps he's the one you should be looking for. Good evening, gentlemen."

Once the sentinels had been escorted out, Fairchild retreated back to his room where he removed his shirt and hung it up beside his coat in his otherwise emptied wardrobe. He took up his glass of brandy and finished what was left of it. He did not notice that the Bene-seneschal's note he had set it on had gone missing.

He went to the washroom, relieved himself, and ran the faucet. While rinsing his face he looked at his own reflection in the mirror. The dimly lit man staring back at him was a weathered shell of the portrait that hung on the landing. Weak and feeble. He would not miss the painting.

He sighed.

Then Fairchild noticed something dart behind him. Before he could turn, something grabbed him from behind. In the mirror he saw his nose and mouth covered by a black leather glove. The grip was so tight he felt as if his jaw was going to shatter. As the blade came across his throat, Fairchild caught a glimpse of a dark figure whose face was masked in a balaclava. The blood shot onto the mirror, covering the reflection of his assassination.

The Vengian gently laid him down on the floor. He turned off the faucet, closed the washroom door behind him and walked out of the room.

The gray turned to night, the drizzle into a storm. A knife and vapor, the Vengian was gone.

CH 31

FREE

The food hatch opened. A tray of boiled cabbage, a piece of bread, and sausage appeared through it. The attending cleric who had served the meal said, "The Maker bless you," before closing the hatch.

"The Maker bless me?" Charles Valkyrie asked mockingly. "How does the Maker bless me when I am forced to eat boiled cabbage day in and day out? All I've had is boiled cabbage for thirty days. Why does a benevolent God create such terrible things, like war, murder, greed, and boiled cabbage?"

Dale walked over to the door and collected his tray. Ignoring his neighbor, he sampled the sausage. It was saltier than he liked but of good quality. It was his first meal since being detained. He was hungry, and so he was thankful to have something to eat.

With his mouth stuffed with boiled cabbage and sausage, Dale asked, "You a Mystic?"

"Nope," Valkyrie replied. "As godless as they come."

"Strange musings for an atheist."

Valkyrie laughed. "Perhaps not so strange, my friend. Even an atheist will speak of the Maker when he needs to blame someone for his troubles. And you? Have you placed your faith in the Maker?"

"No."

"Good for you. People believe what they believe. Who can explain it? It's when they start telling you what they believe,

taking all sorts of creative liberties with the unknown, you end up where the Shaldea and cultists are. You end up spewing all kinds of dogma. I know there's nothing original about my pragmatism, but the way I see it, religion is, at its core, all about self-improvement. Trouble is, once you're all self-improved, it's near impossible to avoid a kind of elitist contempt for everyone else."

"For someone not claiming to be a Mystic, sounds like you've put some thought into this."

"I'm Emmainite. We're born thinking over our heads. I think the Great Ur Aremis had it right when he said, 'Religion is the taint of an unbroken spell that beckons man to believe in the extraordinary.'"

Dale did not understand what this Ur Aremis meant or what made him so great. Dale was not in the frame of mind to try to understand it. He hadn't slept much. All night, every little sound stirred him awake. Each time he sat up, hoping the sound was Selah's promised return. Each time he lay back down in disappointment. The disappointment turned to worry. In his mind, there was a good chance the Shawls had heeded his warning. Replaying the scene at the bakery in his mind, Dale told himself that Uncle Turkish and Auntie Cora Tess were convinced. He thought he remembered that they had agreed to flee. It was too late for the city. Even if the officials and the Benesanti had believed him, it was too late to get everyone evacuated. *Maybe it's not too late to organize a defense. Maybe even a counter offensive.*

And then there was Darius. Sparrow had told him the Ancile would not be able to hold back the invasion. If the Ancile falls, Darius would surely lose his life. *How do I get word to Darius? I got to get out of here.* These had been the thoughts swirling in his head, depriving him of sleep. For hours he had drifted in and out of the waking world, his mind racing with all that Sparrow had forewarned.

Dale finished his meal. He set the tray next to the door. He tried to wiggle the trap door open. It did not move.

"How was it growing up an atheist Emmainite?"

"I wasn't always like this," Valkyrie replied.

"No?"

"Lots of things happened, but I think the turning point was the day I learned the Shaldea were dealing with the *Zaal'mavorte*. I realized if my people were willing to deal with the devil, then God was inconsequential. And all that rhetoric, that radicalism behind the Shaldea, it was all political, not spiritual. So I left."

"You just picked up and left?"

"Pretty much."

"How'd you end up here? I mean, not in this dungeon, but here, in Groveland? In Meredine?"

"I've ended up everywhere in my life at one point or another. Nothing special about here."

For a fleeting moment, Dale felt the sharp piercing of envy. A life of freedom. His childhood dream of life on the sea, journeying to distant shores with no pull neither here nor there. It was a life that died at age twelve, in that alley with Marcus Addy. It got buried at the Academy and aside from these moments of painful regret, long forgotten.

"How'd you make a living?"

"I worked odd jobs mostly. Shepherding. Lumberyard. Deckhand. Even dabbled in smuggling. I ran with some gravediggers for a period. Then one day, while I took up work as a porter for a posse of game hunters, I discovered I was a natural tracker. So I tried to get around people who could teach me about nature, terrain, and survival. Lived with a tribe of druids in the northern coasts, spent a year of solitude in the fjords of the arctic, roamed the Saracen deserts with nomads. Once I felt prepared, I started to hire myself out. Became a freelance ranger. Ran with anyone, from bandits to bounty hunters. Whatever. As long as they paid. And when business was slow, I'd gather ingredients from the Wilds for apothecaries."

"Or swindle them."

"Or swindle them," Valkyrie repeated, appreciating the jab.

"You ever miss it—Loreland, I mean?"

"All the time." After a pause, Valkyrie added, "What I wouldn't give for some fried hallume right now."

Just then the door down the corridor opened. Dale stood and approached his cell door in anticipation. He heard the footsteps come down the corridor and stop at his door. It was unlocked and opened. Standing in the threshold was Sir Thomas Grail. Dale heard a commotion next door.

"Move it, ranger! You too," he heard another templar bark.

Dale was led out into the corridor where he saw his hall mate, Charles Valkyrie, for the first time. Valkyrie's black beard and bushy hair had grown out wild, but he wasn't unkempt. As he did every morning, he dampened his hair and matted it down to one side. He glanced back and acknowledged Dale with a flick of his brows. They both appeared to the other different than envisioned.

They said nothing as they were led out into a connecting passage on the opposite wall of the long hall. They were taken through the temple's less-travelled underground passageways into a dark chamber. At the end of the room was a raised platform with a long desk designed to seat a panel of twelve men, the seal of the Benesanti in the center. Alaric Linhelm was standing in front of the desk.

Valkyrie was stopped at the chamber entrance while Dale was led up to where the senior templar stood.

"Hello, Dale. I am Champion Alaric Linhelm, Marshal of the Vail Templar."

Dale nodded.

"As you have been informed, you've been deemed a saboteur and thus, I cannot offer you Sanctuary. I can, however, offer you your freedom. I've heard you confessed to a great many things during the inquisition."

Dale offered no reaction.

"Something you said is especially disconcerting. It is regarding the Balean invasion. Is it true? Is Duke Thalian planning to initiate a war?"

"That's what I was told."

"But do you believe it to be true?"

"I have no reason to doubt my… source."

"You mean your *friend*."

Dale didn't reply.

"Prioress?"

Selah approached and placed her hand on Dale's shoulder. She held up his sword and his shirt.

"Thank you," he muttered softly, retrieving his effects.

"Sir Grail, escort Mister Sunday out and wait for me in my office. I'll be by shortly."

"Yes, m'lord."

"And see to it he gets onto Republic soil unnoticed."

"Yes, m'lord."

"As for you, I suggest you get out of the city."

"I plan to," Dale replied.

"Good luck, kid," said Valkyrie, as he passed him on his way out.

CH 32

Alaric excused the remaining templar and ordered Charles Valkyrie forward. With no one but Selah present, Alaric addressed him.

"Mister Valkyrie, given your past involvement with the Shaldea, I'm afraid I cannot award you Sanctuary either."

"I figured. But you can grant me my freedom."

"Yes. Yes, I can. Before I do, I have something I'd like to ask you."

"What's that?"

"How familiar are you with the Wilds?"

"Excuse me?"

"You're a ranger, correct? The Wilds—how familiar are you with them?"

"Seeing it's been my home for the past ten years, I'd say I know the Wilds better than anyone. Why?"

"I have a favor to ask of you."

"*You?* You want a favor from *me?* Oh, this is going to be good."

After showing Dale off the temple premises by way of the less-traveled Northern Wall, Sir Thomas Grail sat in Alaric's office, waiting as instructed. Aside from the large windows with their diamond-patterned etchings, the cold, dark gray stone room was nearly indistinguishable from the dungeon cells. The room was largely bare. A rug, a hearth, a desk, and an iron chandelier that held candles were its only features. The marshal's office was located in the part of the temple that was not yet wired for electricity.

When Alaric Linhelm entered, Thomas shot up from his seat, snapped his heels, and with a crisp salute, stood at attention.

"M'lord."

"At ease, Thomas. I have something I want to tell you. Listen very carefully because I will repeat none of it. When I am done, you are free to ask questions, but know that I will be stingy with my answers. I neither have the time nor the disposition to explain myself, understand?"

Clearly concerned, Thomas hesitantly nodded. "Yes, m'lord."

"Kneel."

PASSING THE TORCH

Thomas kneeled before the marshal.

"I, Champion Alaric Linhelm, appoint you, Sir Thomas Grail, my successor and hereby declare you Champion of the Holy Order of the Benesanti, Marshal of the Vail Templar."

"M'lord?"

Alaric stopped him with a raised hand before continuing, "As such, you will be taking over my office and its duties. I bestow upon you all rights, privileges, and responsibilities of this office. Effective immediately, I vacate my seat, and relinquish my sword and shield to you. They will serve as proof of this appointment. The Maker's hand of righteousness be upon you. May he guide you and protect you as you protect all entrusted to your care. Rise, Champion Thomas Grail."

Alaric removed his sword and shield and handed them to Thomas. The young templar hesitated to extend his hand. Alaric thrust it upon him.

"Take it."

"M'lord…?"

"Take it."

"With all due respect, what's the meaning of this?"

Alaric sighed. "I have a war to stop."

"M'lord?"

"That's all I will say."

"This is…I don't understand."

"It's not your place to understand. Take it."

Thomas took the sword and shield pressed into his chest.

"I have nothing but faith that you'll make a greater marshal than I ever was," Alaric said. Then he added, "Inform the Bene-seneschal of my departure and your subsequent appointment at nightfall. Until then, honor me with your silence."

Just as he was about to leave, Thomas stepped in front of the ex-marshal and drew his own sword.

"M'lord, if you're going to stop a war, you will need a sword."

Alaric received it with a solemn nod and rushed out of the office.

CH 33

BLACK

As he ran toward the Central District, dusk was beginning to descend.

The bakery was closed. Still, Dale stopped to take a peek inside. Once he confirmed it was empty, he continued on to his house. There, he took a quick bath and changed his clothes. It was no easy task as he was acutely aware of the wounds on his back. Rushed as he felt, he knew he couldn't risk infection. After haphazardly stuffing his Republican Guard backpack with basic supplies, throwing on a pea coat and lacing up his boots, he stood breathless in the middle of the room. The whirlwind of activity had put him in a daze. The challenge to remember everything for a trip was in this case compounded.

OUT

Suddenly, he remembered his copy of *The Walgorende's Last Stand*. It was in the back pocket of his discarded pants. As he located the book, he also remembered to grab some important documents—the deed of ownership to his house and the breaker. At last, he took up his augmented sword and headed for the door.

The family photographs on the mantle stopped him. Dale picked up the one of his mother and father together, smiling. After a close look, he gently set it back down. With a final scan of the house, he rushed out.

As he ran toward the Central District, dusk was beginning to descend. Dale passed scores of men and women in costume. The closer he got to the city's center, the more costumes he passed. When Dale reached the Halo, everything but the circus was closed. The Concert Hall was empty.

"Damn it." Dale remembered that Mosaic's performance was at the Flora Crystal. He hired a cabriolet. The roads were congested and by the time he reached the Flora Crystal, the sun had set, the city lights had turned on, and the festival was well underway.

The venue, as it turned out, was more a nightclub than a concert hall. According to the cabby, who wouldn't stop talking, the Flora Crystal was famous for making the finest imported drinks affordable for young common socialites. It boasted unrivalled service and an anything-goes environment. When Dale arrived, he saw a line of men and women in a menagerie of exotic costumes waiting to get in. The line wrapped around the building. Whatever they had in the Flora Crystal, people wanted it.

Dale ran past the line, right up to the door. A bouncer at the door stopped him. The line booed and shouted obscenities.

"Hey, that's the line. To the back with you," the bouncer said, still holding him by his coat.

"I need to get in," Dale pleaded.

"Everybody needs to get in."

"I just need to talk to my sister."

"Who's your sister?" asked another bouncer.

"Mosaic Shawl. She's performing tonight. It's an emergency."

"Wait here."

The bouncer disappeared into the club. A few minutes later he reemerged with another man. Dale didn't recognize him behind his makeup and court jester costume.

"Hey, it's me, Terry. We met at the Rapture. I work there, remember?"

"Right. Terry. Listen, is Mosaic in there?"

"Yeah." Terry turned to the bouncer and said, "He's fine, let him in."

Dale was ushered in with a rain of protest from the line. The bouncer spotted Dale's sword and tried to stop him.

"Wait, you can't bring that in here."

"It's okay, Cyrus," Terry replied on Dale's behalf. "It's part of his costume."

"Mister B said absolutely no weapons."

"Don't worry. I'll clear it with Mister B. Relax, Cyrus. It's a party."

Terry then showed Dale into the main room. There was a sea of dancing—hundreds of people molded into a single entity by the throbbing rhythm. The crowd made the large space look small and cramped.

"Thanks."

"What was that?"

"Thanks! For getting me in!"

"No problem. I'm glad Cyrus found me," Terry replied.

"Where's Mo?"

Terry pointed to the stage. A winged Mosaic made up to complete her forest-sprite costume, sat behind the piano, pounding on the keys. Behind her was a full ensemble—drums, strings, horns.

As they made their way through the pulsing crowd toward the stage, one woman after another threw themselves in Terry's path. He staved them off, saying something into their ear. Whatever he said, he left each one in laughter. Just as they crossed the dance floor, the song ended with a shattering of the cymbals. With the crash still ringing in the air, the ensemble started on a softer song. Mosaic was no longer on the piano. She was standing center stage, her lips to a microphone. And as she sang, her mezzo-soprano voice carried like healing magic through the entire club.

Dale stood there in the middle of the swaying crowd like a marble column. The only other person not swaying was a figure making a hurried line through the dance floor, straight toward him. The deep hood attached to his charcoal-gray coat was pulled over his head. In the dim lit club, even as he approached and stood close enough to butt Dale's head with a jerk, Dale could hardly see his face.

"What're you still doing here? What is *she* doing here?"

"Sparrow? What're *you* doing here?" Dale countered.

Sparrow turned and faced the stage. He pressed a flyer to Dale's chest. It was a promotional flyer of the night's performance. Still looking toward the stage, Sparrow said, "I wanted to make sure she wouldn't be here. I told you to take her and get out of the city."

"I know but—" Before continuing, Dale looked around for Terry and saw that he had drifted into the crowd. "I was held up."

"What do you mean?"

"The SSC got me. I was released just a few hours ago."

Sparrow squared up to Dale. He pulled his hood back so Dale could look into his eyes.

"What did you tell them?"

"They drugged me."

"*Rohar,* what did you tell them?" Sparrow repeated, carefully enunciating each word.

"I don't know. Everything."

The music stopped. The stage lights went out. And the dim mood lighting running throughout the club went black. The spell was broken and there was a collective gasp. Then murmurs. Laughter. Then hoots and hollers.

"Get her and meet me in the back," said Sparrow.

Dale rushed the stage. He climbed up and grabbed Mosaic.

"Mo, it's me. Dale."

"Dale? Dale! You made it."

"Listen, we need to get out of here. Now!"

"What's going on?"

"I'll explain later."

"I can't. I'm in the middle of a performance."

"You're done. Come on."

He took her by the arm and rushed her off stage. Unable to see, he led her down a hallway with his hand held out in front of him, like a blind man leading the blind. They managed to shuffle through the crowds and stumble out the backdoor. They emerged onto the back lot, into

pitch black. Dale realized that it wasn't the club that had turned off the lights. It was a blackout. A citywide blackout.

It's starting.

"Sparrow!" Dale called.

"Over here."

He was crouched beside some empty crates.

"What's going on, Dale?" asked Mosaic. "You're scaring me."

"It's okay. Everything's going to be okay. Where are your folks?"

"Home, I think. Why?"

"*Rohar*, we need to get moving." Sparrow stood and walked up to Dale and Mosaic.

"Who is that? Dale? What's going on?"

"The invasion has begun." Sparrow said.

"Invasion? What invasion? Who are you?" Mosaic grew increasingly frantic.

There was a rumble coming from the government quarter. The crackling of gunfire was followed by distant screams. The rumble rose to a steady roar. Dale knew exactly what he was hearing. Nothing sounded quite like a battlefield. The city bells began to toll. In the blackness, a ball of flame rose into the sky. Crowds stood looking up at the ominous sign in the sky. Dressed in costume, the ill-prepared citizens of the city looked pathetic. When one person realized it was a military strike, the crowd exploded into a panicked scurry.

"Follow me."

Sparrow's voice was calm and assertive. Avoiding the main streets, he led Dale and Mosaic into an alley behind a row of restaurants. It was a forgotten passage, considered more a waste disposal location than a street. A waft of the ripening waste hit them in the face. Dale took two deep breaths until his eyes were watery. He turned to Mosaic, who pinched her nose.

Sparrow shuffled through the garbage. Rodents scattered in their wake, causing Mosaic to scream a nose-plugged nasally scream. Sparrow stopped at a specific spot and cleared a mound of waste. Beneath his feet, he uncovered an iron grate leading into Carnaval City's sewer. Sparrow pried it open. It smelled like a sewer.

Still holding her nose, Mosaic looked at them and asked, "Really?"

Sparrow jumped in. Dale lowered Mosaic. When they were all below, Sparrow shut the grate behind them and led them into the dark bowels of the city.

CH 34

SHIT STORM

It was pitch black. They walked along a concrete ledge just a couple feet above the slow-moving stream of sludge. The sounds of trickling water, the rats, the distant, indistinguishable echoes; the stench of all forms of human waste in a damp, enclosed tube—they were surrounded by it. Sparrow was unfazed. Somehow, through the darkness, he knew where to place his steps.

Mosaic turned and said in a hushed voice, "Dale, I'm scared. Tell me what's going on."

As they walked under a world at war, Dale told Mosaic all he knew. She listened in quiet disbelief.

"My God," she finally muttered. "What're we going to do?"

"I don't know."

"Where's your friend taking us?"

"The temple," Sparrow replied. "It'll be the safest place in the city."

"I can't go back there," said Dale. "I need to get word to the Ancile."

"Wires went down with the Spegen," said Sparrow.

"Then I'll need a horse."

"*Rohar*, the Ancile has fallen. It's too late." Sparrow kept a steady pace.

Dale knew Sparrow was right. The invasion about to envelop Carnaval City was proof enough that the Ancile had not withstood the initial Balean assault. Still, he insisted. "I need to go find Darius."

Mosaic was shivering in her costume. She couldn't tell whether it was from the cold or from fear.

While Dale stopped to remove his coat and drape it around Mosaic, Sparrow had a moment to wonder, *What am I doing?* For a childhood friend he hadn't seen in over ten years, he was risking everything—everything he had learned, everything to which he was committed. This singular focus with which he had ruthlessly constructed his life was now blurred. It was a strange feeling—the feeling of internal struggle. This friend had already confessed to divulging everything to the SSC. He knew the right thing to do. He knew what his commitments demanded. But in the sewer with Dale and Mosaic, *to kill* was never a real consideration. Somehow it felt right to risk everything. It felt right to risk his own life.

"Let's keep moving."

After what felt like four blocks of walking, Sparrow stopped and looked up. He climbed the ladder, slid the stone cover back, and poked his head out. Having scanned the area, he waved both Dale and Mosaic up. They emerged onto the middle of an empty, nondescript side street. Dale and Mosaic had no idea where they were.

"This way."

Sparrow led them down a block and then turned at the next intersection. Just beyond was the plaza, south of the temple cloister. The plaza was empty. Mosaic saw the temple and then looked back at Dale.

"Go on, Mo. You'll be safe inside."

"You're not coming?" she asked.

"No, I need to find Darius."

"How are you going to get there? What if you can't find him?"

"I have to try something. I can't just wait around here."

"Yeah, but what if something happens to you?" Mosaic's eyes were welling up with tears.

"Look, when you see Uncle Turkish, tell him I'll try to send word once the dust settles, okay?"

"When will that be?"

"I don't know!" Dale sighed, immediately regretting his outburst. "I'm sorry, Mo. I didn't mean to…I just…remember when you told me that not doing anything was just as bad as doing something wrong? Well, you were right. I can't just do nothing."

Mosaic wept as she gave Dale a long hug. "I can't believe this is happening."

"Me neither."

"Be careful, Dale," she said, still holding him tight.

"I will."

She gave Dale his coat back. And then she turned to Sparrow. "Thank you."

He acknowledged her with a nod.

Dale and Sparrow watched as she ran to the temple and was granted entry by the guard at the cloister gate. Others seeking refuge were beginning to make their way in after her. She looked back one last time with a wan look and waved. Dale waved back. Then Mosaic disappeared into the temple halls.

In the distance, there was the popping of rifle fire over the city bells still tolling.

"Come on," said Sparrow.

With that, Sparrow began to jog. As he had since leaving the Flora Crystal, Dale followed.

"Where are we going?" Dale asked.

"You want to get out of the city, right?"

Sparrow steadily picked up the pace. It had been months since Dale had run like this. He could feel his chest burn and his legs grow heavy. Too proud to ask Sparrow to slow down, Dale pushed himself until the spit turned pasty in his mouth. Ten minutes in, Dale was breaking a sweat. After another mile, he got his second wind. He remembered what it felt like in the Academy—those ten-mile runs in full gear. They ran east toward the outskirts of the city. The endorphins kicked in.

More and more people flooded the streets. People were fleeing the Central District, the site of all the scheduled festivities. Others who had decided to forego the crowded city center poured out of their homes onto the streets. They came out looking for answers. By the reaction of the crowd, Sparrow and Dale could see the word was spreading. The men rushed about. They wore a determined expression, but their eyes were blank. The women gathered children and belongings. Dale wanted to tell people to leave their possessions behind, but he knew it would be futile. He would be trying to reason with an unreasonable crowd until he too, would be swallowed up with them by the advancing army.

When the two reached the fairgrounds, the city had reached a fever pitch. The stables next to the little racetrack appeared abandoned. The main entrance was shut. Sparrow knocked. When there was no answer, he began to pound on the door. It finally cracked open. An old man holding a candle peered nervously out at Sparrow and Dale.

"The hell you think you're doing? You're gonna break down my door."

"Old man, you better get out of the city," said Sparrow. "Balean soldiers have invaded."

"Bale? Is that what all the ruckus is about?"

"Yes. But before you go, we are going to need a horse."

"Horses aren't for sale. Sorry."

"I'll give you a fair price," Sparrow said, producing a coin purse from his pocket.

"You deaf? They are not for sale."

He tried to close the door but Sparrow lodged his foot in the crack. He shoved it open with his hand.

"Old Dingo. I know who you are. You've sold horses before or at least you've supplied some for the Carousel Rogues. You can't take them all with you. So you can take my gold and ready me whatever horse you please, or I can cut your throat and take whatever I please."

The old man frowned.

"You a Rogue?"

Sparrow didn't reply.

The old man glanced over Sparrow's shoulder at Dale.

"There ain't enough gold you can carry for two."

"I only need one," Sparrow replied.

He grumbled. Then he snatched Sparrow's coin purse. As he walked back into the stable, along a row of horse pens, he continued to grumble to himself, "Get out of city? And go where? Is an old man supposed to find another place? Start over?" He scoffed. "I'm staying right here. With my horses. 'Get out of town,' my ass."

the men following him. "You two stay right here. I'll bring out your horse."

At the end of the row, the old man pulled a horse out. By the light of a kerosene lantern he strapped on a saddle. He walked the horse back to them still grumbling, "Damn near impossible to live without light. This one is a standard young colt. He's not the fastest. Truth be told, he's slow as shit. But he's a good horse. He's tough—got good stamina."

"He got a name?" Dale asked, putting his hand on the head of the chocolate brown horse.

"You can call him Shit Storm for all I care. He's your problem now." Then he looked over at Sparrow. "You're not a Rogue, are you, squinty? You're not wearing a black rose."

Sparrow didn't answer his question. He gestured to Dale that they had better go.

As they walked away, the old man followed them back to the entry. "Well, whoever you are, you tell the Silver Fox or whoever's in charge that we're square now. I don't want to see you people around here anymore. I'm done."

Without acknowledging his words, Dale and Sparrow stepped out. Outside they heard a rolling hum. They both looked up to the source of the sound and saw what looked like a belly of a flying whale.

"The hell is that?" Dale wondered aloud.

Just beyond it, they saw another one. And another. A fleet flying past them toward the heart of Carnaval City.

"*Rohar,* you need to leave. Now."

Dale nodded and mounted the horse.

"Head north out of the city through the river mouth," Sparrow continued. "Ride along the northern coast but get off the beach as soon as you can. There's a quarry six hundred strides north of the city. As soon as you pass it, cut across west into the Lowers. You can travel under the cover of trees."

"You going to stick around?" Dale asked.

"I have unfinished business here."

"Well, keep an eye on Mo for me, will you?"

Sparrow nodded.

"I can never thank you enough. For everything."

"You're my friend. You don't have to thank me."

"I know I don't. Thank you, Sparrow."

"Take care, *rohar.*"

Dale kicked the horse into a gallop and started down the road. In his heart, there was a kind of fear he had never felt before.

CH 35
INTO THE WILDS

Dale's heart sank at the sight of the Royal Navy's ironclad warships anchored just off the coast, north of the city. Dozens of landing crafts were launched off the ships and were transporting Balean soldiers to shore. They had overcome the Republican naval blockade. Soon, the waterfront would be overrun and his breaker expropriated by the invading force. Dale put it out of his mind and kept riding. By midnight, he had reached the quarry and was cutting west into the Lowers. As he rode, Dale saw bursts of fire rising over the silhouetted city he had left behind. Solid black forms loomed above the burning skyline, the skyships hanging like castles from the clouds.

For the next few days, he traveled at a steady gait, stopping only to steal some sleep and water the horse. He rode through the night and made his stops during the day, rationing the berries and nuts he had gathered in the Lowers. Extending from the rolling hills near Carnaval City, up along the west and across the foothills of the Borderland Ridge, the Lowers was an expanse of dense forest that separated Groveland from its uninhabitable West, known as the Wilds.

Days passed. The world at war receded. Amidst the trees, lush hills, and open prairies, the scene Dale left behind felt to him like a dream. No crackling of gunfire, no earth-moving cannon blasts, no smell of smoke and powder. Only the sounds of crickets and a running brook nearby. Dale saw in the distance an abandoned farm submerged in overgrowth. The wild grass swayed as it had for thousands of years,

before the Republic, before the war, before him. In this place, in the open, in the silence, everything was as it should be.

A week later, Dale was reacquainted with reality. From the cover of the forest, he saw a Balean checkpoint on the road leading to the Ancile. Dale sat staring at the checkpoint in frustration. If he could remain on his current route, he was only a day's ride from the Ancile. As it was now, he would have to backtrack, travel east out of the Lowers to maneuver his way around the checkpoint. After weighing all the options, Dale retraced his steps along the Lowers until he could no longer see the checkpoint. Then he left the cover of the forest for the first time since his flight out of Carnaval City.

Feeling uneasy, Dale dismounted and quietly walked the horse. There *had* to be other soldiers around. He reasoned that the further he was from the checkpoint, the less likely he was to run into a night patrol. But just as his fear of being discovered began to subside, he heard a shout from the prairie trails to the south.

"You there! Stop!"

Dale looked and saw a small detachment of five Balean scouts on horseback. They were a mere twenty-five paces away. Dale was caught in between the checkpoint and this scout patrol. In the open road, there was nowhere to hide.

He jumped onto his horse, yanked the reins and kicked him into a full gallop back toward the Lowers.

"Hey!"

The shout was followed by rifle fire and the whiz of bullets. Dale looked back and saw the five horsemen in close pur-

suit. Having already extended itself from the long flight out of Carnaval City, Dale could feel the horse faltering between his legs. By the time they climbed a knoll and ventured beyond the tree line, the scouts were on him. As they neared the Wilds, the forest grew dense, the gaps between the trees narrowing.

With his sword drawn, the lead Balean scout came riding up along Dale's right side. Crouching low, Dale gave his horse a swat. "C'mon, Shit Storm!"

Dale heard a "swoosh" and suddenly, he no longer felt the rider beside him. Another rider came up on his left. Dale glanced back to see that he had a pistol drawn. Hearing the same "swoosh," this time Dale turned on the sound to see an arrow hit the rider in the chest, knocking him off his mount. Dale pulled the reins and jumped off his horse. As he regained his balance, he drew his sword and turned to face his pursuers. Imagining that the scouts were upon him, Dale was surprised to see that they had halted near the spot where the other two had fallen.

Trying to control their jumpy horses, they nervously looked about for the source of the arrows. Before any of them had much time to think, Dale heard the sound of three more arrows fly past his head in short order. They each hit their mark. Dale watched as one of the horses galloped away with a body slumped on its saddle. He spun around to look for his hidden deliverer and saw a large man, carrying a huge sword, step out of the thicket behind him.

It was Alaric Linhelm.

"Champion?" Dale was asking himself as much as asking Alaric.

"Ex," said Charles Valkyrie as he emerged with a long bow in hand and a quiver full of arrows strapped to his back. The Emmainite was dressed like a proper ranger—machete sheathed to the side, a leather rucksack full of supplies.

"Man, am I glad to see you guys," said Dale.

"That's the same patrol we were ducking. Of all the trees in the forest, you had to lead them here."

"How was I supposed to know you were here? What the hell you doing here anyway?"

"Long story. You?"

"Long story."

At last, Selah stepped out through the curtain of wild growth behind Valkyrie. Aside from the traditional haircut, in appearance Selah had left everything else of the Benesanti behind. She was outfitted for adventuring—a pair of equestrian pants, knee-high brown leather boots, a long fur-lined coat. And she wore a saber on her hip.

"Hello, Dale."

"Prioress," he said, sheathing his sword.

"No time for pleasantries, unfortunately," Valkyrie said. "These scouts will soon be missed. The dead one, that horse could lead him right back to the checkpoint. We need to hurry."

They determined they had no time to give them a decent burial. The best thing to do was drag the bodies into the thicket. Selah helped Dale remove one of the bodies from the clearing. She appeared unfazed by the violence and death.

"Where are you off to?" she asked as they pulled the body of the other scout by the ankles.

"The Ancile."

"The Ancile? Why? It's likely swarming with Balean forces."

"I need to find my brother."

"Well, forget it, kid," said Valkyrie, as he walked past with the horses he retrieved. "You might as well stroll across the border waving the Meredian flag."

"Where are you all going?"

The ranger looked to Alaric for an answer.

"North," the ex-templar curtly replied on their behalf.

Valkyrie slipped his bow over his shoulder and began un-strapping the horses from their harnesses. "We were on the main roads most of the way," he said. "We cut into the Lowers when we saw the first patrol."

Valkyrie removed the saddles from both the scout horses and their own, and sent them running off to the south.

"What're you doing?" asked Dale.

"The Wilds' no place for horses. You better do the same with yours if you plan to join us."

Dale looked around. He didn't have much of a choice.

Valkyrie drew his machete and began hacking away at the vines. Alaric knelt next to the bodies and bowed his head in a moment of prayer.

"It's the first time he's seen battle since taking his oath," Selah explained.

Dale held his gaze on her and said, "It's good to see you again, Prioress."

"Selah. You can call me Selah."

As the others ventured into the dense growth, Dale lingered a moment with the bodies. There was no mourning. He relished the fight. These Baleans had invaded his country and aggressed war against his people. For the first time, he identified with Emmainite villagers—the villages he'd raided as a Republican Guard. How they must have longed to see him as he saw these Balean scouts.

Dale walked over to his horse and stroked his muzzle. He was grateful for Shit Storm's faithful service. After giving the horse what was left of the nuts and berries, Dale sent him south with the other horses. Then he followed his new companions into the Wilds.

CH 36

THE KISS AT THE WORLD'S END

A trek by foot through a pathless labyrinth of stubborn growth required a certain tenacity that few possessed. The dense forestry and the wall after wall of thorny, and at times poisonous, growth made some areas of the Wilds virtually impenetrable. And what paths they carved were not much better, often cutting along treacherous slopes. The cover of night, once their ally in the Lowers, had become their nemesis in the Wilds.

Aside from Charles Valkyrie, at one point or another, each member of the party found him or herself either caught or tripping on vines and dead foliage. Only the ranger seemed to know where to find sure footing. Leading the group, he had the benefit of the dim light cast by their only lantern illuminating his steps.

For Dale, walking through the Wilds with Selah did not feel so burdensome. As soon as he saw her, he was again captivated. Whatever happened on the Groveland Express had not worn off. But his feelings were torn. This journey for him started with Darius. His brother was Dale's singular thought as he rode out of Carnaval City, getting to the Ancile his only objective. Dale's commitment to finding Darius had muted any feelings he had for Selah. It was impossible for him to feel that strongly about two unrelated things at once.

He saw it—his heart for Selah. As they walked through the challenging terrain, he would extend a hand to help her over a stream or scale a steep rock. Each time she took it, it thrilled him. He saw all the evidence of his feelings but he was unable to give himself to them. To enjoy her company was unimaginable. He recognized the part of him that wanted to linger with her in the Wilds, and yet he wanted more than anything to get out of there, to be at the Ancile. The painstakingly slow pace frustrated him.

I need to find Darius. I need to know that he's okay.

Selah saw it in him—the troubled look, the surfacing elements of a man frantic inside. She understood that Dale feared for his brother, for his family, for his country.

Finally, they arrived at the borders of the Wilds Deep. Valkyrie recognized its borders by the line of trees leaning eastward. They leaned as if warding off trespassers tempted to venture further. The trees were in fact bent by the offshore winds from the World's End and lack of direct sunlight within the Deep. It was said that the Wilds Deep was more perilous than the Wilds themselves, but Valkyrie assured them the change of environment would be a welcome break. And he was right.

The air was temperate, lightly salted from the steady ocean breeze. More importantly, there was plenty of space, clearing after clearing between the pillars of the legendary evergreens. They were known appropriately as the Skywards. Skywards were not only the largest trees in the world, they were the oldest. They were as wide and as high as a castle tower or city building. Their far-reaching branches and translucent leaves at the top created a seamless canopy through which the moon cast a soft green glow. The forest bed, having never been touched by unfiltered sunlight, was carpeted in moss. Around the base of the trees grew fungi in a myriad of bright colors. It reminded Dale of a candy store.

"Maker be praised." Selah was especially awestruck. She ran her hand against the trunk of a Skyward. She stopped to take in the breeze. She raised her head with her eyes closed as if basking in the green-tinted moonlight. "This feels like a dream."

It was no wonder to her why the grandeur of the Wilds Deep was inspiration to so many druidic songs.

Beside a little stream known among rangers as Portis Creek, the group set up camp on an embankment sheltered from the wind.

"How much longer in these deep roads?" asked Alaric, dropping an armful of gathered wood.

"We just got here, Champ. You eager to move on already?"

"From here? Yes. This place…it's strange."

"A welcome break, is what it is. I suggest you take it while you can. Tomorrow, we set off in the early morning and don't stop until sunset. At least here we can move by day. If we keep pace, we should be in the borderlands in two nights."

They refilled their canteens, started a fire, and snacked on some rations Selah had prepared—bread, thin slices of cured pork, dried persimmons, a dollop of preserves, pickled eggs, and a wedge of cheese. Dale stuffed his mouth and chewed vigorously, breathing heavy through his nose. After a week of nuts and berries, the modest meal prepared by campfire was an epicurean delight.

When they had finished supper, they took turns bathing in the stream. Selah took her bath first behind a hedge of long grass. Alaric Linhelm kept an eye on the men.

"Keep your eyes abroad, gentlemen. This is no show tease."

Dale had to concentrate, keep his eyes fixed on the fire. Valkyrie however, was shameless in his voyeuristic attempts. He stole glances whenever he could. Alaric caught him and gave a stern warning. "Look that way again and you'll get a close look at my fist."

The men went in as a group after Selah got out of the stream. Dale found the stream to be tolerably cold. When they finished and were dressed, Selah approached Dale by the fire. She asked Dale to pull his shirt up so she could inspect his back.

"They've healed up quite nicely," she said, "your wounds."

"Yeah. But it itches like nothing else."

Valkyrie held up two little mushrooms. "Do you know that it's because of these little things that I'm stuck here with you?" he asked of Alaric Linhelm. In one hand, he held an elf ear. In the other, he held a karis truffle. "Can you tell the difference? No, you can't. You know why? Because there is none."

"Swindling is swindling."

"You want to talk about swindling, talk about the snake-oil salesmen who push this nonsense…"

They carried on bickering like they were old men with nothing else to do. Across from them, Selah sat beside Dale.

"So how far north do you plan to go?" Dale asked her.

"Valorcourt," Selah replied.

"Valorcourt? What for?"

"Alaric and I intend to make an appeal for peace to the duke."

"And why would he listen to you?"

"We're the only two Baleans represented in the Benesanti." She sighed. "It is difficult to believe that an appeal will accomplish anything. I cannot imagine the duke listening to us. But we must do something."

"What do you plan to say to him?"

"'Stop this nonsense, right now.'"

Dale smiled at her attempt at humor.

"I don't know," Selah continued. "I think Champion Linhelm will do most of the talking. We have plenty of time to think about it."

They sat in silence for a while. Dale noticed her saber.

"You know how to use that thing?" he asked as he tapped its handle.

"I wouldn't be carrying it otherwise."

"Never heard of a cleric that swings a sword."

"What about you? You seemed reluctant to use yours back there."

"Didn't get a chance to, thanks to the ranger. But you're right. I've used this thing enough as a Guardsman."

"Do you believe in the sanctity of life then?"

"Not sure what I believe. But yeah, I didn't much like killing anyone. Doesn't it bother you—all that death back there?"

"By the Maker's grace, I have never

> *"This place...it's strange."*

had to use the blade so I can't speak for taking a life. But death is nothing new to me. As a cleric, I've seen many depart this world for the next."

Alaric stood and walked a stone's throw away from camp.

"Where's he going?" asked Dale.

"To pray."

Across the fire, Charles Valkyrie was already fast asleep.

"Your brother—the one you seek at the Ancile—he's also a Republican Guard?" Selah asked in a hushed voice.

"Yeah. He was transferred around the time I was decommissioned."

"Older or younger?"

"Older."

"Are you close?"

Dale frowned. "Close enough to have our disagreements and still get along. You? You have any brothers or sisters?"

"I was an only child. What's your brother's name?"

"Darius."

"Well, Darius will be in my prayers. I can see you're burdened for him."

"I appreciate it."

Despite the sincerity of his words, Selah could sense Dale's skepticism.

"You don't believe in the Maker, do you?" she asked.

"Like I said, not sure what I believe about anything. I believe I'm here with you. And I believe I need to find Darius. That's about all I can manage right now."

Alaric returned to camp. As he walked past, he said, "You two should get some sleep."

"I would, but it'll be the end of me if I fall asleep with wet hair," Selah replied. "Can't afford a cold while trekking the Wilds, can I?"

"You won't fare any better fatigued. Get some rest."

Alaric Linhelm lay down next to the fire and crossed his arms. In a matter of seconds, he was snoring.

"Incredible," said Dale.

"What's that?"

"How he can fall asleep like that. Guess it's true. A clear conscience is the best nightcap."

"And how's your conscience?"

"I'll keep you company until your hair dries."

They sat quietly listening to the popping of the campfire. In the background, they could hear the distant roar of the ocean. Dale looked up at the glowing ceiling of leaves. There was a full moon out. A harvest moon, hidden somewhere beyond the veil. The scent of the salted air made him miss home. He wished he had a smoke.

"You know, I'm glad that kid pickpocketed me," he then said.

"Oh? And why's that?"

"When I first saw you on the Groveland Express, the day I came into the city from Pharundelle, I thought you were the most beautiful girl I'd ever seen. In fact, the whole ride from Lumarion, I was trying to come up with some clever way to talk to you. But nothing came to mind. And when I got off that train, I thought that was the end of it. I'd never see you again. Then that kid stole my coin purse and…" Dale glanced at Selah and couldn't ignore her expression. With every word, she appeared to grow increasingly dejected. For weeks he had fantasized about telling her exactly how he felt. He imagined many scenarios, but her dejection was not one of them. "I'm sorry, is this inappropriate?"

"No," Selah replied, trying to perk up. "I'm sorry. No, it's not inappropriate. It's just—"

"Is it because you're a cleric?"

"Don't be absurd. We're encouraged to exercise temperance, obviously, but that doesn't mean we're forbidden from romantic relationships."

"Is that what this is? A bit forward of you, don't you think, Prioress?"

She smiled. Selah had a look that was both vexed and flattered. "It upsets me because I'm flattered that you find me attractive."

"I don't get it."

"We hardly know each other. And you just think I'm a pretty face. That's it. I shouldn't be thrilled by that. So it's disappointing that I am."

"I can always take it back."

"No, you can't." She laughed.

Dale looked at her and thought she looked more beautiful right then than he had ever seen her. "In that case, why don't you tell me about yourself?"

"And what, exactly, is it that you want to know?"

"Anything. Everything. Where did you grow up? What were your parents like? Did you always want to become a cleric or did you lose a bet?"

"I don't gamble. I grew up all over, from Valorcourt to Trinsington to Lumarion. As for my parents, I don't know much about my father and I lost my mother when I was young. I was sent to the temple orphanage under the care of the College of Sisters. When I turned sixteen, I felt that it was my calling to go into service of the order that looked after me. So here I am. Satisfied?"

"How did you lose your mother?"

Selah's shoulders curled and she looked away.

"She was killed."

Despite his piqued curiosity, Dale could tell by Selah's curt reply, bare of an explanation, that she did not want to talk about it. Fearing her precipitous withdrawal from their conversation, Dale quickly volunteered his own past. "I never knew my mother. She died on the delivery table while giving birth to me. From what I hear, she was a good woman. And my father passed away a little less than two years ago from heart failure. I was still on tour so I didn't get to say goodbye."

"I'm sorry."

Dale shrugged. "We weren't very close. I mean, I know he loved us and everything, but he was distant. Sad."

Selah studied Dale under the soft light. "The apple doesn't fall far from the tree, does it? Seems we share that much. A bit of sorrow in our story."

"Yeah." Dale smirked. Returning her gaze, he said, "See? I feel like we know each other a little better now and I still think you're beautiful."

She shook her head, smiling, and finally surrendered. "Thank you."

"You're welcome."

Then she abruptly stood, stretched, and dusted off her bottom.

"It's quite amazing, isn't it?" she asked, looking up at the green ceiling above. "All of this. Strange, really. Never could have imagined a place like this actually existed."

"Yeah. It is pretty amazing."

A thin layer of fog-like dust had settled in around them.

"You ever see the World's End?" she asked, looking down at Dale with a glint in her eye.

"Only on a map."

"It's a terrible shame to be so close and not see it." Her voice had now taken on a playful tone.

"Yeah, it is."

"Shall we, then?"

"What, you want to go see it?"

Selah nodded with an intrepid smile.

"Now?"

"My hair's still wet."

Dale shrugged. "Okay."

With an eye on Alaric, they quietly climbed the embankment like mischievous children. A ten-minute stroll through columns of Skywards, and the canopy above showed signs of thinning. Then the sky opened up. A dark blue sky sprinkled with stars. A haze had settled on the ground of the forest like morning mist. The ocean grew louder.

"Come on!" said Selah, taking Dale by the hand.

They ran against the breeze and stopped just shy of the cliff's edge. Some two hundred feet down the ocean lashed into the base of the cliff. They stood, side by side in silence, still holding hands. Selah was beaming. At the World's End, they were children again—vulnerable and free, without pretense or doubt. And the world was as it should be.

"Did you know, according to the scriptures, humanity was born of the Maker's kiss?" Selah asked.

Dale gave her hand a gentle tug. She looked at him and their eyes locked. His heart racing, he leaned over slowly enough to give her time to pull away. She didn't. She closed her eyes and they kissed.

CH 37

THE SERMON IN THE MUD

On their walk back, Dale and Selah noticed that the fog had grown thicker. They thought nothing of it until the earth below their feet began to shift.

"The ground is moving," said Selah. "You feel it too?"

When they arrived back at camp, they found Valkyrie and Alaric awake, and busily moving about. The fire was put out and the camp packed up. Their eyes were wide and their pupils dilated. Alaric looked

panicked. And Valkyrie stood, just staring at his hands.

"Where were you?" Alaric barked at Selah.

"We went to see the World's End," Selah replied. "What's wrong?"

"I'm sorry," Valkyrie replied, looking up. "It's the spores. Of all the luck."

"What spores?"

"The kind that make you go mad. Grab your things. The longer we stay… the longer we stay…wait, did I just say that?" Valkyrie shook his head and started rubbing his eyes. "Hurry! I'm starting to see things."

"Me too," said Selah.

Dale looked at her and saw a halo radiating from her skin. He was beginning to feel dizzy. As he gathered his things, it felt as if time had slowed. His short-term memory became spotty and everything felt like a disconnected set of snapshots.

Ever since entering the Wilds Deep, they had been exposed to its perils. The effects of the spores were so subtle that they had gone undetected until it was too late. If Valkyrie had not been there to guide them, the party would not have known to run back into the Wilds. Alaric lumbered behind Valkyrie with his eyes fixed on his heels. Selah and Dale trailed close behind. Once they passed the east-leaning trees, the mist was thin. They kept running until Alaric was convinced the vines were swallowing him up.

"Maker save us! We've fallen under a curse!" he cried.

Then he collapsed where he stood and fell unconscious.

Valkyrie stopped and looked up into the exposed sky. He mumbled like a madman as if trying to solve some algorithmic equation.

"Are we safe?" asked Dale, immediately wondering if the question had escaped his lips. When no one replied, he resolved he'd only thought it. His legs were heavy. So were his eyelids. He looked at Selah. She was already asleep. It was the last thing he saw, the last thing he remembered when he woke up the next morning.

Everyone else was still lying awkwardly where they fell on a bed of wild vegetation. Valkyrie had fallen asleep sitting up, with his legs crossed in front of him and his head hanging over his lap.

The first to rise, Dale began to rustle the others awake. Slowly, everyone came to. They were groggy as if coming out of a drug-induced slumber. Even awake, they moved about in a daze. They managed to eat their morning rations. As their minds cleared, they tried to understand the previous night's experience.

"So what happened?" asked Dale.

"The toxic mist," Valkyrie replied. "There's a reason why they say the Wilds Deep is more treacherous than the Wilds. Once a month, all those mushrooms release their poisonous spores. No way of knowing exactly when. Some luck we have to camp on that day. Any longer and it would've been the end of us. Thank the Champ he took a piss when he did."

Selah shot Alaric a bemused look.

"I woke up to relieve myself and felt inebriated," the ex-templar explained. "Something I'm sensitive to since I've not imbibed a drop since taking my oath. I assumed it was the result of our rations so I woke the ranger."

As the talk continued, Dale sat silently, wondering if the kiss had been poison induced. He remembered that before telling Selah how he felt about her, he had not given it any thought. It just flowed out of his mouth. There were no nerves, no second-guessing. He had been strangely calm. The more Dale thought about it, the more convinced he became that he had not been acting himself the night before. He looked over at Selah to see if there were any signs from her. She was fixed on Valkyrie and Alaric's talk about the mushrooms.

"Strange night, huh?" Dale asked, fishing for a sign.

"Yes, very."

There was no inflection in Selah's

voice. No twinkle in the eye. Nothing to indicate that anything lingered from what had happened the night before. She was back to her guarded, distant self—the proper, disciplined cleric. Even though Selah gave Dale no encouragement to pursue it, he could not let it lie in suspended ambiguity.

"About what happened last night, at the World's End—"

"The spores," said Selah. "Clearly I wasn't myself. None of us were."

And that was that. There was nothing more to discuss. "Right, that's what I thought. Glad we could clear that up."

Whatever it was, whatever it could have been had come to an abrupt end before it started. *Good*, thought Dale. *I've got to get to Darius. Those mushrooms made me stupid. What were you thinking anyway? There's no time to be playing with a girl in the woods.*

In the ensuing days, Dale kept a distance from Selah. He occupied himself with the thought of getting to Darius. He stuck close to the ranger, watching and learning. Charles Valkyrie's vast and detailed knowledge of the Wilds impressed Dale. Valkyrie knew by sight, which fruits were edible, which were not. He knew which plants were poisonous and which were useful for different medicinal purposes. Dale asked him questions about shelter, plotting a course, how to find water, and how to trap game. With nothing else to do but walk, Valkyrie eagerly instructed his new apprentice. Without Valkyrie, the party would have been hopelessly lost, starved, and dangerously exposed to the elements.

"How long you been doing this?" asked Dale.

"Living in the Wilds? About ten years," Valkyrie replied.

"Must be freeing. No accountability or obligations, no attachments to anything or anyone."

"That's the very definition of loneliness, kid. When no one expects anything of you, you've done it—you're completely alone."

"Doesn't sound so bad."

Valkyrie stopped as they came to a steep, muddy incline. "It's no way to live. Trust me." Then he looked back at Selah and Alaric. "Get your boots strapped in tight. It's going to get messy."

As they labored up the trail, Valkyrie continued. "The way I see it, we're social creatures. We're meant to be dependent. Without other people, it's easy to lose your grip on reality. Why do you think prisons use prolonged isolation as a form of punishment? It's mental subjugation. People like me, we're either looking for something or running from something."

Dale heard a piece of himself in the statement. He didn't like what he heard. When he beat up Marcus Addy, his father had told him that he should have run. When things got to where he couldn't deal with it anymore, Dale had left the Republican Guard. And back in Carnaval City, he had forfeited his childhood dreams of sailing the Amaranthian Sea to settle on a life at the breaker.

"And what are you running from, ranger?" asked Alaric, having eavesdropped on their conversation. "What do you seek?"

Valkyrie chuckled. "It doesn't matter. Because I already know that whatever I look for, I'm never going to find it. And whatever you run from, it'll eventually catch up to you. It always does."

"Perhaps you're looking for the wrong thing," said Alaric.

"Perhaps. Or perhaps life is a ruse. A losing game. And the sooner we understand that, the sooner we can learn to cope."

"The wisdom of a cynic is despair," said Alaric. "But hope comes from the Maker."

"The Maker." Valkyrie snickered. "Where is this *Maker* now? Where has he been all these years of suffering?"

"The world is not so simple. You know this."

"I also know that there is no Maker. And thus, with him no hope."

"You can dismiss the existence of God. You've worked to rid yourself of your need for him. But for those of whom you speak—the suffering—hope is all they have. They believe there is something greater, someone who will deliver them. This resilient hope, the will to live, speaks of something beyond what we see."

"It's called instinct. Look, if God exists, he's negligent at best, cruel at worst. And until he can prove otherwise, the world and its history attests to that fact."

"Those sound like the words of a Mystic spurned by the Maker. Are you sure your professed atheism is not in reality the tantrum of a child who has not gotten his way?"

Valkyrie laughed. "I should've known better than to bait a templar into a theological discussion. I assure you, Champ, the inability to see the Maker or hear his voice is no act. It requires far less of me to believe tales of magic and dancing fairies than to believe all that nonsense."

"I can see you are a man determined. Only a fool keeps pushing something that cannot be moved. And I am no fool."

Dale walked and listened. With all he had been through, he was in no mood to comment on the Maker. Merely listening got him annoyed. He fell back a ways so he would not have to listen to the discussion. A few paces back, Dale journeyed with his thoughts as mired as his steps. If there was a Maker, he had some explaining to do—not only for what had transpired in the last twenty-four hours, but also for all that led up to his flight out of Carnaval City. A few more steps and his mind flooded with thoughts of Darius. All along the journey, Dale had been telling himself, *Darius would have gotten out. When things got bad, he would have led a few men out of the Ancile before it fell.*

Without much care about what he did or did not believe, and not knowing to whom he was talking, Dale prayed.

Please, let Darius be alive.

№ 04

CH 38

THE SAD BOY AND THE SONGSTRESS

In a matter of days, the Balean assault on Carnaval City had decisively turned into an occupation.

The Steam Powered Electric Generator was shut down, which effectively cut off all communication. As the initial assault bore down on the city from the northwest, the City Guards could not warn the other parts of the city. The severing of communication along with the aerial assault made for an attack of overwhelming speed. Within the first few hours, most of the City Guards had been neutralized. With no forewarning, they were ill-prepared to defend themselves, let alone mount any sort of counter-attack. Most were killed in the first wave of the assault. The survivors abandoned their positions and disappeared into the city. Once the city was secured, order was swiftly restored. By the time news reached Pharundelle, Carnaval City was a garrisoned Balean foothold.

Balean generals and Shaldea groups victoriously marched their troops through the city's main streets, the citizens forced to bear witness. Because of the speed of the invasion, much of the city remained intact. There were only a few buildings left smoldering. The Spegen was restored as soon as Balean officials were given full access to the switchboard stations. Speakers were installed throughout the city to blare daily announcements and propaganda. The first week, a curfew was instituted. A few businesses were eventually re-opened, mostly for the pleasure of the occupying forces. The entire Waterfront District, including Dale's breaker, was taken for use by the Royal Balean Navy. The occupying forces were strategically stationed throughout the city. By week's end, the transition from war to governance was well underway.

First priority was restoring the rule of law. Looters were shot on sight. Aside from a handful of incidents, the threat of being shot was an effective deterrent to would-be opportunists. Ruthless as they were, to their credit, the Balean occupiers were no hypocrites. Their law did not exclude them. Four Balean soldiers found guilty of raping a young woman during the assault on the city were hanged. The judgment and sentencing came swiftly. The hanging was public. The bodies were left on display for three days. As intended, it evoked both terror and respect from the locals.

The only thing the Balean occupation failed to anticipate was a threat to their fragile alliance with the Shaldea that came in the form of the Emmainite community living in Carnaval City.

With the invasion aided by the Shaldea, the city's Emmainite diaspora went from being a marginalized minority community to the ruling party overnight. They came out into the streets to enjoy their newfound status. Some of the suppressed frustrations were vented. Abuses occurred under the watch of, and at times assisted by, the Shaldean fighters. Indiscriminate in their commitment to the law, however, the Balean occupation was forced to intervene and subsequently execute some Emmainites. This would have led to an extraneous uprising had the Shaldea not quickly intervened. Aware that they could not afford a conflict with the Kingdom of Bale, the Shaldea responded by bringing their people under control and justly punishing them themselves in accordance to Balean law.

In the midst of this governing transition, the temple sanctuary became the largest of the many makeshift refugee camps throughout the city for displaced residents who flooded in from the outlying villages. These villages had either been sacked or consumed for use as military outposts.

For weeks, Mosaic waited in the sanctuary for news of her parents. She passed the days scouring boards set up as communication centers for missing persons. Her hope never waned. One afternoon, after posting yet another note, she left the temple to comb the city. The streets were covered in crystal pools from sporadic rain. The sky was a misty gray. She made her way down to the waterfront, where she stopped at the bakery. The doors stood open. The inside was bare.

The clouds thundered. It began to drizzle. Mosaic went inside to take shelter from the rain. The furnishings were gone, and the shelves and cupboards were barren. Spiking inflation and widespread rumors of food shortages made it the most sought-after commodity.

Walking through the kitchen, Mosaic saw her mother's apron left trampled on the floor. She picked it up, dusted it off, and slipped it on. On the counter, she saw a trace layer of flour where dough was dusted and kneaded daily. She ran her fingers through it. Then she wept.

There was a rapping on the window. Mosaic quickly wiped her eyes, leaving the tip of her nose and cheeks dusted with flour.

"Mosaic? Is that you?"

She looked up. "Sebastian?"

Peering in was her friend, the bespectacled literary elitist. "I thought it was you!" He was with three others—two men and a woman she did not recognize.

Mosaic rushed out and gave him a long hug.

"How are you?" Sebastian asked.

Mosaic tried a smile between her tears. "It's good to see a familiar face."

"Where are you staying?"

"The temple."

Sebastian shook his head. "Listen, those camps, they're there to monitor you, you know that, right?"

"Really?"

"From what I hear, for every ten refugees, there's one Balean mole. Temple or not, they're running the show. Not the Benesanti. If you want, you're welcome to stay with us. We got a little place near Trivelka Square."

"Thanks but I'm waiting to hear from my folks."

"Yeah. I heard about Hoche." With a grim expression, Sebastian then asked, "You know they got Terry, right? That night at the Flora Crystal?"

"What do you mean 'they got Terry'?" Mosaic asked in alarm.

"They killed him."

Mosaic put her hand to her mouth.

"They fired into the crowd," Sebastian continued. "We rushed some soldiers that were beating a city guard to death, so they just shot at us." He paused and grit his teeth. "They shot Terry. They killed him."

Mosaic's eyes began to well. "What about Rudy? Where's Rudy?"

"I don't know." He glanced over his shoulder, scanning the quiet streets. "I have to go. Look, a few of us are getting together later this week. You should come join us."

"I'd like that."

"Good. Meet me at the dry fountain in Trivelka Square on the Fifth Day. Sixth hour of the night, sharp."

"That's just before curfew."

Sebastian hushed her. "Sixth hour. Fifth Day. Got it?"

Mosaic nodded.

"And don't mention it to anyone else. Especially no one at the temple. I'll talk to you soon."

Then he jogged back into the rain to his waiting companions. The four walked swiftly around the corner. When they were out of sight, a hooded figure emerged from within the shadows of the adjacent alley. He entered the bakery unnoticed.

"Bad idea."

Mosaic darted around to see Sparrow standing just inside.

"Oh my God, you scared me. Where'd you come from? How long have you been standing there?"

"You get caught past curfew, they'll jail you."

"Where's Dale?"

"The last I saw, he was on a horse headed for the Ancile."

She gripped her apron and closed her eyes. "Is he okay?"

"I don't know. But he was on a good horse and it was early. The Shaldea and the Baleans wouldn't worry themselves with one scurrying soul."

Mosaic opened her eyes. She stared at Sparrow for a beat, to see if he was telling the truth. Comforted, Mosaic walked back into the bakery. As she walked past Sparrow, she asked, "Why are you here?"

"Don't go to that meeting in Trivelka Square. Your friend doesn't know what he's doing."

"What is he doing?"

"They're organizing a resistance. But they are just going to get themselves killed. And you with them, if you go."

"How do you know all this? *Why* do you know this? And why do you care?"

Sparrow walked up close to Mosaic so she could clearly look into his eyes. When he saw that he had her full attention, he said sternly, "Go back to the temple, Mosaic."

She paused, both intimidated and intrigued. Then with equal gravity in her voice, she replied, "I don't have an umbrella."

Sparrow turned around. At the door of the bakery, he pulled the hood of his jacket over his head, cinched his collar, and ran out into the rain. Mosaic walked over to the front window and watched him sprint across the street and disappear around the corner.

"Okay, bye," she muttered to herself.

She went behind the counter and opened random drawers, looking for nothing in particular. In the glass of the emptied display counter, Mosaic saw a reflection of herself. Still wearing her mother's apron and with her hair pinned up, she saw that her face was smudged with flour. As she leaned close to get a clear picture, she thought, *He could've said something.* After wiping the flour off, Mosaic took another look to make sure she got all of it. Through the display counter, she saw Sparrow standing on the other side. She darted up to see him holding a red umbrella.

"Let's go," he said, standing in the threshold.

"Where'd you get that? Did you steal that?"

"We're going to the temple."

"You're coming with me?"

Sparrow nodded.

Mosaic walked around the counter and under the red umbrella. They set off shoulder to shoulder for the Central District. It wasn't more than two blocks before Mosaic broke the silence.

"So did Dale put you up to this?"

"Yes."

"Is your name really Sparrow?"

"No."

"What's your name?"

"Jūng-geun."

"So why does Dale call you Sparrow?"

"I don't know. He's always called me that."

Mosaic stopped dead in her tracks. "You're the sad boy! From Azuretown! I remember you! You're Dale's friend from when you guys were little."

"Keep walking."

They rounded a corner after a few more blocks.

"You don't like to talk much, do you?" asked Mosaic.

After a few more steps, Sparrow replied, "You ask a lot of questions."

Mosaic bridled at the comment but made no retort. They were passing Balean soldiers standing post at a checkpoint. Every few blocks there seemed to be a checkpoint, and soldiers on the move, patrolling in between. The occupying presence was stifling.

When they reached the temple's West Gate, the templar on post asked them for their papers. He gave an obligatory glance at the documents, not thorough enough to distinguish Mosaic's authentic papers from the forged ones Sparrow presented. They passed through the West Gate and started up the gray marble steps to the main sanctuary's double doors.

"I didn't know you were staying here too."

"I'm not."

Mosaic was going to inquire further but held her tongue on account of his last comment.

They entered the vestibule where the watchman cleric greeted them. Once she had confirmed that they were not in possession of any weapons, she sprinkled them with myrrh and gave them a blessing.

Just inside the main sanctuary, Sparrow handed Mosaic the umbrella. "Keep it." And just before leaving her, he grabbed her by the shoulders. "Mosaic, listen to me. I don't know when I'll be able to check on you again. Do not leave the temple. Don't get mixed up with anyone. Mind your own business, and stay alive. Okay?"

"Okay."

With Mosaic looking on, Sparrow walked toward the altar at the front of the sanctuary. There, he knelt down. A minute later, a man in common merchants' attire walked over and knelt down beside him. With his head cast down as if praying, he whispered, "You are late."

A PROMISE KEPT

Magog was in disguise. He had applied make-up to add some tone to his pale complexion and cover parts of his facial tattoo that weren't hidden below an artificial black beard. In the inconspicuous attire of a common merchant, he looked like any number of the refugee men.

Magog took a peek back to see if Mosaic was still watching. Seeing that she had moved along, he peered sideways at Sparrow. With his head still bowed at the altar he said, "Against my better judgment, I granted you permission to warn your friend. The matter was settled when your friend was warned. Who is *she?*"

Sparrow didn't respond. Magog turned his head back toward the floor. "Are you forgetting who you are?"

The Samaeli were the keepers of night, the great equalizers—an organization, the origin of which was veiled in mystery. It was as if they had no beginning, as if they had always been. They were the last line, the final option. When all else failed to reset the balance of power, then and only then were the Samaeli summoned. They did not, therefore, have the luxury of morality, to struggle with "right and wrong." Ideals, values, they were all laid at the feet of what needed to be done. They were pragmatists who dealt in absolutes, each sworn member unwavering in his commitment to his calling. Disciplined like machines.

Sparrow knew this well. It was not long after he had been initiated that Master T'varche was killed—assassinated by the very organization he'd sworn allegiance to. When in his rage Sparrow sought revenge, it was Magog who had explained to him that this was the nature of the Samaeli and that Aleksander T'varche had welcomed his fate. Having proved himself an adept pupil, it was against this backdrop that Magog had extended the invitation to Sparrow to become the Samaeli's hand of judgment. And when Sparrow accepted, he knew exactly what he would become— what he was. Vengian.

Magog rose to his feet and hovered over him.

"Are you forgetting who you are?" he repeated.

Sparrow stood and met his glare. They postured up like two fighting dogs before the altar, out of touch with fear, unfamiliar with retreat. Sparrow knew that his long time co-conspirator had no qualms about killing him. Though he was no Vengian, he was just as capable. In the blink of an eye, he would set aside years of close partnership. Sparrow had seen Magog do it before. He himself as the Vengian had done it.

"No," he finally replied.

Though unsatisfied and still suspicious, Magog dropped the matter by proceeding. "Meet me in the south transept when you're ready." Then he disappeared into the refugee camp.

Sparrow noticed Magog had left a satchel where he'd been kneeling. Sparrow grabbed it and walked briskly into the washroom.

Sparrow put on the brown, templar squire uniform he found in the satchel. Then he went to join Magog in the south transept. They walked down a dimly lit corridor to the Bene-seneschal's study. There was a single squire posted at the door.

"Good evening, brother," he said, as they approached.

"Is the Bene-seneschal in?" asked Magog.

"He is, but I'm afraid he's not taking any visitors at the moment. Is there something I can do for you?"

"As a matter of fact, there is."

Magog lunged forward with a poison-laced needle between his fingers. Before the squire could react, the needle was in his jugular. His eyeballs rolled back as he extended an arm to grip Magog's outer garment. When he collapsed to the floor, the Vengian caught him and gingerly laid his body down.

Magog knocked. There was no reply. He knocked again.

"What is it?" a voice called from within.

Magog opened the door and entered alone.

"Gaius, I told you I don't want to be disturbed…who are you? Where's Gaius?"

From his one encounter all those years ago in that desert outpost of a town, Magog recognized him. Yusef Naskerazim. There were wrinkles where there was once smooth skin. The hair had whitened, and the years out of the desert sun had softened his complexion. His overall look was quite a departure from the once feral, black-bearded *Rajeth* of the Shaldean Riders, but the eyes were the same. And in his eyes, Magog saw that he too was recognized.

"Bene-seneschal, I have come a great distance to see you," said Magog, exposing his silver teeth in a satisfied smile.

As he stepped forward, Magog took note of the chessboard in the corner. The white bishop was indeed sitting on the square, *g2*, just as the note Sparrow had retrieved from Fairchild's bedchamber had indicated.

"My name is Magog Siberion." He removed the beard. "I am the face of an organization your people refer to as the *Zaal'mavorte*." The blood-red tattoo of the palm over his mouth confirmed for Yusef what he was already dreading.

Magog flung a dart. Like the squire, Yusef had no time to react. He didn't know what was happening. The abrupt movement startled him. With a jolt, he grabbed the armrests of his chair. Feeling the sting

dart buried there.

"Soon, you will be dead." Magog started around the desk toward Yusef. Yusef began to heave for air. His eyes, wide and desperate, followed Magog around the desk. Magog came alongside him and whispered into his ear. "I warned you that I would undermine all who would profit from this war. I warned you and your Shaldea. How strange it is to see you now, wearing the sacred adornments of the Benesanti. Oh, how far you've come from the days of riding the Saracen as your people's deliverer. If they could see you now—working with Enlil Fairchild in the guise of the cloth. The irony!" Magog snickered. After removing the dart from Yusef Naskerazim's chest, Magog stepped toward the door.

Unable to resist, he stopped. Once more, he turned to Yusef who was slumped back in his chair. His head was hanging to the side. The eyes were open but Magog could not be sure whether Yusef was still there. His breaths were shallow. They could have been as much a result of lingering reflexes as they were living breaths.

"You asked for justice, Mister Naskerazim. This world—Parabolis—this is perfect justice: that we, the unjust, are condemned to live an unjust existence. You are no more innocent than this Republic you've cursed. And that you've crawled into the heart of it to die here is fitting. Go now, naked before your Maker, and be

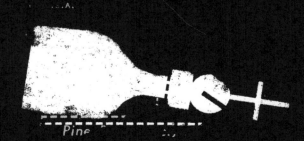

CH 40

LIVING FOREST

A day later than Valkyrie had predicted, they were in the borderlands. The region was noticeably cooler. The prevailing mist they had grown accustomed to since traveling along the coast seemed to linger deeper into the day. The climate changed, but the severity of the terrain remained the same. The dense forestry and the rugged topography of the Wilds extended to the borderlands.

A mile from the Ancile, Valkyrie stopped and held his hand up.

"Hold it," he whispered.

Everyone froze.

"What is it?" asked Alaric.

Valkyrie slowly crouched down and parted the fern at his feet. He fingered what appeared to be an iron mechanism. There was a snap. A noosed rope went flying up into the air.

He looked back at the others. "We're not alone."

Then they heard a voice not far off in the distance. "Damn right ye not!"

Alaric, Selah, and Dale all drew their swords and carefully stepped toward the voice. Valkyrie drew his bow and aimed an arrow toward heavy foliage over their shoulders.

"Drop ye weapons."

"Like hell," Valkyrie said, still not seeing who spoke.

"Ye got twenty rifles trained on ye, sandworm. If yon arrow flies, the sound of rifle fire will be the last thing ye hear."

Selah and Alaric lowered their weapons. Dale followed suit.

"We are emissaries from the Holy Order of the Benesanti," said Alaric.

"Then tell yon Shaldean companion to lower his aim lest ye all suffer for it."

"Charles?"

The ranger reluctantly eased the tension on his bow and dropped the arrow. The forest immediately came alive around them. Not five feet from where they stood, shrubs levitated from the earth on the helmets of soldiers. Like paper cutouts, some of the vegetation strolled out from the dense foliage. Men dressed in ghillie suits. Even their faces were caked over with mud. There were only ten of them, but they were each armed with rifles. The squad leader had in his hand a large war hammer. As he walked past, Dale noticed the weathered red of a Republican Guard's uniform below his camouflage.

"What brings ye this way?" asked the squad leader, propping his hammer over his shoulder.

"We're looking for safe passage," Valkyrie tried, before he was cut off.

"Nay was I addressing ye, sandworm."

The squad leader looked at Alaric and the sword at his feet. "By what order of business have ye been sent into these Wilds, templar?"

"To escort this cleric to Valorcourt and make an appeal for peace," Alaric replied.

"Templar, my ass," said another soldier. "He sounds Balean. Looks like we got ourselves some coalition spies."

The squad leader then began eyeing Selah.

"If nay ye be a templar, then mayhap yon lass nay be a cleric. In which case, a party we be having tonight with her."

The other soldiers hooted and hollered.

"That's a cleric of the Benesanti you're talking about, soldier," said Dale.

"Aye? And as far as I be concerned, she's got a hole that needs a plugging which I intend—"

Before he could finish, Dale jumped forward and punched him in the mouth.

The squad leader stumbled to the ground. Two of his comrades grabbed Dale from behind and kicked the back of his knees. The others raised their rifles and fixed them on Alaric and Valkyrie.

The squad leader spat out some blood. He got to his feet and bellowed a crazed laugh. Looking at Dale with a bloody smile, he cast his hammer aside, and instructed his men, "Let him go. I like this one."

"You're wearing the uniform of a Republican Guard," said Dale. "If they're yours, then you're in violation of the Guard's code of conduct, *Sergeant*."

"Am I?" The squad leader punched Dale in the stomach. Dale fell to his knees. Leaning down, the squad leader then mocked him. "How about now, chatterbox? Am I still in violation?"

He took a step back to drive his heel into Dale's face. Just as he took a big step forward, the squad leader was sent flying from a push kick delivered in his flank. Standing there was his commanding officer with a reconnaissance detachment of six men.

"You got a reason for beating on my kid brother, Sergeant Bixby?" asked Major Darius Sunday.

The sergeant scrambled to his feet. With a dumbfounded expression, he muttered, "Bloody hell, sir. Nay did I know—"

"Nobody hits my brother but me, is that clear?"

"Aye, sir."

Dale jumped to his feet and hugged Darius. With an embarrassed chuckle, Darius reluctantly hugged Dale back. With his head on Darius' shoulder, Dale remembered where he was, the people around him and quickly pulled back.

Darius with his hand on Dale's shoulder gave the men orders. "Take the sandworm and get your men back to camp."

"Aye, sir."

"Hey, wait. Dare, he's with us. Charles is a good guy," Dale tried on behalf of Valkyrie.

"The Shaldean? He's with you?"

"He's no Shaldea. He's a ranger."

"So?"

"He killed Balean scouts to save me. I owe him," Dale pleaded.

"Look, we'll get this all sorted out when we get back to camp," Darius replied. To assure him, he instructed the sergeant not to mistreat him. Valkyrie was bound with rope and led onto an unmarked trail with the squad. Darius looked at Dale. "You all right?"

"I'm fine. Dare, you got to let Charles go. You can't leave him with *that* guy."

"He's going to follow orders. Don't worry about him. What are you doing here, anyway?"

"I came to find you."

"What the hell for?"

"I don't know. We heard the Ancile was taken. The wires were down, so I couldn't call."

"*You* wanted to check up on *me?*"

Darius shook his head and looked at his kid brother. Feeling as if he might cry, he wrapped his arm around Dale in a semi-headlock. "It's damn good to see you. Uncle Turkish and everyone else okay?"

"I don't know," Dale replied. "Carnaval City's gone."

"So is the country."

"Pharundelle?"

"An unconditional surrender just a few days after the initial attack. Quickest in history. I'm guessing they lost their will when they saw those flying ships. I don't blame them."

"But if Pharundelle surrendered, what're you guys doing here?"

"No one said *we* had to take it lying down." Darius then gave Alaric and Selah a wary look. "What's going on with them?"

"Oh, right. Sorry. These are my friends. That's Alaric Linhelm of the Vail Templar and Prioress Selah Evenford."

"You'll forgive my men if they're a bit suspicious of wanderers. We meant the Holy Order no disrespect. Major Darius Sunday."

"Well met, Major," said Alaric.

"You *are* Balean, then?"

"Our allegiance is to the Holy Order of the Benesanti."

"That wasn't my question."

"Yes. By birth, we are Balean."

"What brings you this way?"

"We are on a mission to Valorcourt. We intend to appeal to the duke for an immediate and unconditional withdrawal of his forces."

Darius scoffed. "Good luck with that." Looking back at his recon team, Darius said, "Let's get moving, boys. Sir Linhelm, Prioress, if you'll come with us."

Darius' recon team led them through the growth along the unmarked trail. As they walked, Dale asked Darius, "Where'd you find that asshole anyway?"

"Who? Bixby? He's not so bad. Definitely the kind of guy you want on your team when you go into a fight. He's a Berserker."

"That explains a lot."

The Berserkers were the nomadic tribesmen of the Hesperian Highlands, known for their passion for a brawl, brute strength, and heroism on the battlefield.

"We lost a lot of good men during the invasion. We're thankful for the ones we have."

"I'm sorry I wasn't there with you guys."

"I'm not. In fact, you shouldn't even be here now. We'll get you fed and rested. Tomorrow morning, I'm sending you back."

"Like hell you are."

"We need to get word to Brookhaven."

"Send a runner. I'm here to watch your back."

Darius shot his brother a sideways glance then shook his head. "Stubborn shit."

CH 41

THE GUERRILLA RESISTANCE

The makeshift camp was a scantily supplied gathering point for a Republican Guard platoon sewn together from survivors of various battalions. In the camp, there were also a handful of irregulars—armed civilians and scattered members of self-appointed militia who were forced to flee from their homes in nearby villages.

"This everyone?" asked Dale.

"Pretty much."

"No reinforcements?"

"Other than the occasional irregulars, no. Everyone's rallying in Brookhaven. We heard they've set up a provisional government down there under some senator. Can you believe it?"

A young soldier approached Darius. "We're all prepped, sir."

"Good. Be ready to move out by midnight. Oh, and Mills, this is my kid-brother, Dale."

"Pleasure to meet you, Dale."

Dale saw by the bars on his collar that the soldier was the same rank as he had been when he left the Republican Guard—a lieutenant. Mills' face was ashen but his eyes had a fire in them. That fire had been long extinguished in Dale. Looking into those eyes, Dale envied this lieutenant.

"Get the templar and cleric situated, will you?" Darius instructed. "The sandworm, too. Post a guard and keep Bixby away from him."

"Yes, sir."

Darius then showed Dale into the tent that served as their command center.

"So you're in charge?" asked Dale.

"The colonel was killed in the assault," he explained. "We're keeping rank, but we're not under the flag anymore. You're looking at the first resistance."

"How many, exactly?"

"Twenty-four riflemen and twenty-five light infantry."

"That's a full platoon."

"Forty-nine able-bodied men willing to fight on."

"Fifty," Dale replied, gripping his sword.

"We'll see about that. Lemme see that thing."

Dale drew his modified sword and handed it to Darius.

"The hell you do to it? Feels light. Incredible balance." Darius then took his own standard steel sword and offered it to Dale in exchange. "Here, you can have mine."

"Nice try. Give it back."

"You gotta introduce me to the smith who did this."

Dale started to tell Darius about Sparrow. The talk of the sword quickly transitioned to all the strange events leading up to the invasion. Dale told him everything: The Carousel Rogues, being reunited with his childhood friend, the warning, the inquisition. If it was anyone but Dale telling him, Darius would not have believed half of what he heard. Dale went on to tell him about his flight out of the city, how, as he rode out, he saw the skyships.

Then Darius told Dale of the assault on the Ancile. How the skyships had rolled over them. As they tried to make sense of what they were seeing, the Shaldean Riders were already at the gate, followed closely by an overwhelming Balean ground force. He explained how he and his men barely escaped, fleeing into the Wilds—how they'd been on the run for a week before finally regrouping. After setting up a camp, they began to launch attacks.

"Guerrilla warfare. Hit and run. We use the Wilds as cover and attack patrols when we can, disrupt supply lines. But this, this is going to be our biggest operation yet," he added, holding up a large leaf.

"It's better to be the head of a hare than the tail of a tiger."

It was part of a crude diagram made up of stones, twigs, and leaves. They marked the position of the Balean forces—checkpoints, patrol and supply routes. Darius placed the large leaf back on the diagram.

"What, a leaf?" asked Dale.

"The skyship."

"There's only one?"

"Once the Ancile fell, the rest of the fleet was sent off. Apparently to Carnaval City and Pharundelle."

"So what's your plan?" Dale asked.

"We're going to bring it down."

"How?"

"We got a good look at it. We think it's just a boat hanging from a large hot air balloon. So we're going to pop it."

"And how are you going to manage that?"

Darius opened a crate on the other side of the tent. "It's incendiary ammo. Raided it last week. They're like miniature missiles. Instead of delivering a slug, the bullet delivers a small explosive. Upon impact, it's supposed to detonate." Darius closed the crate and returned to the diagram. "The only problem is, it's currently out of range. We're going to have to lower it. It's tethered to a windlass on the west end of the Ancile. If we can wind the winch just enough…"

When Dale had seen the naval ships enter the bay just off of Carnaval City, he had given up all hope for the city. The thought of fighting against the invasion never even entered his mind. With the city's fall a foregone conclusion, Dale had quickly shifted to thoughts of Darius. For a moment, he had ventured off the path of saving his family to explore the possibility of warning the city at large. The exploration led to nothing but trouble. As he rode out of Carnaval City, he had chastised himself for getting caught up in Mosaic's idealism.

Once he found Darius, he was confronted once again with the ideals: patriotism, country, honor. Even after the fall of the Republic's symbol of invincibility, Darius was undeterred. Against impossible odds, he was still leading men. He was still fighting. Dale was inspired by his brother's defiant attitude.

"So what do you think?"

"Sounds risky," Dale replied. "Where do you want me?"

Darius chuckled. Then he sat down and took a sip from a tin of cold coffee. "You know, the last time I saw you was before you left the Guard."

"I know, but—"

Darius held up his hand.

"Let me finish. I regretted not telling you that I'm proud of you. And I know Dad would've been proud of you too."

Dale threw up his hands. "What the hell you talking about?"

"Hey, will you shut up and let me finish? This isn't easy, okay? You remember what Dad used to say? 'It's better to be the head of a hare than the tail of a tiger.' Well, I think that's what you've become. A leader."

"Okay, Major."

Darius glared at Dale. "That doesn't mean anything. It's just a title. I've always been the tail. I followed orders, always did what I was told and what was expected of me. But you—you've been the head of your own life. That's why you don't have to do this. You said you weren't like me. You're not a soldier. And you were right. You're better than that."

"You got irregulars out there who aren't soldiers either. This is my fight as much as it is theirs."

With an expression of resignation, Darius said, "Let's get some warm food in your belly. We'll talk in the morning."

"Dare, forget the talk. Just brief me. When's the strike?"

Darius shook his head. "Tomorrow night," he relented.

"Good. Where do you want me?"

"Take a seat."

Darius brought in some hot coffee and meal rations, and laid out their strategy.

"We're going to stage a diversion,"

he continued. "A raid from the east end led by Mills and his squad. My recon team will take the west flank and access the windlass. Once the ship's lowered to range, all fireteams will unload on the balloon from just outside of the Lowers. The irregulars will be on standby and fill in the holes. Supply, reinforcement, auxiliaries, the basics. That's where I want you."

"On standby? No, I'm going in with you."

"If something happens to me, I need someone who will know how to pull the men back in an orderly retreat. Besides, the irregulars don't have a field commander. Most of them don't even have battle experience. You're a civilian, you lead them."

"Assign that asshole Berserker to them."

"I am. In fact, I'm assigning him to you. He's going to watch your back."

"Hey, I don't need a babysitter."

"It's either this or you're on a horse early morning."

Dale sighed. "Okay."

"Okay, what?"

"Okay, I'll lead the irregulars."

"Good. As for your friends, none of them are going anywhere until after the operation. I don't care how close you guys are. At the end of the day, they're still Balean and an Emmainite. And we can't risk any leaks. They're free to move out when we do."

"Fine with me so long as you can guarantee their safety."

After a dinner of gruel, canned fish, nuts and roasted wild game, Dale got a chance to brief his traveling companions. They were not included in the plans to down the skyship. They were told that they would not be allowed to continue on to Valorcourt until the day after the next. Darius had posted guards outside their tent as a precaution. Valkyrie was content so long as he was fed and the Beserker sergeant remained a safe distance from him. Alaric and Selah occupied themselves in prayer.

Darius ordered Mills to take his squad and get into position just after midnight. It would be a long trek across the plains to the far side of the Ancile.

"Good luck, Lieutenant."

"Thank you, sir."

"We'll see you on the other side."

Dale watched as the men marched out of camp. As they disappeared into the darkness, he was startled by the thud of an arm draped over his shoulder.

"So ye think me an asshole, do ye?" asked Bixby with a wry smile. "According to yon major, this asshole's not supposed to let ye out of me sight. Looks like ye and me, we were meant to be together, aye Little Sunday?"

"Shit."

CH 42
EVENING SUN

The few remaining officers and others selected to lead a fireteam were called into the command center for a final briefing. Six men who were either wounded or deemed to have the least combat experience were assigned to guard the campsite and its guests. Despite their disappointment, there was no protest. After the briefing, the rest were sent to their respective teams to go over the specifics of their part in the operation. Each team then went through their normal equipment and weapons check. The operation was scheduled for sometime in the evening. They waited for word from Darius.

Dale spent a good portion of the day

making his own camouflage suit. He gathered nearby foliage and meticulously wove them onto his jacket. By evening, like the rest of the resistance, Dale was prepared to blend into his surroundings.

During dinner, the men ate quietly. With his untouched ration sitting in a small bowl on his lap, Dale slowly rubbed his palms against his trousers.

Alaric watched him. "There's talk of a battle brewing among the men. This won't be your first, will it?"

Dale looked up at the templar and replied after a long pause. "No, it won't."

"But you can't eat."

"Guess I'm not hungry."

"Are you afraid?"

Dale gave thought to the question—a question he did not want to consider.

"The prioress and I have prayed for you."

"I'm not so much afraid of dying as I am of taking another life."

Alaric nodded.

"You ever kill anyone?" Dale then asked.

Alaric sighed. "More than I care to remember."

"How do you reconcile that with your faith?"

"I don't. There are questions to which there are no easy answers. One can only wrestle with them for so long. Life does not wait. We must live on—move into the darkness. In the end, my only hope is that the Maker is forgiving. You should eat. You have a long night ahead of you."

Dale forced down a spoonful of gruel. Not long after, Darius emerged from the command center.

"It's time, gentlemen."

The men rallied together, fully dressed for battle, camouflaged and armed with rifles and swords. A company of tree-men. When they were ready to march, Darius stepped forward.

"I'd say something to stir your hearts, boys, but I'm not big on speeches. Besides, we have with us members of the Holy Order. A cleric from the College of Sisters and a templar." Darius turned to Selah. "I'd like to ask you, Prioress. Would you bless us?"

Selah hesitated. But when her eyes locked with Dale's, she nodded. The men bowed their heads as she began.

"By your grace, O Maker, we beseech you, go before these men. Steel their hearts with your nearness. Grant them strength in their weakness and the courage to overcome fear. May your favor go with them and may you keep them in their darkest hour. *Alunde andra.*"

"*Alunde ver ti,*" the men responded in unison.

Dale surveyed the men as they lifted their heads. With the exception of Sergeant Bixby, who had a ravenous look on his face with his war hammer in one hand and an axe in the other, everyone looked scared.

"First dibs on a kingsman be mine!"

shouted the Berserker, pumping his weapons in the air. "Lest any of ye quaking boots have something to say about it!"

"Quaking boots my ass, highlander! No Berserker will feed before me!" cried a voice in the back. "My country; my right!"

The others erupted in a collective roar.

"Let the blood of the Baleans stain our swords!" another shouted.

Another roar.

The sergeant's bravado stirred the men into a zealous uproar. With each primal roar, the men forgot their fears. But as they marched out, the somber reality resettled over them. In silence they passed Selah who watched them with her hands clasped and pressed to her lips. As Dale walked by her, he gave her a reassuring nod. She closed her eyes and bowed her head.

Two hours later, they reached the edge of the Lowers, marked by a precise tree line against the prairie. The air was crisp. The sky was well lit by a low-hanging moon. The light gave clear definition to the dark silhouette of the skyship hovering high above. For the first time, Dale took a careful look. Instead of sails attached to the masts, there were large hot air balloons. There were propellers at the ends of wings on both sides of the hull. A third propeller was mounted on the back in place of a rudder. It was armed with a battery of cannons and a hatch on its belly for bombing. It was like nothing Dale had ever seen. The Balean's answer to the Ancile.

From their position, Dale could also see the Ancile. The outer walls had been leveled. Breached and overrun. The Republic's symbol of security and strength was now a monument to its great collapse.

Darius and his recon team took turns staking out the fortress through a spyglass. They took note of the guards and planned the most effective approach. Then Darius stooped low, made his way over to where Dale waited with his men.

"You ready?" Dale asked.

"Yeah."

"How long do we wait?"

Darius checked his watch.

"Any second now."

Not a minute later, there was a rumble. And then the crackling of rifle fire in

> *"If they didn't, this mission's about to be compromised."*

the distance. The Ancile came alive. Balean soldiers scrambled to reinforce the east wall where Mills and his men were in full frontal assault.

"This is it. Wish me luck."

"Wait, Dare…be careful."

Darius and his team of six men charged into the open field hunched low like a pack of wolves. The moonlight did not help their approach, but their camouflage gave them some cover. They ran in spurts, spread thin, until they vanished from Dale's vision.

Dale summoned his men and had them line up with the other fireteams. Their rifles were loaded with the incendiary ammo, fixed on the skyship above. An explosion erupted on the east end of the Ancile.

"Damn," said Bixby, with a smirk. "Mills be making quite the ruckus." Then he looked at Dale. "Just give us the word, Little Sunday, and we'll rain hell on yon balloon boat."

They waited. Fifteen minutes passed. The skyship did not budge.

"It's taking too long," Dale muttered.

"Eh?"

"He should be there by now. Where's the windlass?"

"The west wall. Over there," Bixby said, pointing. Then handing Dale his spyglass, he added, "There be a contraption of sorts between the fourth and fifth enfilades on a raised platform."

"I see it."

At the bottom of the magnified image cropped in the lens, Dale noticed six rustling shrubs inching up to the platform. There were two guards posted on it. Dale panned the lens across the wall. Just south of the platform, he saw a figure emerge from the top of the southwest parapet along the fifth enfilade. It was a patrolman. And by the angle of their approach, Dale knew Darius couldn't have seen him from the ground.

He handed Bixby the lens.

"Southwest wall, the guard overlooking the target."

"Nay was he there before."

It wasn't what Dale wanted to hear.

"Suppose ye the major noticed?"

"It's a difficult angle," Dale replied. "If they didn't, this mission's about to be compromised."

He looked back at his team and called forward the archer and an infantryman. "Christoph, Barret, on me." Turning to

Bixby, he said, "Sergeant, I'm guessing you're coming with me as well."

"Aye."

"The rest of you, keep an eye on that ship. When it's in range, fire."

"Yes, sir."

Dale led the three men on a reckless run to the platform.

Meanwhile, Darius and his men had swiftly and stealthily dispatched the two guards standing beside the windlass. But as soon as they began winding the winch, the grating noise drew the attention of the guard on the parapet above them. He peered down and saw Darius' team.

"Enemies at the windlass!" he cried, and blew the trumpet.

"Christoph!" Dale shouted as soon as they were within an arrow's distance.

The archer propped himself up on one knee, aimed, and released. The patrolman was struck. But the trumpet's call was already in the air. In response, the gates were raised. The first wave of infantry came rushing out, fifteen strong, followed closely by a cavalry of five troopers.

While two of Darius' men continued to wind the winch, the others set up a perimeter around the platform. They readied themselves for the closing infantry.

The skyship was slowly sinking.

The five troopers on horseback spotted Christoph and galloped to his position. Dale and his men sprawled in the tall grass. Their archer continued to fire on the troopers closing in on him. He managed to fell two of the horsemen. Just as the other three reached Christoph, they were ambushed by Dale and his men.

Bixby threw one trooper off his horse with his hammer. A follow-up swing crushed the trooper's head like a melon. Barrett cut down the horse of another and was in a sword fight. With little battle experience, he was being driven back by the strength of his opponent. The last trooper, not seeing Dale, tried to circle around to Barrett's flank. As he was about to overtake Barrett, Dale struck him from behind. Bixby came to the assistance of Barrett and split the last trooper open with his axe.

With all of the riders down, Dale and Bixby mounted the nearest horses and made straight for the windlass. Christoph and Barrett retrieved the other two horses and followed closely behind.

From fifty paces away, Dale saw the Balean infantrymen line up and prepare to fire on Darius' recon team. Dale whipped his horse. It was already in full gallop. He gripped the reins white-knuckled, desperate. "Please, God. O Maker, please."

He could see the Balean soldiers. It was too late. He looked to the recon team and immediately spotted Darius among his men. "Darius!"

Darius turned to him—his eyes wide, his lower jaw slack. They locked eyes and Dale heard the shots. Dale saw Darius blink and flinch as the dust burst off his jacket in a violent jolt. The lifeless body collapsed.

As Dale turned to the Balean line, he heard bullets whiz past him. Some of the Balean soldiers, seeing Dale and Bixby approaching, had turned their rifles on them. By the time the rest of the line realized what was happening, Dale had drawn his sword and was riding through them. As his horse stampeded through the line, Dale hacked away indiscriminately. Once he had ripped through, Dale jumped off his horse to go after what was left of the Balean unit. He saw that Bixby had already dismounted and was wielding both hammer and axe on a group now in total disarray. Some were trying to reload their rifles even as Bixby was bearing down on them. Still others were dropping their rifles and in a panic trying to draw their swords. Christoph and Barrett rode in to what was quickly becoming a slaughter.

Dale saw three men running back toward the gate. He gave chase. Dale cut down the one trailing behind the others. The second spotted Dale and turned around. Before he could bring his rifle up to defend himself, Dale lowered his shoulder and plowed through him. A few paces from the Ancile, he caught the frontrunner and tackled him from behind. Dale bounced to his feet and saw that the soldier was unarmed. Lying on his back, he raised his hands. Before he could say anything, Dale swung his sword through his arms and down onto his neck. Without hesitation, he ran for the soldier he had knocked down. He was on his feet, picking up his rifle. Dale charged him with the point of his sword and ran him through.

Lying on top of the soldier with his sword buried in him, Dale heard himself. It was a cry, a yell from somewhere deep inside a person. A place where there is no inhibition. When he heard it, he stopped. There was silence. He slowly got up and pulled his sword out. When he turned to where they had met the Balean infantry line, he saw Bixby and the two other men standing motionless, staring at him, their weapons hanging limp at their sides.

Dale dropped his sword and ran toward the windlass. As he started for his brother, all he saw were strewn bodies. There was no movement. When he got to him, there was blood everywhere. He turned him over. Darius' mouth was full of blood; his eyes were open and empty.

"Dare…Darius. Please." He held him over his lap. Bursts of air escaped Dale's lungs through his nostrils in muted convulsions. He cursed in spits like the rattling lid of a boiling pot.

Bixby and the others ran behind Dale to the windlass. Bixby ordered Christoph to work the windlass, as he and Barrett stood by with an eye on the gate. Any minute, reinforcements were sure to stream out of the Ancile. The skyship began to descend.

As the low-hanging skyship eclipsed the light of the moon, the resistance emerged from the shelter of the forest and ran out onto the field. A column-

formation of trees, six riflemen in rank and four in file, the irregulars standing by. They stopped twenty paces out. Rifles were lined up to the balloon. The incendiary ammo left trails of light as they darted through the air. An ascending meteor shower. When they reached their target, the gas in the balloon ignited into an enormous fireball.

The sky above the Ancile was set ablaze. A momentary evening sun. As the explosion dissipated, it rained fire. And as if the favor of the Maker were guiding its descent, the hull came crashing down directly on top of the Ancile. Over the shower of flaming debris, a collective cheer could be heard erupting from the resistance on both ends of the fortress.

Dale didn't see any of it. Even as he sat right under the explosion and ensuing crash, he did not take notice. He sat hunched over the body of his dead brother.

The skyship's fall on the Ancile halted the Balean soldiers streaming out of the gate. They looked up and then scurried away from the burning debris. Under Bixby's orders, Christoph and Barrett were already mounted and retreating across the field to regroup with the others. Bixby jumped on a horse and rode over to Dale.

"We best be moving, Little Sunday!"

Dale did not respond. Clutching Darius, he slumped onto his side. Bixby jumped off his horse, grabbed Dale under both arms and forcefully pulled him away from Darius. Dale did not release his grip.

Seeing that he was dragging both bodies, Bixby lowered himself over Dale. He grabbed him by the collar and shook him violently.

"He's dead! And soon we be joining him if ye nay get on your feet!"

Dale turned to him with his eyes peeled back like a lunatic. He beat Bixby off him with a flurry. And again, he plopped down next to Darius.

Bixby looked back toward the gate. The Balean soldiers were beginning to regroup. Even as the darkness of night was restored, at such short distance, standing near the platform, Bixby was in plain sight. And from the commotion, he knew he had been spotted. He could see a wave of soldiers starting toward him. Some even from a distance began to discharge rifle rounds. Bixby stepped around Dale and kicked him in the side of the head followed by a punch. Then he hoisted a dazed Dale over his shoulder, slipped him onto his horse, and saddled up. As Bixby turned his horse toward the tree line, he looked back and saw that the Balean soldiers had stopped running toward him and were instead taking aim. Behind them, he saw Shaldean Riders on their Saracen Gliders speeding out of the Ancile.

With a yell, Bixby gave the horse a strong kick. Bullets whizzed by his head as he made himself as small as he could. Curled over Dale, Bixby rode toward the tree line.

CH 43

BORDERLAND RIDGE RUN

"We're not leaving him!"

"Listen, Prioress. The kid wasn't part of the agreement. My job is to get you and the Champ safely to Valorcourt. If you want to compromise that, that's your call. But don't expect me to wait around here for Baleans in a fury to find us. Especially harboring a Meredian resistance fighter."

Dale's eyes opened. When he sat up, the commotion in the room ceased. They all turned to him. Selah and Valkyrie were in the center of the tent and Alaric stood at the door. Selah walked over to Dale, crouching to look into his tear stained face. The tears had smudged the blood and dirt. His eyes were swollen and his lips dried and cracked. He was still half-dressed in his battle raiment, tree branches and leaves hanging off his body.

"By the Maker's grace, you're alive," said Selah. She sat beside him. "How do you feel?"

Dale was sore in so many places that his head was throbbing.

Selah sat beside him and studied his barely opened eyes. "It appears you were grazed by a bullet. We dressed it. Your hand as well. You may have broken it but we can't be sure."

Dale looked at his hand. It had been bound in bandage.

"We don't have time for this!" barked Valkyrie.

"Time for what?" Dale mumbled through clenched teeth.

"They're gone, Dale," Selah replied. "The resistance. They've scattered. They said if and when you woke up, to tell you that they were planning to rendezvous with the others along the South Pass."

"You smell that? That's smoke," said Valkyrie. "They're setting fire to this forest as we speak. They'll send the hounds next. We can't afford to sit around and explain all of this. We need to move, now."

"He's right," said Alaric. "Can you walk?"

Dale rose to his feet. He was dizzy. Although he could barely stand, he looked at Alaric and gave a nod. Valkyrie tossed him his backpack. Dale slipped it on and emerged from the tent to an empty camp. There was a smoke in the air. Ashes were already beginning to fall from the sky like early winter snow.

"The Berserker left you this," said Selah, handing Dale his sword. "You have him to thank for your life."

Taking the bloodied sword, Dale remembered that Darius was dead. He closed his eyes and let out an exhausted moan. His legs went wobbly.

Selah reached over and grabbed his arm. She went to his side so he could lean onto her arm.

"Dale, I'm so sorry about your brother."

Dale said nothing.

"What'll it be, kid?" Valkyrie was antsy. He knew how pressing the situation was. "You coming with us or regrouping in the South Pass?"

"I don't care. I'll go with you as far as the ridge."

"And after that?" Selah asked.

"I don't know."

Valkyrie and Alaric gathered their things and led Dale and Selah back into the Wilds. They started north, hoping to make a run for the Borderland Ridge. Within an hour, they heard dogs barking in the distance.

"Shit." Having to abandon the run for the ridge, Valkyrie veered out of the Wilds and started east toward the Lowers.

"Where are we going?" asked Alaric.

"We're doubling back. They won't come searching for us near the tree line."

"Wouldn't it make more sense to go west? Maybe back into the Deep?"

"The spores won't clear for another two days. It's the dogs I'm concerned about. We've got less than a mile on them."

Valkyrie studied the leaves around him. As he walked, he ripped some off, rubbed them between his fingers and smelled them. Then he did the same with others.

"If I can just find the right one," he mumbled to himself, while continuing the pattern. Suddenly he stopped. "Here!"

He stood next to a small tree that didn't look any different from the countless others they had passed. As he began to rip its leaves off he instructed the others to do the same.

"Get as much as you can. Chew it up and rub it all over yourself. Like this."

Valkyrie demonstrated and the others followed suit. The chewing left their mouths tingling and numb. Breaking up the leaves and mixing it with saliva resulted in a bitter paste.

"It's the stuff metholine is made of," Valkyrie explained. "Hopefully, it'll throw them off our scent."

"If not?" asked Alaric.

"Then our journey's going to end real quick."

When they had fully lathered themselves with the paste, they continued out into the Lowers.

Dawn was breaking.

Where they stood, the forest was intact. Just a mile to the south of their position, the land was scorched. The fire burned out of control, blackening the sky. An entire legion of Balean soldiers was lined up along the edge of what was once a lush forest. The cavalry on horseback stood with torches in hand. Between them, the Shaldean Riders on their Saracen Gliders, led by their *Rajeth*, Haddu.

"Wait, do you hear that?" asked Valkyrie.

"Hear what?"

"*Shh*. Listen."

Dogs.

"Bloody hell!" cried Alaric. "The stuff didn't work."

"Move!"

They followed the ranger northbound as he weaved between the trees. The pack of dogs gave close chase, and the Shaldean

---

Just a mile to the south of their position, the land was scorched.

Riders responded to the barking. Under Haddu's command, all twenty-four of them kicked their horses into a full gallop. A detachment of Balean cavalry joined the chase from a distance.

The party ran as fast as they could, but with each minute, they gave ground to the dogs, and now to the Riders. Dale tried to keep up, but he kept trailing back. Still dizzy and exhausted, he could not find the will to struggle. Selah kept looking back to see where Dale was. She slowed just enough to spur Dale on. When he saw that he was putting Selah in danger, Dale pressed harder to keep pace.

They reached the base of the Borderland Ridge. A steep incline of solid stone that led to the top where the ground was level—a plateau at the end of which was a waterfall overlooking the Hesperian Highlands to the north. Valkyrie sprinted up the slope with the ease of a mountain goat. Dale collapsed just a few steps up. Selah and Alaric picked him up and slung his arm over their shoulders. They steadily climbed as Valkyrie watched from above, his bow drawn.

The dogs emerged from the Lowers and raced up the ridge. As soon as they were in view, Valkyrie fired his arrows in rapid succession. It only slowed the pursuit. Just as Selah and Alaric got Dale to the plateau, the Shaldean Riders rode out of the Lowers.

The party continued running along the ridge toward the waterfall but the

Riders were already cresting the plateau. With nowhere else to go and no chance to outrun them, Alaric and Selah drew their swords. Though he could barely stand, Dale also drew his sword. Valkyrie fell to a knee, drew an arrow, and leveled it along the horizon.

They appeared one by one in his line of sight—twenty-four Riders. Valkyrie held his breath and aimed for their *Rajeth*.

"Charles! Wait," said Alaric. "We can't take them all."

The Riders came up to them and rode around them in circles, waving their scimitars in the air. Alaric stepped forward to meet them.

"*Durmaq!*" Haddu finally shouted. Immediately, reins were pulled to a stop. When the dust settled, he pointed his scimitar at Alaric Linhelm. "Are you a templar or a member of the resistance?"

"Neither," Alaric replied.

"You carry a templar's sword."

"I am Alaric Linhelm, former Marshal of the Vail Templar, Exile of the Royal Crimson Knights."

"A Crimson Knight? You are Balean then?"

"Aye."

"Tell me, knight. Why were you running?"

"We were running from the fire. And then we were running from the dogs."

"And where, exactly, were you running to?"

"Valorcourt."

"That's quite a run. Why?"

"To make an appeal to the duke."

"What kind of appeal?"

"To end this senseless war."

Laughter broke out among the Riders.

"Even if I believed you, Champion Alaric Linhlem, former Crimson Knight, your traveling companions, they raise much questions. You, there. You're an Emmainite?"

"By blood only," Valkyrie replied.

Haddu dismounted and walked up to the ranger.

"Blood is everything, *shadiq*," he said. "What are you doing with these *ostra?*"

"You ride with the Balean invasion force," Valkyrie replied. "You tell me."

"I bring our people justice. You?"

"I do as I please, Shaldea."

Haddu scoffed. Then he looked at Selah.

"And you, woman? What business have you traveling with Champion Alaric Linhelm?"

"I am a cleric, nothing more."

"And yet, you are armed. What cleric serves the Order as if she were a templar? This war is not against the Benesanti, Sister. You would be safer in your robes within temple walls. Why risk your life out here in the wild?"

"She is my attendant," said Alaric. "She is here under my leave."

"An armed cleric working at the behest of an ex-templar, guided by an Emmainite who thinks himself a peach. A most peculiar party, indeed."

Then he looked at Dale, still dressed in what remained of his ghillie suit. Haddu leaned in and closely examined the twigs and foliage hanging from his outfit.

"This looks a lot like what the Meredian dogs were wearing last night. Those natives fighting for the liberation of their land against foreign occupation. In their terms, terrorists. You wouldn't happen to be one of them, would you? A terrorist? Tell me, peach, what's your name?"

Dale's eyes were vacant, his expression weary, and his voice flat as he replied.

"My name is Dale Sunday and I *am* a terrorist. I am a former lieutenant of the Republican Guard and I killed five Emmainite villagers while deployed in Loreland. Last night, I was with the resistance. We brought down the skyship."

There was silence. Protruding his neck, Haddu took a close look. Then he smiled.

"Such insolent bravado. Is this courage or foolishness?" He removed his cape and handed it to one of his minions. Then he began twirling his sword in his hand. "To boast of your exploits insults me, Dale Sunday. It is only fitting that you should die by the hand of an Emmainite. Draw your sword. You've killed villagers. Let's see how you fair against a proper warrior."

Selah, knowing Dale's condition, tried to intervene.

But Dale had already unsheathed his sword and turned to face the *Rajeth*. He stood straight up, barely holding the sword out in front of him. With a puzzled look, Haddu casually slapped Dale's sword with his scimitar. Dale's sword went flying out of his hand.

"Is this a joke?" asked Haddu. "Pick up your sword."

Dale picked it up and again, it was quickly struck out of his hand. This time, Haddu struck it in anger.

"What kind of a Republican Guard were you?"

The Riders burst into laughter, jeering and taunting Dale.

"Pick it up, Lieutenant. You terrorist. Fight!"

Dale sighed and stood upright, his sword still at his feet.

"You think I won't cut down an unarmed Republican dog?" Haddu continued, "You are an ant. An insignificant mark. I will remove your head and roll it down this ridge."

"So stop talking and do it," Dale said.

"Dale!" cried Selah. "What're you doing?"

Haddu shook his head. And with a shrug, he swung his scimitar. It was stopped short by Selah's saber. She followed the block with an upward thrust, driving the blade under the *Rajeth's* sternum, piercing his lung.

He collapsed and died. After a moment's shock, the Riders burst into an uproar. They dismounted and drew their scimitars. Alaric pulled Selah back behind him. Dale and Valkyrie formed a feeble shield around them.

"The girl will die a slow death!" the Riders began to shout. They took cautious steps forward. As they closed in, the Balean Calvary arrived.

"What's going on here?" asked the ranking Balean trooper.

"A curse be upon you, *ostra* whore!" cried the Shaldea. "She killed the *Rajeth*."

Alaric stepped forward and shouted, "Protect your queen! Protect the queen of Bale!"

"Quiet! All of you! Who are you, templar?" the Balean trooper then asked.

"I am Balean born *Sir* Alaric Linhelm, exile of the Crimson Knights. And here stands before you Cyrene Evenford Leawen, daughter of the late King Aegis Leawen, heir to the Balean throne. For the kingdom and the crown, do not deliver her into their hands."

Dale turned around to look at Selah. She looked at him. She looked like a girl—a little girl, startled and scared. Dale turned back around and sat down on the ground.

"Kill them! Kill them all!"

"Royal troopers to arms! *Verunda!*" the trooper then shouted.

With their blades drawn, the Balean cavalry rode in between the Shaldea and created a tight barrier around Alaric, Selah, Dale, and Valkyrie.

"Stand down, Shaldea. These four are now under the custody of the crown."

"She killed our *Rajeth!*"

"And there will be reckoning. But if you harm her, woe to Loreland and all its inhabitants, for the wrath of Groveland, both Meredine and Bale, will rain upon it. Now return to the Ancile before you make a blaze of a spark."

The Shaldea reluctantly mounted their Gliders and turned them around. And before they started back down the ridge, one yelled back, "The general will hear of this."

The trooper replied, "Indeed. Tell him then that we've found the princess."

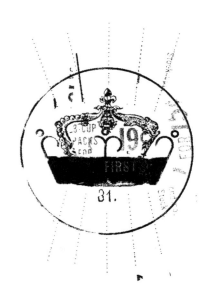

CASUALTIES OF WAR

Mosaic was lying on her cot, reading a copy of the Mystic Tome that the clerics had distributed to the refugees. It was a collection of sacred writings and stories on which the Benesanti faith had been established. Engrossed in its dense content, she was unaware of the ensuing commotion around her until her neighbor peered over the partition that separated them.

"I think they're calling you."

"What?" Mosaic asked.

"They're calling all men and women between the ages of eighteen and thirty." The older lady pointed to the center aisle of the main sanctuary. A templar was gathering young women into a line. "I bet it has something to do with the Bene-seneschal's murder."

"What does our age have to do with it?"

Her neighbor shrugged. "You better

get up there."

Mosaic set the tome down and started toward the growing line. A cleric approached and greeted her.

"Young lady, how old are you?"

"Nineteen," Mosaic replied. "What's going on?"

"Please, wait right over."

"What for?"

"You needn't be concerned. We're assisting the Baleans in their effort to reunite lost sons and daughters with their families."

"Well, why not everyone else? Why not the little ones first?"

"It's all just part of the procedure," the cleric replied. "It will only take a few minutes and you'll remain under the protection of the Benesanti."

The cleric then went on to fetch others. There were whispers and rumors, but no one spoke with any level of authority. Within five minutes, Mosaic was in the vestibule where the line ended.

"Next!" a senior templar shouted, standing out in the courtyard.

He waved her over and directed her to one of six tents that were set up along the West Gate: three for the women, three for the men.

When she entered the tent, another templar was standing in the back behind a panel of three unarmed Balean officers who sat at a table. The officer in the middle was a blonde woman in her late thirties with a humorless face, thin lips, and hair pressed tight against her scalp as if it had been painted on with a fine brush.

"Sit," she said.

Mosaic sat in the chair provided.

"Name, date of birth, and residence before the occupation."

"I'm sorry. May I ask what this is regarding?"

"We're conducting a search. The sooner you answer the questions, the sooner you'll be excused."

"Mosaic Shawl. I was born on the Third Day of the Seventh Month. This is my nineteenth year. And my home is in Hoche, Barrington Prefecture."

"Hoche, Hoche, Hoche—let's see, ah! There we are. Yes, the Shawls. You are the missing daughter of Turkish and Cora Tess, I presume?"

Mosaic sat up alert.

"Cora Tess, yes. Do you know where they are?"

"They were your natural parents, then?"

"I'm sorry. *Were?*" Both her hands slipped off her thighs. She gripped a leg of the chair to try to steady herself.

"I regret to inform you that they were unintended casualties of war. They were your natural parents, yes?"

She didn't hear the question. "Casualties of war? What do you mean? What happened? How do you know?"

The officer remained cold and spoke with matter-of-fact authority. "We do not have that information. These records were relayed from the field. They are accurate. And then she reiterated her question. "They were your natural parents?"

With tears beginning to stream down her face, Mosaic answered, "Yes."

"Miss Shawl, do you know anything regarding the Bene-seneschal's recent demise? Any affiliates, perhaps, that expressed disappointment with the Holy Order, or someone who entered the premises without proper papers?"

Again, Mosaic did not hear the question. At that moment, there was nothing she cared about.

"Miss Shawl?"

She looked up, her vision blurred.

The female officer glanced at her comrade. He shook his head.

"That will be all," she said. "We ask that you remain here on the temple grounds for the time being until our investigation is complete."

Mosaic stood and walked out of the tent, her movements severed from her will. The line outside the tent looked to her for answers.

"It's about the Bene-seneschal, isn't it?"

"What do they want in there?"

"Are there Baleans in there?"

"I'm talking to no goddamn Balean if I can help it."

She ignored them. When she got past the gauntlet of questions, Mosaic stumbled toward a wall. She fell to her knees and wept.

Back in her partitioned space, she lay on her cot. Time was without pity, carrying along with a mocking bounce in its steps. For days she lay there, hardly eating, hardly speaking. She fell asleep hoping to wake up in the next Realm, reunited with her mother and father. But her eyes opened to the present—a partitioned wall, alone in her own corner of a cold temple sanctuary, the ambient murmurings of fellow refugees. An unflinching reality.

After several days, when her tears were depleted, her grief exhausted, she finally sat up. Slowly, she distributed the weight of her wilted body onto her legs, and stood. Shuffling one foot in front of the other, she managed to bathe, eat a proper meal, and dress herself. And by the time Sparrow visited her later that evening, she was gone.

"You just missed her," her neighbor explained. "She's been lying there in a bed of tears for days, just up until this morning."

"Where did she go?"

"Beats me. She found out her parents were killed in the invasion."

"What day is it?"

"The Fifth, I believe. I'll tell her you stopped by when she comes back. What was your name again?"

Sparrow checked his watch. It was nearing curfew.

CH 45

THE FINAL

Mosaic met Sebastian at the fountain in Trivelka Square. He quietly explained to her that they were forming a resistance group, just as Sparrow had warned. They were congregating at an undisclosed location. Although Sebastian had initially invited her, he hadn't expected her to show up. He was suddenly reluctant to bring her along but Mosaic insisted on going.

"Are you sure?"

"They killed my parents, Sebastian. As far as I know, they've killed Dale and Darius. They've taken everything. I can't just lie around the temple and wait to see what happens next."

Despite his unease, he finally relented. Sebastian led Mosaic down an alley in what appeared to be an industrial part of the city. There was an inconspicuous green door. When they approached, a lookout peered through a small, curtained window adjacent to the door. Recognizing Sebastian, the young man with a gaunt face and

DIRECTIVE

black hat let them in. It was a small, out-of-place café. No one who was not from the area would ever expect to see a café on that street.

The air was stale in the dim, candlelit room. A clerk kept wiping down an already spotless bar while patrons quietly sat around tables with drinks and smokes. They were all young. Not much older than Mosaic. They trained their eyes on her as she trailed behind Sebastian. It didn't take long for Mosaic to realize the whole scene was set up as a front.

One of the patrons arose from the table and got in front of Sebastian. "Who's this?"

"She's with me," Sebastian replied.

"That's not what I asked."

"She's the one I was telling Max about. Her brother's a Republican Guard."

Mosaic made no attempt to correct him as the unconvinced man scrutinized her. Then with a reluctant head toss, he gestured them to the back where there was a small gathering around a table. A young man who appeared to be about thirty years old greeted them. He was in a black turtleneck. Considering the circumstances, he appeared cheerful and carefree.

"Max, this is her," said Sebastian. "This is Mosaic."

"Welcome, Mosaic. Welcome. I've seen you before. The muse of the Halo. You have the most beautiful voice."

"Thank you."

"It's a pleasure to meet you. I wish it were under different circumstances. Please, sit with us."

In a couple minutes, three facts about Mosaic were communicated: She was a close friend of Sebastian, an artist who performed regularly at the Halo, and the younger sister of two Republican Guardsmen. The information seemed to appease the nervous room. They made room for Sebastian and Mosaic at the table where they continued to plot their next course of action.

Mosaic looked around the room. The group was comprised mostly of young men. There were only a handful of women. It was unlikely that a single one of them had any type of military training. They appeared to be mostly students, maybe a few artists and literary types. By candlelight, she could see that they were either terrified or filled with idealistic zeal. It was telling of their naivety, their ignorance. As Mosaic surveyed the room, she thought Sparrow's warning was more of a clear prediction. These people were going to get themselves killed.

"Well, how can we trust the Shen detective?" someone asked.

"Because the Eagle trusts him," another replied. "He's the only source we have on the inside."

Sebastian leaned over and explained to Mosaic that "the Eagle" was the leader of the nascent resistance, a sentinel of the State Security Command that happened to be in town when the invasion began. Just as he finished, the lookout at the window whistled.

"Someone's coming!"

Immediately, candles were blown out. The café went dark. Everyone froze and held their breath. A minute of taut silence was broken by a loud crash. The little green door was blown into the café and Balean soldiers poured in like rodents through a sewage pipe. There was screaming as the room scattered in a panic. A couple of the men who were at the tables tried to put up a fight, but were quickly subdued or killed.

Once the front room was secured, a Balean soldier started to yell for everyone to get down on the ground. Max and the others who sat at the table were already running through the kitchen. Sebastian and Mosaic followed closely behind. They squeezed their way between the narrow counters toward the backdoor. As they burst through, they were met by a squad of soldiers. Max and several others were apprehended, but a few broke through the squad.

Pulling Mosaic by the wrist, Sebastian managed to get them past. As they ran down the street, they could hear soldiers in close pursuit.

They turned the corner into a wider street. One of their pursuers caught up and dragged Sebastian to the ground. In the process, he knocked Mosaic down on the cobblestone road. Another soldier joined them and began to club Sebastian. With the first couple blows he split Sebastian's scalp. He was knocked unconscious. They kept beating him, smashing his glasses onto his face.

"Sebastian!" Mosaic cried. "Stop it, you're going to kill him."

She got up, ran at them and jumped on one of the assailants. He grabbed her and lunging forward, threw her off of him. As she tried to get to her feet, he ran up to her from behind and kicked her on the small of her back.

He returned to Sebastian, who was being shackled. The soldiers were out of breath and irritated. Sebastian was bleeding profusely but the soldiers did not seem rushed. The one who had kicked Mosaic returned to her. She was still lying face down on the ground.

"You are in violation of curfew and hereby charged with unlawful assembly. You and your friend are coming with us."

As he spoke, Mosaic remained unresponsive. Then the other soldier spoke up.

"Wait. Did you hear that?"

"Hear what?"

There was silence. But the soldier hovering over Sebastian couldn't shake the feeling that someone, or something, was lurking in the darkness of an alley just a few paces from where he stood. He removed his pistol and locked his gaze into the black. "Someone there?" he called.

Again, silence.

"What is it? You see something?" his comrade asked.

With all attention honed in on the alley, no one seemed to notice the charcoal gray figure walking up fast from behind. He grappled the armed soldier in such a way that the barrel of his pistol ended up tucked below his chin. There was a pop. A poof of blood and brain matter dissipating. Without pause, the figure drew his blade and lunged toward the soldier who had kicked Mosaic. Backpedaling, the soldier raised his pistol. In a panic, he flinched and set off an errant shot. When the smoke cleared, he had

There was a pop. A poof of blood and brain matter dissipating.

With the hood of his jacket pulled far past his brow, his face in shadow and a bloodstained blade in hand, Sparrow looked down at Mosaic. She was trembling. He knelt down next to her, "Can you walk?"

"Sebastian."

Sparrow left her side to examine Sebastian. Then he came back to Mosaic. "He's not going to make it."

"No." Mosaic closed her eyes.

"Get up," Sparrow said, extending his hand down to her.

His voice was even and cold. She looked up and then took his hand. Mosaic stood and looked over at Sebastian. Seeing him with his crushed skull, bleeding to death, she wanted to crumple to the ground. Her hand went limp in Sparrow's hand.

He grabbed her tightly and began to run. She ran to keep from falling. As they ran, Mosaic began to weep. Her cries deepened until she was barely running. Feeling the weight, Sparrow stopped so he wouldn't drag her to the ground.

Mosaic staggered aimlessly. She finally fell to the ground. Sitting with her head in her hands, she convulsed, trying to regain composure.

Sparrow squatted next to her and said, "Mosaic, I didn't come to save you."

Thirteen hours earlier, he had been sitting with Magog in the bathhouse within the lair of the Carousel Rogues. They had discussed their imminent departure from the city. After going over some specifics of their exit, Magog had then issued the final directive.

"Remy will remain here. For now, he will continue to run the guild and monitor the state of affairs. But before we depart, we need to address something. Mosaic Shawl. That is her name? Your strange behavior these recent days necessitates a show of commitment. We have lost confidence. Go and restore it. It is what the Umbra demands."

As the Vengian, he had responded with a nod. But now, here, he was sitting next to the woman—a woman who as a child had shown him kindness. Looking at her, the thought of taking her life for the purposes of a "show of commitment" was absurd. He remembered the feeling when he was asked to accept the murder of the only father he knew. Magog had told him that Aleksander T'varche had welcomed his fate. And there was the same sense then—a wanton, absurd waste.

Mosaic looked up at him. Looking into her big tear-filled eyes, Sparrow thought of the cake Mosaic had handed him when they were children. The song from her lips. He thought of Dale's final request before their parting. He thought of Dale, his friend. *Rohar*. The potato shared with a starving Goseonite boy.

"I'm so sorry," he said, as he drew his blade.

It was dark.

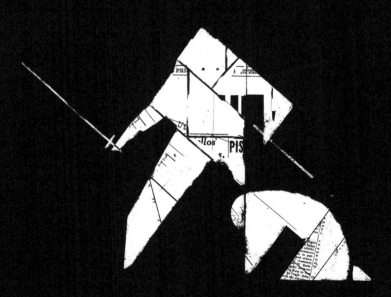

CH 46

A CONFESSION

"I promised him Sanctuary."

"So give it to him."

"You know it means nothing now. What he needs is immunity."

"He's not a part of the coalition. He's not Shaldea."

"I owe him. The queen owes him."

"She's not the queen," General Arun Kilbremmer replied. "Not yet."

He wasn't much older than Alaric Linhelm. The general sat across from the ex-templar in full, dark plate armor, decorated with a gilded coat of arms. His sheathed gold-hilted broadsword lay across the table between them. They were in the general's makeshift office that once belonged to the colonel of the Republican Guard. They were arguing like they used to years ago, when they were friends and colleagues.

"Why didn't you just come to us from the beginning?"

"We couldn't be sure," Alaric replied.

"Sure of what?"

"Whether or not reintroducing the child would be welcomed by the current regime."

"You don't trust the duke?"

"His Majesty had me swear that I would protect the child. For years, I have taken great care to do just that. And nothing in this world is more dangerous than a power-hungry man near a throne. Besides, with our plan, no one had to know. We did not set our eyes on the throne. Our plan was only to seek audience with the duke to make an appeal for an end to this madness. To plead for the restoration of peace."

"This *is* the path to peace, Alaric. Order and justice. And if she had no interest in reclaiming the throne, you shouldn't have openly declared her our queen."

"I already told you. She killed a Shaldean *Rajeth* to save our companion. I only revealed her identity to save her life."

"The duke is not corrupt. He is as committed to the law as the king was. Had you come to us, he would have understood."

"Like I said, it was a risk I could not take. You sit on a seat of power; you of all people ought to understand my reluctance. It is a difficult seat to relinquish. Very few men do it voluntarily."

"The duke is a better man."

"Is he? I was not willing to stake the child's life on what I did not know. And now I am glad I didn't. This war reveals the nature of your duke. You and I know it is an unjust war."

"I'm a soldier, Alaric. I don't have the luxury of making judgments on the throne, regardless of who sits on it. The voice that comes from it must be heeded."

"And yet, you tell me he's a better man. Which is it? It's a dangerous thing, Arun, to judge and vacate judgment as it suits you. Crimes come in the form of commission and omission. You must know that making no decision is also a decision."

"Is that what they teach you in the temple?"

"It's what every human ought to learn in their youth. Let's dispense with all this. We're not getting anywhere. Now, how do you suppose he'll take the news?"

"The duke? You'll have to tell me. I'm sending you both to Valorcourt immediately. I would've preferred to send her by way of the skyship, but seeing as how your friends destroyed it, that's no longer an option."

"The sky is for the birds."

The general shook his head at his stubborn old friend.

"Arun," Alaric explored, "if the regent is unwilling to defer to the rightful heir, who will you support?"

"That's a decision I hope I will not have to make." The general sighed. "It's a different world we live in, isn't it, old friend? Alliances with terrorists. You, an ascetic. Me, an armchair general. What happened to us? What happened to the glory days of the king and his Crimson Knights? When good was good, and bad was bad."

"The world shrank," Alaric replied. "In the days of old, wars were waged between us and them. Now, it's all just us."

The general nodded. Then he said, "I'll give him free passage on the main roads. But that's it. He gets himself in trouble, he's on his own. That's all I can do for an Emmainite ranger."

"Thank you. And now, about the Meredian."

"You have the audacity of a thief," the general said, shaking his head in disbelief. "No! He admits to serving the resistance. He took part in taking down the skyship and the killing of my men."

"Yes, I know Arun. I'm not asking for immunity."

"Then what do you want?"

"It's not what I want. It's what *she* wants."

When Dale had been brought into the Ancile, the structure appeared to him like a king on his knees. Most of the western and northern perimeters had been leveled. Debris from the night before was still being swept and gathered. On every parapet that was still standing, Royal Balean banners flew where once flew the golden eagle crest and star of the Republic.

Dale was allowed a bath before he was taken into a cell. He discarded the camouflage he wore into battle and put on his regulars. As a captive, Dale experienced firsthand the level of Balean commitment to law and order. His captors, some of whom had to have been his combatants on the field the previous night, treated him fairly. They stuck strictly to protocol—never even verbally attacking him. When Dale was shown into his cell, he nearly thanked the guard.

Alone at last, Dale curled up in the corner of his cell. He thought of Darius. His death. His life. With the memories playing in his mind, there was a stifling pain in his chest. Then he thought about the men he had killed in response—how easy it had been.

He wept.

"Dale," a soft voice called from behind.

Selah stood on the other side of the iron bars. When he saw her, he quickly averted his eyes. With his head still bowed, he rubbed his face in the palms of his hands.

Without a response, Selah turned away. She pressed her back up against the iron bars and crouched down. After a long silence, Selah began what sounded like a confession.

"My mother was executed for treason when I was nine years old. Her brother, my uncle, was discovered to have ties with an insurrectionist group. He was arrested. At trial he was found guilty of treason and sentenced to death. My mother tried to free him but failed. When she was implicated, she was defiant. Even as she sat on the throne, she spoke against it and what she thought was tyrannical rule. With the queen speaking out, people wondered if she would usher in political reform. In the end, she was executed along with her brother. My father gave the order."

She spoke with a muted numbness—a detached recollection as if telling the story of another.

"I was sent to the College of Sisters. Soon after, Alaric Linhelm was sent by my father to be my guardian. Early on, from time to time, he asked me if there was anything I wanted to tell my father. I wanted to curse him, but I said nothing. I got letters—letters I never read. Then one day, Alaric told me that my father had passed away. Later, I found out he killed himself, overcome with grief. I felt nothing."

Selah sighed. "I've forgiven him. It

took me years to realize it, but he was just a man. Torn, like so many others, between ideas, beliefs. Could he have changed the law for his bride? What would have become of the country if she were pardoned? I realized he suffered under that decision until he could bare it no more. When I forgave him, I felt as though I could finally live—like I was released."

She glanced over her shoulder.

"You're a good man, Dale. Don't give up."

She stood and looked at him. With his head bowed, he did not stir.

"I…" She appeared as if she had wanted to say something more but stopped herself. "Good bye, Dale Sunday."

Then she turned and walked down the cellblock. Dale finally looked up at her. He thought about calling out to her. But he didn't. He just watched her leave.

Two hours later, the guard entered with his ring of keys in hand. He unlocked the cell gate and held it opened.

"On your feet, Meredian," he said.

Dale did as he was told.

"Turn around."

The guard shackled Dale's hands behind his back. Once shackled, he was led out of the cellblock through the bunker at the center of the star fort. When they emerged from the building, dawn was hardly breaking, a soft glow in the distant horizon. The cold morning air swept across Dale's face. His nose went numb. He saw a blood-stained chopping block in the middle of the court and a hooded guard standing by it with a battle axe. An executioner. Dale braced himself for the unknown. But he was escorted past the chopping block and through the east gate, beyond the outer wall where Valkyrie was waiting for him. The guard unshackled Dale and left him. Confused, Dale stared at the ranger, who handed him his backpack. It was stocked with rations. Valkyrie also handed him his sword.

"Try to hang on to it this time," Valkyrie said with a smile.

"What's going on?" asked Dale.

"We're free to go. Can you believe it?" Valkyrie held up an official document signed by the general granting him safe passage through Balean-occupied territory. "You know what this is? Balean Sanctuary. We can go wherever we want now."

"Where's Alaric and Selah?"

"They're gone. Left about an hour ago for Valorcourt."

Dale's heart sank.

"That reminds me." Valkyrie folded the document, slipped it into his purse, then removed from it a sealed envelope and presented it to Dale. "Here. Selah, or should I say, *Her Royal Majesty*, wanted me to make sure you got this. I'm guessing that's your copy."

Dale took the note and ran his thumb over the seal bearing the royal crest of the Balean Kingdom.

"This whole time, we were traveling with royalty. A princess. One familiar with swordplay no less." Valkyrie shook his head. "Did you see her move with that saber? She knew what she was doing."

"I never got to thank her," Dale muttered. Already, he hated himself for having said nothing to her.

Valkyrie glanced back at the Ancile. "Come on. Let's get out of here before the Baleans change their mind."

As they began to walk, Valkyrie asked, "You know where you're going?"

Dale shrugged. "Carnaval City."

"Are you crazy? After everything you went through to get here?"

"There's nothing left for me here."

"There's nothing left for you back in Carnaval City, either."

"I have family," Dale replied. "I have to make sure they're all right."

"Well, you won't help them any getting yourself caught. I say you stick with me at least until the dust settles."

Dale gave it some thought. "Where are you going?" he then asked.

Valkyrie pointed east. "Muriah Bay."

"What's in Muriah Bay?"

He saw a blood-stained chopping block in the middle of the court

---

"It's not what's there. It's what isn't there—namely, this war. If we're lucky, we might even find a job as a deckhand. Always wanted to take to sea. It'd be nice to leave the West for a while."

Dale looked back at the Ancile. Behind it was a lingering star, the last vestige of the autumn's evening sky.

"So what'll it be, kid?"

Ahead of them on the horizon, lighter skies heralded the rising sun. Dale gestured Valkyrie to lead the way.

"Good. It'll be a few days before we reach the coast. Less than a week if we keep a steady pace and stay on the main roads." Valkyrie looked at the envelope in Dale's hand. "Aren't you going to open it? Better keep it handy in case we run into a patrol."

Dale broke the seal. He removed a piece of paper from the envelope. It wasn't an official document. It was a simple note, written in ink with schooled penmanship.

Dale,

I'm sorry I did not have the courage to be forthright with you before. I want you to know, that night at the World's End, it wasn't the spores. It was me. The real me. The one that I wish I could be, always. Perhaps someday we will meet again under more favorable circumstances. Until then, I pray you'll find a measure of peace on your journey through life.

Yours,
Selah

Dale folded the note and tucked it into his breast pocket close to his heart.

"So? What's it say?" asked Valkyrie.

"Sanctuary."

As they walked toward the new day, Valkyrie noticed Dale's steps liven, his countenance lift.

CH 47

SHADOW IN THE NORTH

Duke Merrick Thalian was pacing at the foot of the throne when Eli entered.

"We just received word from General Kilbremmer," said the royal advisor. "They found the princess."

"Where?"

"She turned up at the Ancile with the exile." Eli handed Duke Thalian the note. "They're on their way here."

"Send out a detachment of Royal Guards to meet her."

"I've already sent my own Ciphers."

"Good." The duke sighed. He wandered over to the crystal windows. Outside the window, he could see the balcony from which the late king often addressed Valorcourt. The duke gazed out and said, "Very good."

"What will you do?" asked Eli.

"I don't know. A change in power in the middle of a war could be disastrous."

"The war is over, Your Highness. Only a small resistance remains in the cities. The provisional government in Brookhaven has already sworn fealty to the throne."

"I was praying we would find her in good health," said the duke, "but this is too soon." He turned and approached the throne. "Do the people know?"

"There has not been an announcement. But news like this travels fast."

The duke slowly sat on the throne. He ran his fingers over the contours of the armrest.

"Feels wrong to sit here."

"It suits you, Your Highness."

The duke smiled. Then he looked to his left where the crown rested on a velvet pillow. It was veiled under a silk cloth.

"The law is the law. And it belongs to her. All of this."

"Yes, it does."

"Eli, which is truer? Adhering to the letter of the law or executing its true intent?"

"These are dangerous questions, Your Highness."

"Yes, they are. We've won the war, but there is still much to be done before a united Groveland is to be realized. Much can go wrong. Can we entrust the course we've charted to a child? We are so close to securing peace for generations to come. It is too soon."

"Your Highness, you are regent. There has been no coronation. Until the girl's formal investiture, your word stands as the Maker's own."

"Yes. And the weight of responsibility torments me."

There was a knock. The duke quickly rose to his feet and stepped away from the throne. "Enter."

The cupbearer entered with two goblets of wine. "As you requested, sir," he said, approaching the royal advisor.

Eli removed the goblets from the tray. With a sleight of hand, he sprinkled a pinch of powder into one of the goblets before handing it to the duke. "I thought you may want a drink after hearing about the princess."

"You know me too well, Eli."

Just as the cupbearer turned to leave, Eli ordered him to wait. Then he raised his glass and said, "Duke Merrick Thalian, here's to your reign and the glory of Bale."

They both took a generous sip. The duke lowered his glass and smacked his lips. With a tilted head, he turned to Eli with a troubled look. He convulsed and doubled over. Gasping for air, he fell to his knees and began to cough. Then he fell over on all fours and spat up blood. His coughs became more violent, strands of blood and saliva hanging from his mouth, his eyes white with terror.

> **"These are dangerous questions, Your Highness."**

The cupbearer, startled, took a few steps back before Eli grabbed him by the shirt. He shouted for the guards. Just as the Royal Guards rushed in, Eli removed a dagger and repeatedly plunged it into the cupbearer's belly. At last, he dropped the body and ran to the duke who was by then laying on his side. "Summon the physician!"

"Yes, sir." One of the guards ran out of the throne room.

He checked the duke's pulse. "Guard!"
"Yes, sir?"
"Forget the physician. He's dead."
"Shall we summon him for you, sir?"
"I'm fine."
"But your shirt, sir."
Eli looked down and noticed that his shirt had been stained heavily with the blood of the cupbearer.

"Summon the alchemist to analyze the wine before you clean this up, and hold everyone in the kitchen for questioning. I want to know if the cupbearer acted alone."

"Yes, sir."
"And have the runner assemble the Royal Court."
"Yes, sir."

Eli then removed his bloodied shirt and draped it over the face of the duke. As he left the duke's side, he held his hand over his chest to hide the tattoo that, like Remy Guillaume's, marked him as a Shadow of the Samaeli.

CH 48
FAILED

The traffic of people and goods through the harbor only intensified with the Balean occupation. New Balean regulations and procedures were introduced to maintain order to the harbor. But it had the reverse affect. Fisherman and merchants who had for generations navigated the harbor by methods handed down from fathers to sons were forced to learn and comply with regulations that made no sense to them. Balean soldiers not properly trained to serve as customs officials only added to the confusion and delays.

Amidst the hectic crowd, Magog stood at the foot of a boarding ramp set off the side of a docked schooner. Aside from the scarf over the lower half of his face, he looked like so many other contracted seamen who wandered the area. He checked his watch.

Magog had not seen the Vengian after sending him off on his final assignment. Although he was not expected to present himself to Magog, the Vengian's silence coupled with his late arrival for their departure made Magog uneasy.

"Sir, we need you to board now," said the deckhand.

"According to my watch, there are still seven minutes left."

The deckhand, unsure as to how to respond, walked away for the moment only to return seven minutes later.

"Sir? It's time."

Magog shot him an impatient glare. And just as he was about to ascend the ramp, he caught a glimpse of the Vengian. He stood conspicuously still in a moving crowd. Magog waved him over. He did not move. He just stared down the pier at him from the esplanade. Magog told the deckhand in no uncertain terms to keep the schooner where it was. Then he walked up to the pier to the Vengian.

"What are you doing? The ship is about to sail." As he drew near, he saw something in the Vengian that made him reach for his blade.

The Vengian already had his blade in his hand, and he lunged at Magog. He grabbed Magog's arm before he could unsheathe his blade, and ran him through.

"It's finished," he whispered into Magog's ear.

The brazen stabbing was witnessed by the crowd. With yells and screams, the crowd scattered away from the men locked in a fatal embrace. With the Vengian still holding his arm, Magog buckled onto his knees. Balean soldiers rushed to the scene with their rifles ready.

"Drop the blade and put your hands behind your head!" one of them shouted.

Magog's body fell over as the Vengian released his arm and quietly complied.

"Now get on your knees!"

With his hands interlocked behind his head, there was no thought of running. The Vengian did not try to figure out which was the best of multiple opportunities for escape. He thought instead about the previous night. About his struggle. About her innocence.

"What are you sorry about?" Mosaic had asked. In the silence, she did not avert her glassy eyes or yield to doubt. She had looked at him. And as she had done as a child, she believed in him.

"I said on your knees!" the Balean soldier repeated.

Sparrow looked down at Magog. His eyes were vacant. He thought about Mosaic—how she would live to bring more beautiful songs into the world. Then he fell to his knees and surrendered.

CH 49

MURIAH BAY

In little over a week, Dale had grown to appreciate nature, both its cruelty and its kindness. He slept in the snow. He walked in the rain. He was well fed with food he did not sow. He learned how to set his own traps, dress game, and cure meat. He learned that Valkyrie's Grovish name was inspired by Olafur Charles, the father of botany, and Zainah Valkyrie, an adventurer credited with charting the Winter Pass. He was exposed to the disparity of accounts in common history, especially when viewing the Emmainite people through the lens of an Emmainite. He had tested his boots. He had read *The Walgorende's Last Stand* cover to cover.

Two uneventful passes through Balean checkpoints, three blisters, and countless excursions into the surrounding forests later, Valkyrie and Dale reached the eastern seaboard.

When they finally strolled into Muriah Bay, it was near dusk. The town glimmered with evening lights from the densely stacked buildings built into the slope of a cove. The lights at dusk danced off the slow rippling surface of the water between the many anchored ships. It reminded Dale of Carnaval City's waterfront. It reminded him of home. But the beautiful scene was abruptly disturbed by the message on the defaced archway leading into town: *Enter at your own risk.*

They found the nearest tavern in search of drink and some proper accommodations— things they had not seen in weeks. Before entering, Valkyrie offered Dale a bit of advice.

"Stay away from the women. There aren't many around. And if they're not spoken for, they're probably carrying something you don't want to catch."

Once Dale nodded, they walked a few more paces. Valkyrie stopped him again, "One more thing. Everyone is dangerous. Everyone."

At the lowest part of town, right along the water, was the town's center. It was a stark contrast to the quiet country they'd been wandering for weeks. They followed the sound of after-work revelry to a local watering hole. Inside the smoke-filled establishment was a decidedly male crowd. There was heavy action at the gambling tables and heavy action at the bar. The few women who braved their company looked meaner than the men.

Valkyrie stopped the first woman that passed by.

"Well, aren't you a sight for sore eyes?"

Without acknowledging his attempt at charm she asked, "What do you want?"

"Look, sweet thing, we need a hot meal and a warm bed."

"I'm no tavern wench, *sweet thing*," she replied curtly.

"My mistake."

She turned and began to walk away. Valkyrie grabbed her by the arm.

"Look, we're not from around here. Who can we talk to about some food and a bed?"

"Look around, genius. No one here's from around here. Try the bar."

She yanked her arm out of Valkyrie's grip and walked away.

Dale scanned the eclectic room. There were islanders with their tribal tattoos, traders from Silverland, Azurics with their varying hairstyles, and even some Lorean slavers.

"She wasn't kidding," he said.

"Yeah, how about that."

Valkyrie led them over to the bar where they happily discovered they could order a meal from the kitchen. He ordered a plate of fried fish with a side of oysters, and a couple of pints of beer. The first sip of beer made them turn to each other—their eyebrows raised. They knew what the other was thinking. They ordered a second pint before finishing their first. As they sat talking about boarding options in Muriah Bay, the fried fish and oysters were served. After a steady diet of foraged food, they had forgotten how good a prepared meal was. Neither spoke a word while they ate. On his third pint, Dale leaned away from the bar and looked around the tavern.

Sitting next to him at the bar with his back to Dale was a large man who kept looking over his shoulder at Dale and Valkyrie. After yet another sideways look, the large man said something to his friends down the bar. They all looked over and began to chuckle.

"I'm getting a bad feeling about this guy," he quietly told Valkyrie.

Valkyrie glanced over at the broad-shouldered man and the four others drinking with him at the end of the bar. "Finish your drink," he said. "Let's get out of here. There has to be a quieter place in town to sleep."

Dale stood and was clearing his glass when the broad-shouldered man deliberately stumbled back into him. Dale's beer splashed his face and spilled onto his shirt. The man turned around with a smirk. Dale looked at him holding his empty glass. Faced with him directly, he was even bigger than Dale had thought. It was difficult to place where he was from. His hair and clothing were non-descript—it was only clear that he made his life out at sea. His skin was dark and thick with deep creases on his neck like a walrus. He had hair all over his face—his beard ran up high on his cheeks and his eyebrows extended near his hairline. On his tightly cropped head, he wore a knit hat that must have come with him from some distant shore. The dark, unruly face highlighted his gray, almost silver eyes.

"Be a little more careful next time, peachy. Now run along and give your Emmainite dog a bath. My mates can smell him from all the way at the end of the bar."

The end of the bar burst into laughter.

Charles Valkyrie put his arm around Dale. Pulling him away he said, "Yes, yes. I'm perfectly stuffed. I do believe it's time for us to get going."

But Dale was tired. He was tired of being attacked, of running, being forced to go here and there. He was weary of people—weary of being subject to their control and abuses of power. He shrugged Valkyrie's arm off his shoulder.

"I think you owe my friend an apology," he said.

"No, no." Valkyrie continued, trying to placate the escalating situation. "I was thinking the same thing. A bath is what I need."

"I don't owe anybody anything," the big man said as he got out of his seat. His four friends did the same. He hunched over Dale and shoved his finger into Dale's chest. "Now, you listen to your dog and run along before I turn ugly."

Dale dropped his glass and reached for his sword. The man shoved him. The shove knocked Dale and Valkyrie stumbling against the bar. People cleared the area. All activity stopped as everyone in the tavern turned to see the commotion. The four companions drew their weapons. The instigator grabbed a barstool and wielded it like it was a small stick.

Just then a man jumped into the middle. "Dale Sunday! Is that you?"

He spoke in a lilting manner with a defining lisp. Dale recognized him immediately.

"It's Leon. Leon Getty. I was just over there in that booth telling Cassiopeia,"— he pointed toward a booth on the other side of the tavern. All of the combatants straightened up and looked over at the booth. Cassiopeia smiled warmly and waved at Dale—"that looks like Dale Sunday. We couldn't be sure. Here you are. What in the world are you doing out here in Muriah Bay? And what is this you're wearing?" Leon turned to the big man holding the barstool. "I see you've met Ratto."

The big man looked sedated, like he'd been put into a trance by Leon's lilting voice and hisses.

"Ratto, this is Dale Sunday. A friend. He runs the breaker yard in Carnaval City.

Dale dropped his glass and reached for his sword.

You remember." And turning back to Dale: "Ratto is one of the best deckhands around. When you build a crew, you first find Ratto and then you get a crew. Isn't that right, Ratto? He's done everything there is to do on a boat. Knows everything. It's good that you're here, Dale.

We've been wondering what's become of Carnaval City. We've only heard bits and pieces." He stepped over to Dale and put his arm around him. "You need to come over to our booth and tell us all about it." As they stepped away from the bar, the tavern's reveling tone was restored. Leon turned to the bar as he walked away with Dale and Valkyrie in tow. "Ratto, you boys sit back down. Bartender! A round for the boys on me."

As they walked toward the booth, Valkyrie introduced himself.

"A pleasure to meet you, Mister Valkyrie," Leon replied. "Leon Getty, Captain the Saint Viljoen."

"You don't need to introduce yourself. I've heard much about you and the Saint Viljoen. To meet you in the flesh— I can't tell you what an honor it is."

Leon chuckled. "Flattery will get you everywhere, Mister Valkyrie."

Dale was still brooding. His hands still shaking from the confrontation.

"Thank you for what you did back there," Valkyrie added.

"Please, do not mention it." They reached the booth. "Cassiopeia, you remember Dale."

"How can I forget?" She extended a hand.

"And this is his friend, Charles Valkyrie."

"A pleasure to meet you."

"Good to meet you."

"Please, join us."

They scooted into the booth. More drinks were ordered.

Late into the night, they sat sipping rum and smoking. Dale and Valkyrie told the Submariners about their journey. They listened, shaking their heads, stopping them on occasion to ask for details—details about things that, until then, were mere rumors. The story ended with how the two were now in Muriah Bay.

"That's quite the story."

"And what about you?" asked Dale. "What are you still doing here?"

"We're stuck." Leon sighed.

"Goddamn marks turned to shit as soon as the war broke out," Cassiopeia added. "There was hardly enough funds to pay the crew."

"So you're stranded?"

"For now," Leon replied. "Unless you know someone interested in a briefcase full of devalued currency. We can't even afford the docking levy. They're holding the Saint Viljoen as collateral."

"Who's 'they'?" asked Valkyrie.

"The Bay House of Judicators."

"No offense, but you're pirates," said Dale. "Why don't you just leave?"

"Do not mistake pirates for thieves. A petty thief is dumb and reckless. We Submariners live by a code. The Judicators are appointed by the Pirate Lord Del Rasa. To defy them would be to defy Del Rasa himself. And making the wrong enemy is as costly as making the wrong friends."

"Every horse-shitting second we stay aground, that levy adds up," Cassiopeia

bemoaned.

"As you can see, it's a bad time to be here," said Leon.

"It's a bad time to be anywhere," Dale replied.

Then he rummaged through his backpack and removed the certificate of ownership to the breaker.

"You think I can buy the Saint Viljoen back for you with this?"

After a quick perusal, Leon passed it on to Cassiopeia.

"This is a bad idea," she said.

"Yeah, they can't claim it now," Dale conceded, "but the war won't last forever. And the deed is universal. It'll hold up in Balean courts."

"The Judicators are opportunistic men," said Leon. "They will not lightly dismiss your offer. Cassiopeia is not worried about that. She's worried about you owning the Saint Viljoen—you being her captain. If we use your asset, then the boat will be released in your name."

Dale smiled. "I have no ambitions of captaining a ship."

"That is not a negotiable term with the Judicators. There is no room for misrepresentation. Every recorded book in the seamen's codex will declare you the new captain of the Saint Viljoen."

Cassiopeia scoffed. "That's not going to happen."

"If you've no ambition to be a captain, why exchange your business, such prized property, for a ship?" Leon then asked.

"I got family in Carnaval City. An aunt, uncle, cousin. I need to get them out."

"A stop in Carnaval City is out of the question. You'd fare better strolling into Valorcourt."

"The offer is good only if we head into Carnaval City and try to get my family out," said Dale. "That's it."

"Good luck, then," Cassiopeia replied. She looked at Leon imploringly. Seeing Leon deep in thought, she protested. "Leon! You're not actually considering this, are you? We're not pawning the ship to some random brimcake."

"Which alternative is more preferable, love? Oh, that's right. There is no alternative. We've been ashore too long and you said yourself, in more colorful terms, that our debt grows with every idle second. A drowning person has no say in what form the rescue takes."

"There's no way we're going back to Carnaval City. We'll all end up in a Balean dungeon if not dead at sea."

"Cassiopeia, this is what we do. We take impossible chances to smuggle things out from under the noses of the powers that be. Dangerous? Yes. But I'm warming to the idea. Besides, what choice do we have? There are no guarantees either way." Leon looked at Dale and gave him a nod. "Assuming I take your offer?"

"If we do this, I'm captain in documents only," Dale replied. "Let's get it quietly squared away with the Judicators, by the book, and let the papers say what they say. But we needn't tell anyone else. This is your show, Leon. I'm just looking for a ride to Carnaval City. Take me and Charles on as hired hands and we'll play it from there."

Cassiopeia shook her head, but she took some solace in Dale's deferential tone. Leon smiled and held his hands out toward Dale as if he were presenting Cassiopeia with a show prize. "You see, love. There's more to this dove than meets the eye. He just might make a great captain after all."

CH 50

A MEASURE OF PEACE

Valkyrie couldn't keep his eyes off Cassiopeia. He watched her from afar as she reviewed the pre-departure schedule.

"I think I'm in love."

"Get in line," Dale replied. "You've got a boat full of competition."

"You call those other brutes competition? She'll be sharing my bed. You'll see."

Cassiopeia glanced over and met Valkyrie's gaze. He winked. She returned it with a steely glare.

"Not before she castrates you," said Dale, watching the exchange.

"Well, she's worth the risk."

Dale shook his head. "Good luck."

With the Bay House Judicator's approval, Dale was the official captain of the Saint Viljoen. A small crew had been assembled. They were hand picked from a number of trusted and able-bodied men—men who had organized their lives in a way that made them available at a moment's notice. Once the paperwork was finalized, they were ready to embark. They had already settled into their bunks and prepared for departure. The crew did not need to be told what to do. Assuming their responsibilities, the boat took on a working tone.

Dale and Valkyrie went above deck where they walked around and took in the view. It was the only part of the Saint Viljoen not made of matted black steel. Instead, it was layered with wood, designed as a lounge deck for when the vessel was docked or cruising on the surface.

"How many days to Carnaval City?"

"Who knows," Dale replied.

"Some *captain* you are."

"Not so loud, *Sayeed Errai*. Or I'll make you walk the plank."

"Does this thing even have a plank?"

Dale removed the tattered copy of *The Walgorende's Last Stand* and handed it to Valkyrie. "Here. To help you pass the time."

"I've been meaning to ask you about this." Valkyrie flipped through its pages. "Is it any good?"

"It's sad."

"My kind of book."

The Saint Viljoen's engines were activated, steam spitting before settling into its perfect purr.

"Guess we're moving out," said Valkyrie.

"Guess so."

"You coming below?"

"In a bit."

"Well, don't get caught up here when we dive." Valkyrie tucked the book under his arm and started toward the hatch. Then he stopped and looked back at Dale.

"Hey, kid. Thanks for getting me aboard."

"You're my friend, Charles. You don't have to thank me. Besides, you might not be so grateful when we come across a Balean armada."

The ranger laughed heartily as he climbed down the hatch.

The Saint Viljoen began to move. Dale leaned up against the railing and looked out into the endless stretch of water. The air was crisp, the wind in his hair. Alone, riding on the wings of his childhood dreams, his thoughts began to roam. He thought about mortality, the origins of man, the longing heart. He thought about Darius, Sparrow, the Maker. He thought about Selah. Dale removed her note from his breast pocket. He unfolded it and read it twice over, relishing every word.

I pray you'll find a measure of peace on your journey through life.

The alarms went off accompanied by a flashing red light on deck indicating the vessel's imminent descent.

Dale held the note up. For a minute, he watched it flutter in the wind. It rattled violently, threatening to tear. Then he let go. A gust of headwind carried it over the rail and out to sea. It disappeared somewhere in the wake of the Saint Viljoen.

Dale smiled. Then he went below.

ACKNOWLEDGEMENTS

Editors: Kyu-Ho Lee and Deena Drewis

Beta-testers: Sam Nguyen, David David Katzman, Kyle Runnels, and Zainah Al-rujaib

Special Thanks To: My Mom and Pops, the Merlo Family, Fred and Sarah Chun, Daryl Burney, "Airforce" Dan Kim, Jessup Pyun, Sam Joe, Eugene Kashida, Linda Peters, Vikram Advani, Brett Bozeman, and Jesse.

And our undying gratitude for the support of Cassie Marketos and the entire Kickstarter Community.

EDDIE HAN

THE AUTHOR

Eddie Han was born and raised in Orange County, California. He has a degree in Studio Art from the University of California Irvine. He paints in acrylic. He writes in his boxers. His favorite movie villains are Roy Batty and Neil MacCauley.

Parabolis was inspired by lonely nights abroad, joyless jobs, window gazing, video gaming, good friends, good bourbon, faith, hope, love, and the music of Sigur Ros, John Coltrane, Blue Sky Black Death, Ulrich Schnauss, and Yann Tiersen.

Parabolis is Eddie's first novel.

CURT MERLO

THE ARTIST

Curt Merlo grew up in Fresno, California. He graduated from the University of California Irvine with a degree in Studio Art and began his career as a freelance editorial artist shortly after. Since then, his work has been featured in several publications including the covers of L.A. Weekly, Businessweek, The Village Voice, and U.K.'s instrumental post-rock band, Minion TV's third album, the Last Projectionist.

Curt's influences include Constructivism, Euro Deco, Gerd Arntz, Charley Harper, David Plunkert, Goncalo Viana, Lotta Nieminen, Don Draper, Thom Yorke, NPR podcasts, and a bunch of other cool shit